THE HANGED MAN

THE HANGED MAN

T.J. MacGREGOR

KENSINGTON BOOKS
http://www.kensingtonbooks.com

KENSINGTON BOOKS are published by

Kensington Publishing Corp.
850 Third Avenue
New York, NY 10022

Library of Congress Card Catalog Number: 96-079085
ISBN 1-57566-266-3

First Printing: June, 1998
10 9 8 7 6 5 4 3 2 1

Printed in the United States of America

Again and always, for Rob and Megan,
and Mom and Dad

Thanks to my agent, Al Zuckerman, and to my editor, Kate Duffy, who helped sculpt the story; to Renie Wiley and Phyllis Vega for their input on the complexities of the tarot; to Linda Griffin, who endured all those practice readings in Seattle; and to Nancy Pickard, master of the hexagrams.

I: The Murder

"We can rest assured that the secrets of psi and its application will be available to whoever chooses to commit the necessary resources to unlocking them."

—Richard S. Broughton
Parapsychology:
The Controversial Science

1

The immediacy of the noise enveloped her, surrounded her, a whispery sound, the voice of wind through leaves. But outside, absolute stillness gripped the darkness, a waiting stillness, as if nature held her breath.

Mira pushed up on her elbows, blinked hard to dispel the darkness, but it remained, as black as India ink. She strained to hear the noise again. There. It seemed distant at first, faint, then grew louder, urgent murmurs punctuated by angry staccatos. Somewhere in the house, two men argued.

In her house.

Her thoughts flew to Annie, asleep across the hall. Blood pounded in her ears as she slipped out of bed. Where had she put Tom's gun? The bureau? The nightstand? No, no, the closet, on a high shelf in the back where her daughter couldn't reach it.

The voices grew uglier and louder as she groped her way through the dark. She stumbled over one of the cats, curled up on the rug, undisturbed by the intruders. Only then did she realize the voices originated in her head, stronger than echoes, brighter than memories.

—*Take it easy. Careful with that thing.*

—*Shut up. Move back nice and slow.*

—*Look here . . .*

—*Move!*

She wrenched back, patting the nightstand for a pad of paper, a pen. She dropped to the edge of the mattress and listened hard, eyes shut.

External sounds: frogs, crickets, an isolated splash in the lake behind the house. More distant still, traffic hummed. She focused on a dot of light inside her head and willed it to expand, to open. The light brightened and melted like butter across her inner vision.

She saw them now—not their faces, just their legs, two pairs of legs in a dimly lit room. Two men. One of them wore running shoes with lime green laces, the other was barefoot, his muscular legs covered in very dark hair.

Mira could no longer hear them, but somehow knew they continued to argue. Without opening her eyes, she scribbled down what she saw. It wasn't enough, she needed more details.

A child appeared in the left-hand corner of her vision, a young boy of three or four. Sleepy eyes, black hair. He clutched a teddy in the curve of his arm and peeked out from behind a door. Mira was sure the men didn't see him. Sound suddenly clicked back in, the hiss of air-conditioning. She couldn't tell if it came from her room or belonged to the awful scene that unrolled across her inner vision.

A sharp, abrupt pain pierced her chest and she gasped and doubled over, the pad and pen slipping to the floor. One of the men had been shot. She was locked into him, zipped up inside of him. Blood rushed out of him, out of her. He slammed into the wall and air blasted from her lungs.

He wheezed and so did Mira. She saw through his eyes, saw blood pouring out of him and across the floor. She heard what he heard, soft, low laughter and a voice: "Tough luck, Sherlock."

The connection ruptured.

Mira slid to the floor, her body collapsing like a beach chair. The hot, bright pain in her chest began to subside. She sucked at the air and rubbed at her chest, just below the sternum where the first bullet had entered. She didn't feel any blood, any hole.

She lurched for the lamp, hit the switch, and rocked back on her heels, rubbing frantically at the front of her T-shirt. No blood. She jerked the shirt down, certain she would see blood, exposed muscle and tissue, a gaping hole just below her breasts.

Her skin bore no marks.

She felt only a phantom sensation now, a terrible numbness that spread across her chest, as though she had been injected with Novocain. The man, she thought, had known his killer and had died with that low laughter rumbling in his ears.

"*Qué haces en el piso, Mami?*"

Mira opened her eyes and peered at Annie, kneeling in front of her, staring at her.

"I slipped off the bed."

"That's a dumb thing to do."

Mira laughed. "For sure." She pushed to her feet, sat down on the edge of the mattress. Better, she thought. Much better.

"You sure you're okay, Mommy?" Annie asked. She frowned slightly, hands on her narrow hips, a forty-year-old woman trapped in an eight-year-old's body. "You look sort of funny."

The sweet perfection of her daughter's features struck her just then, the even blend of genes. Annie had her Cuban father's dark, fathomless eyes, the high sweep of his forehead, the shameless sensuality of his mouth. The rest of her mirrored Mira: the rounded chin, the aquiline nose, high cheekbones, curly dark hair.

"I had a bad dream." Mira picked up the pad and pen from the floor and quickly jotted down the rest of her impressions.

"You write down your bad dreams, too?" Annie asked.

"If they seem important." She included the date—Thursday, October 23—glanced at the digital clock, and added the time as well. 5:32 A.M. She put the paper and pen into a drawer, stood. "What're you doing up so early?"

"Seuss woke me up."

The black and white Tom that Mira nearly had stumbled over had been born here in the neighborhood six months ago, the runt in a litter of wild strays. She and Annie had rescued them from the atrium of a home whose owners hated cats. Whose owners probably would have drowned the kittens. Annie and her friends had tamed the kittens within thirty minutes and Annie had chosen Seuss for herself. He slid between Annie's legs now, begging for attention, for food, for whatever she might give him, thank you very much.

"Mommy, you don't look okay."

"I'm fine. Really. C'mon, let's brush our teeth and get some breakfast." But her racing heart told her she wasn't fine.

Annie clasped Mira's hand, her way of making sure that her mother had returned from wherever she'd gone. Her daughter understood that Mira sometimes saw pictures and heard voices in her head. But she didn't know for sure what any of it meant.

Some years ago, Annie had mentioned her concerns to a preschool teacher, who had related the conversation to Mira. Fortunately, the teacher didn't equate psychics with devil worshippers; she had made an appointment for a reading and subsequently had become a friend.

But Annie, older and more curious now, had begun to question the entire process. *What kind of pictures do you see, Mommy? What kinds of sounds do you hear? Is it like a daydream? I think I like it better when you just do the cards.*

Mira actually preferred the tarot cards, too. She controlled them, not the other way around. She could read them or not read them. They didn't shoot into her awareness the way her psychic impressions did.

The nagging, gnawing question, though, centered around timing. Had the events occurred at the moment she perceived them? Or last year? Or would they happen next week? What was the time frame? And hell, what did it have to do with her?

The drone of morning cartoons drifted through the house, a comforting noise, utterly familiar. Mira rubbed the steam from the bathroom mirror and stared at her blurred image. She hadn't put her contacts in yet, but she didn't need the contacts to peer upward and to the right of her reflection. Here, she could sometimes see replays of whatever she had tuned into.

She knew some detail of the experience had escaped her. It happened sometimes, a psychic blindspot, a tiny black hole in her mind's eye. She sensed the detail's shape, its reality, but she couldn't seize it. She kept seeing only herself, her black hair still wet from her shower, her dark eyes pinched with worry.

Look harder, her grandmother always told her. *If you don't see it right away, keep looking until you do. That's what your name means. To look.*

She leaned closer to the mirror, but nothing changed.

Screw it, she thought, and picked up a jar of face cream that her grandmother had given her last Christmas. The stuff supposedly removed dead cells from the skin and thus make wrinkles less pronounced. A youth cream, Nadine had said. She herself used it all the time and did she look eighty?

Nadine had never looked her age. A runner long before it was fashionable, she'd been practicing yoga and meditation since her twenties and meat hadn't passed her lips since she hit eighteen. She had outlived two husbands and two of her five children. A broken hip last year had slowed her down, though, and her bad fall had frightened her enough to sell her home and move into the apartment above Mira's bookstore.

Mira dabbed the cream on her face and rubbed it in. She wondered what she would look like if Nadine had not been her grandmother. After all, Nadine had encouraged her to become a vegetarian twenty years ago, when she was just seventeen, had taught her yoga, had guided her into herself and out again after Tom's death.

Nadine had liked Tom on sight. But even without her grandmother's tacit approval, Mira had loved him from the beginning. Only later had she realized he came from a family that represented everything she wasn't. They ate meat, his mother was a rigid Catholic, and his father was a practicing *santero* who sacrificed animals. Tom had been none of those things, but a product of all of them.

We choose what challenges us. Nadine's slogan.

Mira supposed it might be significant that she thought of this now, as she tried to recall some slippery detail of a vision. She felt sure she didn't know anyone in the scene she'd glimpsed. It had nothing to do with her and Annie. And yet, its power had to indicate a connection to her. But how? In what way?

By the time Mira and Annie finished breakfast, the sun had come up and the neighborhood ducks had congregated in the backyard, fussing for food. The ducks numbered about fifty now and they made their home on this small, placid lake in the Fort Lauderdale suburbs. Everyone fed them, but she and Annie made a ritual of it.

They walked down to the lake with a jar filled with birdseed and poured it into the feeder under the banana tree. The ducks descended in a feeding frenzy. Annie moved among them on her hands and knees, stroking this one, talking to that one, feeding a white duck out of her hand. Her dark hair shone in the sunlight, the cool October breeze ruffling the ends. She had turned eight on September 15, the five-year anniversary of her father's death.

Annie came running across the grass, shouting that she didn't want to be late for school. And suddenly the trees and the lake and the ducks dissolved. Mira stared out of someone else's eyes at blurred greens, high grasses, a patch of blue sky, all of it seen as though the person—a woman?—lay flat on her back.

Mira shut her eyes quickly, opening herself to it. She didn't see anything, but she heard an odd scraping sound, like a broom brushing against metal, and she smelled water. *Canoe. Tall grass.* Then it dissolved. She couldn't tell if it had a connection to the other vision or not. It felt eerie, scary.

"We going or what?" Annie asked, tugging impatiently on her hand.

She opened her eyes, relieved that the world had solidified again. "We're gone," she said with a smile, and they ran up to the porch.

Mira sat in the office of her bookstore, one hand on the phone. She knew she would regret it if she didn't make the call to the police. The vision would haunt her. She would wonder what might have happened if she had called.

Her limited experience with cops had been, for the most part, unpleasant. The three cops she'd worked with on half a dozen cases or so over the years lived forty years in the past. They automatically dumped psychics in the weirdo category, along with witches, vampires, and things that went bump in the night.

None of the cops had ever informed her whether the information she had given them was accurate, had never offered any feedback at all. They could have been reincarnated priests from the Dark Ages who had made the reading of the cards punishable by burning at the stake.

So forget it, she thought. She had a business to run, she didn't have time for this shit. Why get involved? Why invite complications? Right now, she needed to focus her energy on the psychic fair for Halloween weekend, about nine days from now. She still had a million loose ends to tie up.

The city of Fort Lauderdale, in conjunction with local businesses, put on the street fair every year. Bands, art booths, food concessions, clowns and jugglers, a costume contest. This year's fair would include one block of exhibits devoted to "alternatives"—alternative lifestyles, alternative futures, alternative anything. Her job was to sign up psychics, card readers, health food and vitamin advocates, everything allied with alternative living.

It would be held on Las Olas Boulevard, Lauderdale's less pretentious equivalent of Palm Beach's Worth Avenue. City officials expected two hundred thousand people to attend over the course of three days. The exposure would expand her store's visibility, bring in new customers and, she hoped, would boost the profits, which this year had been only marginal.

She pushed the phone out of reach, swiveled her chair around, and felt dismayed by the stacks of papers on her desk. Book orders, special orders, a dozen yellow notes about the fair stuck to files, envelopes, her wall. Call so and so. Confirm with so and so. Get money from so and so.

Through the rear window, she could see the yoga class in session in the garden, in the grassy shade of a pair of banyan trees. Nadine taught most of the yoga classes, her body as supple as a child's despite her eighty years and a broken hip twelve months ago.

One World Books & Things had never been just a New Age bookstore. From its inception, she'd envisioned it as a place where people could find alternative answers to their spiritual, emotional, and physical needs. As a result, the shop now offered services that ranged from yoga to channeling, the prosaic to the esoteric.

Nine years ago, Nadine and Tom had financed the property, two lots on Fort Lauderdale's New River. Even then, waterfront property had been enormously expensive, but they'd gotten the land in a foreclosure sale for a fraction of its worth. The price had included a two-story house of crumbling coquina rock, limestone embedded with fossils, the peninsula's DNA.

Built in 1942 by a wealthy citrus baron for his partially para-

lyzed mother, the place had numerous amenities for the handicapped. She and Tom had retained some of them: the rickety
elevator that connected the two floors, the dumbwaiter in the
kitchen, the single closet shared by two rooms, the wheelchair
ramps. But the house had needed so many repairs, Tom had
taken the summer off from the firm where he practiced law and
they had gone to work rebuilding the place.

Mira had been pregnant at the time, an easy pregnancy for
a twenty-seven-year-old woman, easy except for the wild mood
swings and the vivid, horrifying dreams.

No, that wasn't accurate. There had only been one dream, a
soap opera of the unconscious that had expanded in detail every
time she had it: Tom pulling out of the driveway one evening
at dusk, Tom walking into a store where he was gunned down.
She had never told Tom about the dream.

In real life, it had happened three years later and Mira and
Annie had driven to the convenience store with him. Annie,
exhausted from her birthday party, had fallen asleep in the backseat, so Mira stayed in the car while Tom went inside. The details
of the actual incident had differed sufficiently so that initially
she didn't recognize them as what she had dreamed.

By the time the man charged out of the store and she realized
what was happening, the damage was done. Tom already lay
in a pool of blood inside, one of two victims shot by a masked
assailant during a robbery. The bastard had gotten away with
maybe two hundred bucks and had never been found.

That had been her first experience with a cop, an aging cynic
who believed only in what his five senses told him. She hadn't
succeeded in convincing him otherwise. Despite countless
attempts, she never had been able to pick up anything on the
killer and had begun to doubt her ability. Now she realized she'd
been too close to it to separate her grief from her impressions.

But this situation differed, she needed to remember that. She
wasn't too close to it, she didn't know either of the men she'd
seen, she *wasn't involved*. What could it possibly cost her simply
to give the cops the information? Then that would be it.

Mira reached for the receiver before she could change her
mind. She called information for the Broward County Sheriff's

Department, then punched out the number. She nervously tapped a pencil.

"Broward County Sheriff's Department. How may I direct your call?"

"Homicide."

"Just a minute and I'll connect you."

Click, buzz, nothing but a void. *Hang up now. This is going to mean trouble for you.* Images of what she'd seen welled up inside of her—the two men, the running shoes with the green shoelaces, the shot, the child. She suddenly had trouble breathing, a wall of perspiration swept across her back, her stomach knotted.

I can't do this, she thought, and started to hang up when a gruff male voice said, "Homicide, Detective Ames."

She tried to even out her breathing, to speak normally. "My name's Mira Morales. I, uh, have some information about a murder."

"What sort of information, Mrs. Morales?"

Another thing about cops that she didn't like was that they called all women "missus." "Psychic information."

Silence. She could almost see his derisive smile, the roll of his eyes. Then he said: "What's the information?"

"White male. Shot in the chest below the sternum by another male. There was one witness, a boy of maybe four. Later on, I saw a boat, maybe a canoe, gliding through tall grass. I saw it early this morning, but I'm not sure of the real time."

Spoken aloud, it sounded foolish, demented. The cop didn't laugh, but he didn't sound too impressed, either. He actually sounded somewhat bored. "Was there anything else, ma'am?"

"No, that was it."

"We appreciate the call, Mrs. Morales. If we need to speak to you again, where can we get in touch with you?"

She knew he'd dismissed her as a flake. Just the same, she gave him her phone number and address.

"One World Books is where you work, ma'am?"

"I own the store." *I'm not a complete flake, turkey.*

"Very good, ma'am. Thanks for calling."

The line went dead.

2

The sawgrass scraped against the canoe, a noise like fingernails drawn over a chalkboard. He paddled faster, faster, propelling the canoe through a flowing river of grass with dagger-sharp teeth.

In junior high school, Hal Bennet had read about this river of grass, the very essence of the Everglades. He had read about the way it whispered to people who listened, that the tiny ridges on its leaves were sharp enough to flay the skin from a man's hands. Something in the description of such wilderness had captivated his imagination and held it through all the years since.

The grass ended and he paddled out into Hell's Bay, an open lake that shimmered like a sheet of aluminum foil. The sun beat down, heating up the top of his head. But it didn't scoop him raw inside, didn't suck him dry, didn't bake his bones. This didn't even come close to the heat in July or August or even September, when the sun burned white against the sky and mosquitos filled the scorched, breathless air.

He paddled rapidly, tirelessly, propelled by the fear that had dogged him since he had left Steele's home. At times, the fear became a vague, protoplasmic thing, a thick mass that lodged in his throat or pounded between his eyes. Other times it molded itself into something quite specific: that he'd overlooked something at the house that would enable the cops to identify him. The fear pierced him now as he crossed the open lake, completely exposed, vulnerable.

He wished he had used the airboat. He kept it hidden in the mangroves not far from where he lived, his fast ticket to civilization, noisy but efficient, like driving a Porsche versus a golf cart. It would have gotten him across this lake in the blink of an eye.

The woman lay on the floor of the canoe and had been sighing and weeping much of the time, but now seemed to be slipping into oblivion. Hal had injected her with enough Darvon to catapult her into next week. He hoped she would stay out for awhile now; her whimpers and groans and sighs irritated him. He found it easier to paddle and think when she remained silent.

On the other side of Hell's Bay, the mangroves sprang up, hiding him again. The trees looked like green umbrellas with long, bushy tassels that nearly brushed the water. The branches sagged so badly they created narrow, eerie tunnels through which he paddled, traveling up and down trails that had been created by the force and power of the water itself.

Some of these trails, labyrinthine and hidden, didn't exist on any maps and couldn't accommodate airboats—not his, not those of the park service. The trail he followed emptied into a lagoon surrounded by dense mangroves. At its deepest, the water went down about six feet.

Hal had stumbled upon it after he'd maxed out his sentence for fraud nine years ago. No land surrounded it, just the ubiquitous mangroves, their nest of roots thrust deeply into the black, rich soil.

The mangroves hid the chickee so well you couldn't see it unless you knew it was there. It looked like a snug wooden box with four skinny legs that lifted it eight feet out of the water. The Seminole Indians had built the first chickees in the Everglades, spare, open-sided habitats that kept them high and dry but little else. In the last fifteen years, the park service had constructed a number of them for campsites. Hal felt sure, though, that his had been the genuine Seminole version.

When he'd found the place, it had resembled a lean-to with a leaky roof and a rotting platform. Over many months, he had hauled in supplies by canoe, enlarged the platform, built walls, put on a tin roof and covered it with branches and leaves for camouflage. Then he proceeded to make it not only habitable, but comfortable.

He had added two rooms—a kitchen with a waterproof storage closet and a family room. The kitchen had most of the modern amenities—a gas stove, a small fridge that ran off a generator, a sink with running water that he pumped from the lagoon, even a small microwave. He had sanded down the wooden floor, filled in the spaces between the beams, and sealed it in polyurethane.

The family room impressed him; sometimes he wondered how the hell he'd constructed it. The shelves against one wall housed his extensive collection of videotapes, a small color TV, a CD boom box with a stack of CDs, a laptop computer, and a cellular phone. Hal enjoyed his creature comforts and had gone to great lengths to make the chickee not just a refuge, but a home.

From the beginning, the chickee's bathroom had been a problem. It had lacked plumbing and he couldn't bring himself to pollute the lagoon by flushing waste into it. So he'd stolen parts from various Jiffy Johns at the campsites and had made a smaller, more compact unit. Whenever it filled, he pumped the contents into a fifty-five-gallon drum, hauled it to the nearest campsite, then emptied it into another Jiffy John.

The park service probably had blamed the missing parts on vandals; he felt sure he had nothing to worry about in that department. But now, with one more person here, he would have to empty it more often.

He considered the shower his best invention. A wooden stall outdoors, it used water hand-pumped from the lagoon or from the small cistern on the roof.

Hal paddled to the ladder at the back of the chickee. In the shadows by the mangroves, he saw Big Guy, the ten-foot gator that had been a fixture here for the last four years. He fed the gator often enough to keep him around because nothing would discourage an intruder faster than a gator with an appetite for fresh meat. His small reptilian eyes peered just above the surface of the water, watching Hal, waiting for the canoe to tip or for Hal to slip on his way up the ladder.

"Not a chance, fucker." He slapped the water with the paddle.

Big Guy sank out of sight.

Hal tied the canoe to the ladder and began unloading his

supplies. Since he had started living out here about six years ago, he never wasted a trip into town. Prison had taught him the importance of being prepared and Andrew Steele had taught him, among other things, to trust no one.

On the rare occasions when he got lonely, he went into town for dinner or a movie. Or he *reached*, his consciousness soaring across the distance that separated him from other men until it found the perfect host. During his isolation here, he had gotten good at *reaching*, much better than even Steele had ever imagined.

In the early days, he occasionally picked up some sweet young thing from one of the bars on Lauderdale beach. But the last time, the whole thing had ended in disaster.

The woman, a college student looker from Maine, was so drunk she didn't remember him in the morning. She refused to have sex with him, refused even though she'd loved it during the night when she was bombed. He told her she could swim back to Lauderdale. She took it literally and leaped into the lagoon.

Hal, locked in horror at the edge of the platform, had watched Big Guy attack her. For weeks afterward, he had remained out here, too terrified to venture into town. Every night he'd dreamed of prison and every morning he'd awakened with his throat tight and dry, his heart racing.

When he couldn't stand it any longer, when his need to know overpowered his fear, he had ventured into the library in Florida City and looked through the back issues of the local papers. The only reference he found was a short piece in the local section— "Mystery of Missing College Student Remains Unsolved." He had never brought a woman out here again, until now, and this woman wasn't just any woman.

Once he'd piled the supplies on the platform, he climbed back into the canoe and knelt beside her. Zipped inside the sleeping bag, she was completely out of it now. Her mouth had opened slightly, her dark hair curled like punctuation marks against her forehead and cheeks.

It thrilled him to see her up close like this. All the waiting and the planning had paid off. Hal particularly liked her mouth, full and sultry, a Kim Basinger mouth. Her skin, as creamy and smooth as whipped butter, spoke of eternal youth. Her thick lashes left shadows on her cheeks. He could love a woman like this, had loved her at one time, maybe loved her still.

But considering how wrong things had gone at her house, maybe he should've killed her back there. Maybe he should do it now. One silenced shot between the eyes, then let Big Guy get rid of the evidence.

The idea tempted him. If he killed her, he wouldn't have to deal with the possibility that his plans might fail, that she might not grow to love him, that she, in fact, might discover he had killed her husband. But hell, he'd brought her this far, risking his ass, so he picked her up, sleeping bag and all, draped her over his shoulder like a load of dirty laundry, and climbed the ladder.

Hal carried her into the big room in the chickee, set her on the futon cushion, flung open the four shutters to admit air and light. It got awfully hot when the place was closed up, but the shutters cut down on roaches, rats, and other undesirables.

He glanced slowly around, wondering how she would react to it. Even though the room didn't begin to compare to her luxury with Steele, it possessed a certain uniqueness. In his considerable spare time, he had made most of the furniture—the pair of swinging chairs that hung from the center ceiling beam, the frame for the futon, the coffee table, the bookshelves, even the shutters.

Drawings and sketches covered the walls, charcoals and pencil sketches he'd drawn of her during the months he'd been watching her. Rae on the street, her hair blowing out behind her. Rae getting into her snappy Mercedes. Rae on the beach. Rae on a playground with her son. The sketches hardly qualified as great art, but he didn't think they were half bad, either.

He knelt beside her, brushed her hair away from her forehead and face. She got prettier every time he looked at her. He pressed his face into her blonde hair, breathing in the scent of sweat and grime and the faint fragrance behind it, some expensive shampoo. He ran his fingertip down the bridge of her nose, across a cheek. Christ, skin this soft should be against the law.

He unzipped the sleeping bag, peeled it open, and looked at her, taking her in. Bare feet with polished toenails. Gray leggings that covered long legs, muscular, shapely thighs. A long rose-colored T-shirt with "Nassau" written across the front in pink letters. She and Steele used to fly to Nassau just to shop.

Hal raised her T-shirt bit by bit. Nice. Very nice. Hips like blades, not an ounce of fat at her waist. He raised the T-shirt higher. She wasn't wearing a bra. He stared at her breasts, pale as moons, not too large, not too small. Beautiful, just beautiful. A mole stood alone under her right breast, a dark, mysterious eye that stared back at him.

Sooner or later he would have to sketch that breast, that mole, and add it to his collection. But not now. Now he would indulge himself in a private celebration for a job well done.

Hal sat beside her, legs crossed Indian-style. He rested one hand lightly against her forehead, the other clasped his knee. He shut his eyes, focused on Rae, and *reached*. With her conscious mind numbed by the Darvon, his energy coursed into her swiftly, unimpeded. In seconds, he found the dark, shuttered room that held her primal fears, a Pandora's box that he would open for his own dangerous pleasures and then use to control her.

Her husband, after all, had been his best teacher.

When Hal surfaced awhile later, sweat soaked his clothes. He shrugged off his T-shirt, went into the kitchen for the foot ladder, and carried it back into the room. He set it in the corner, climbed onto it. He reached into a space between the tin roof and the wall, a nook, a cranny, a hole in space and time, and let his fingers trail over the three aluminum tins hidden there.

Two of the tins held about thirty grand, a fraction of the money from the scam that had sent him to prison. The third tin, the one he selected, contained a .38 and two boxes of bullets, several pairs of handcuffs and their keys, and a wallet he hadn't touched in more than four years. He plucked out a pair of handcuffs, put the lid back into place, returned the tin to its hiding place. Then he returned to the woman. To Rae.

Hal snapped one cuff around her wrist and locked the other around a vertical strut on the rocking chair. He had bought the cuffs at one of the sex shops in Lauderdale, heavy-duty suckers that even Houdini couldn't wiggle out of.

He sat back on his heels, staring at her, tempted to *reach* inside of her again, to do it just for fun this time, like he used to do when he lived in Miami. He called himself Reverend Hal back then, counselor to the numerous suckers willing to pay him a bundle to clean their lives of negative vibrations, remove curses, protect them from psychic attack. He'd lived like a king.

Then some of the Cuban *santeros,* pissed off because they lost their clients to him, had blown the whistle. He was arrested for fraud, his attorney advised him to plead not guilty, and he'd gotten seven fucking years.

Now, though, he was wiser and in full command. Steele had always cautioned him to pace himself between *reaches* so that he could maintain control. Restraint, Hal now knew, proved vital to the process. So he left her alone. Besides, he had already filled her with the image that would prey on her darkest fears, that would discourage her from doing what the coed had done.

Rae Steele, ex-beauty queen, ex-prison teacher, widow of a multimillionaire, didn't know how to swim. Water terrified her. And that, Hal thought, would be the pivotal point of his control over her.

Unless she discovered that he'd killed her husband. Then she would do everything she could to get out of here.

It scared him to think about the things that might go wrong. Even if she didn't find out about Steele, she might never come to love him, and then where the hell would he be? Or, even worse, suppose the cops found him and pinned the murder on him? He wouldn't just go back to prison; he would end up at The Rock, the worst prison in Florida. And he wouldn't be in just any cell, he would be on Death Row, getting set for Sparky, Florida's electric chair.

Hal had read about electrocution, how your skin burned and sizzled and smelled like bacon, how your organs turned liquid, how your brain fried. When he was younger, he had always thought it couldn't happen to him. Now he knew better. It could happen to anyone.

A slow, piercing chill moved through him. He squeezed his eyes shut, clasped his arms at his waist, and rocked back and forth, again and again, until the cold, crippling fear had passed.

3

On Friday morning, October 24, the budget cuts in the Broward County Sheriff's Department hit Wayne Sheppard where it really hurt. Due to his low seniority—five years—he would no longer have a cruiser at his disposal except for emergencies. A homicide investigation didn't qualify as an emergency, which was why he was driving his aging Camaro up a winding driveway to a crime scene.

You'll get mileage, Shep, Captain Young had assured him.

Like twenty cents a mile would buy him a new car when the Camaro died. It now sputtered and coughed its way toward ninety thousand miles, at least thirty past its natural life. He expected that before the end of today, he would have to drop it at the garage for yet another repair in a string of repairs that had been eating him alive. The front axle, the alternator, the AC, an oil leak. The ravages of entropy.

And now, without the cruiser to fall back on, it would be a matter of weeks before he was forced to sink more deeply into debt for a new car.

Debt obviously didn't concern the family who lived at the end of *this* driveway. Sheppard drove through a virtual forest of seagrape trees and Florida pines and passed beds of wildflowers that exploded with color. The air smelled fragrant with gardenias, pine, ocean. A faint breeze rustled the leaves as he passed. He guessed the estate covered five acres or so, not much for someplace like Montana or Texas. But here in South Florida, a beachfront spread this size qualified as a kingdom.

The trees ended just short of the mansion, a sprawling split-level made of cedar, pine, and glass. The house seemed to blend into the land, as though it had grown from the soil itself.

The Camaro rattled and spewed black smoke as he turned off the engine. Christ, what now? The muffler? The alternator? Something altogether new? Cancer instead of just arthritis, he thought.

If Gabby couldn't patch whatever was wrong and he had to leave the car overnight, he would have to beg for the use of a cruiser. Or rent a car, which he couldn't afford. He had bought a town house not long ago and with the mortgage, taxes, the repairs, and furniture purchases, not to mention his mounting credit card debt, he was in hock up to his eyeballs.

He headed up the sidewalk, past the forensics' van and the paramedic trucks, to the open front door. He cracked his knuckles and counted silently backward from a hundred, the best way he'd found to detach himself at a crime scene.

He stepped into the marble hallway and saw Paula Crick at the end of it, a silhouette against a burst of sunlight behind her, the only black coroner in the state. She spoke quietly into a mini cassette recorder, then turned it off when she saw him and hurried over.

"I thought I heard your heap farting up the driveway, Shep. What'd they do, take away your cruiser?"

"You got it. We aren't even a month into the new fiscal year and they're doing more than just trimming fat."

"Shit, tell me about it. I lost two assistant positions and that's going to mean three days minimum for an autopsy."

The grapevine already buzzed with rumors that certain positions in the sheriff's office had been earmarked for elimination. If they made this decision on the same basis as the allotment of cruisers, then he was screwed.

"What've we got?" he asked as they walked up the hall, deeper into the house.

"White male, late forties, shot through the chest. My guess is that it happened sometime yesterday morning; he's been dead at least twenty-four hours. Name's Andrew Steele."

"The criminologist?"

"The same."

"Christ."

"You knew him?"

"Not well. He taught a couple of workshops back in the days when no one worried about the budget. He wasn't just a criminologist, he was also a shrink."

"What'd you think of him?"

"Brilliant man. I admired him." And envied his sophistication, smoothness, his obvious breeding.

Crick didn't offer an opinion about Steele. "His four-year-old son was found in the kitchen, unconscious and curled up in a fetal position. The housekeeper says he's a diabetic. She had the presence of mind to give him a shot of insulin when she found him, which may have saved his life. He's at Holy Cross Hospital now. The mother is missing."

In other words, Crick believed the mother was the primary suspect. "She shot him and split, leaving her injured son behind? Is that what you're saying, Paula?"

"Honey, no conclusions yet. I'm just telling you what I know so far."

"Where's the housekeeper?"

"Out by the pool, waiting for you. She had Thursday off and came in around eight this morning. She's been working for the Steeles since they got married ten years ago, and comes in five days a week. Cleans, picks up the son from preschool, helps with dinner."

"Any relatives?"

"Maternal grandmother in California. The housekeeper has a call into her."

"What kind of work does the missus do?"

"The worst imaginable, if you don't include what we do. High school English teacher. Rae didn't show up for work yesterday."

ABC, she laid it out. Paula Crick had been Broward County Coroner for almost twenty years, was now pushing sixty and sharper than ever. Very little got past her. People respected her, but found her abrasive and opinionated, the very qualities that Sheppard liked about her. The standing joke was that Crick preferred the company of the dead because they couldn't argue with her.

The hall opened into a magnificent room that overlooked a swimming pool and deck and the grand sweep of the ocean.

The Savould rug in the center had probably cost more than his annual salary. A small fortune in jade and crystal figurines graced a display case against the wall. Lithographs and paintings adorned the walls.

And there, next to a hewn stone coffee table, sprawled on the marble floor, lay Andrew Steele. Fruit flies hovered over him, an army of ants marched from the sliding glass doors to the corpse and then over it. They swarmed across his face, into his nostrils and out, busy little fuckers marching across the bloodstain shaped like Sicily on the front of his silk pajamas. Steele's head was turned toward the sliding glass door, as though he had hoped to glimpse the ocean one last time.

Sheppard said, "I knew Steele was well off, but I didn't realize it was this kind of money."

"Family money on his side. His grandfather owned half the county back in the thirties. Rae was his second wife, their son is his only child. With him dead, they inherit everything."

"How much is everything?" he asked.

Crick threw out her arms, a gesture that embraced not only the house, but the whole complex package. "Shit, I don't know. Five million? Ten? Twenty? More than we're likely to see in our lifetimes."

He would have to live as long as Moses to even take a baby step close to twenty million. *Get off it, Shep. One second at a time.* Right. Be in the moment. Focus, for Christ's sake. Focus.

He walked over to the body and moved around it slowly. How many corpses had he seen in his life? Three years on the streets of Miami, five with the FBI, five with Broward County: the bodies added up. You had to shut off the part of you that cared and he did it by counting backward from a hundred. It kept his left brain busy and calmed him.

He began the countdown and by eighty-eight, Steele looked pretty much as Sheppard remembered him: lean, solid, sinewy. A runner's body. Once, he'd been Cary Grant handsome, hair fading to white at the temples, sensuous mouth, bold bone structure. Now his bloated body looked sickly white.

Judging by the angle of his body, the way he was lying, and the splatter of blood, Sheppard figured he'd been shot from maybe fifteen feet. He probably had stumbled back and tripped over the hassock that stood about six inches from his feet. Blood had seeped around him, thick and dry now.

He thought about Moses again, nine hundred years of burning bushes, burning seas, burning miracles, and he thought about how fast and brightly twenty million would burn. Andrew Steele, brilliant and wealthy, at the apex of his life, had seemed invulnerable to Sheppard, protected somehow by his wealth, his opportunities, his silver spoon. But here he lay, just one more corpse, one more goddamn South Florida statistic.

"When can you autopsy him, Paula?"

"Like I said, hon, these budget cuts . . ."

"C'mon."

She rolled her eyes. "Barring a catastrophe, I should be able to do him by Monday at the latest. I don't anticipate anything unusual, but you never know. Maybe it'll be easy and I'll find coke in his blood."

"His secrets smell more complicated than that."

"One thing's for sure. Anyone with this kind of money has all different problems than we do."

"We'd deal with the problems, Paula, if we were in his shoes."

Paula Crick folded her arms at her waist, nodded slowly. "This girl hears you loud and clear, Shep honey. I play the Lotto every week, same as you. But c'mon, if we won, we'd fuck it up, same as he did." Her arms unfolded from her body like wings and made a gesture that encompassed the house, the beach, the rarefied air of Steele's world. "The only difference is that we wouldn't end up murdered, you and me, because it's something we know more about than he did."

Sheppard's head began to ache. He didn't want to be standing here. He didn't want to be in this house, having this particular conversation with the coroner while Andrew Steele's corpse lay at his feet. It reminded him of his own mortality, which had gotten all mixed up with money issues.

"Any idea how much alimony goes out to the ex?" he asked.

"No alimony, at least according to the housekeeper. Wife number one lives in Boston, has remarried, and hasn't had any contact with him for at least twelve or thirteen years. Wife number two met him when she was teaching at Manatee Correctional up the coast. She's ten years or so younger. The housekeeper hinted that things weren't going too well."

They had moved past the body to make room for the police photographer and stopped in the kitchen doorway. She pointed at a black X on the marble floor. "That's where the son, Carl, was found. You want to talk to the housekeeper?"

"Not yet. I'd like to poke around first." He needed to be alone in these rooms, to pull the silence into himself, to mull it over. Maybe, just maybe, the silence would tell him something about why Steele had been murdered.

Sheppard pulled a pair of latex gloves from a pocket inside his windbreaker. "See you in a bit."

The house was—what? Six thousand square feet? Eight? Ten? Whatever the exact measurements, it would take a team of cops days to search it well. But any home search could be narrowed down initially to just two rooms, Sheppard thought, the victim's bedroom and office.

Sheppard climbed a winding staircase from the second floor that opened into a large cupola made almost entirely of glass. The astonishing view of the glistening Atlantic and the beach three floors below literally stole his breath. Gulls wheeled past the glass, their shrieks echoing in the morning stillness. French doors, also glass, opened onto a wide porch that wrapped around either side of the cupola. Wicker patio furniture, painted the same shade of blue as the sky, stood under an awning.

He walked out onto the porch and peered straight down into the swimming pool area. He glimpsed a pair of brown legs poking out from under an umbrella that covered a patio table. Probably the housekeeper. Toys floated at the shallow end of the pool.

Sheppard stepped back inside the cupola. He wondered what it would it be like to wake up every morning in a house like this, walk into this office in the morning and feast on this sky, this ocean, this sunlit paradise?

Money: hello again. The grim reality depressed him. He was pushing forty, two thousand bucks stood between him and bank-ruptcy, and the credit card companies loved him so much they kept sending him new cards with lower interest rates and higher limits.

The two grand he'd managed to save had been marked for a trip to the Peruvian Amazon. Every day it became increasingly apparent that the trip wouldn't happen within the next six months. If he lost his job, the only way the Peruvian trip would happen at all would be if he lived as long as Moses.

Sheppard pulled a notepad from his shirt pocket and jotted notes. When he glanced up, his own reflection gazed back at him: that of a muscular man with sandy-colored hair who stood six-four in his bare feet. The slight stoop to his shoulders had started in eighth grade, when he'd shot up a full foot and towered over every other kid in his class. The stoop irritated him. It was a throwback, a habit, one of many that he had trouble breaking.

He straightened his shoulders, cracked his knuckles. Another habit. Trace that one back to his last cigarette years ago.

The moment, he reminded himself. Live in the moment. Sure. The Zen of homicide. Forget the corpse, forget the millions, forget his imminent unemployment.

He turned, his gaze sweeping through the office. Books. Everywhere he looked, he saw books. The things a man read, the books he collected, often told more about him than what he kept in his desk drawers. Sheppard climbed the wooden library ladder that moved from wall to wall along a metal track. The books ranged from true crime to a large collection on metaphysics to heavy psych tomes. Freud, Jung, Adler, all of them accompanied by numerous pop psychology books.

Sheppard had started out as a psych major and after a year of boring bullshit, switched to criminology. It had its share of bullshit, too, but it had held his interest. After three years as a Miami cop, he'd found the stress unbearable and had gone to law school. He'd come out of the University of Florida with a degree, a wife, and the certainty that he and the practice of law would soon part ways. It, too, was riddled with bullshit. But his law degree had gotten him into the FBI.

By the time he'd quit the Bureau, his marriage had fallen apart. He'd saved quite a bit of money, so he traveled around for a while. He had taken up running and regular workouts at a gym as ways to deal with stress. He had ceased pouring energy into what had gone wrong and had tried to define what had gone right in his life. By the time he'd put himself back together again, he was ready to move on and had ended up in Fort Lauderdale.

Now, as one of two floaters in the department, he worked wherever he was needed. He'd been assigned to every major department, he liked the variety. And the floater spots, he thought, probably headed the budget shitlist.

None of the women in his life fell into the "special" category. He traveled even when he couldn't afford it and preferred foreign destinations. His passion for very old places didn't quibble about continents, as long as the site held mystery.

He collected things when he traveled and now had an impressive array of pre-Columbian artifacts. He hoped to open an import/export business someday, which would allow him to indulge his need for travel and his fascination with ruins. But that dream seemed about as close as the moon.

Sheppard had been on several archaeological digs as a volunteer, had seen the sunrise over Machu Picchu, and he had spent four hours alone inside of the Great Pyramid, listening to the whispers of a civilization that had been dead for millennia. Those kinds of experiences constituted his vision for the future, on a full-time basis and not just as some expensive hobby.

Homicide work bore an uncanny resemblance to digging around in ruins; the past told its secrets to those who listened. Perhaps in this way he and Andrew Steele differed only marginally and the secret lay in finding their commonality, however small.

So Sheppard selected several of Steele's books, set them to one side of the desk to take with him. The desk, he noticed, was probably the most normal object in the room, wood-paneled, six feet long, with two shelves at the back and six drawers. The arrangement of contents smacked of an organized, efficient mind, everything just so: pens and pencils, Scotch tape, computer supplies, paper supplies, printer ribbons, two boxes of Christmas cards.

He found a small photo album with pictures of a striking

young woman and a small boy, probably Steele's wife and son. Sheppard looked more closely, noting the strain in the wife's smile, the hesitancy in the boy's eyes. A bad day? Or a life that hadn't measured up?

He knew the feeling, all right. He'd felt like this when he and his wife had split. Even Steele's money would not have fixed the marriage. Then again, money wouldn't have fixed Sheppard's marriage, either.

He opened the deep bottom drawer on the left side. No files, no papers, nothing that he'd expected. Instead, he removed two colorful tins of chocolate; a jewelry box that held a lady's silver watch studded with amber and lapis lazuli; a second jewelry box that contained a deep green emerald set in gold; small velvet bags that held a jade monkey and an elephant made of some black stone, maybe obsidian. The last item was a pendant of quartz crystal.

Sheppard set everything on the desk and popped open the lids on the tins. None of the chocolates had been touched. But resting on top in the first tin was a plain white envelope. Inside he found a sheet of paper wrapped around seven cards. He recognized them as tarot cards, but knew nothing about them.

He smoothed the paper flat. Someone, presumably Steele, had listed the cards one through seven and next to each had jotted REC'D, a date, and one of the items now sitting on the desk.

He felt that first familiar ripple of excitement at discovering something that clearly didn't fit. That was the thing with police work; you never knew when or what you might stumble upon that would lead you somewhere. He enjoyed the hunt, piecing together the seemingly disparate parts, the search for the whole picture. It fit that part of him that continually searched for answers to his own dilemmas.

Sheppard removed the empty trash bag from the wastebasket next to the desk and put everything inside of it. He included several of Steele's books and half a dozen patient files.

He started to boot up the computer when he heard someone coming up the stairs. Crick stopped in the doorway. "A girl could kill herself on these stairs," she said, her voice slightly breathless.

"Some room, huh?"

"I'd never get a lick of work done up here. Listen, the house-keeper's chafing at the bit. You'd better talk to her while you have the chance."

The computer would have to wait. "I'm finished in here for now." He pocketed the envelope, tucked the trash bag under his arm, and carried it downstairs. He set the trash bag down in the kitchen, then walked out to the pool area with Crick.

She introduced him to Augusta Lee, a middle-aged black woman whom Sheppard pegged as Trinidadian. "I realize you've been through a terrible experience, Mrs. Lee," he said. "But I only have a few questions."

"And I have no answers." She held a pink handkerchief to her nose and blew. "Except that Mrs. Steele did not do this."

"No one has accused Mrs. Steele of anything."

"Not in so many words. But I know how it looks. A young woman who has disappeared, an older, wealthy husband . . ."

"When was the last time you saw the Steeles?" he asked.

"Wednesday evening. She and I fixed dinner, he was doing laps in the pool. He exercised a lot."

"Did they act unusual in any way?" Crick prodded.

"Not that I noticed."

"What time did you come in this morning?" Sheppard asked.

"Eight. I . . . I found Carl first. He's a delightful boy, very polite, very smart, we . . . I . . ."

Her composure broke, her voice cracked, tears leaked from her eyes. "He was still alive. Still breathing. I . . . I picked him up, set him on the couch. I . . . I knew he was in insulin shock. In my country, I was a nurse. I sometimes gave him his injections.

"I ran to the refrigerator for the insulin, gave him the shot, then . . . then called 911. The cord stretches a good ways and that's when I . . . I saw him. Mr. Steele. I knew just by looking at him that he wasn't alive. But . . . but after I hung up, I went over to him and felt his wrist. His robe had fallen open and I found somthing strapped around his waist. Then . . . then I backed away from him and waited with Carl until the paramedics arrived.

She set an object on the table that resembled a remote control device for a television. Sheppard didn't pick it up.

"I understand you've called Mrs. Steele's mother."

Her head bobbed. "She and her husband—her second husband, Mrs. Steele's stepfather—live down in San Diego. She's a pediatrician, semi-retired, I think. Nice lady. I got her answering service and left a message."

Sheppard handed Mrs. Lee his business card. "Please have her call me as soon as you talk to her."

"She'll be on the first plane out here. I know that much. Carl is her only grandchild."

"Mrs. Lee, can you tell me anything about these?" He removed the tarot cards from the envelope and fanned them out on the table in front of her. "I found them in Mr. Steele's desk."

She nodded and stuffed the hanky in a pocket in her skirt. "They came in the mail. Every few months for the last year or so, Mrs. Steele got a package in the mail and one of these cards was with it. She thought one of her students was sending them."

Students didn't send expensive watches, rings, or jade figurines, he thought. "What were in these packages?"

"Chocolates. That's all I saw. Anyway, when the last one arrived, Mr. Steele was quite disturbed by it. He said he . . . he was going to have the police look into it."

Sheppard made a mental note to check on that.

"I really am not feeling very well. I'd like to leave now."

"Just one more question," Sheppard said. "Do you think the difference in age was a problem in the Steeles' marriage?"

He expected her to answer quickly, just to get out of here. But she considered the question carefully. "Their problems were about his absences, not about their ages. Besides, it was only ten years."

"Was he seeing someone else?" *Is that what this is about? Another woman? Infidelity? Is it going to be as common as that?*

But Augusta Lee looked at him as though he were crazy. "There wasn't any room in his life for anyone else. He was always working. His life was about work."

"What about Mrs. Steele?"

Augusta's prolonged hesitation didn't bode well. She looked down at her hands. Flicked at something on the tabletop.

"Anything you can tell us, Mrs. Lee, will help us out," Crick said softly.

She rolled her lips together and looked up at Crick, then at him. "Yes, I think she was seeing someone. Sometimes when Mr. Steele was out of town she called me at the last minute and asked me to sit with Carl. She was never gone all night or anything," she added quickly. "But she often came in quite late, two or three in the morning."

"Was this recently?"

"No, maybe six or seven months ago. My birthday's in March and it was around then that she stopped calling me at the last minute."

"Do you have any idea who the man was?" Sheppard asked.

She shook her head. "No." She stood then. "I really don't feel well. I'll be glad to answer your questions some other time." She started to turn away, then gestured at the object she'd removed from Steele's body. "I don't know what it is, but maybe it's important."

Sheppard nodded and thanked her. As she and Crick walked across the deck and out of sight, he fiddled with the small knobs on the device, but nothing happened. He turned it over and slid open the piece that fitted over the battery compartment. He removed the four triple A batteries, which appeared to be new, and put them in again. The device still refused to work. Sheppard pocketed it to turn into the lab later. But a part of him gnawed at the puzzle of the device. Why would Steele wear the contraption to bed?

He walked around the pool, eyeing the forlorn toys, the lone raft. Down below, on the beach, sunbathers gathered despite the cool air. By noon, they would be out in droves with their umbrellas, their colorful towels, their sunblock #50. Beyond them, the Atlantic stretched forever, clear and calm, waves breaking gently against the sand. Sandpipers scurried about as the waves receded. A slice of paradise where something had gone very wrong, he thought.

Crick strode back across the deck toward him. "Sergeant Jenks said to tell you he and Franklin are going to start their rounds with the neighbors." She motioned toward the tarot cards and wrinkled her nose as if she had bitten into something sour. "What do you make of those?"

"Do I look like I know anything about tarot, Paula?"

"Honey, you look like you know stuff I'd love to learn." Then she winked and laughed. "Hey, that was a joke, Shep. C'mon, lighten up. The closest New Age bookstore is that one over by the river. You'll probably find someone there who knows about tarot."

Sheppard glanced at the toys floating in the pool and felt the descent of that ethereal black cloud again. "How do people like this end up as statistics?"

"Oh c'mon, Sheppard. You've been spending too goddamn much time on the wrong side of the tracks. Rich people fart, they hurt, they make bad choices."

He didn't think it was quite that simple, but he couldn't say it eloquently.

In Venezuela, where he had lived much of his childhood, the poor occupied hillside shacks called *ranchitos* which surrounded the rest of the city. In Iquitos, Peru, they lived in huts on stilts in the middle of the Amazon's tributaries. In Rio they roamed the streets in gangs and slept where they happened to be when they got tired. People like that didn't have access to the basics, much less to power and privilege.

He supposed this held a message for him, but damned if he could figure it out.

4

Her eyelids felt as if they had been glued together with some cheap substance that had dried on her lashes. Her mouth tasted of sand, deserts. Her left arm had gone numb. Her bladder threatened to explode. The hollow ache in the pit of her stomach told her it had been awhile since she had eaten.

Rae Steele rolled onto her back, felt the cool, indifferent pressure on her left wrist, and opened her eyes. Metal. A metal object encircled her wrist. Gradually, her field of vision expanded to include the rocking chair to which the metal was attached. Handcuffs.

She lifted her head. Walls, wooden walls. Charcoal sketches on bright white sheets of paper covered the walls. She raised up a little higher and stared at the sketches.

All of them depicted the same woman involved in various activities. The longer she stared, the clearer the women's face became. She was the woman.

Panic fluttered like a trapped bird at the back of her throat. She sat all the way up, the handcuff pulling hard on her right wrist, her other senses kicking in. She was lying on some sort of cushion, sweat had soaked through her clothes, she smelled water.

She squeezed her eyes shut and sank back against the cushion, desperately seeking the safety of sleep. It eluded her, but she still didn't open her eyes.

Andy and I were arguing, I left in a huff, drove out to the cabin, and on my way home . . . What?

Headlights. She remembered headlights shining in her rearview mirror as she had crossed the bridge to the beach. It had been early, just past seven, and the car had followed her closely. Once she reached the other side of the bridge, she'd lost sight of the headlights and figured the car had turned off. She'd been more concerned then about what she would say to Andy, that things between them would have to change if she continued in the marriage.

She had parked, gone into the house, and found a note from Andy saying that he and Carl had gone out for a bite to eat. Ten minutes later, the doorbell had rung, and . . .

Don't think about it now.

Rae opened her eyes again, sat straight up, and looked around slowly, taking in the room, the details other than the sketches of her. The odd chairs that hung from a ceiling beam. The handmade furniture. The high sheen of the floor. The colorful hammock strung up near a window. The beanbag chair with a big red *H* on it. On the wall to her right, she saw a childlike sketch of a hanged man, the kid's game, guess the letters or hang in the noose.

Through an open doorway in front of her she glimpsed trees. She couldn't tell from here what kinds of trees these were, but they looked dense. Impenetrable. She felt fairly sure that water surrounded this weird little house.

Gradually, noises impinged on her awareness. Clicks and hums, the soft whisper of water, birds. She sat up slowly, careful not to rattle the handcuff, and craned her neck to peer over the edge of the window. Trees, sky, water, afternoon light.

She heard a noise and glanced quickly toward its source. A dark figure stood in the doorway on the other side of the room, face lost in shadow. A man. Five-foot-ten or so, brawny shoulders, muscular legs slightly spread. He held a tray. When he stepped forward, out of the shadows, something monstrous swelled in her throat. She tried to swallow it back, failed, tried again, and air rushed past her teeth. The monstrous thing sank to someplace deep inside her; her mind snapped into clarity.

A sequence of events loomed in her head and collapsed into a single event. This man had rung her doorbell, slapped something over her mouth, brought her here, handcuffed her.

Rae watched him as he crossed the room, his movements assured, deliberate. She'd seen her share of cons when she had worked at Manatee Prison. These days, they called prisons "correctional institutions" and convicts were "inmates," as though the labels mitigated the truth. But she knew otherwise. She knew that the worst cons, like Bundy and Manson, were the exceptions, not the rule.

Men like the one in front of her didn't make the news, no books had been spawned from their lives, they hadn't been featured in TV movies or documentaries. But that didn't diminish their evil. The only quality they seemed to share with the likes of Bundy and Manson was that they rarely looked the way she imagined killers should look. Sometimes they even looked like this man did.

Forget Freddy Krueger and Hannibal Lechter. This guy's eyes burned blue, a brilliant, guileless blue, the focus of his attractive face. No acne scars pitted his cheeks; his skin was smooth, bronze, like rich, dark honey. His hair and beard were blonde. Someone's heartthrob, a model on the cover of a magazine, that was what he looked like.

His quick smile attempted to assure her there was nothing wrong with her being handcuffed to a rocking chair, inside a weird house in the middle of Christ knew where. He looked to be in his early thirties, but she knew he wasn't. Before last night, she hadn't seen him in nine years.

"I made some soup," he said, setting the tray on the wooden crates and pushing them over to the cushion. "I figured you'd be hungry. You've been out a good while." He unrolled a cloth napkin with a soup spoon inside of it. "This is fish soup with potatoes." He dipped the spoon into the soup and raised it toward her mouth. "Open up now. It's really delicious."

Rae's unshackled arm flew up, knocking the spoon out of his hand. "How much money do you want?" she hissed. "Just tell me! How much?"

He stared at her with murderous eyes, then grabbed her unshackled arm with one hand and her jaw with the other. He leaned into her face, leaned so close she could smell the sweat on his skin. "I don't want your money. This isn't about money. We clear on that?"

Tears filled her eyes and she whispered, "Yes."

He released her jaw, rubbed his palms over his jeans, gestured at the soup. "You want this or not?"

"I . . . I have to go to the bathroom."

A deep furrow formed between his eyes, he looked injured. "You don't even remember me, do you?"

"I remember."

"You're just saying that because you're afraid. If you really remember me, what's my name?"

The *H* on the beanbag, she thought, and the name popped up from some thick, ugly darkness inside of her. "Hal. Your name is Hal."

No last name. But apparently the first name satisfied him; his frown vanished, his eyes brightened like a kid's. "I never forgot your name either, Rae." He set the bowl in front of her, the spoon inside it. "You need to eat."

He sat back on his heels, watching her. Rae leaned over as if to pick up the spoon, but instead swept up the bowl and hurled it at him. Hot soup splashed into his face, the bowl hit a beam behind him, and she leaped up and ran toward the door, dragging the rocking chair behind her, her breath exploding from her mouth.

She burst through the doorway, the rocking chair banging against the floor, into sunlight and heat. A startled flock of blue herons lifted from the nearest trees, their wings beating against the stillness. She gaped at the water, at the mangroves. Sweet Christ, she was in the Everglades.

Then he tackled her and Rae crashed to the wooden platform and sank into a place beyond hunger, despair, beyond fear.

Hal unlocked the handcuff from the rocker, picked her up, and carried her back inside the chickee. He set her on the cushion. Stupid bitch.

But he sympathized with her fear. He knew what it was like to feel trapped. He had felt that way every day during his stint in the joint, except for the brief respites when he *reached.*

He left her on the cushion and went into the kitchen for the Darvon. A nurse he had met during one of his lonely periods had provided the Darvon, syringes, and a number of other vital medicines for his first-aid kit. You didn't live in the Everglades unless you were prepared.

The big drawback to the Darvon was that he had to run the generator to power the fridge so he could keep the stuff cold. Nothing he could do about it now. He needed the Darvon because it silenced the chatter in her head and allowed him access to the deeper levels of her personality.

He gave her less than before, then waited for the Darvon to take effect. The first time he'd *reached* into Rae, they'd been sitting across from each other in her office in the education building on the Manatee compound.

In those days, she was a teacher and guidance counselor and they were discussing the college courses he would take. He'd been enthralled with her Cupid's bow mouth, the soft blue veins that ran through her eyelids, the shiny thickness of her hair, a sunlit river that flowed down her back.

He had *reached* ever so gently, seeking contact, nothing more, and had found Steele right there at the surface of her thoughts. It was how he'd discovered that she and Steele recently had become lovers.

He had leaped away from her and back into himself so suddenly, so violently, she had felt it, he knew she had from the way she winced, as if afflicted with a sudden, very bad headache. After that, he'd *reached* into her only when they weren't in the same building. It had required more effort on his part, greater concentration, but as long as she was on the compound, he had managed to do it once a day.

For months, he had spied on her in this way, a psychic voyeur. She had become his obsession, his fix, his addiction. On weekends when she wasn't working, he'd suffered agonizing withdrawal, an anguish that seemed, at times, almost physical.

He finally had gotten to the point where he couldn't stand it anymore, so one weekend he tried to *reach* beyond the compound. He'd failed miserably and repeatedly. He couldn't get past the buzzing static that emanated from several hundred inmates, guards, visitors. He couldn't move past his *need*.

Hal had continued his attempts for weeks until, at the pinnacle of his frustration, Steele had inadvertently given him exactly what he needed to make the difference. He had handed Hal a photograph of a man who could have been anyone.

Reach for this guy, Hal, and tell me what you get.

His success at extending himself had begun then and had brought him to this moment in time, with Rae. And this was what he'd wanted, right? Rae with him. But not like this, Rae terrified, trying to escape, Rae doped up on Darvon. But he didn't know what else to do, didn't know how to make her trust him.

Her breathing evened out; the Darvon had done its job. Hal sat at her head, placed both hands at the sides of her face, fingers at the temples. In the movie *Resurrection*, Ellen Burstyn had done this in a revival tent, while healing a sick child. Hal couldn't recall what the child had, couldn't recall much of anything, in fact, except for the shape of Burstyn's hands against the boy's head.

He would have to watch that movie with Rae, he thought. He needed to remind himself that Burstyn's talent in *Resurrection* differed from his own only in the intent. She healed and alleviated suffering; he had been trained to gather information, to injure, to destroy. He needed to learn how to redirect that training so that he could ease Rae's fear of him.

Hal shut his eyes and *reached*, trying to fill her unconscious with peaceful images. His cellular phone pealed, interrupting him. Manacas was the only person who had this number and if Hal didn't answer now, Manacas would keep calling until he did. He got up with enormous reluctance, retrieved the phone from the kitchen, and walked out to the edge of the platform, well away from Rae's range of hearing.

"Yeah, Eddie, what's up?"

"I told Indrio about Steele. He drove by the place earlier today and said the estate's swarming with cops, so it looks like they found the body."

"Good. Then it won't be long before Fletcher shows up."

"Indrio wants us to meet in the next few days."

"I'm tied up right now. I'll call you tomorrow sometime and we'll settle on a place."

"Indrio wants to meet tomorrow, Hal."

"It's not convenient for me. Look, I've got to go. I'll talk to you later."

He disconnected before Manacas could reply, walked out to the edge of the open platform, and sat down. Was it worth it? Rae was worth it, yes, but Rae was his personal business; she didn't have anything to do with the original scheme he, Indrio, and Manacas had concocted.

Way back when they had first discussed getting rid of Steele and Fletcher, he had only wanted to get even with them for using him, for using all of them. Now he knew that as long as either of them was alive, it would be nearly impossible for him to have a life outside of the Everglades. This was especially true as long as Fletcher was alive, because she had a personal score to settle with him for walking out on her. And, of course, the higher she climbed within the FBI's hierarchy, the more pressure she would feel to bury Delphi and its numerous errors.

There was no question in Hal's mind that Steele's death would bring her to Florida. She would conclude that he or Indrio or Manacas or the three of them were behind it and she would pull out the plugs to hunt them down. The plan, of course, was that they would get to her before she got to them. But even the best plans rarely worked the way they were envisioned and, quite frankly, now that Rae was in the picture he wasn't sure if he wanted to take the risk.

He needed time to work on Rae, to bring her around, to gain her trust, before they left the chickee and the Everglades and moved out into the world.

And go where, buddy boy? Just where the fuck you going?

And what would he do once they got there? He supposed he could play psychic reverend again, but building a clientele took time and he had no burning desire to repeat that part of his past.

What he wanted most of all was to find some secluded place where he and Rae could live in relative comfort and seclusion. A farm in Iowa, forty acres in Washington state; the place wasn't as important as a house, a family, a life. Assuming he could pull any of that off, would he still be looking over his shoulder for Fletcher?

He slid his thumb over the edge of the phone, then quickly punched out Fletcher's home number before he could change his mind. She picked up on the third ring, her voice soft and hoarse with sleep. "Yes? Hello?"

Hal shut his eyes, pulling her voice into himself, then *reached.* Static, that was all he got, it was all he usually had gotten in the past. It was enough to convince him that as long as she was alive, he would not be free.

He pressed his thumb over the button and disconnected.

5

At eleven Friday night, Lenora Fletcher and two dozen other people sang happy birthday to Keith Krackett, the deputy director of the FBI. He then blew out sixty-eight candles on a cake nearly as large as his dining room table. His diminutive wife proceeded to slice it into small, tidy pieces, as though she thought there might not be enough to go around.

Fletcher's feet ached from standing and the knot in her gut now weighed about forty pounds. But she still managed to notice these small, stupid details about the gathering. Yes, tonight was important. Yes, there would never be another night quite like it. But oh Christ, she wanted to soak her feet in warm Epsom salts. Wanted to get a massage, sit in a sauna, bake on a beach. She hungered for privacy and silence.

Now Krackett tapped his knife against his crystal water glass and everyone fell silent. She had to pay attention, had to slide the Fletcher mask into place.

Krackett pushed to his feet. His bearing had always made him seem taller than he actually was and younger than sixty-eight. He had a full head of salt and pepper hair, a trim physique that he maintained through daily games of tennis, a meticulous diet, all the right health choices. His face seemed remarkable only because of the shrewd intelligence in his eyes.

"I'd like to make an announcement," he said. "As all of you have undoubtedly heard by now, I'll be retiring in the next three to six months. That means that while you're slaving away in D.C., I'll be out here in Virginia, playing tennis and lazing by the pool."

Laughter. Fletcher glanced quickly at the faces around the

table. Except for Krackett's wife and the maids, all of these people were Krackett's intimates within the Bureau and political circles in Washington. They, like everyone else who mattered, had heard rumors for months that he planned to retire; this announcement merely made it official.

Other rumors had been circulating, too, about Krackett's successor. She knew she had a good shot at it, better than most because Krackett stood so firmly in her court. But the director had other favorites, two men with less seniority who had sucked up to the right people over the years. They were both here as well—a Harvard boy with an impeccable record and a good-looking stud who dressed and acted like the fed on *The X-Files*.

She had no doubt that her qualifications surpassed those of both men. But she also had enormous internal conflicts about handling the job. These stemmed, she knew, from the errors she had made during the Delphi business, serious errors in judgment.

"The director and I have discussed at great length the qualities we're looking for in my successor," Krackett went on. "Although he couldn't be here tonight, we agreed this would be a good time to share our decision with you.

"Up until the early seventies, when I became deputy director, there had never been a female agent within the Bureau. The woman who broke that tradition was a twenty-six-year-old attorney fresh out of Yale. She blazed her way through the ranks and has become something of a legend at Quantico, where she is now in charge of the training program for recruits.

"She brings twenty-two years of experience with her and will be the first woman in the Bureau's history to hold this position. Ladies and gentlemen, I'm delighted to introduce you to the next deputy director of the FBI, Lenora Fletcher."

The applause, loud, prolonged, sincere, thundered inside of Fletcher, reverberated against her very bones. She lit up like a Christmas tree and locked eyes with Krackett, who grinned from ear to ear like a new father. But behind that grin, inside those shrewd dark eyes, flashed a message she didn't miss: *We pulled it off, Lenora, but now you have to tie up the Delphi fiasco.*

Her head spun as people came up to congratulate her. The Harvard boy shook her hand, his smile as stiff as his hair; Mr.

X-Files looked totally stunned. She no longer felt her aching feet, jammed into high heels that only TV women wore. The knot in her gut began to dissolve. Her mind raced, calculating the odds.

The formal announcement wouldn't be made for at least another six weeks, but this was the first important step. By tomorrow morning, the rumor mill would be churning and calls would pour in from minor players scrambling to get into her good graces.

Somewhere in the house, a phone rang, its peal a reminder that beyond these gracious rooms, beyond the rolling green lawn outside, the real world ticked away like a bomb. *Six weeks.* She felt a sudden uneasiness that it wouldn't be enough time to wrap up the Delphi mess, the one glitch in her career that could kill this promotion. Hell, at this point, she wasn't sure that another six *months* would be enough time.

It seemed she had spent most of the last three years either hunting for or getting rid of the seven participants in the project. Four were dead, three were still missing, and she had absolutely no idea where they were. But as long as they were free, they jeopardized her future.

"Lenora?"

She glanced around to see Krackett's wife, her smile cockeyed, as if she'd had too much to drink. She was, in fact, a teetotaler who had had a stroke about a year ago, one of the reasons Krackett was retiring. "It was a lovely dinner, Anita."

"I didn't cook one bit of it," she replied with a laugh, then leaned closer. "Keith would like to speak to you privately in the study."

"Thanks."

Fletcher hurried down the wide hallway and knocked at the door of Krackett's study. "Come in," he called.

The tremendous room shone with genuine eighteenth century antiques. A large fireplace dominated one wall, shelves of books climbed another. But the room might have belonged to anyone. None of Krackett's degrees and commendations graced these walls, no family photos stood on the oak desk. It looked like a room in an expensive, historical inn.

Since he was still on the phone, she sat down in one of the

leather chairs in front of his desk. Her hands perspired, her heart drummed, she didn't like the expression on Krackett's face.

"Right, I understand," he said. "I'll be in touch."

"I hope that was a birthday greeting," she said lightly as he hung up.

"Andrew Steele has been murdered."

As soon as the words sank in, walls of muscle and bone collapsed inside her and she nearly choked on the debris.

"His son is in intensive care, his wife is missing."

"Missing? What the hell does that mean? Is she a suspect?"

"Yes."

"How did Steele die?"

"A .38 to the chest."

"Then it doesn't involve Delphi."

Krackett leaned forward, his face skewed with emotion and urgency, blood pouring into his cheeks, his eyes burning with passion. "We have no way of knowing that for sure." The words hissed through his clenched teeth. "And until we know otherwise, we're going to assume that it *does* involve Delphi. That Manacas or Indrio or Bennet is behind it."

Or the three of them were in it together. With this thought, her promotion sprouted wings and flitted away.

Krackett paced, his shoes squeaked against the polished wood floors. Her mind scrambled for answers and came up with a big, fat zero.

"I would prefer the local sheriff's department know as little as possible, Lenora."

These marching orders would cast her out of D.C. at the very time when she should be here. Lenora Fletcher, fallen angel. She suddenly realized Krackett had stopped talking, that he was staring at her.

"What, uh, did you say?" she stammered.

"How soon can you get a surveillance team down there?"

Down there: as if Florida lay somewhere near Australia, a dark, untamed continent she would have to traipse across, to conquer. "It'll take two calls. Who's the cop in charge of the investigation?"

"Wayne Sheppard, a five-year vet with the Broward Sheriff's Department." He reeled off the rest of what he knew, which wasn't a hell of a lot at this point. "The best way to proceed is low profile until we're better informed. If Mrs. Steele is still missing, we call it a possible abduction, step in, and take over the investigation even if there isn't a ransom demand."

"Jesus, Keith. Without a ransom demand, it's tough to call it an abduction. That alone could stir suspicion."

He turned, his eyes as bright as aluminum. "We can live with suspicion. But we can't live with exposure. Let's hope to Christ Steele's murder is unrelated to Delphi. But if there's a connection . . ."

He didn't finish the sentence. He didn't have to. They both knew the consequences. If the machinations that had formed and sculpted Delphi ever came to light in the press, heads would roll and hers and Krackett's would lead the parade.

The mood of the American public toward government had hit an all-time low, cynicism was king. Joe Smith in Iowa wouldn't give a shit why Delphi had been created. The only thing ole Joe and all the others like him would understand was that the government had funded a covert project with prisoners and had made some grievous mistakes along the way. Her political allies would side with public opinion if it ever came out that the bulk of Delphi's funding had been funneled through the CIA. And she would be pounding pavement in search of a new job. Waitressing, for instance, or tour guide at a Florida park.

"I'd better make those calls," she said, and realized she needed to make one other call as well that Krackett wouldn't know about.

As she got up, she felt like the kid who had to stick his finger in the hole in the dike to save Holland from a flood. The big question remained: would she be able to find the hole before the dike exploded?

Light spilled across the front of the Vietnam memorial wall. Fletcher's eyes roamed this vast black continent of the dead, searching for the names of the two men the war had stolen from her.

Her older brother, her only sibling, had died in a raid on a Vietnamese village when she was in college. His closest friend, the kid next door whom Fletcher probably would have married, had died in a POW camp. She still couldn't look at this wall without a lump of emotion rising in her throat.

"Early morning musings on philosophical questions certainly isn't the route to good health and longevity, Lenora."

She turned at the sound of the voice behind her. The man in the black leather jacket and tailored slacks no longer looked as fierce as he once had. The ravages of age and cancer had sunken his cheeks, paled his blue eyes, and left his skin a soft, sickly white. Chemotherapy had stolen most of his leonine white hair. But he still possessed an indisputable presence that you could feel, she thought, even if you didn't know he once had been one of the most powerful individuals in the CIA.

"You don't feel anything when you stand in front of this wall, Richard?"

His small, shrewd eyes darted from her to the wall, then back again. "Sure. I feel disgust that we lost the goddamn war."

"Hell, you people are the ones who started it."

His smile smacked of a paternalism she'd once found comforting, but which merely irritated her now. "You were always prone to exaggeration, Lenora. By the way, I heard about your promotion. Congratulations."

"Thanks."

"But I don't suppose that's why we're meeting at this ungodly hour."

"Of course it is. I'm gloating."

He laughed then, a quick laugh, a shell of the robust explosions she remembered. "Touché. Let's sit down." He gestured toward a nearby bench and they walked over to it.

Fletcher noticed that Richard Evans moved more slowly than he had the last time they'd met. He'd never told her what kind of cancer he had, but she didn't have to be an M.D. to recognize that the prognosis wasn't good. When he finally sat down, he seemed winded from the short walk.

"How're you feeling, Rich?"

"I've got good days. But today isn't one of them. But hell, I'm seventy years old and I've only got a few regrets. In all, it hasn't been a bad life."

She reached out and squeezed his hand, a gesture she never would have allowed herself in the old days. "It's about—"

"Andrew Steele," he said before she could finish. "I'm not that far out of the loop. I got a call about one this morning."

"From who?"

Evans just smiled and clicked his tongue against his teeth. "Lenora, Lenora. You never give up. Even if I told you the name, it wouldn't mean anything to you. The labyrinth is far more complex than it used to be. It's extended into the private sector as well. Did you realize that once Delphi began to fall apart, Andrew used Bennet and some of the others for his private clients? I understand he made quite a bit of money at it, too. That didn't set well with anyone in the Agency."

"Are you saying this was an Agency hit?"

Evans winced at the expression. "We've never been hit men, Lenora. There's always been a broader purpose. But in answer to your question, no, I couldn't find any evidence that the Agency is behind Andrew's murder. I think one or all of your missing boys are behind it."

"Maybe."

For years, Evans had been her Deep Throat in the CIA, the man who brought her information, funding, and finally, the truth about Delphi. By then, of course, it had been too late, the damage had been done. But she rarely had doubted what he'd told her and she didn't doubt it now.

"Are you going down there?" he asked.

"Later today."

Evans reached into his jacket pocket and brought out three CD-ROM disks, each labeled with a number. "All our Delphi files are on here. Those on Bennet, Indrio, and Manacas are on the first disk. I doubt if you'll find anything you don't already know. After all, you worked with them, Lenora."

"I worked with them under false pretenses, though. I wasn't fully informed until it was too late."

"Believe it or not, that's one of my regrets in life. But at the time, I couldn't pass the information on to you without risking my own neck."

"I'm not blaming you, Richard." She dropped the disks into

her purse. "I'm just saying that I never saw the Agency's files, so there might be something in here that'll help." She kissed him quickly on the cheek; his skin felt dry and old. "Thanks."

He started to get up, but didn't have the strength. Fletcher quickly grabbed onto his hand and pulled him to his feet. She held onto his arm as they made their way away from the wall. "Call my cell number if anything comes up, okay?"

"I'll call regardless," he replied.

She walked him to his car and watched him get inside, a frail and sick old man. As he drove off, she stood there with the chilly morning air nipping at her legs and wondered if she'd just stared into the face of her own future twenty years from now.

She would rather be dead.

II: The Players

"Research over the last fifty years by little-known but forward-looking thinkers has shown there is a vast creative potential in the human mind that is as yet totally unrecognized by science."

—Edgar D. Mitchell, *Psychic Explorations*

6

At noon on Saturday, Sheppard pulled into the crowded parking lot of One World Books & Things. In a glance, he knew it was not his world, but it looked like an interesting place to visit.

As he opened the glove compartment to get the envelope that contained the tarot cards, a stack of envelopes tumbled out. Bills. He had stuck them in here a few days ago to mail. By Monday his answering machine probably would short-circuit with calls from his creditors.

A hard knot formed in the center of his chest. He rubbed at it, forced himself to take several deep breaths. Angst, he thought. Sometimes it manifested as a hard, pounding ache between his eyes, sometimes it lodged like an old bullet in his intestine. But when it concerned money and his creditors, it nearly always swelled in his chest.

Zen, he reminded himself. Be in the moment and all that. He got out of the car.

The wind chimes that hung from an awning over the front porch tinkled in a breeze that blew off the river. Bird feeders, swinging from branches, had attracted flocks of twittering black birds. Beneath the trees on either side of the house stood thick, lush gardens that imbued the place with a kind of magic. The peaceful grounds soothed him, dissolved the lump in his chest.

Ten years ago the so-called New Age had existed as an esoteric movement populated mostly by weirdos and social misfits. But at some point between his stint with the Bureau and his move to Fort Lauderdale, it had gone mainstream and become a multi-million dollar industry that included everything from health foods to vision quests. The shop looked to be flourishing in this favorable clime.

He strolled through the open front door. Flute music issued softly from unseen speakers, the air was redolent with the sweet scent of incense or candles. His older sister had taken him into head shops in the Sixties that had smelled like this; the aroma brought back the wonder and confusion of his adolescence.

To his immediate right he saw a small room where half a dozen women browsed through displays of crystals, polished stones, and a selection of Southwestern jewelry. To his left a much larger room housed a pair of cages and a pair of tall, wooden floor perches. A magnificent Amazonian parrot occupied one perch, a toucan stood on the other. A pair of white doves cooed softly from a large cage near the window.

The birds probably violated health codes, but they were a nice touch.

As he turned, he nearly collided with a pretty little girl of eight or nine. "Oops," he said. "Sorry."

She dropped her head back and gazed up at him with her huge, dark eyes. "Wow," she breathed. "You're about the tallest guy I've ever seen. You a basketball player?"

Sheppard laughed. "Nope. Those your birds?"

"Well, sort of. They're One World's mascots, but yeah, they're mine. I feed them, change their cages, stuff like that. The toucan's name is Iquitos, because he comes from the jungle around there. The parrot's name is Blue. He's from the Amazon, too. You ever been to the Amazon?"

"A couple of times."

"C'mon." Her eyes widened. "For real?"

"For real."

"Is it true they have pink dolphins down there?"

"Absolutely. They're smaller than the dolphins you see in Florida."

"And they're really pink?"

"Like bubble gum. Supposedly they're able to transform themselves into people. The legends say that whenever there's a celebration in a village, one of the dolphins becomes a man and goes to the party, where he dances with the prettiest women.

People recognize him because he wears a hat over his blow hole."

"Awesome."

He didn't tell her the rest of the story, that the transformed dolphin seduced the prettiest woman, took her to the river, and impregnated her. That way when an unmarried woman got pregnant, she could say the dolphin had done it.

"And did you see piraña?"

She pronounced it in Spanish, the ñ rolling off her tongue in a way he had never mastered. "I went fishing for piraña."

"And you ate them?"

"Definitely."

She made a face and he laughed. It was hard not to like a kid like this. If he and his ex had stayed together, a daughter might have been a reality. He thought about it more often than was healthy, thought about it at moments like this, when a kid asked him questions, when a kid caught his eye in a crowd. He was grateful, though, that she'd distracted him from a nagging doubt that he was completely off track with this tarot stuff. The way his luck had been running lately, he doubted the cards had any connection whatsoever to Steele's murder.

"Are they any good? The piraña?"

"A little bony, but tasty. *Es Cubana?*"

"*Medio.*"

Half Cuban. He extended his hand. "I'm Shep."

His hand swallowed hers. "I'm Annie. If you're here for the Voyager workshop, it's down the hall. That's where everyone is."

It sounded like a workshop for alien abductees. "What's a Voyager?"

She giggled. "It's a tarot deck."

"I'm just looking for the tarot books."

"I'll show you where they are."

He followed her past a display of angel books and entered the heart of the shop, three large rooms designed for browsing, exploring, poking around. Sunlight formed warm, buttery pools on the throw rugs. Comfortable chairs invited him to sit down, kick off his shoes, and stick around a while.

"The tarot books are at the very end of the shelves, under tarot," Annie said.

"Thanks a lot."

"Sure. If you need anything else, I'll be up front." She smiled and wandered off.

Sheppard walked the length of the shelves that lined the north wall, topics clearly marked above each section. Angels, aliens, crystals, herbs, health, channeling, meditation, the spectrum of alternative strangeness.

He felt uncomfortable just being in here. Maybe this stuff got into your system through osmosis. Or sound waves. Hell, if the magnetic field emitted by a transformer could cause cancer, no telling what disease he might pick up here.

When he finally reached the tarot section, he was shocked at the sheer number of books and decks. Angel decks, Jungian decks, herbal decks, feminist decks, mythical decks, even the Voyager deck.

"Do you need help finding something?"

The elderly woman had approached him on feet of silk. She barely stood five feet tall and had to drop her head back to look at him. Her eyes captivated him, dark eyes like Annie's, eyes he could drown in. Her curly salt and pepper hair was short, stylishly cut. A pair of glasses hung from a chain around her neck. She wore jeans, a Guatemalan shirt, and Venezuela *apragatos,* colorful woven sandals. Her face belonged to another age, Europe of a century ago, South America when the Incans had walked there. He couldn't guess her age

"Actually, I'm looking for a book on this particular tarot deck." He slipped one of the tarot cards out of his windbreaker pocket. The Lovers.

She put on her glasses, glanced at the card, and nodded. "The Rider-Waite deck." Her long, bony finger trailed across the spines of books on a lower shelf and plucked out a thin book. "This book should do."

"I had no idea there were so many decks and books on tarot."

She laughed. "I don't even try to keep up with everything that's coming out these days. Not that long ago it was impossible to find more than a couple of decks."

"Do the meanings of the cards change from deck to deck?"

"Minor changes. The differences are primarily in the focus of the particular deck. Some are best for predictions, others are best as tools for self-knowledge and spiritual growth. It depends on what you're looking for."

Most things did, he thought.

"That card, for instance. The Lovers. In one deck it might indicate that you're facing serious choices in a relationship. But in another deck, it could point to a duality in your nature that you must come to terms with before you can move on with your life. Do you understand what I mean?"

Yeah, Sheppard thought. You either banished your demons or learned to live with the little fuckers. "I think so. Do you read the cards?"

"My granddaughter, Mira, is the tarot expert."

"Is she here?"

The woman smiled at that. "Most of the time. This is her store. Would you like to speak to her?"

"That'd be great. I'd like to get this book, too."

"I'll ring it up for you. By the way, I'm Nadine Cantrell."

"Wayne Sheppard."

Something changed in her expression when they shook hands, a small thing, a fleeting nuance too brief for him to determine what it meant. "It's a pleasure, Mr. Sheppard." She headed toward the register, leaning lightly on her cane. "Are you new to the area or just down here for the season?"

"Neither. I've been here about five years."

"But you travel a great deal."

His smile mirrored his astonishment. "It shows?"

"A lucky guess. You look like the sort of man who moves around a lot."

It was news to him. Most people who knew him remarked that he looked like the kind of man who had never left his birthplace. In other words, a throwback to a simpler time.

"Are you and Annie related? She's a real charmer."

"She's my great-granddaughter."

"That's hard to believe," he blurted.

She laughed with obvious delight. "Who's the charmer, Mr. Sheppard?" Then she rang up his sale and paged Mira.

Sheppard picked up a schedule of monthly events at the store. Lectures, workshops, classes, daily yoga sessions, something scheduled nearly every day of the week. Most of it looked like weird shit, the nut fringe of the New Age—a woman who allegedly channeled "group energy from the Sirian star system"; a pair of UFO abductees; a psychic dentist. He fully expected the granddaughter to look and act strange.

But she surprised him: a slender build, five-foot-six or so, curly black hair that brushed her shoulders. Her black Levis hugged her narrow hips and tiny waist; the flecks of silver in her shirt drew his eyes to her silver earrings, miniature Kokopellis, the Hopi symbol of fertility. A Kokopelli pendant hung from a chain around her neck, his delicate fingers playing a flute made of amber.

She wasn't a knockout, he wasn't certain she was even pretty. But something about her struck him immediately and made him feel tongue-tied, awkward, like some teenager with wild, fluctuating hormones. Too long between women, he thought.

Nadine introduced them, then handed Sheppard his book and the receipt, and left them alone. Mira folded her arms at her waist, as if she felt the sudden need to protect herself. "What can I do for you, Mr. Sheppard?"

He flashed his badge. "It's actually Detective Sheppard. I'm with the sheriff's office."

"You're kidding. It took Detective Ames a while, but he actually came through."

Sheppard thought he'd missed something. "Excuse me?"

"Detective Ames sent you, right?"

"No."

"Then I'm confused."

Sheppard laughed. "So am I."

She shifted her weight to her right foot and tucked her fingers into the pockets of her Levis. "I, uh, spoke to Detective Ames Thursday morning. I had picked up some information on a murder and felt that I should report it. I thought he'd sent you."

"Picked up information?"

"Psychically."

No wonder Ames had been mute. He lumped psychics under a broad category entitled "horseshit." Sheppard supposed he meant well, but Ames was basically an idiot who belonged behind a desk in an administrative job. "I haven't talked to Ames since early last week. I'm actually here because I need some information on tarot that's related to a case. Your grandmother said you're the expert."

"*Me?*" She smiled. "I learned tarot from her. But I'd be glad to help you out."

"Great."

"Let's sit outside."

They exited through a fire door in another room and headed toward the garden behind the building. Bloodred bougainvillea blooms blanketed the trellis at the entrance of the garden. The depth of their color seemed like a portent to Sheppard, symbolic of a fool's bleeding heart. He blamed it on his sexual drought.

They settled at a rickety picnic table where the air smelled faintly of gardenias. "What information did you give Detective Ames?" he asked.

"Not all that much, really. Two men arguing, one of them was wearing green shoelaces. A little boy was watching them, peeking out from behind a door, I think. The guy with the green shoelaces shot the other man right about here." She touched her breastbone. "Through the sternum or just below it."

A chill raced up Sheppard's arms and shot through the center of his chest, an arrow of ice. Steele, she was referring to Steele. But how could she possibly know that Steele had been shot through the sternum? The news in this morning's paper hadn't mentioned specifics about his physical injury; that information hadn't been released to the press. The story had focused mostly on Steele's professional life. So even though she might have read about the murder, she couldn't know something this specific.

He'd worked with psychics a couple of times during his stint with the Bureau, but always on the sly. Not much had ever come from the leads. Maybe this woman would be different. Sheppard felt that quick, hot ripple of excitement again.

"What did Ames say?"

"That someone would get in touch with me if the cops had any questions. I figure he wrote me off as a nutcase."

Undoubtedly. But by now, Ames had to know about Steele and if he knew, he should have told Sheppard about Mira's call. In a homicide investigation, you pursued every lead, regardless of how it struck you personally.

"Did you pick up anything else?"

"Later I did. A canoe, tall grass. The view was what you would see if you were lying on your back. Does this fit something you know about?"

"It might. Could you tell where the canoe was?"

"No. But the energy I tuned in on was female."

Energy? What energy? "I don't understand."

She leaned forward, the scent of her perfume drifting toward him, a light, pleasing fragrance that stroked his libido. "Most of the time, I perceive energy. Men and women have different types of energy and this was female. If I encounter it again, I'll recognize it. To me, energy is as unique as a fingerprint."

Sheppard wondered if his energy reflected the pathetic state of his financial affairs or the possible loss of his job. "Can you tell me anything about this, uh, female energy you perceived?"

"Just that she seemed to be lying on the floor of a canoe." Her lovely eyes narrowed, focused on something over his left shoulder. "Her vision was blurred. I felt a thick, crippling lethargy, like she was drugged. That's about it."

Jesus, Sheppard thought. Was it possible that she had tuned in on Rae Steele? But if Rae had killed Steele and split, why would she be drugged and lying on the floor of a canoe? Because she didn't kill him, he thought. Because whoever had killed Steele had abducted his wife.

This scenario certainly made more sense to him than Paula Crick's theory that Rae Steele had killed her husband and split. But if she had been abducted, why had there been no ransom demand?

"You look puzzled, Detective Sheppard."

"Blown away is more like it." He withdrew the envelope from his windbreaker pocket, took out the tarot cards, and fanned them out on the picnic table. The light made their colors look luminous. "These cards were found at a murder scene. The victim had been shot through the sternum."

She stared at them, chin cupped in her hands. Then she turned those deep, dark eyes on him. "Where were they found?"

"In a tin of chocolate." He showed her the slip of paper that listed the tarot cards and the item that had been mailed with each card. "These were supposedly mailed to his wife, who's missing."

She studied the list. "So this is the order in which the cards were received?"

"It would seem so. Do you have to know the order to tell me what they mean?"

"No, but it would help. Do you know anything about tarot, Mr. Sheppard?"

"Not really."

"With tarot, with any kind of divination system, you use spreads, positions that have particular meanings. A simple three-card spread might represent past, present, future. Seven cards could be laid out any number of ways."

Sheppard arranged the cards according to the list. The Lovers, the Tower, the eight of cups, the Wheel of Fortune, the eight of swords, the ten of swords, the Hanged Man. "Can you give me some idea what these cards mean in this order?"

Mira, sitting across from him, turned the cards so they faced her. "I'm glad it's not my reading."

Sheppard, tarot neophyte, particularly disliked the card that depicted ten swords sticking out of some poor sucker's back. "Do any of these cards mean death?"

"There's no single death card in tarot. You have to look to the surrounding cards. If anything, what I see here is the ending of a cycle, a way of life."

She rearranged the cards in what looked, roughly, like a star. As she explained the meanings of the cards, weaving them into a kind of story, Sheppard felt as if he'd stumbled into some ancient past, where the future could be read in the toss of a handful of bones. He didn't understand how this woman did what she was doing; at some elemental level, it terrified him. And yet, it also fascinated him.

When she finished talking, he grappled for something to say. "So basically the cards are telling us that whoever sent them is dealing with issues having to do with love, sudden and unpredictable changes, with unions and new partnerships, and choices related to all of those things." He paused. "Right?"

"Yeah, pretty much." Her smile held a hint of embarrassment. "Actually, it seems pretty general when I say it out loud."

"It's more than I had before I came here. What else do the cards say?"

"Because of the catastrophe that slams into his life, he loses faith in himself, in his world. Nothing is what it seems." She tapped the eight of cups. "He walks away from a situation or from a relationship that he's finished with." Her finger moved to the fourth card, the Wheel of Fortune. "This card always reminds me of the wheel of fortune in *The Dead Zone*." She glanced up. "You ever read Stephen King?"

"I used to. In *Dead Zone*, the wheel of fortune was at the carnival, right before Joe or Jack or whatever the hell his name was gets hurt."

"John Smith."

"Played by Christopher Walken. I loved the movie."

"Me, too."

Her gaze held his; he felt an odd tightening through his chest. Chemistry. Ridiculous. He could never get involved with a woman like this; she spooked him. He would always be wondering if she was tuned in, peering into him. No thanks. Besides, so what if they liked the same movie? He and his ex had also liked the same movies and what good had that done them?

He'd noticed, though, that she didn't wear a wedding ring .

"So this man is now riding the wheel of fortune," she said. "It could stop anywhere. He's accepted the risk." She paused, laced her fingers together, rested her chin on this steeple of bone and skin, and studied the cards. "But when the wheel stops turning, he feels trapped. Or he makes someone else feel that way. I mean, look at this woman. She's blindfolded and gagged, her arms are bound and she's surrounded by eight swords that stick up out of the ground."

"A bad hair day," Sheppard said with a wry grin, and she

laughed. He tapped the Hanged Man, a guy suspended upside down by an ankle. Yeah, he could identify with this one, all right. It fit how he felt right now, how he felt in the middle of any investigation that appeared to be going nowhere. "What about this card?"

"Since he's hanging upside down, the Hanged Man doesn't see the world the way the rest of us do. The card indicates a complete reversal in one's affairs. Sometimes the Hanged Man is about spirituality, about psychic abilities." She glanced up. "Does the murdered man have a son?"

He nodded. "Right now Carl Steele is in intensive care, being treated for an insulin reaction. He's conscious, but not out of the woods yet. I'm hoping I'll be able to talk to him tomorrow."

"He may have seen what happened."

"That's occurred to me. Right now, his mother is the primary suspect simply because of what she stands to inherit. But I have a few problems with that. Why would she kill her husband when her son was in the house, then split without taking him with her? She knows he's a diabetic. It doesn't make sense."

Mira gathered up the cards. "I'll see if I can pick up anything else, Mr. Sheppard, and give you a call when I do."

It disturbed him that he anticipated seeing her again, even if he had to talk about murder and tarot cards to do it. But as soon as he'd thought this, his emotional censor shook a finger at him, reminding him again that she spooked him. "Great, I appreciate it." He jotted his home and beeper numbers on the back of a business card and handed it to her. "Call any time, don't worry about the hour. If I'm not in, leave a message."

They walked toward the front of the building, their shoes crunching over woodchips, the scent of jasmine suffusing the air around them. They made small talk about books and movies, about her store and his job, and he suddenly wanted to linger in her world, to explore it a little longer.

Sheppard felt strangely comfortable around her, as though they were old friends who hadn't seen each other in a long time and now had a great deal to catch up on. Except that he wasn't thinking about friendship. He was thinking about how nice her hair would feel between his fingers.

Watch it, big boy.

When they reached the driveway, they were discussing *Dead Again*. She had liked the movie, but not the way it had depicted reincarnation.

"That was what made the plot work," he said.

"Hollywood's rendition of reincarnation is too linear. I think the Self is far more creative, that consciousness is multidimensional."

Sheppard didn't have any idea what the hell she meant. Her world loomed like some exotic country in his mind, its culture too strange even for an experienced traveler like himself. Let it alone, he thought.

"I'll call you in a few days, Mr. Sheppard."

"Shep. Mister makes me feel old."

"And I'm Mira."

When they shook hands, he felt the chemistry again and knew it wasn't in his head this time, that she felt it, too. He also sensed that the handshake communicated something psychic to her and quickly reclaimed his hand.

As he hurried down the gravel driveway to his car, he still felt the phantom pressure of her hand against his palm.

7

Mira stood at the window in the front office, watching the old Camaro pull out into the street. An odd stew bubbled up inside of her that was uneven parts of dread and delight. Dread that her involvement had now extended beyond what she'd intended, delight that the extension concerned a man to whom she was physically attracted.

An electric warmth lingered on her palm; she could still feel the shape of his hand against her skin. This had happened only once before, the day she'd met her husband fifteen years ago, the two of them waiting in line at the courthouse to pay for speeding tickets. It had been the tourist season, the line was long, they had started talking. She couldn't remember now what they had talked about, yet she clearly recalled how, in his presence, she'd felt as if she had returned home after a long journey.

Now he was dead and the possibility that she might have prevented it still haunted her. Nadine, of course, was more sanguine about it. *If you'd told him about the dreams, he might still have died.* This particular "what if" remained one of the great riddles of her life.

His death had left an emotional void inside of her that she initially filled with Annie, with the store, with her clients. These elements still mattered to her, but not in the same way. Annie was older and more independent now, and with Nadine actively involved in the business, the store didn't demand the time it once had.

As a result, she often experienced bouts of intense loneliness, a hunger for the kind of intimacy and companionship she and Tom had known. She'd been involved with two men since Tom's death. One man had felt threatened by her clairvoyance, the other had hung on because of it. Neither relationship had provided what she needed.

In the last year, her social life had shrunk considerably— family events, outings with friends, several short vacations with Annie. She hadn't met a single man who remotely interested her. Until now.

But Christ, a *cop?* Why did he have to be a cop?

Even more to the point, why did their meeting have to involve a murder? How could anything positive come from this? Despite her physical attraction to Sheppard, she felt that the single violent act of Steele's death would taint whatever might develop between them, that it was a kind of curse. In other words, forget Sheppard. He would be nothing but trouble.

"Mom, the workshop people are taking a break."

With some reluctance, she turned away from the window. "Is that pot of coffee done?"

"Yup. And I put out cups and sugar and stuff."

Mira slipped an arm around her daughter's shoulders. "You just got a raise, kiddo. Two bucks an hour."

Annie grinned and rubbed her hands together. "I'm going to get this new CD-ROM I saw advertised. It's called Crystal Skull and it's about a search for a magical crystal skull that's really powerful. And there's an underground city and stuff where you get your clues."

"My computer whiz kid," Mira murmured.

"That guy you were talking to? Shep? He told me the most incredible story about the pink dolphins in the Amazon."

As she chattered on about the myth, Mira realized that a man who could talk about magic and transformation with an eight-year-old couldn't be a typical cop. But it didn't change her mind about getting involved any more deeply in this investigation. One vision was enough; she didn't want a repeat performance.

As soon as Sheppard hit Sunrise Boulevard, the needle on the temperature gauge swung into the red zone. Thanks to the oil leak, he had been adding oil to the engine every other day and he'd forgotten to do it the last two days.

He drove another two blocks and turned into Gabby's Garage. Gabriel Jacinto worked twelve hour days, seven days a week, unless his wife threatened to divorce him. This week she apparently hadn't threatened him.

Cars were lined five and six deep in front of the three stalls, typical for Gabby's. Other mechanics in town were as good as or better than Gabby and certainly cheaper. But no other mechanic was as honest.

Sheppard parked at the side of the building, got out, raised the Camaro's hood. The stink of scorched metal floated into the warm October afternoon. If Gabby couldn't do a quick patch-up job, Sheppard would be up shit's creek. He tried to remember which of his credit cards hadn't maxed out and which one had the lowest interest rate. Visa from First Union? Master Charge from Sun Bank?

"Hey, *amigo*," Gabby's voice boomed behind him and he slung an arm around Sheppard's shoulders.

Gabby was short and thin, a Cuban with jovial dark eyes and a Ricky Ricardo smile. His thick, dark hair had begun to pale at the temples. He wore stained jeans and a blue work shirt unbuttoned halfway down his hairy chest. Nestled in the mat of hairs was a gold St. Christopher's medal.

"I've got major problems, Gabby."

He wrinkled his nose. "You have one problem with many facets, *amigo*. A new car would solve everything."

"I can't afford a new car. I've spent too much money trying to keep this one running."

Gabby's frown caused his bushy brows to melt together so they formed one continuous line above his eyes. "We work out something on this one, *amigo*. I owe you."

The debt Gabby referred to went back to when they'd met. His garage had been broken into and thousands of dollars worth of tools were stolen. It had taken Sheppard four months to track the leads to a ring of car thieves. During those months, he and Gabby had gotten to be friends. Sheppard was now a godfather to Gabby's three kids and a regular guest for the rowdy Sunday dinners when the entire extended family gathered at Gabby's. Sheppard was, in the words of Gabby's wife, an honorary Cuban.

"It's the other way around. I still owe you for labor on the muffler."

"What labor? You did the work. I just showed you how."

Sheppard didn't remember it that way. "Charge me what's fair and square, Gabby."

"No way I can have this ready by tomorrow. I'm booked through the middle of next week." He stabbed a thumb toward the silver Porsche he had bought a year ago in an estate sale. Sleek as a bullet, it would make it from Lauderdale to Miami in the blink of an eye. "You take Angelita."

Little Angel. "And I'd be in debt to you for the rest of my life if something happened to it."

"Shit, man, nothing's going to happen to it with you behind the wheel and my saint on the dashboard." He touched the St. Christopher medal around his neck, then tossed Sheppard the keys. "Now I sleep good at night and I can take my time with the Camaro, no?"

Sheppard felt absurdly grateful for the break, but he didn't want to take advantage of Gabby's generosity. "At least let me pay you something for the use of the Porsche."

Gabby made a face. "Look, *amigo,* you are doing me a favor, *me entiendes?* I drive the car to work so my son can't use it. Sixteen years old and he thinks he should be driving a Porsche, no? Ridiculous. Now I can tell him Shep is using it and he won't say a word. He likes you too much to complain."

End of discussion. Gabby now poked around under the Camaro's hood. "I thought you were diving for skeletons or something this weekend."

"I didn't leave town soon enough." Sheppard told him about the homicide; Gabby had never heard of Steele. No reason that he should have. Gabby's contacts were extensive, but they began and ended with the Hispanic community in the tri-county area. "I'm hoping to get some leads from a psychic."

Gabby raised his head, obviously amused. "You and a psychic, *amigo?* I thought those people spooked you."

"They do. You know anything about One World? That New Age bookstore over by the river?"

"I know the woman who owns it. Mira Morales."

The world, Sheppard thought, had only a thousand people in it. "She doesn't look Cuban."

"She's not." His head vanished under the hood again, where he examined the dipstick. "She was married to a Cuban."

Sheppard noted the past tense. "She's the psychic I mentioned."

"I myself don't know whether she's any good as a psychic. But I knew her husband, Tomas. He was a lawyer who did much free work with Cuban refugees. Five years ago he was shot and killed during the robbery of a convenience store. *Una lástima,* a man like that. The killer was never caught."

"Did it happen here in Broward County?"

"*Sí, claro.* That store at the corner of Powerline and Northwest Tenth."

Sheppard knew the store he meant. It was about two blocks from the worst crack neighborhood in Lauderdale. "It must've happened before I started. Otherwise I'd remember the case."

Gabby grinned and held up the dipstick, which was bone dry. "You remember names, *amigo,* but you can't remember to put oil in the car."

"Guilty."

"I don't think there is too much damage to the engine, but give me a few days, no?"

"Take as long as you need, Gab. And I can't thank you enough for the use of the Porsche."

His options on this Saturday afternoon depressed him. If he took the rest of the weekend off and drove over to Warm Mineral Springs as he had planned to do yesterday, he knew he wouldn't enjoy himself. He would worry about the investigation and about how he couldn't afford the trip. Forget Warm Mineral Springs.

If he stayed home and completed some of the projects he had begun shortly after he had moved, he would also worry about the case and fret over his unpaid bills. Forget staying home. That left one choice: go to work.

The dozen detectives in the department supposedly rotated their weekends so none worked more than one weekend a month. But at this time of year, vacations and the flu took their toll on the order of things. As a floater and the man with the lowest seniority, Shep had gotten stuck filling in for the last six weekends. Seven, if he counted this weekend, even though he wasn't filling in for anyone. So it surprised him to see that nearly every desk on the third floor was occupied. Everyone bustled around.

Budget cutbacks. The layoff rumors had brought in the troops. Put in an appearance, make it look good, and do it for comp time not pay, the route to job security. All of these guys had more seniority than he did and if *they* were worried, then he was fucked.

Don't think about it. Zen.

Sheppard made a beeline for the very small office he shared with Pete Ames. As usual, Ames's side of the room looked like it had been ransacked by a gang of thugs stoned on speed. The chaos had spilled over the imaginary line that separated his area from Sheppard's, files and folders stacked haphazardly on his chair and *his* half of the windowsill. The air smelled suspiciously of the sickeningly sweet spray freshener that Ames used to cover up the stink of his cigarettes. Goddamn slob. Ames was one of the main reasons that Sheppard didn't spend much time here.

He shut the door, grateful that the office had only two windows—one that looked out into the street, another in the door. It gave him a modicum of privacy. He moved Ames's files from his desk chair, pushed it up to the computer, and sat down.

He booted up the computer, then suffered several moments of excruciating indecision. His job demanded that he cull information about Steele and his wife and that he do it immediately. If he could come up with something tangible in the next couple of days, it might save his ass from unemployment.

But first, he wanted information about Mira's husband.

Sheppard initiated a search for a Tomas Morales. If the perp who had killed him had never been caught, then the case would still be open. Sure enough, the name came up with a cross reference to the cold cases division. He accessed the case number and printed it out.

The investigating officer, Guy Hotchkiss, had retired. Sheppard vaguely remembered him, a sour-faced man with a beer belly who had once commented that the cold case division, where

Sheppard was working at the time, should be abolished. Hotch-kiss now worked as a security guard for Motorola up in Boynton Beach, a fitting place for the man.

According to the investigation report, the murder had happened about the way Gabby had described it. Morales had been in the wrong place at the wrong time and the perp had gotten lucky. He wore a mask during the holdup. The description pegged him as about six feet tall, between a hundred and seventy and a hundred and ninety pounds, with light hair, which probably fit half the men under thirty-five in Broward County.

Hotchkiss had taken copious notes on his dealings with Mira. *She claims to be psychic, but hasn't come up with a single lead that has checked out.* Snide SOB.

The door suddenly opened and Ames lumbered in, as graceless as a rhino in heat. "Hey, Shep. I hear you got stuck with the Steele homicide."

"You got it. And I hear you took a call that could be related to it."

"What?" Even when Ames's blue eyes widened, they still seemed very small, like shiny blue buttons stuck onto his soft, pudgy face. "What're you talking about?"

"The woman who called in Thursday morning with a tip about a homicide."

Ames looked puzzled. Like a slow computer, the outdated microchips in his head struggled to make connections from the stored information. When he finally brightened, Sheppard expected to see smoke billowing from his large ears.

"Oh. That." Ames chuckled, moved the files from his chair, and sank into it. "C'mon, man, she'd had a vision, for Christ's sakes. We get about ten calls like that a week. Who told you about it?"

"She did."

His cocky smile vanished. "I'm not following."

"You don't need to follow it, Pete. Next time you get a call like that about a case of mine, let me know about it."

"Chill out." He grabbed a file off one of the stacks, rummaged through one of his messy drawers, and pulled out a bag of peanuts. He proceeded to consume them with great, noisy gusto, adding to Sheppard's general misery.

Sheppard returned to the computer printout on Morales. For a long time, the thick, stale silence in the office reminded him of that in a nightclub on a Sunday morning. Ames hated silence and finally broke it.

"You heard the news, didn't you?" he asked.

"Which news?"

"It won't be official until Monday, but they've narrowed the cutbacks in our department to four positions."

Sheppard went utterly and completely cold inside; liquid nitrogen ran through his veins. He suddenly knew what death would feel like six feet under. "Who?" he croaked.

Ames looked as smug as a pig in shit. "Captain doesn't know yet. But that's why everyone's working on a Saturday."

He numbered among the targeted four, he was sure of it. He was equally sure that Ames had figured it that way, too.

"We're all looking for the big one that will save our asses," Ames went on. " 'Course, even overtime isn't going to help if you don't have the years in."

"And how many years is that, Pete?" *You dumb shit.*

His smug little grin widened. "I hear at least six."

The knot of anxiety hardened in his chest again and swelled in direct proportion to the widening of Ames's grin. He couldn't stand looking at the man any longer, so he turned his attention back to the file.

For the first few moments, the words kept blurring, sentences ran together like melting wax, and he saw himself in an unemployment line. The unemployment office would smell of sweat and heat and frustration. The clerks would be deadbeats counting the minutes to their next coffee break. Christ help him.

Focus, focus, focus.

He rubbed his eyes and went back to the beginning of the file. Hotchkiss never turned up any significant leads. The convenience store clerk who gave the description on the perp had gone into the freezer to get the man ice cream and when she'd come out, two men were dead and the perp had split with a couple hundred bucks.

When I asked her why she'd gone into the freezer and left her register untended, Hotchkiss wrote, *she seemed confused, said she didn't know why she'd done it, she simply had. Despite repeated questioning about the perp's appearance, she was able to recall only one other new detail, that the guy wore lime green shoelaces. I never mentioned this fact to Mrs. Morales. I hoped she would come up with it in one of her "visions." She never did.*

"Sweet Christ," Sheppard whispered. Lime green shoelaces.

He shot to his feet, scooped up the rest of the file, and hurried out of the office, vaguely aware of Ames's eyes glued to his back. He went into the Xerox room, shut the door, and leaned against it, the file pressed to his chest, his eyes squeezed shut. Blood pounded in his ears.

You imagined it.

No, he hadn't. He patted the wall for the switch and turned on the light. He moved the file away from his chest, smoothed the wrinkled top sheet with the palm of his hand, and read the line about the green shoelaces again and again.

The killer in Mira's vision had also been wearing green shoelaces. His deepest instincts said it had to be the same guy. The odds were too great for it to be otherwise. This discovery wasn't just a vital link in the case; it might save his ass from the unemployment line.

Sheppard made four copies of the page—overkill, for sure, but what the hell. He decided not to say anything to the captain yet. Gerry Young, a pragmatist, wouldn't give much credence to Mira's version of what had happened to Steele. But if Steele's young son confirmed that the killer had worn green shoelaces, then he would have something solid to present to Young.

He returned to his office. Ames had left, thank Christ; he needed some privacy. He shut the door, then called pediatrics at Holy Cross Hospital, gave his badge number, and asked for an update on Carl Steele's condition. The head nurse said that Carl Steele had improved sufficiently so that Sheppard could talk to him tomorrow sometime. She cautioned him to keep it short and to proceed as gently as possible. Sheppard assured her he would.

"I certainly will. Thanks for your help."

The phone rang almost as soon as he hung up. "Detective Sheppard."

A man with a soft, raspy voice said: "I have some information on the Steele homicide that will interest you."

"And your name?"

The man ignored the question. "I'll be at the Elbo Room on Lauderdale Beach next Thursday evening at ten."

"How will I know you?"

"I'll know you," he replied, and hung up.

Sheppard sat there gripping the receiver, the man's words ringing in his ears.

8

Tom had taught Mira that without a dream, life was tragically diminished, a parody of itself. Even if the dream never materialized fully, the striving mattered.

In the days and weeks and months after Tom's death, she'd thought often about striving to reach her dreams without Tom cheering her on in the background. As the child of Cuban immigrants, he'd known a few things about dreams. He and Nadine had envisioned One World, believed in it, long before she had.

Now she climbed the stairs to the apartment they had lived in during that long, hot summer when they had been making the dream a reality. In her memories, Tom usually was laughing, a rich, robust laugh that had marked him as surely as the rich black of his hair.

He had been one of those rare individuals whose optimistic nature called a day partly sunny, not partly cloudy. He hadn't been a complicated man, perhaps because his priorities had been utterly clear in his mind. But his depth had awed her.

Tonight a kind of menacing gloom accompanied her up these stairs, the result of Sheppard's visit, of his request for information and help. She felt anxious, uneasy, spooked by the smallest sounds here in the stairwell. The creak of the old wood, a scratching she couldn't identify, the muted whisper of the wind: the internal made manifest. She knew it wouldn't stop here.

The tension already had begun to appear in her body. Her head throbbed, her stomach felt weird, the vague, irritating ache in the small of her back begged for the soothing heat of a long bath. Everything she felt at the moment, in fact, screamed for her to forget Sheppard's request, to just let it be. She had seen what she had seen, she had reported it, she had answered his questions to the best of her ability. No spoken or unspoken code obligated her to do anything more than that.

But she couldn't dismiss it because she didn't understand why she had tuned in on the murder of a man she had never met. After struggling all these years to understand the nature of her ability and how it worked, she knew at least one thing: it didn't reach out randomly and scoop in psychic garbage just because it was there. So why Steele? What was it about him that had triggered the connection?

She didn't know. No matter how she looked at it, how she turned the equation around, she found only a looming black question mark.

At the top of the stairs, Mira rapped on the door of the apartment, then let herself in. Nadine had moved in here about a year ago, after the fall that had broken her hip. Up until then, she had been living alone in a large house in nearby Hidden Lake that she once had shared with her second husband, a millionaire who had died eleven years ago.

She had transformed the place, bringing her own eccentricities to these rooms. But rather than molding them to fit her requirements, it was as if Nadine had released their essence.

The bamboo chairs, the Mexican tile floors, the wild profusion of plants, even the sparse furnishings, coalesced into some breathing, organic whole with which Nadine coexisted. Her grandmother always had lived at the border between the visible and the invisible, the tangible and the ethereal, equally at home in both.

Mira's parents, on the other hand, clearly belonged in the realm of the visible. They lived in an ocean condo on Vero Beach, belonged to the local yacht club, played golf four times a week, and attended their church regularly even though they didn't believe a word of what was preached. To them, Mira and Nadine were the eccentrics of the family, the affable weirdos who cruised in for a visit every few months, then returned to their inexplicable lives.

The cats greeted her with fussy meows that made it clear they didn't appreciate being hauled from the house to the apartment.

Annie and Nadine lounged on the couch, Annie reading and Nadine watching the late news, which she hadn't done in at least a decade. "You just missed seeing Detective Sheppard," she said, glancing away from the TV. "He was giving a statement about the murder of a man named Andrew Steele. Does that have anything to do with the tarot cards he wanted interpreted?"

Mira nodded and dropped her purse in one of the bamboo chairs. "I don't know if what I told him helped very much."

"Nana and I saved you some veggie chili, Mom," Annie piped up.

"Thanks, sweetie. It's past your bedtime, don't you think?"

"Aw, c'mon. Tomorrow's Sunday."

"Thirty more minutes."

Annie blew her a kiss and reached for the TV clicker.

Nadine picked up her cane and pushed to her feet. "Let's talk in the kitchen while you eat."

Tin boxes lined wall shelves in the tiny kitchen, each a different shape and color, each containing a deck of tarot cards or one of its permutations. A myriad of other psychic tools were displayed as well—runes, I Ching coins, shells, pendulums, even a collection of bleached white bones and a crystal ball. A wind chime made of different colored crystals hung in the only window, its wooden shutters open to the night.

Despite the window, this little hobbit kitchen always made Mira feel as if she were underground, in some dry, firelit cave. Everywhere she looked, she saw tree frogs: the miniature collection that lined the top edge of the stove, the dish towels with tree frogs on them, the frog-shaped soap dish, the ceramic frogs that held a pair of unlit red candles. Nadine considered frogs to be her talismen.

"I want to hear it from the beginning," Nadine said, setting a bowl of chili and a glass of iced tea in front of Mira.

She started with the vision she'd had Thursday morning. For as far back as she could remember, Nadine had been her sounding board, her mentor, teacher, and close friend. She'd helped Mira understand and deal with the clairvoyant impressions she'd had as a child, had taught her how to focus her psychic ability, and how to shut it down. Nadine had dealt with psychic matters most of her life; if an explanation existed for why Mira had tuned in on the murder of a man she'd never met, Nadine would help her find it.

"The first question you have to ask yourself, Mira, is why you picked up on this man's murder. You didn't know him, had no personal connection to him whatsoever. So why him?"

"That's what I'm hoping you'll tell me."

Nadine hobbled over to the kitchen drawer where she kept her special tarot cards. They shared space with some of Annie's toys, with pens and pencils and old grocery lists, with everything that didn't fit elsewhere. By contrast, Mira kept her decks wrapped in silk of different colors and stored in a cool, dark place. But Nadine had never been big on ritual.

She selected two decks, the Voyager and a Rider-Waite deck. The first, the subject of the workshop this afternoon, was a unique permutation of the original tarot, designed for the next millennium. No art graced these cards; each consisted of a photo collage that was utterly magnificent. The second deck was the same one Sheppard's cards had come from.

"What were the cards again?" Nadine asked, rolling the rubber band off the Rider-Waite deck.

"The Lovers, the Tower, the eight of cups, the Wheel of Fortune, the eight and ten of swords, and the Hanged Man."

Nadine slipped on her reading glasses, which hung from a chain around her neck, and removed the respective cards from the deck. She fanned them out face up and slipped the four major arcana cards out of the fan. The Lovers, the Tower, the Wheel of Fortune, and the Hanged Man.

"Since these are majors, they're the only ones that are important right now."

Major Arcana cards concerned character and destiny and depicted archetypical situations: birth, death, change, growth, love, marriage—the biggies. The minor arcana, the four suits of cups, wands, swords, and coins, concerned behavior and circumstances.

"When you interpreted the cards for Sheppard, were you just giving him the definitions or were you reading the cards?"

In other words, had she tuned in? Nope, she hadn't. "I was trying to listen to the cards, I didn't want to tune in."

"You were afraid to, you mean."

It wasn't a criticism; Nadine simply stated the truth as she saw it. Mira nodded.

"This murder thrust itself into your awareness for a reason, Mira, even if we don't know what that reason is yet. By fearing it, you're denying your own power. So your first decision has to be whether or not you can continue to be involved."

"I'd rather not be involved. But I want to know why I picked up on the murder."

"Fine. Then let's see what kind of story we can create from these cards." She glanced down at the four majors. "Since the cards were sent to Mrs. Steele, I have to interpret this story as one of romantic obsession. Our Hanged Man's love for Steele's wife is a dark, twisted emotion. He's willing to do almost any-thing to possess her. He takes enormous risks. Perhaps he even kills Steele and abducts her. In that case, the majors point to the destiny between Mrs. Steele and this man."

"If you believe in destiny," Mira remarked.

Which neither of them did. With each choice you made, with each belief you discarded or adopted, life changed. This was part of the problem with doing predictive tarot, predictive anything. When Mira read for a client, she tuned into the path or paths that were most probable *at that moment*. The point of power resided in the present. Change what you believe and your life changes.

So what belief of hers had drawn this experience to her? "The problem with all this, Nadine, is that the cards were sent before the murder. Everything may have changed since then. Also, I don't know what spread to use."

Nadine made an impatient gesture with her hand. "You're too obsessed about spreads. You don't need a spread to read the cards. They are what they are. You know that."

The cantankerous undertone to her voice put Mira on the defensive and cranked up her body aches and discomforts another notch.

"They're nothing but a particular placement. The cards are

what matter." Nadine picked up the Voyager deck, snapped off the rubber band. "Think of a question and pick three cards. But keep it simple, okay? I'm too tired to get into a big deal."

Mira thought of her question, chose her cards, set them facedown on the table, nothing fancy, one two three, right next to each other. Nadine quickly turned the cards over. "Your past is holding you back. You need to release it before you can move forward in your life. A man that you meet through work will help you break those patterns."

"That's it?"

"Yes."

She laughed. "What bullshit, Nadine. I asked if I was going to have a guest bathroom in my next house."

"That's a frivolous question."

"Not to me."

Nadine picked up the cards, shuffled them back into the deck, snapped the rubber band around them again. "That's exactly my point. It doesn't matter what question you ask. The cards will give you the information you need about where you are in your life."

"But you're the one doing the interpreting. That doesn't count. You know me too well."

She rolled her eyes and reached for her cane. "That was just an example to make my point."

The knot in Mira's stomach tightened, she pushed the half-eaten bowl of chili away from her. "It was a blatant attempt on your part to get me thinking about Sheppard."

"You need to get out more, Mira. That's a fact. And he seemed like a perfectly nice man."

"He's a cop."

"Better a cop than a convict," Nadine replied with a laugh.

"Very funny. Is Ben around?"

"No, Ben isn't around." Nadine sipped from a mug of hot chocolate—sipped noisily, an unattractive habit, but what the hell. Her age entitled her to a few quirks.

"You're just angry that I called your bluff."

"I'm not angry."

"If you weren't angry, Ben would be around."

For at least fifteen years, her grandmother had been channeling an entity who called himself Ben. She didn't do it for clients; outside of the family, the only people who knew about Ben were Nadine's oldest friends.

Ben claimed that by working through Nadine, he accelerated his own spiritual growth. Mira still didn't know what, exactly, Ben was. At times, she thought he might be part of Nadine, some disassociated piece of her personality. Other times, she felt sure he was what he claimed to be: an "energy essence" no longer focused in physical reality.

Regardless of what he was or wasn't, his accuracy had proven impressive. Although the specifics of some of Ben's predictions had differed from the actual event, that was typical for any psychic reading. The bottom line, though, had remained unchanged for fifteen years: when Ben came through, Mira listened.

"C'mon, Nadine, I've got a couple of questions for him."

Besides, Ben owed her. He hadn't warned Tom to stay out of convenience stores (but then again, neither had she) and hadn't given her any information whatsoever about who had killed him. He'd only discussed why it had happened, which wasn't what she had wanted to hear five years ago. She had said all this before, but she said it again now.

"Okay, okay, Mira."

Nadine sipped once more from her mug, then sat back, palms flat against her thighs, and shut her eyes. Her breathing deepened, that was all.

When she opened her eyes again, they seemed to be all pupil, as black as wet streets. Her spine had straightened, she looked younger, more energetic. Mira knew from experience that Nadine wouldn't need her glasses now to read, that her hearing would be sharper, that she wouldn't use the cane if she got up from the table.

Many channelers manifested similar changes, a phenomenon Mira likened to what happened to people with split personalities. One personality might be a diabetic, for instance, but the condition didn't exist in another personality, even though both used the same physical body.

When Nadine spoke, the voice was hers, but it sounded huskier, lower. "It's nice to see you again, Mira."

"You, too, Ben. I've been puzzled by a few things." And scared. "Did you enjoy the chili?"

"It was a trifle spicy. But it keeps Nadine's palate sharp."

Ben claimed he had been a gourmet cook in his last life, chef on a yacht that sailed the seas around southern Spain. "I was wondering if you could tell me anything about this murder, Ben."

"Your vision was essentially correct. Detective Sheppard will find confirmation when he speaks to the dead man's son."

Mira decided to take notes. She started to get up for a pencil, but Nadine stood first and walked over to a drawer, walked without her cane, with barely a limp. She returned with a pencil and some paper and began to speak as soon as Mira had made her notes.

"Can you give me a description of this man? Or tell me his name?"

"He goes by many names. I believe his preferred name has an *H* in it. The cards are his story. The green shoelaces are important."

She hadn't mentioned the shoelaces to Nadine, but it wasn't uncommon for Ben to know things about Mira or her life that Nadine didn't. "Anything else?"

"There are actually three men who play prominent roles. But the man with the green shoelaces is the most important. He's very powerful, Mira. He's able to project his consciousness in an unusual way and is also able to shield himself."

"Psychically? Is that what you're saying?"

"It's more complicated than that, but yes, basically he has a highly developed psychic ability. But it's misdirected, corrupted."

"Don't take this the wrong way, Ben. But since you know all this, why can't you give me a description or a full name?" *Why can't you tell me why this happened?*

"I perceive energy essences. It isn't as if I'm up *there* somewhere peering down, Mira. There's no bird's eye view where I am."

"Why did I pick up on this murder?"

"At some level, you were open to it."

"But why?"

Ben ignored the question and continued. "A man will approach Detective Sheppard with certain explosive information."

Explosive. Mira didn't like the adjective. "What do you mean by explosive? Who is he?"

Again, he failed to answer her question and went on as if he hadn't heard her. "This entire situation demands the utmost caution on your part, Mira. I can't stress this strongly enough. You'll be up against—"

The phone suddenly rang, snapping Nadine out of her trance. Mira grabbed it before it could ring again. "Yes? Hello?"

"Mira, it's Shep. Sorry to be calling so late. I tried your house, but there wasn't any answer."

Her body reacted to the sound of his voice in the same way it had when they had shaken hands outside of the store. An odd something fluttered in the center of her chest. "We're still up." *Talking to Ben.* "I should have some more information for you by tomorrow."

"Great. Could we, uh, get together sometime in the afternoon?"

"That'd be fine. What time?"

"Well, I was wondering if you could walk through Steele's house to see what impressions you pick up."

Utmost caution: Ben's warning echoed in her ears. When she hesitated, he rushed on.

"I'd be glad to pay you for your time."

She shut her eyes and rubbed the aching spot between her eyes. "You don't have to pay me." *And I don't have to do this.* "I don't think I'd be able to give you the information you need." *I don't want to do this.* And all else aside, she had Annie to consider. "Quite frankly, Shep, I don't want to get any more involved in this."

There. She'd said her piece. But Sheppard wouldn't let it go. "Look, it won't go any farther than the two of us, if that's what you're worried about. Your name won't be mentioned or associated with this investigation in any way, Mira. I give you my word. I'm just looking for leads."

Christ, she thought, staring at her toes as they curled and uncurled against the floor. He would browbeat her, plead, beg, keep her on the phone the rest of the night if that's what it took. "That's only part of it. I just don't feel good about any of this."

"We're the only two who will know about it."

She rubbed her forehead, massaging the ache. "If I consent to try, Shep, that will end my involvement. You have to understand that."

"No problem. I really appreciate it, Mira. How about one tomorrow afternoon? I can pick you up."

"Okay, see you then."

"You see how things work?" Nadine said with a small, annoying smirk. "Once you decided to be involved, the universe gives you the opportunity to find the truth."

"I don't want to read Steele's home, but maybe I'll pick up something that will explain why I tuned in on his murder. And whether I do or don't pick up anything, this will end my involvement."

Nadine didn't look convinced, but she didn't say anything.

"Is Ben still around? He was right in the middle of something."

"Why should he do your work?"

Because the dead were supposed to have at least some of the answers. "Would you please try again?"

"He's gone."

"C'mon, Nadine. Don't be so stubborn."

"He's gone," her grandmother repeated.

Annoyed now, Mira leaned forward again. "Gone where, for Christ's sakes?"

"I don't know." Nadine shrugged, finished her hot chocolate, and got to her feet, ending the discussion.

Mira sat there, anxiety rolling through her again, and wished she'd told Sheppard to forget the whole goddamn thing.

In the dream, she and Tom sat on an emerald hillside that overlooked a city. She knew this place, they had met here many times since he'd died. The sky always seemed to be a deep violet, like a bruise, the way it looked before sunrise or sunset. Although a breeze stroked her face, nothing around them moved—not leaves or blades of grass, not even the clouds. The air was still. "I want to stay here," she said.

"You can't, Mira. This is just a spot in the between." He took her hand then, his thumb sliding over the knuckles. "C'mon, I'll show you where I live."

As they walked away from the hill, the sky didn't change colors, the violet didn't deepen, no stars popped out. It was as if time literally held its breath. And yet, she felt the softness of the grass beneath her bare feet, the warmth of Tom's hand in her own, the heat of her desire for him.

He talked, his voice moving through her like some magical liquid, touching her all over inside. She clung to his words, the sound of his voice, the smallest details. She knew that most of what she experienced here would slide away from her when she woke.

"You like him," Tom said.

He meant Sheppard. "Yeah, I like him."

Tom squeezed her hand. "Good. It won't be easy, you'll fight it like hell. But don't cheat yourself. It's okay to let go."

She suddenly stopped and threw her arms around him, hugging him fiercely. She didn't want to let go of him, of her memories, of what they'd had. She didn't want to let go of any of it. "I'm afraid," she whispered. She buried her face against his chest, filling her lungs with the scent of the fabric. "Don't leave me."

Tom's hands, his large and wonderful hands, slipped along the sides of her face and he stood back slightly. "I'm not leaving you, Mira. We'll always meet here. But we both need to move forward."

She didn't want to hear about moving forward, about moving anywhere. She groped at his shirt, her mouth crushed his, and she came to with the pillow smashed against her body and her face damp with tears.

Mira squeezed her eyes shut and tried to sink into the dream again, to draw it around herself, to wrap herself up inside of it. But the dream had disappeared and so had the hill. The only part of Tom that remained was a phantom's touch, like the ghost pain an amputee feels around a severed limb.

9

In the moonlight, Hell's Bay glinted like pale aluminum. The airboat flew across it, eating up the miles between here and Florida Bay with the hunger of some exotic sea monster. The engine thundered in Hal's ears. He would be half-deaf for hours, but it would be worth it just to get to the bay and back before sunrise.

Rae wouldn't be stirring before then; the shot of Darvon he'd given her before he'd left would last a good while. Just the same, he worried about what might happen if she came to before he returned. Although he'd handcuffed her, suppose she struggled so hard she broke her wrist or her hand? Suppose she stumbled off the end of the platform like the college coed?

Suppose this, if that—fuck it. Right now he needed to focus on the meeting with Manacas and Indrio. This would be the first time they'd seen each other in nearly six months. Of the two, Indrio would be the most likely to discover the truth about Rae. He, of course, would tell Manacas, who would confront Hal.

They would see it as a deception and it might seed distrust among them at a time when they most needed to be unified. The point now was to get rid of Fletcher so the three of them could get on with their lives. Their best chance of doing that was to work with each other, to share whatever information they had.

But in all fairness to himself, Hal thought, he'd been living alone all these years while Manacas had a wife and an infant son. The woman Indrio lived with had helped him and Manacas obtain new identities back in the late eighties. She had offered to help Hal, too, but he hadn't been ready then. Even if he had, he wouldn't have accepted her help, he hadn't wanted to feel indebted to anyone. He always went his own way.

So how could they blame him for needing the same thing they already had?

But they *would* blame him. By bringing Rae into this, he might be jeopardizing The Plan.

When Hal docked at the Bay Pub, he still hadn't made up his mind how to handle it. So he shoved Rae into the back of his mind and made his way through the crowd on the pub's dock. Jukebox music pumped through the cool, salty air, laughter drifted out over the painted waters, the place was jammed.

The pub catered mostly to boaters who hung around the tip of the peninsula—fishermen, shrimpers, tourists, rednecks, misfits of various shapes and sizes. Some frequented the place only during the tourist season, others showed up on weekends, and still others probably warmed the stools every night of the week. The pub was the bay's neighborhood bar, an open-air chickee in the middle of nowhere, which ran off half a dozen generators. Only one rule existed here: you didn't fuck with anyone else's space

Hal spotted Vic Indrio first, tall, thin, uptight, a chain-smoker who literally vibrated with energy. A scar angled down the left side of his face, a vestige of prison. He leaned against the railing, tossing food to the fish, but even at rest he twitched, he fidgeted, his feet shuffled. Hal wondered if Indrio moved when he slept.

Hey, bro, Hal thought at him.

Indrio's head suddenly snapped up and he glanced around. He grinned, bobbed forward like a man on a pogo stick, and threw a skinny arm around Hal's shoulders. *Goddamn, you're looking good.*

Hal never knew for sure whether what he heard in his head was exactly what another person was thinking or whether he picked up merely the pattern of words, filtered through his own subconscious. Even Steele hadn't known for sure. But what he heard was close enough. He stood back and gestured at the cigarette burning between Indrio's fingers.

Still sucking on those cancer sticks?

"Shit, it's made of ginseng and it smells like pot." He laughed and tossed the butt over the railing. "Ruthie gets pissed if I smoke anything else. C'mon, let's go over to the other side. Ed was trying to get us a table there."

"You two been here long?"

"Half an hour." He patted Hal on the back. "Good work with Steele. That's the best goddamn news I've heard since Ruthie handed me new ID. But what's with the wife? The radio said she's missing."

Not exactly.

Indrio stopped and stared at Hal with his dark, spooky eyes, eyes that had always seen too much. Indrio had been sickly as a child and had spent most of his early childhood bedridden. Hal believed his telepathic ability had developed then, a means for him to stretch the narrow confines of his world. Under Steele's tutelage, his ability had flourished. Even though he couldn't *reach* like Hal could, he could read a man's thoughts with astonishing ease and Hal's were so close to the surface Indrio barely had to extend himself.

"Christ. That was stupid, man, fucking stupid."

He'd figured that Indrio would be more disturbed about Rae than Manacas would, but his vehemence startled him. "Easy for you to say. You haven't been living alone."

"But why her? Why Steele's wife? This could fuck things royally."

"It won't."

Indrio ran his hands over his thinning chestnut hair. "Ed doesn't know yet, does he?"

"No. It doesn't change our plans and it may just bring Fletcher here even faster."

"Ed thinks she's already here. He couldn't find her at any of her usual spots in D.C."

Ed Manacas, remote viewer, had been able to keep loose tabs on Fletcher since he'd split from Delphi in the late eighties. Hal had never understood why Manacas was able to locate her while he had been unable to *reach* into her except on rare occasions. Manacas couldn't explain it, either. But then again, Manacas rarely thought very deeply about such things; he was too busy reacting.

He sat alone at a table at the back of the pub, a big, muscular man with a head so bald it seemed to glint in the starlight. He stood as soon as he saw Hal. There was no bear hug from him; he had always been more formal than Indrio. But he clasped Hal's hand in both of his own, his grin slicing the bottom part of his face in half. "Good to see you, man. It's been too long. Have a seat. We've got plenty to celebrate."

As they sat down, Indrio looked at Hal, brows lifting. *Well, bro?*

Yeah, yeah, just give me a chance.

Manacas couldn't read either of them, but he knew them well enough to realize something was going on. "So? Anyone going to let me in on the secret?"

"I've got Steele's wife," Hal blurted.

Blood drained from Manacas's face. His hazel eyes caught the light, hurled it away again. He glanced at Indrio, then at Hal, and exploded with laughter. "Jesus, you almost had me fooled, man." But his smile faded like a tan when neither Hal nor Indrio said anything. "It's a joke, right?"

Hal shook his head; he suddenly felt vulnerable, exposed. He'd made a major mistake by mentioning Rae.

"Aw, fuck."

"You got it," Indrio agreed.

"Steele had a kid. You take him, too?" Manacas sat forward, his face skewed with anger.

"He wasn't there." As soon as Hal said it, he realized he didn't know that for sure. A terrible cold fluttered deep down inside his chest, the wings of death brushing his heart.

Where the hell was the kid?

He quickly slammed a door on the thought, but Fletcher's face rose unbidden in his memory. He blamed her for all of this, her and Steele. He wouldn't be sitting here now if it hadn't been for them. Yes, Steele had taught him how to sharpen his abilities. Yes, he probably wouldn't be able to *reach* as he could now if it hadn't been for Steele. And yes, Fletcher had upheld her end of the bargain when he'd gotten out of the joint. But there had been nothing benevolent about any of it. Steele and Fletcher had used him, had used Indrio and Manacas and the others, to further their own agenda. And behind their agenda, he thought, had lain another, something darker, murkier, labyrinthine, that he'd never quite figured out.

On one level, their agenda had been incredibly simple. The seven participants in the Delphi project were psychic spies for the government. Mission Impossible shit with a twist. But on another level, Delphi had been their private secret weapon, a means to benefit personally. Hal knew Fletcher was the guiltier party in this respect, that she had advanced through the Bureau ranks because of information he'd given her, because of jobs he had pulled for her.

If it hadn't been for information Hal had given her about one of the Colombian kingpins, she wouldn't have been able to make the bust that had put her in the running for the assistant deputy slot. If Hal hadn't fucked with the head of an agent who had been harassing Fletcher, he wouldn't have ended up in the psych ward of a local D.C. hospital and she wouldn't have assumed his job.

Or how about that trip to Russia after he'd been sprung? Even though the Bureau supposedly handled only domestic cases, he and Fletcher had flown to Moscow so he could *reach* into Boris Yeltsin for information about a capitalist venture. Fletcher had passed the information on to someone in the CIA whose allegiance she had sought.

Roll over, Hal. Bark, Hal. Sit up, Hal. Do your tricks, Hal. And Fletcher had never given a shit about what time of the day or night it was; she charged in with her questions and fuck whoever got in the way.

Manacas tapped Hal's arm. "You still with us, man?"

Hal snapped back and said, "With Rae missing, they may call it an abduction and that'll get Fletcher involved right up front. It'll make it easier for us."

Indrio looked dubious, but Manacas, always the pragmatist, brightened. "He may have something, Vic. It might just work to our advantage."

Indrio shook his head. "I don't like it. The whole thing sucks." His bushy brows knitted together. "Did you plan this shit with Rae from the beginning, Hal?"

With Rae. Like Indrio knew her personally. Hal felt like sinking his fist into Indrio's ugly mouth. "No." Hal knew Indrio was reading him, but since he had answered the question honestly, he didn't care. "At least not that I was aware of. But I've always had a thing for her, so maybe the thought was there from the beginning, I don't know."

"Well, shit." Manacas waved one of his massive hands. "It's done. We just work with it. I'm more interested in how we're going to get to Fletcher."

"You're sure she's left D.C.?" Hal was relieved to get off the subject of Rae.

"I scanned every coordinate we've got for her haunts in D.C. She wasn't at any of them. Any ideas where she'd stay in Lauderdale? You know her a hell of a lot better than Vic and I do."

Yeah, Hal had a good idea. Fletcher, a creature of habit, always had a cigarette with her Cuban coffee in the morning, a hot lunch and a light supper, six hours of solid sleep, and a room with a view. "My first guess is Pier 66. A penthouse room or suite."

"That'll be easy to check out," Manacas said. "If you're right, Vic and I will keep tabs on her just so we have some idea how many people she's traveling with, what she's up to, where she's most vulnerable." He grinned, his teeth lining up in his mouth like an old, stained picket fence.

Indrio regarded Hal through a cloud of smoke. "It'd be easier if you could just, you know . . ." He sliced the air with the side of his spidery hand. "Fuck her head up real good, Hal."

"I can't *reach* into Fletcher. I've never been able to." Except for rare times that were none of their business.

"There's one other thing we need to consider," Indrio said. "I picked up that the local cops are working with a psychic."

Manacas shrugged. "So what? That doesn't mean the psychic's any good."

Hal didn't dismiss it as quickly. "You pick up anything on the psychic?" he asked Manacas.

"Yeah, a woman. She's surrounded by books. She has a couple of big birds."

"Books and birds?" Indrio laughed and rolled his eyes.

"C'mon, man, if you're going to take her seriously, you've got to do better than that."

Manacas looked pissed at the remark. "I don't see you picking up squat that's useful, Vic."

They argued for a few minutes, but Hal didn't follow it. He tried to wade through the ramifications of a psychic helping out the cops. It disturbed him, made him feel that the investigation had taken a new and unexpected turn. But most of all, it scared him.

He had known many psychics during his years in Miami: frauds with charisma who hoped to cash in on a burgeoning business; a handful of astrologers who could predict the future through the movements of certain planets; palm and card readers who made predictions with reasonable proficiency. True clairvoyants were rare, but he suddenly felt certain this woman fell into that category. He had nothing to base this on, but he *knew*.

"We need more information on the psychic," Hal said.

"And on the local cop who's investigating the murder," Manacas added. Then the pitcher of beer arrived, Manacas filled three glasses, and picked up his own. "Here's to the end of the bitch on wheels, however we take her down, and to the cop and the psychic and whoever else gets in the way. *Salud, amigos.*" He tipped his glass to his mouth and drank it down.

Hal drank, too, but the only taste in his mouth was fear. Fear that this psychic, whoever she was, might very well be far more dangerous to him than Manacas and Indrio, more dangerous, in fact, than Fletcher.

10

To Fletcher, the construction site resembled the ruin of some ancient city that had been abandoned long before Columbus had sailed in. The blocks of concrete and the dunes of dirt glinted in the starlight. The air smelled the way it always did in South Florida, of the rich lushness of her childhood here, part ocean, part Everglades, part something she couldn't define.

Fletcher spotted the van, parked exactly where Jim Hood had said it would be. Hood might be eccentric, she thought, but he was dependable. They had worked enough jobs together so that he knew what she expected. Even so, Fletcher felt tense and irritable about all this. If Steele's murder had no connection to Delphi, her presence here was a waste of her time. But if one or all of the missing three participants were responsible, then she would face the most important challenge of her career: finding them before they found her.

She pulled her rental car alongside the van and got out. She had driven straight to the hotel from the airport, checked in, showered and changed clothes, then called Hood. Since Krackett had instructed her to play it low-key initially, she would have to work behind the scenes with Hood until she could determine just what was going on.

She found the whole process enormously frustrating. It seemed more prudent to just step in and take over the investigation, thus eliminating problems with the local players. It was a more direct route to the answers she needed. But because she needed Krackett's continued support until her promotion was publicly announced, she would play it out until she decided it was time to seize control.

Sand seeped into her Adidas as she walked over to the van and rapped at the door. "It's Fletcher."

The door swung open and Hood motioned her inside. He sat on a stool in front of a complex array of electronic equipment. The headphones he wore looked like they grew out of his skull. A coffee stain bloomed on the pocket of his guayabera shirt, which looked a size too small, the buttons straining.

Hood's greatest weakness was food and it didn't seem to matter what kind of food. If it was in front of him, he ate it, and he obviously had been doing a lot of eating during his hours in the van. Crumpled cellophane wrappers and empty plastic bags littered the floor; the air smelled of chocolate, peanuts, old coffee. Personally, he revolted her. But she respected his expertise and reliability. Hood, if nothing else, had been an excellent foot soldier in the past.

"Where's Laskin?" The second man in her operation.

"Taking a leak," Hood replied. "There are two calls that concern us." He handed her a set of headphones. She slipped them on and Hood fiddled with dials and knobs on his equipment. "One came in this afternoon and the other came in a couple hours ago."

The first caller, a man, sounded like he had a bad cold. ". . . information . . . Steele homicide . . . Elbo Room . . . next Thursday night." Something familiar resonated in this voice, but she couldn't pinpoint it. "Any idea who it is?" she asked Hood.

"Nope. The call was made from a public phone in Lauderdale."

The second conversation didn't rouse her interest until she heard, ". . . see what impressions you pick up."

"A psychic?"

"That's what it sounds like. She's going to read Steele's house tomorrow afternoon."

Good, Fletcher thought. It would be an ideal time to drop by and introduce herself.

The rear door opened and Bruce Laskin climbed in. "Hey, Lenora." He snapped his chewing gum in greeting.

"Did you hear the tape, Bruce?" she asked.

"Yeah." Crack, snap, went his gum. He had quit smoking a

while back and now consumed gum and breath mints with enormous relish. "Guy sounds like he has major sinus problems. Maybe he knows something, maybe he doesn't. Either way one of us should be at the Elbo Room."

Laskin, a Miami-based agent whom she worked with by default, irritated her. But they'd worked together before and he took orders well.

Hood tore open a pack of peanuts, popped several in his mouth and pushed them into his cheek, like a hamster. "I'll go there. Bruce looks too much like a cop." Hood said it as though Laskin weren't present. His cold dead eyes gazed out at her from the cherubic face of an adult Gerber baby.

"I'll go myself," Fletcher said. "And I want to know more about this psychic. Is she any good? And if so, how good? Does she make her living as a psychic? What's her background? Everything."

"I'll do that," Laskin said.

The psychic actually worried her more than Sheppard's anonymous caller because she knew just how powerful a true psychic could be. At the peak of the Delphi project, Vic Indrio had been able to walk into a room crowded with politicians, read whomever she told him to read, and walk out with the information she'd been looking for. Or take Eddie Manacas, remote viewer. Armed with nothing more than geographical coordinates or a random set of numbers, Manacas had been able to "see" whatever was happening at the target. The ideal psychic spy. Hal Bennet, the most powerful and erratic of the three, stood in a class by himself. He could *reach* into most people with frightening ease and fuck with their heads.

Fletcher considered psychics of this caliber to be mutants. She suspected that Sheppard's psychic was only mildly intuitive or, better yet, a phony. But still, it worried her and until she knew more about the psychic, Krackett didn't need to know about this part of it.

The deputy director, despite his participation in Delphi, had never been comfortable when he didn't play by the rules. So he tried to compensate by walking a thin line between worlds, trying to meet the requirements of both.

But to Fletcher, something was either efficient or inefficient. At the moment, the most efficient course coincided with Krackett's directive: remain low-key. But when that ceased being efficient, she would do whatever she thought was best. And before she did anything, she would talk to Evans again.

"I'll be in touch." She climbed out of the van.

Her cell phone rang just as she stepped into her room. "Lenora Fletcher."

"It's Richard. Can you talk?"

"Yes, I'm alone. What's up?"

"What've you found out?"

"Not much yet." She told Evans about Sheppard, the psychic, and the call Sheppard had gotten.

"After we talked, I decided I need some Florida sunshine. I'll be arriving Monday and staying in my place over on Lauderdale beach. There's plenty of room, Lenora."

The offer stunned her. In the nearly twenty years she'd known Evans, she couldn't recall him ever making this kind of gesture. "Is this your penance or something, Rich?"

He laughed. "In some respects, I suppose. But I also have a personal interest in your success."

Of course. Once she became deputy director, she would be privy to information that Evans might use for leverage in his dealings with his old cronies in the Agency. "Retired but not really."

"Something like that."

"Give me a call when you get here. If nothing else, we'll get together for dinner."

"Good enough. Oh, by the way, your boss called me personally to tell me about your promotion."

"Knowing Krackett, that wasn't his only reason."

Evans chuckled. "Quite right. He wanted the Agency files on Delphi."

"What'd you tell him?"

"That there weren't any files."

"And he believed you?"

"I don't know. But he couldn't very well call me a liar, even if that's what he was thinking."

"Thanks, Rich."

"Don't mention it. Talk to you tomorrow."

As Fletcher hung up, she felt vaguely uneasy about Krackett's call to Evans and wondered what the real purpose of the call had been.

Shortly after sunrise, Fletcher woke suddenly and sat straight up in bed. Her senses strained to detect a noise, a voice, traffic. But the penthouse's location insulated her from traffic sounds and no sounds came from the hall.

Light seeped in around the edges of the curtains, briefly tempting her to get up, order a cup of Cuban coffee and enjoy it with a cigarette out on the terrace. But Christ, she was tired. She had slept fitfully for the last few months and it was beginning to catch up with her. Just one more hour, she thought, and eased her body back to the mattress.

But as soon as she shut her eyes, they snapped open again, darting through the incomplete darkness like terrified rats. A presence, she felt a nonphysical presence. She knew she was being scanned psychically, a focused, deliberate scan as real as a searchlight, but utterly invisible.

Sweat erupted on her skin, her heart slammed into overdrive, blood drummed in her ears. She bolted forward and grabbed the ELF device, damning herself for turning it off last night. She fumbled with the switch, turned it on, felt the difference instantly. The extremely low frequency radio waves that it emitted created a screen of white noise that blocked the scan.

Fletcher leaped out of bed, the ELF device clutched in her hand, and lurched toward the curtain that hung in front of the balcony's sliding glass door. Air, light, fast. She threw open the door and hurried onto the balcony. The early light poured over her, a primal relief filled her. She felt like a cave woman who worshipped the flicker of a flame.

Fletcher rubbed her arms against the morning chill. The blue vastness of the sky surrounded her like some huge transparent dome. Her eyes slid down its cold smoothness to the horizon, a narrow band of violet light where sky met sea. It grounded her, rooted her. Now she allowed her eyes to move closer in, to the boats moored at docks in the intracoastal canal, to the gulls pinwheeling through all the blue. And when she felt full and calm again, she walked back into the suite.

She stood motionless in the center of the room, her muscles tight, her heart still pounding. She was fairly sure the scan had ended, but she needed to be absolutely certain so she turned off the ELF. Nothing, zip. She quickly turned the device on again and moved to the foot of the bed, deeply shaken by what had happened.

A deliberate scan. She knew of only two individuals capable of such a thing. One was dead. That left Eddie Manacas.

Manacas, the first of the three to flee Delphi, had vanished like some Houdini prop in the late eighties, while still on parole. He had vanished so completely, Fletcher suspected he'd had professional help: cosmetic surgery, a new identity, a new life. He might be right under her goddamn nose and she wouldn't be able to recognize him. Unless he pulled a stunt like this.

Fletcher set the ELF on the oscillating mode, just in case Manacas attempted to scan her again. The device, a permutation of a prototype that had been used experimentally in riot control, was calibrated to match electrical impulses emitted by the brain. In this mode, it would alternate between theta waves—one to three cycles per second—and delta waves, which pulsed between four and seven cycles were second.

Most of the Delphi participants, while working psychically, had fluctuated between these two states. At home, she usually removed the device at night, a habit that had become as automatic as brushing her teeth before bed. But given what had just happened, she sure as hell wouldn't be turning it off at night or any other time, not as long as she was here.

So what had prompted the scan? Steele's murder? Her arrival? Her hand trembled as she lit a cigarette. *This is what they do to me.* She got up and paced the room, paced because it was easier to think as long as she was moving.

Go through it again, Lenora. Three men are missing. Indrio, Manacas, Bennet. The names marched through her head with a terrible impunity, a threat to everything that she was or might become. The deadly trio of mutants, the Frankensteins she, Steele, and Evans had helped create.

Her thoughts turned toward the past, to questions she had asked herself a million times before. The lethal trio had known about each other since Delphi's genesis, so didn't it make sense that they had kept in touch after they had vanished? She seized on this thought and her mind ran with it, chasing it up and down the highways of the past, the mazes of probabilities.

She called Hood in the van. He sounded groggy when he answered, she was sure she woke him. "Jim, run a voice print on that call Sheppard got tonight and compare it to our tapes on Hal Bennet, Ed Manacas, and Vic Indrio."

Hood let out a low, soft whistle. "Jesus, Lenora, you may be onto something. I'll call you back in an hour."

"I'll be in my room."

And for the next hour, she paced and smoked and thought, figuring the angles. But it all boiled down to only one question: if she was right, what the hell did it mean?

Hood called back sixty-five minutes later, the longest sixty-five minutes in her life. "That voice print matches Indrio's perfectly."

Fletcher squeezed her eyes shut, her emotions careening between elation that she was right, that Manacas and possibly Indrio and Bennet were in the area, and despair that her worst nightmare had begun.

11

Light touched Rae's face like a warm hand, but she didn't open her eyes. She listened first. Bird songs. A breeze skipping through branches. Splashing in the lagoon. Sounds so ordinary they made her feel safe, protected, almost peaceful.

But another part of her whispered, *Nothing is what it seems.*

As soon as she thought it, a serene image swelled in the depths of her mind and drifted upward until it filled her: a beach at sunset, waves breaking gently against pristine sand, the sun a burning orange disk against the horizon. A postcard image.

She couldn't explain the contradiction, couldn't bridge it with something that lay between the two extremes. So Rae pushed it out of her head and opened her eyes enough to peer out through her lashes.

Early morning on the chickee. She didn't see Hal, didn't hear him. But the aroma of fresh coffee drifted in from the kitchen, so she knew he was here.

Rae lifted up on her elbows. The handcuff, still snapped around her left wrist, wasn't attached to anything. She sat all the way up, her joints clicking and snapping, her body bright with pain in a dozen places. Her bladder ached. Nausea from whatever drug he'd given her mitigated her thirst and hunger, but overall she felt as if she'd been dissected and slapped recklessly back together.

She vaguely remembered eating and sipping at something sweet, maybe juice, but these memories burned like fireflies in a dark gray fog. She didn't know where they fit in time.

She rolled onto her knees and stood slowly, her legs unsteady. She made it to the nearest window and leaned out into the morning air. Rae rubbed her hands over her face, trying to shake her torpor. But she felt as if her bones had been filled with some thick, heavy substance that weighted her. She stared down at the lagoon, eight or ten feet below her. A sinkhole, she thought. Unimaginably deep.

A sinkhole? In the Everglades? Another contradiction that she couldn't explain. It frightened her. She sensed it wasn't right and yet her memory of the fact was intact. *There are sinkholes in the Everglades:* she repeated this silently to herself, testing it, and it just didn't feel right. *Why not?*

She concentrated on the color of the water, copper, like a rich tea, from the tannic acid. Mangroves shaded the water, except in the middle, where a hole opened to the blue sky. The only way she would get off the chickee was to become a bird and fly through that hole. Or she would have to take a boat. She couldn't swim to the mangroves. She didn't know how to swim, water terrified her.

Andy claimed he understood her terror of water, but he really didn't, not as a shrink, not as a husband, not as one human being to another. Sometimes he rubbed her nose in it by humiliating her in front of their son. *Your mom's afraid of the water, Carl.* Or by taunting her. *C'mon, Rae, the water's wonderful.* Or by making her feel that her fear was ungrounded. *There's nothing like making love in the water, Rae.* Andy had never been particularly supportive.

At the moment, in fact, she wasn't sure why she had married him. His charm, his brilliant mind, their home: none of it compensated for his frequent absences, his moody silences, his self-absorption. And sex, she thought, hadn't been very good between them for a long time.

And what're you thinking now, Andy? Has Hal made a ransom demand?

She had been missing for—what? Two days? Three? Longer? She didn't know. Her sense of time had vanished. Perhaps Hal hadn't made any demands yet. If not, then Andy probably thought she'd gone somewhere to mull things over after their argument. She'd done that before, why should he think differently this time? Since he regarded her teaching career as merely her hobby, he wouldn't remember that she never had split when school was in session.

So if he believed she'd just taken off for a while, then he simply would wait for her to return. Therefore, he wouldn't notify the police that she was missing. He would tell Mrs. Lee and whoever else asked that Rae had gone to visit friends.

All things considered, she wasn't in any particular hurry to get home. Although she worried about Carl, it thrilled her that Andy would now live in her shoes for a while. The realities would be forced on him: grocery shopping, cooking, meals, child care, doctor visits, preschool, the lawn man, Mrs. Lee. Let him juggle his personal and professional lives for a while. Let him wake up in a blind white panic at night because he'd neglected to update Carl's immunization forms for preschool.

Anger, she felt anger most of all. She'd been angry four years out of the ten they had been married. Angry because most of the time her husband acted as though their son's conception and birth had happened independently of him. Angry because he made her feel like the hired help, the nanny and the cook and the whore, all rolled into one tidy little bundle. And worse, she'd allowed it.

When Carl was diagnosed as a diabetic, Rae remembered, Andy had acted as if it were some kind of curse, something they had to hide from their friends, their professional associates. He had never once given Carl a shot of insulin; to do so would be to acknowledge a problem existed. The bottom line, she thought, was that it wouldn't take much to despise the man she'd married.

Oh God, my baby, where's my baby now?

She pressed her knuckles to her mouth, stifling a sob.

Stop it.

Rae paused in the doorway and peered out. Hal stood on the left side of the kitchen, where the stove and sink were, his back to her. He hummed softly to himself, tapping his foot in rhythm to some internal tune. The scent of bacon mixed with the odor of coffee.

He wore gym shorts and a tank shirt. No shoes. He looked the way men in campgrounds looked, sated and sappy.

"I'd like to take a shower and put on some clean clothes," she said.

Hal spun around. She had startled him and realized it pleased her. "I didn't hear you." He looked quickly back at the stove and began to lay strips of bacon on a spread of towels on the counter. "You hungry?"

Famished. But she kept her response simple. "Yes. But I'd like to shower and change clothes first."

He set the spatula down, wiped his hands on a dish towel. "I brought some of your clothes from the house. They're right here."

He went over to the cabinet under the sink to retrieve the leather bag Andy had bought her on their honeymoon in Brazil. He carried it over to where she stood, set it at her feet, and stepped back. "There's no razor. Nothing you can use as a weapon. But otherwise you'll find everything you need."

She unzipped the bag. He had packed her things with an obsessive neatness, shorts over here, T-shirts there, panties on top. It nauseated her to think of his hands pawing through her dresser drawers, touching her clothes, folding them. But her disgust didn't last long; it wouldn't change a thing.

Rae selected clothes, a towel, picked up the baggie filled with toiletries, and stood. "Would you mind removing the handcuff? It's scraped my wrist practically raw."

He thought about it a moment, then reached into a pocket in his shorts and pulled out several keys. As he unlocked the cuffs, his fingertips brushed her skin, a deliberate touch that nearly caused her to wrench her hand away.

"Where's the shower?" she asked, rubbing her wrist.

"On the open platform." He pointed at a wooden stall just beyond the edge of the roof. "You have to pump it a couple of times to get the water flowing. It's clean enough, but I don't recommend that you drink it. Breakfast should be ready when you finish."

She nodded and started past him, but he caught her arm. Caught it gently. She looked down at his fingers on her arm, then looked up at him, into the fathomless blue of his eyes.

Something passed between them, a kind of current that connected them at a level too deep for words. She had the distinct impression that he could read her mind, that he had actually wormed inside her skull and looked out through her eyes at himself, at the two of them.

His hand dropped away from her arm. "This was the only way I could think of to get your attention, Rae."

The remark clearly smacked of psychosis and only fueled her fear of him. She felt her bones and organs compress, felt her skin shrivel, felt herself growing smaller and smaller, as if she were in the process of vanishing altogether. But when she spoke, her voice sounded surprisingly calm.

"It's a bit drastic."

"Until the other night, I was just some con who did time in the prison you worked at. There were only sixteen women on the compound in those days. You have no idea how great it was to watch you women come into work every morning, Rae. You all smelled of the free world. You gave us hope."

Deny a person something, deny it long enough and harshly enough, and pretty soon that something became the individual's obsession. She understood that, too, because Andy had felt that way about her in the beginning.

"You barely remembered my first name," he said. "I doubt if you could dredge up my last name. I bet you can't even remember what I did time for."

Her only clear recollection of Hal involved a single incident. They'd been sitting in her office on the compound, going over the courses he would take in the college program, when she'd suddenly developed a throbbing migraine. There had been no warning. The pain had swept from her cheekbones, across her forehead to her temples, then over the top of her skull.

This odd detail had lodged in her memory despite the hundreds of inmates who had passed through the education department at Manatee during her four years there. Then again, when she thought about some of the inmates who had worked for her, men she'd seen five days a week, fifty weeks a year, she often conjured a face to go with a name. Her connection to that Rae back then hung by the most tenuous, illusory threads.

"You're right. I don't remember."

"Fraud." He said it with a kind of gleeful pride. "But we'll talk about that later. I just want you to know that it's never been my intention to hurt you. I kept you drugged for your own safety."

Sure. Rae walked past him.

The shower smacked of originality, she would give him that much. Three wooden walls shot up around a showerhead that descended from the edge of the roof. It was open on the side that faced the western part of the lagoon, so Hal couldn't see her. But the walls didn't reach the floor, so he could see her legs from the knees down, see her clothes as she peeled them off.

That made her distinctly uneasy. If he walked over here, if he tried to . . . *Stop thinking about it.*

She put her clothes and the baggie on the high shelf that ran along two walls. A cheap plastic soap dish shaped like a shell was wedged into a wire container that hooked around the showerhead. It held a fresh bar of Dove soap, her favorite soap, the only soap she had used for years. Coincidence? Or had he known that?

Since the stall stood open at the top, she could drop her head back and stare up through the hole to the sky. *Fly through it; that's your only way out of here.* Rae peeled off her clothes, worked the pump. The water, plentiful and tepid, came from some sort of pumping system that used water from the lagoon.

When she finished, she wrapped the towel around her body and watched the water roll down through the cracks between the floorboards. *Drip drip. Drip drip.*

If all water eventually emptied into the ocean, then maybe these drops would someday touch the beach behind her house. Maybe her son would be running along that beach and these drops of water would touch his feet. If the connection between all things ran as deeply and simply as that, then by licking away the drops she would taste Carl's skin.

A hole opened inside of her then and she began to cry, deep, silent sobs for her son, for herself. Grief, fear, anxiety, all of it mixed up inside of her like some crazy salad. She pressed the heels of her hands to her eyes, pressed until stars exploded deep in her retinas.

Stop it stop it stop it.

"Asshole," she whispered. Crying changed nothing.

But it had released the horrible pressure that had been squeezing up against her heart. Clothes, she thought. Clean clothes. That was the secret: put one foot in front of the other.

She gathered up her soiled shirt and leggings and stepped out of the stall. The mangroves loomed around her, a dense green prison pierced by shoots of chalky light. How fitting that an ex-con's sanctuary would be a prison.

When she entered the kitchen, she saw that Hal had set the table. It was pine, just like the two chairs. Florida pine, homemade furniture. Hal's handiwork. Hal, she suddenly recalled, had taken woodworking in prison.

An empty plastic bottle that had once contained Evian water now held three long, purple flowers. Fresh flowers. Wildflowers. Never mind that the plates and utensils were plastic, that the tablecloth looked like something you'd see in an Italian restaurant where the food was bad and the service was worse. He'd gone to great lengths to create a certain atmosphere and it deepened her suspicion.

She claimed the chair closest to her, at the north end of the table, and Hal sat directly opposite her. He began passing her the aluminum bowls and plastic platters of food, a virtual feast. Bacon, fish, fresh coffee, scrambled eggs, grits, hash browns, toast smothered in honey. She saw wedges of oranges, halves of pink grapefruit, strawberries so perfectly red they looked fake.

Rae forced herself to eat slowly, allowing her stomach time to get used to the idea of food again. Neither of them said a word. "I'm curious," she finally said. "How much ransom did you ask?"

He dabbed at his mouth with a paper towel. "None. I told you before, Rae, this isn't about money."

Her husband's net worth totaled about twelve million dollars, give or take. "I don't believe you."

He started to laugh, a deep, rumbling laugh that puzzled her, chilled her. It ended abruptly, as though someone had pulled a plug and his amusement swirled like water down a drain.

"I don't want his money." He stabbed a piece of bacon from the platter. "I don't need it."

"Then what do you want?" she asked.

"You. The only thing I want is you."

His words slapped her like a wet towel, sharp, stinging slaps that pierced her to the bone. Rae quickly lowered her eyes and kept her hands on her knees so he couldn't see that they were shaking.

It didn't matter to Hal that she didn't say a word throughout breakfast. It thrilled him just to have her sitting across from him, eating food he'd prepared. She seemed to particularly like the fish, bass that came straight out of the lagoon, so fresh it practically melted on your tongue.

He had his sketch pad handy and drew her as she sat there, her hair drying, the strands curling like springs. She had sharp, wonderful features, and bore a vague resemblance to Jessica Lange, one of his favorite actresses. He had every movie she'd been in, even her first, a remake of *King Kong* that he enjoyed watching just for the touch of class she had brought to the film.

When Rae had worked at Manatee, her hair had been like Lange's, much longer, those blonde curls brushing her shoulders. Now she wore it to her chin, a loose casual style that softened the bold angles of her face. Her brows looked a shade darker than her hair and possessed a kind of untamed beauty that he tried to capture in his sketch. He had never been much good at drawing people until he began drawing Rae.

It took her a long time to finish all the food on her plate. Then she sat back with the mug of coffee clutched in her hands and watched the sketch as it emerged. He stared at her long, graceful fingers, the unpolished nails cut almost straight across. A peasant's nails, he thought, not those of a millionaire's wife.

"How long have you been drawing?" she asked.

"Since I moved out here." He struggled to get her mouth just right, the sensuous pout, the fullness. "I started with birds, then Big Guy . . ."

"Big Guy?"

"The ten-foot gator who lives in the lagoon."

"How long have you been watching me, Hal?"

"Awhile."

"You sent those gifts and the tarot cards."

"Yes."

Andy turned everything over to the police."

Hal made sure he spoke of Steele in the present tense. He still worried that she would somehow find out Steele was dead before he had won her trust. "Maybe that's what he said he would do, but I doubt if he did it. The police would ask too many questions that he wouldn't be able to answer."

"What do you mean?"

"Your husband's involved in shit you don't know anything about."

"That doesn't surprise me."

"Oh, I think this would."

She shrugged, looked away from him, her profile etched clearly against the backdrop of light. He knew he'd piqued her curiosity. But now he had to proceed very carefully. He needed to reveal enough so that she understood just how duplicitous Steele had been, but not so much that she guessed Hal had killed him.

While her head remained turned away from him, Hal *reached* into her ever so gently. A violent maelstrom swept him up, a swirling fury of dark, dense colors. He heard shouting, glass breaking. Then her head snapped toward him and he was flung away.

Patterns, he thought. The pattern of her marriage to Steele had been one of arguments, disagreements, shouting matches.

She frowned, rubbed hard at her temple. "So tell me what sort of shit Andy's involved in, Hal."

"Paranormal research." Spy games, death games.

"*What?*" She laughed. "Andy? C'mon."

Yeah, good ole Andy. He nodded.

"Since when?"

"Years." Maybe his whole fucking life. Maybe Steele had been one of those introverted, brilliant kids who had an imaginary playmate and fell asleep with spirits whispering in his ear. "Probably as far back as the sixties."

"No way." She laughed again, nervous, uneasy laughter this time. "He couldn't hide something like that from me. If he was interested in the paranormal, then it was only as an adjunct to psychiatry."

"Think about the books in his library, Rae."

Tragedy burned briefly in her eyes; Hal knew this was how the light of a dying planet would look.

"How do you know what books are in his library?"

"Because when your housekeeper was out, I looked."

Surprise, shock, and disbelief flickered like lightning across her features.

"I figure there must be more than two hundred books in his library that deal with some facet of the paranormal," Hal went on.

"What kind of fraud were you busted for?"

It irritated Hal that she abruptly changed the subject, turning the conversation back to him. *He* wanted to control what they talked about and when. But now that she'd asked, he would go along with it as long as it suited him.

"Psychic fraud. That isn't what they called it, but that's what it amounted to. I had a lot of clients who were paying me from five hundred to a thousand bucks a shot to clean their auras, remove curses from their lives, to advise them on business transactions, that kind of stuff."

"You're a psychic?"

"I was a *metaphysical advisor.*" He smiled at that. The New Age was big on labels, so he had found a label that suited what he did. "There's a difference. I didn't do psychic fairs, didn't read cards or tea leaves or shit like that. I *advised.* Most of my clients were satisfied, they were repeat business. But some of the *santeros* in the Miami community felt I was invading their turf. They got a couple of my ex-clients to file complaints against me, there was an investigation . . ." He shrugged. "I ended up at Manatee."

"What does that have to do with Andy?"

She leaned forward now, he had her full attention, he controlled once again. "I spent my first three months at Lake Butler. I got into trouble, fights mostly, and was transferred to Manatee. Dr. Steele was supposed to do some shrink tests and evaluate me to see if I'd be a threat to the inmate population. Turns out he was more interested in what I was busted for. He did other kinds of tests. I did pretty well, because he started working with me."

"Working with you how?"

Hal kept sketching as he talked, covering the page with Rae in various poses. "Telepathy experiments at first."

She laughed. "Telepathy. Right."

"Believe what you want."

"You mean he would think of something and you'd have to guess what it was?"

"Same idea. But the actual experiments were more complicated than that."

"Give me an example."

"One of the first things we did involved the assistant superintendent."

"Which assistant superintendent? We had three in the four years I worked there."

"Colmes. The guy who laughed like Groucho Marx."

She made a face. "One of my least favorite human beings. He took early retirement."

Yes, indeed, Hal thought. He sure did. But only because his other option had been prison. "Well, this was around the time when Colmes was doing the evaluations on employees in supervisory capacities, including Dr. Steele. He asked me to see what I could pick up on his evaluation, which he hadn't seen yet. So I did."

"Was this before Andy and I were married?"

He nodded.

"And what happened?"

"I picked up that Colmes was giving him a conditional evacuation."

"Andy was hired by the Department of Corrections in Tallahassee. Colmes didn't have anything to do with his job."

"But Colmes was the one who evaluated him for Manatee, then that report was sent on to the DOC."

"How do you know so much about how things worked?"

"I made it my business to know."

He knew this made sense to her. She'd worked in prisons long enough to understand the real rules. "So go on."

"A couple weeks later, he asked me to find out if Colmes was involved in anything shady."

"Andy wouldn't take the word of an inmate," she blurted.

Hal bristled at her arrogance. "I wasn't just *any* inmate, Rae. That's the whole point."

"Look, I didn't mean that the way it sounded. But you know as well as I do what sort of hierarchy exists in prisons. It's always them against us. They drum it into your head during your job orientation. 'These are cons, ladies and gentlemen. They're manipulative. They'll pit you against your fellow workers if you give them half a chance.' That kind of mentality. Andy was rigid that way."

"The difference was that he wanted something from me. I knew he would verify whatever I picked up and that if it checked out, he would be in my court from then on." He set the sketch pad aside, got up to replenish their coffee. "What I found out was that Colmes had a taste for young boys. He was taking guys from the outside grounds detail to his trailer and fucking them."

She didn't react.

"You already know this, don't you," he said.

"There were rumors when his retirement was announced. What did Andy do when you told him?"

"I guess he looked into it, talked to some of the inmates, confronted Colmes. Not too long after that Colmes announced his retirement and Dr. Steele got a great evaluation."

"So you were Andy's spy."

In more ways than you know. "That was one of my roles."

"What were your other roles?"

Enough, he thought. He had whetted her appetite for information, raised her curiosity, and fueled her existing doubt about what sort of man Steele was. "That's it for now. C'mon, I'll show you around."

He felt a certain pride as he gave her the grand tour of the chickee. She didn't comment on the padlock on his study door, but seemed to like that room the best. She asked how long it had taken to do this or that, where he'd gotten his supplies, did the TV actually work? He told her about the satellite dish he'd installed, the generator that supplied power to the chickee.

"I've got about five hundred movies," he said proudly. "Have you ever seen *Natural Born Killers*? Or *Pulp Fiction?*"

"No." Then: "How long have I been here?"

Exasperated that she didn't want to talk about movies, he snapped, "What difference does it make?"

"It makes a difference to me."

"Today's Sunday. I brought you here on Thursday."

"Then the police are probably looking for me by now."

"Probably."

"I can live without Andy," she said softly. "But I can't live without my son." Then her eyes filled suddenly with tears and she walked away from him, out of the room.

Her son, that pesky detail again. He needed news. His small satellite dish would pick up Lauderdale, but he didn't want her to overhear anything about Steele. Not at this point. They had made a nice start, he wanted to build on that.

He walked out onto the platform where Rae stood, arms clutched against her. She had been crying and was now watching Big Guy cruise silently through shadowed waters. "If you can do what you say, then tell me how Carl is."

"No matter what I say, you'll think I'm making it up to placate you."

"Then prove to me first that you can do what you say you can. Tell me something about myself."

"What kind of something?"

"From my childhood."

Easy enough. He'd already done his homework. "When you were young, two or three, a relative—an older cousin or an uncle—decided it was time you learned how to swim and tossed you in a pool. You nearly drowned. That's why you're a non-swimmer now."

"You could've learned that from Andy."

"Yeah, I could've. But I didn't."

She didn't say anything; he knew she believed him. "If you still want me to try Carl, I'll need a photograph of him or something that belongs to him."

She hesitated, fear coiled snakelike in her eyes.

"You want to know, right?"

"If you have my purse, there's a photo in my wallet."

"I'll get it." He retrieved her purse from the storage closet, dug out the wallet, and returned to the platform. He handed it to her.

She slipped a photo out of one of the compartments. As she stared at it, the compassion and pain in her eyes brought a deep, terrible ache to the center of his chest. He didn't want her to be in pain.

"It's not a recent photo, does that matter?"

"I don't know."

She handed it to him and he sat down on the platform floor, the photo pressed between his palms. Then he gazed into the boy's eyes, eyes just like his mother's, and *reached*.

He had never *reached* into a kid before. He felt as if he swam in a primal sea where the intensity of emotions fluctuated like light. *Mommy. Need. Hurt. Scared. Teddy bear. Hospital. Don't like. Mommy, where's my Mommy* . . . Hospital. He seized on the word and *reached* deeper, but his reasoning mind interfered now, tossing up possible reasons for why the boy was in the hospital. He couldn't find what he needed.

"He's scared, he misses you, he's confused. He has a teddy bear he can't find. It's a washed-out brown, with a broken ear."

Rae, sitting in front of him, nodded, her eyes brimming with tears. "And Andy? Is Andy taking care of him?"

"That's all I pick up." Hal handed her the photo.

For a long time after that, she remained out on the platform, in a pool of warm light, staring at her son's picture. Hal watched her, torn between his need to possess her, to do whatever it took to accomplish that, and his fear that regardless of what he did or how fast he did it, he still might fail utterly and miserably.

12

"Wake up, Sheppard, I need to talk to you."

The captain's voice boomed from the answering machine, rousing Sheppard from a sound sleep. He groped for the receiver and glanced at the clock. 7:03. "The sun has barely risen, Gerry," he said without preface.

"I guess you haven't seen the paper yet this morning."

"Not yet." Sheppard didn't tell him that he'd cancelled his subscription to the *Fort Lauderdale News* to save money. "Steele's homicide was the lead story yesterday, so it can't be that."

"On page three there's a short piece about how the day before the body was found, the cops got a call from a psychic who had tuned in on the case. The source isn't named, but I'm betting it was Pete Ames."

"Christ." Sheppard sat up in bed, fully awake now. "Did they print her name?"

"No. But Ames won't be giving any more unauthorized statements to the press, I'll guarantee that."

"He got canned?"

"Don't sound so hopeful. Ames has been with the department for ten years. My guess is that he's going to be transferred to another department."

"And what about the cuts, Gerry?"

His subsequent silence, though brief, didn't bode well for Sheppard's future. "We'll talk about it at the hospital. Can you meet me in the coffee shop at nine-thirty?"

"Yeah, I'll be there," he replied, and hung up.

Sheppard ran four miles around his complex, showered, ate breakfast, and walked into the hospital coffee shop shortly before nine-thirty. Gerry Young had claimed a booth at the back and waved when he saw Sheppard.

The head of homicide wasn't a particularly large or imposing man. Half a foot shorter than Sheppard, he had a thin, wiry body, and thinning hair that had started to gray. Since he worked in a profession where people judged you by the way you looked, others often mistook him for a weak or plodding man. Sheppard knew he was neither.

Young had been his ally since he'd started with the department five years ago. Perhaps he saw a younger version of himself in Sheppard, maybe he felt paternal toward him, maybe their common interests had forged a bond between them. Whatever the reason, Sheppard always had felt grateful for his support.

"So give me the bad news first," Sheppard said as he slid into the booth.

Young looked like he'd had a bad night. Dark circles ringed his eyes, an air of gloom hung over him. Sheppard wondered if it had to do with the budget cuts or an ex-wife. "I spent most of Friday and Saturday arguing with the chief and the county jackals. Christ, if they want to save money, let those assholes take a fifteen percent cut in pay."

On Young's shitlist, the county bureaucrats filled the top slots, right along with reporters and lawyers. "So?"

"On November first, the department is losing a total of ten positions, two per department, including the two floater positions. All other positions and salaries will be frozen for at least a year."

Sheppard felt a hard, almost painful constriction in his bowels. "That's six days from now, Gerry."

Young continued as if Sheppard hadn't spoken; his words smacked of a prepared speech. "You'll be eligible for unemployment, of course, and there'll be eight weeks of severance pay that—"

"Screw that. Unemployment won't even cover my mortgage." Not to mention his credit cards bills.

"Anyone who's got six years with the department isn't getting cut, Shep."

"What about job performance? Doesn't that count for shit

with these people? Stupid question, forget it. Either way, I'm screwed."

Young looked about as miserable as Sheppard felt just then. "Well, you're not alone, if that's any comfort, Shep. We'd had so many unsolved homicides the last few years my job's on the line, too. I've got two ex-wives and three kids who are going to be mighty unhappy if that happens."

"The chief told you your job is on the line?"

"Not in so many words. But hell, I'll be fifty-five my next birthday and I've got twenty-five years in with the department. He'd love to bring in a younger guy he could push around who would do the job for half the pay. At this point, I need a major coup to keep my job."

"Is the Steele homicide major enough?"

"It might be. If we can solve it before the end of the month, it'll still be in the press on November first."

"In other words, do it by Halloween."

Young nodded. "If we crack this one, Shep, I'll be able to draw on a modest reserve budget that will allow me to save one job. Yours. That's the good news, for what it's worth."

"I appreciate it, Gerry. But I don't know how the hell we're going to pull this off by Halloween. I don't have much to go on yet."

"Let's hear what you *do* have and then go upstairs."

He'd intended to wait before telling Young about the possible link between this homicide and that of Mira's husband. Now he felt he didn't have a choice. Young listened without interruption until Sheppard had finished.

"Did Hotchkiss ever tell Ms. Morales about the green shoe-laces?" Young asked.

"According to his notes he didn't. I think if he had mentioned it to her, she would have said something about it. I'm hoping Steele's son saw the green shoelaces, too. That would confirm what Mrs. Morales saw and would provide a tangible link between the two murders."

"Yeah, it would. In the meantime, see if Ms. Morales will, uh, read Steele's house."

"She's going through the place this afternoon." Bemused, he

added, "I never thought I'd hear you encouraging me or anyone else to use a psychic."

Young shrugged. "Look, Shep. We're after information and I don't give a damn if it comes from a psychic or a talking donkey, as long as it's confirmed by someone or something else. Maybe this mysterious caller you're meeting at the Elbo Room will be an unexpected bonus."

Maybe, yeah. But he couldn't count on it.

"One more thing," Young went on. "As of right now, we're working this one together. Any information you get on the case, whether it's through Ms. Morales or someone else, should be taped. I want a record. If you need to tap into computers we don't have access to, say the word and I'll pull the strings that will get you in. I'll cover anything having to do with Mrs. Steele— her friends, fellow teachers, whatever. I'll take up the slack. Agreed?"

"How can I refuse a deal like that?"

"Oh, you could say you'd rather work with Pete Ames."

"Right." They both laughed. "C'mon," Sheppard said. "Let's go see the boy."

On the way upstairs, Sheppard explained that he'd already spoken briefly to Rae Steele's mother. She'd called him after her conversation with the housekeeper. "She may be a royal pain in the ass."

Young nodded soberly. "Yeah, she's a pain. She was in the kid's room when I got here. But I know your innate charm will nudge her into our court, Shep," he added dryly.

The cop outside Carl Steele's room in pediatrics glanced up as they approached. "How's he doing?" Young asked.

"Better. His grandmother is in there with him. Elizabeth Baylor." His eyes met Young's. "Her name's on the list."

"Yeah, I know," Young replied. "I made the list." He pushed the door open, and he and Sheppard stepped into the room.

Elizabeth Baylor looked like a corporate CEO on vacation, not like a pediatrician. A slender, attractive woman in her mid-sixties, she was an older version of the Rae Steele in the photo Sheppard had seen. Her chocolate-colored slacks fit her like a glove, her silk print blouse enhanced the flecks of amber in her dark eyes. A cat's eyes, he thought, alive with a shrewd intelligence.

"Morning, Dr. Baylor," said Sheppard, extending his hand. "I'm Detective Sheppard. We spoke on the phone."

She smiled, but the smile didn't touch her eyes. "Yes, of course. Nice to meet you."

"And you've met Gerry Young, head of the homicide division."

She nodded. When she turned to her grandson, the sun shone in her eyes. "Carl, honey, these policemen would like to talk to you for a few minutes."

The young boy stacked his Legos neatly and precisely on the moveable table that swung across the width of the bed. The beauty of the kid's face struck Sheppard as an advertiser's dream: freckled cheeks, sandy hair that fell across his forehead, big blue eyes. A Tom Sawyer for the nineties.

"You don't look like police," he remarked.

Sheppard held out his badge.

The boy took it, ran his thumb over the shield. "Cool."

Cool. Sheppard was pretty sure he hadn't known that word, used in that way, until he was at least twelve. "What're you building?"

"A world."

"What kind of world?"

"One that's better."

I'm with you, kid.

"How're you feeling, Carl?" Young asked.

"Okay." He snapped together a pair of Legos, then perused the remaining pieces. "My sugar's better. Mrs. Lee saved my life, you know."

"So I understand," Sheppard replied. "We'd like to ask you a few questions about . . ." He hesitated mentioning Carl's father and didn't know what to say about his mother. His eyes darted to his grandmother for help.

"About the other night," she said quickly. "Tell them about your Mom and Dad arguing."

Carl's tongue slipped slowly across his lower lip as he sought to fit a large Legos on top of a smaller one. "They argue a lot."

"About what?" Sheppard asked, noticing that the boy used the present tense.

Carl shrugged. "I dunno. I don't like it when they argue. I go in my room and shut the door."

Young asked, "What happened the night you got sick?"

"I got sick because I didn't get my shot. Mommy and Daddy were arguing and they forgot about my shot. I guess I forgot, too. I went into my room and turned on the TV. I fell asleep. When I woke up, I was in the hospital."

"That's all you remember?" Sheppard prodded. "Waking up in the hospital?"

"I've already been through this with him, Detective Sheppard." Dr. Baylor had folded her arms across her chest and positioned herself at the side of the bed, a paragon of protection. "He doesn't remember anything else."

"Not," Carl said.

Sheppard's brows lifted. "Not?"

Dr. Baylor smiled. "That means I'm wrong. Tell us what you remember, Carl."

"When 'Legends of the Hidden Temple' was on, I heard Mommy's car leave. When 'Salute Your Shorts' started, Daddy came into my room and asked if I want to go to McDonald's. I can eat some stuff there if the carbos are right."

Four years old and he knew about carbohydrates. "And then what happened?"

"Daddy and I went to McDonald's and I was at the playground there for a long time. Then we came home and I went to bed because I wasn't feeling good. Daddy forgot to give me my shot. I forgot to remind him. I got up when it was dark and real quiet outside. I heard arguing in the hall. I thought it was Mommy and Daddy at first. But I didn't hear her voice and I opened my door a little and peeked out. I was scared."

"What did you see when you opened the door?" Young asked.

"Daddy in his pajamas and another man. They couldn't see me because I was behind them. I got scared and hid under my bed."

"Can you tell me what this man looks like, Carl?" Young asked.

"I didn't see his face."

"Did you see his shoes?" Sheppard asked.

"Uh-huh."

"Do you remember anything about them?"

"The shoelaces. They were green, like sherbert."

Goddamn. There it is. He felt like throwing his arms around the kid. "We really appreciate your help, Carl." He looked at Dr. Baylor. "Where're you staying?"

"I haven't checked in anywhere yet. I drove here from the airport."

"There's a motel just down the street, about two blocks from the hospital," Young said. "It'd be better if you didn't go into the house until forensics is finished."

Forensics had long since finished their job, Sheppard thought. Young simply didn't want complications from the grandmother.

"I ... I want my mommy," Carl said softly, his voice trembling.

"We're trying to find her," Young replied gently. "But we need your help, Carl. Do you have any idea where she might have gone after she and your dad argued?"

"Daddy was saying that she probably went to the cabin."

"What cabin?" Sheppard asked.

"I don't know. I was there only a couple of times. Daddy says it's where Mommy goes to think."

"You have any idea where this cabin is, Dr. Baylor?"

"No. This is the first I've heard of it."

Terrific, Sheppard thought. "Do you have any idea what your dad and this man were arguing about, Carl?"

"I didn't hear them too good. But they were angry and it scared me. That's why I hid under my bed."

"Mrs. Lee found you in the kitchen," Sheppard said. "Do you remember going out there?"

"Uh-uh." He pushed the moveable table out of the way and laid back against the pillows. "I want to go back to sleep now, is that okay?"

His grandmother fussed over him, pulling the covers up over him, smoothing the hair off his forehead. "Of course it's all right, Carl. I'm going to talk to the policemen, then I'll be right back."

She walked out into the hall with them and as soon as the door shut, Young said, "If you'd rather not tell him about his father, one of us can do it."

The mere suggestion offended her. "I'll do it. Carl is my responsibility. His doctor would like to keep him under observation for a couple more days, then we'll stay at a hotel on the beach until my daughter is found."

"We hope to have some leads on her whereabouts very soon," Sheppard said.

"I can tell you this much, Detective Sheppard. My daughter would not voluntarily leave her son."

"Did she discuss the marriage with you?" Young asked.

Baylor combed her fingers through her salt and pepper hair. "Yes, she did. She hasn't been happy for some time. She'd been considering divorce, but she was afraid that Andrew would fight for custody and she would lose."

"And she never mentioned this cabin to you?" Young asked.

"No. But some of the teachers she worked with might know. Mrs. Lee gave me several names you can check."

Young jotted down the names. He apparently had every intention of following through on his end of things, Sheppard thought. But even so, a clock ticked loudly in his head, marking off minutes, hours, the days between now and Halloween.

"Have you ever seen *The Postman Always Rings Twice?*" Hal asked.

"No."

"I was going to show you the original version first, but maybe you'd like the remake better."

"It doesn't matter. You decide."

Rae, seated in a rocker in the den, watched him as he plucked two videotapes from the shelves on the wall. She didn't want to be in here, but when he'd asked if she would like to watch a movie, she said sure. A large ceiling fan whirred softly to her left, cooling the air that drifted through the open shutters. She hoped that by being involved in a movie, he would leave her alone.

"The remake," Hal said, and popped the tape into the VCR.

He turned it on, fine-tuned the picture. Light from the window glinted against the TV screen, so he hurried to the rear of the room and closed the shutter. She was relieved when he sat near the coffee table instead of in the chair next to her. He propped his bare feet on the edge.

"You want anything to drink, Rae?"

Hal, gracious host. It was part of his *everything-is-okay* routine. Fine. She could play it, too. "No, thanks."

"Is the fan on too high?"

"It feels great."

A big smile from Hal, then he settled back to watch the movie.

She had her favorite films, with *Body Heat* and *Siesta* right up there at the top, but she had never been a fanatical moviegoer. Carl had changed that to some extent—Barney, Winnie the Pooh, *Aladdin, Free Willy, Andre,* movies he must have watched a hundred times each. She doubted that Hal had those in his collection.

Thinking about her son brought a lump of emotion into her throat. Rae swallowed it back and tried to pay attention to the movie. She suspected that movies were as integral to Hal's life as children were to hers and sensed this might be some sort of test. Maybe he would quiz her on it later.

But her thoughts wandered. This was the longest period of time in which she had been conscious without that thick and terrible fear gnawing at her. Her fear hadn't vanished, it had gone underground. But it existed within tolerable limits right now. As long as the movie rolled, she didn't think he presented a threat to her. His absorption in the movie seemed to be a complete immersion in which just about everything else ceased to exist.

In her head, she replayed Thursday's events up to the point where she had opened the door to Hal. Between then and waking up on the chickee, she could find only one other memory, a sensation of movement, a blur of green and blue. She wasn't sure where it belonged.

He claimed that a ransom didn't interest him, that she was all he wanted. She had begun to believe him and wondered now if she might be able to use it against him somehow. The most obvious way to do this would be to sleep with him, just like

Jessica Lange in this movie, like Kathleen Turner in *Body Heat*.
The idea repulsed her. *And your life may depend on it.*

Her fingers twitched against her thigh and formed a small,
tight fist.

When *Postman* finished, Hal's eyes seemed larger and brighter
than before. "So what'd you think?"

"The ending is a complete shock."

"It's a classic." He hit REWIND, the tape whirred. "There are
some things about the original that I like better, but Christ,
Nicholson is so good."

Actually, she felt that Nicholson had never gotten beyond the
character he had played in *The Shining*, the psychotic weirdo
with the peaked brows. But she wasn't about to disagree with
Hal. "He carries the picture," she said.

He went on for awhile about the story, the plot, the dialogue,
the power of the acting. When he finally paused, she asked, "Do
you have *Body Heat?*"

"Sure. It's Kathleen Turner's best role." His eyes brightened
even more. "You want to watch it?"

"Definitely."

*Woman seduces young man and then convinces him to kill her
husband.* The specific plot didn't fit her situation, but the theme
fit like a shoe. *Woman uses sex to gain her freedom.* It couldn't get
any closer than that: Hal touching her, kissing her, fucking her.

The thought didn't just repulse her, it literally sickened her.
A thick sourness rose in her throat, her head started to ache,
nausea swept through her. But she had to move beyond it if she
intended to escape this place alive.

13

As Mira swung into the driveway of One World, she spotted a spiffy silver Porsche parked next to Nadine's Taurus. Mira didn't know anyone who drove a Porsche and since the bookstore was closed on Sundays, she figured Nadine had company.

She often had imagined that her grandmother had a secret life that included some debonair gentleman whom she saw when it suited her. She'd never asked, Nadine had never volunteered the information, and Mira had never attempted to find out psychically. Some boundaries you didn't cross even with people you loved the most.

"Cool car," Annie remarked as they got out. "Does Nadine have a boyfriend or something?"

"I don't know."

Laughter rang out. Mira and Annie looked at each other. "The garden," Annie said, and they hurried around the side of the house.

Nadine and Sheppard sat on mats in the shaded part of the garden where she held her yoga classes. She was showing him how to do the lotus, but he couldn't force his legs into the position. He looked like a man suffering extreme pain.

"Stiff hips," Mira remarked, smiling.

"Exactly what I told him," Nadine said.

Sheppard untwisted his legs, shook his head. "Not possible." He stood, brushing his hands together, and slipped his sunglasses back on. "I'll never be able to do the lotus."

Nadine gestured at Annie. "Honey, you show him what's possible."

Annie kicked off her shoes and eagerly joined them on the mats. She sat down, folding her legs into a lotus position, then grabbed her right ankle and slowly brought her right foot behind her neck. "I still can't do it with both feet at once," she said.

"You're way ahead of me, Annie," Sheppard said with a laugh.

Annie released her leg and stood again. "You ready?" he asked Mira.

As ready as she would ever be for something like this. "Sure." She gave Annie a quick hug. "I'll be back in a couple of hours."

"Don't worry about us," Nadine replied. "We've got a full afternoon planned."

Annie grinned like a kid with a secret.

"Nice car," Mira remarked once they were inside the Porsche.

"And how's a cop afford it, right?"

"It crossed my mind."

He laughed with obvious enjoyment. "It belongs to Gabriel Jacinto. Mira, meet Angelita."

"Little Angel. That fits Gabby, all right. I guess he told you he and my husband were good friends."

"He also told me how your husband died."

Good, then she didn't have to explain it. "I thought the car belonged to Nadine's secret lover."

"She has a secret lover?"

"I don't know." *And what about you, Shep? Do you have a secret lover?*

The air between them suddenly felt charged, electric. When he shifted gears, their arms brushed and she felt it to her toes. Her skin burned with an unfocused heat, a heat that seemed to be everywhere and nowhere. She found it difficult to breathe. She finally lowered the window so the cool October breeze blew through the car. It helped, but the knot of longing remained in the center of her chest.

"Nadine picked up some impressions last night. You want to hear them?"

"She's psychic?"

"Yeah, you could say that."

"So is this psychic stuff genetic with you all?"

Wiccans claimed that psi ran in families. Some psychics she knew subscribed to the old wives' tales about infants born with caul, a supposed sign of second sight. Mira figured everyone had the ability, but like any talent it needed nurturing to grow. Without that nurturing, it laid dormant and slowly atrophied.

She said as much and added, "I guess I chose a family where it could flourish."

"Your parents are divorced?"

She definitely had missed something here. "No. What made you think that?"

He seemed embarrassed. "I, uh, figured you chose which parent to live with and that parent remarried or something."

"I was talking about the soul's choice. I think the soul, the higher self, whatever you want to call it, chooses the circumstances into which we're born, the parents we're born to, all of it."

As soon as she saw the expression on his face, she realized they didn't speak the same language.

"I chose my sister?" he exclaimed. "Why?"

Mira laughed. "She's that bad?"

"Not bad. Just impossible. The eternal victim."

"I have clients like that."

"How do you deal with them?"

"I try to empower them and encourage them to take responsibility for their lives."

"Does it work?"

"Not often enough."

He nodded thoughtfully, absorbing what she'd said, then changed the subject to Nadine. "So tell me what your grandmother had to say." Sheppard slipped a mini cassette recorder from his shirt pocket, handed it to her. "If you don't mind, I'd like to record this. I'm keeping tapes of everything."

She paged through her notes as she talked, then turned the recorder off. "We got interrupted before I could ask her to clarify this business about the trio of men. But does any of that fit in with anything else?"

"It might. Like the part about this person who will approach me with explosive information. I got a call from someone who wants to meet Thursday night at the Elbo Room. He supposedly has information about Steele's murder. Also, we were over at the hospital this morning talking to Steele's son and—"

"Maybe you'd better not tell me until after I've walked through the house. The less I know right now, the clearer the information will be."

"That's the exact opposite of how I thought psychics worked. Don't you look for cues that people offer unintentionally?"

"That's how cops work," she said. "Not psychics. At least not legitimate psychics."

"What did you pick up on your husband's murder?"

"I was too emotionally involved to pick up anything. Hotchkiss thought I was a phony."

"Hotchkiss is an idiot."

"Maybe so. But I think he would've been willing to listen to any information I could come up with. And since I came up dry, I can hardly blame him for the opinion he formed of me as a psychic."

As soon as she said it, she started worrying that she might not be able to pick up anything in Steele's house and then Sheppard would have the same opinion of her that Hotchkiss did. A dog with her tricks, she thought. Perform or else.

"Look, Mira, you don't have to prove anything to me." As though he sensed her concern. "I already know you're psychic. I'm not judging you. I'm just looking for information."

She wanted to give his arm a quick squeeze, but was afraid it would seem too forward. "I've never done this before, but I'll do what I can."

He turned north onto A-1-A and the Porsche slipped into the snarl of traffic. On her right stretched Lauderdale beach, four miles of open white sand. Sun worshippers crowded the beach— sweet young things in string bikinis, macho muscle men, sunburned tourists, Rollerbladers, men and women with fat thighs pitted with cellulite.

To her left loomed the evidence of big bucks poured into Lauderdale's urban renewal, an attempt to remold paradise. A $47 million bond issue helped revamp the Strip from spring break mecca and its aftermath of pushers, prostitutes, and panhandlers, into a chichi hot spot of jazz clubs, upscale restaurants, and people who might be beautiful one day.

Madonna and Stallone didn't figure into this scene; it wasn't Miami's South Beach. But Lauderdale had its own stars—Wayne Huizenga, John D. MacDonald's Travis McGee, burger baron Dave Thomas. In 1995, *Money Magazine* voted Fort Lauderdale as the second best city in the country in which to live, after Seattle.

Personally, she had mixed feelings about the hoopla. She liked the way the city had been when Tom was alive. But Lauderdale, like her own life, seemed to be in flux.

Mansions blurred past in her window, the driveways shrouded by vegetation—towering seagrapes, Florida pines, ficus hedges trimmed to geometric precision. Lauderdale's wealthy elite. Although Sheppard had told her Steele was wealthy, she hadn't picked up on it and wondered why. Maybe it didn't matter in terms of who had killed him.

They turned into one of these driveways, a winding dark ribbon filled with shadows and dappled sunlight. She realized that with all the cops and forensics people who had been here since Steele's death, she might have a difficult time picking up specific impressions.

"Besides the Steeles, is there anyone else who lived in the house? Or worked here regularly?"

"A housekeeper, Augusta Lee. They probably also had a gardener. Is there anything special you need? Anything in particular I should do?"

"Just answer my questions. Otherwise be quiet." She got out of the Porsche and they started up the walk. A cool breeze blew in from the ocean, thick with the odors of salt and sun and sand, the lure and promise of the Atlantic. With enormous relief, she realized it would be easy to open up in a place like this, surrounded by beauty, the ocean almost close enough to taste. The proximity to water facilitated her abilities, which explained why she lived on a lake and worked near a river.

Her shift in consciousness happened quickly, smoothly, like an autonomic reflex. Before they reached the door, she felt a gentle tug to the left. Mira went with it, stepped off the wood chip path, and went over to the rope swing hanging from the branches of a tremendous banyan tree. She sat on the wooden seat, grasped the ropes, pushed her feet into the leaves.

Don't like it when they fight, it scares me, Daddy shouting, Mommy crying . . . Mira shut her eyes and fixed on the residue of the child's energy, his feeling tone, so that she would recognize it once she got into the house. She kept moving her feet against the leaves, pushing the swing, but not very high. *Don't want to go high. It scares me to go high because when I look down the world is shrinking.*

Mira removed her hands from the ropes, the impression dried up. She walked over to the stoop, where Sheppard waited. He already had broken the crime tape and unlocked the door. She briefly told him what she had picked up. He jotted it in his notepad and turned on his tape recorder.

Inside the house, their footsteps clicked against the marble tile, echoing eerily in the unnatural silence. But beneath that silence she sensed people, voices, confusion. She couldn't sort them out, couldn't find just a single strand to follow. Her chest felt tight, constricted. She had trouble breathing.

Pull back a little, not so close, ground yourself.

She rubbed at the center of her chest, entered the living room, and stopped. Her eyes went to the chalked silhouette on the floor. She moved toward it and immediately felt resistance, as if she struggled to move against an invisible rubber wall.

She turned right. The constriction in her chest eased, she could breathe again. As she climbed the stairs, her hand slipped over the banister, reading the feeling tones of the many people who had touched this wood. But the strongest tones belonged to the people who had lived here. The boy, the father, the mother, each tone distinct.

Rae Steele. She repeated the name in her mind and focused on the texture of Rae's energy. At the top of the stairs, she hesitated, felt a tug to the right, followed it. She was vaguely aware of Sheppard behind her, of the floor's hardness beneath her shoes, of how cool and still the air had become. A part of her floated inside of Rae's energy like a fish in a bowl of water.

Mira slipped off her shoes before she entered the bedroom, twisted her bare feet against the floor. It helped ground her. Then she stepped inside and moved where the energy directed her, toward the dresser.

She flipped open the lid on a wooden music box and strains of "Für Elise" drifted out. Her eyes wandered over the jewelry inside: a watch studded with sapphires, a ruby ring, a pair of ceramic earrings studded with chips of lapis. She felt drawn to the earrings, picked up one, held it against the light. She closed her fingers over it and felt heat rising in her palm.

A highway flashed through her head, homes and trees blurred in her peripheral vision. The image moved too quickly to grasp details, so she shut her eyes, deepened her breathing. Slow it down, she thought. Way down. There.

A major highway. The interstate or the turnpike? *Which one?*

Interstate, whispered a voice inside her.

She had a sudden image of woods—Florida pines?—and a pond. She sensed its importance and froze the image in her mind. Then, very slowly, she distanced herself from it and tried to take in a wider view. "I'm seeing a small house or a cabin." She described what she saw.

"Are there any other cabins or houses nearby?"

Mira scanned the interior picture. "If there are, I can't see them." She kept stepping back from the cabin until she had the mailbox in sight. She tried to see the name on the mailbox. Instead, two images came to mind: a heart and a man. "Heart. Man. I think that's the name."

"How do you spell it?"

"I don't know. I'm just getting images."

"Where is the nearest town or city?" he asked.

She hesitated, searching inside herself for the information. "All I know is you head north on I-95. A man gave her these earrings. I don't think it was Steele." Her eyes opened and fixed on Sheppard. He looked like a man who had just been punched in the gut and was about to gasp for breath and double over with pain. "Does any of that tie in with something you know?"

"Uh, yeah. Yeah, it does. Rae supposedly has a cabin she goes to sometimes. No one seems to know where it is. Steele must have known about it, though, because he mentioned it to his son."

"There should be property tax records."

"Not in Steele's files. But I still have to check through his computer and tomorrow I'll check with the county."

She shut her eyes again, grounded herself with her breathing. *Is there anything else on the cabin?* she asked.

Silence. No new images welled up.

Mira moved across the room, hooked into something else now, following the tug into one of the huge closets, Rae's closet. Her hand trailed over the clothes, soft expensive fabrics that yielded nothing. She stopped at the far end and gazed through a small window as round as a porthole. Ocean. Beach. Sunbathers. She touched her fingers to the cool glass and felt, suddenly, like a prisoner longing for the world that had been denied.

Rae's feelings about her marriage? No, she thought, that was a left brain conclusion.

She shut her eyes, pressed her thumb against her right nostril, breathed in deeply through the left, exhaled through the right. She repeated this several times, then switched nostrils, breathing in through the right, exhaling through the left. She kept doing it until she felt the shift deep inside her body, a radiant heat that burned at the base of her spine. Mira imagined the heat rising upward, spreading through her.

Grounded now, she walked back through the closet until she felt a sharp tug to the left, to the shelf that ran the length of the wall just above the clothes. Mira moved along it, her hands extended, seeking heat. She stopped when she felt it, heat like a blast of dry, desert wind that seemed to be coming from a large cardboard box. She lifted it off the shelf, Sheppard took it and carried it over to the bed.

"What're we looking for?" he asked as they opened it.

"Beats me."

She reached in and removed three large photo albums. She and Sheppard each took one and sat down at the side of the bed to page through them. Although he wasn't sitting particularly close to her, she picked up his exquisite energy pattern.

It reminded her of a complex mosaic, like that of a stained

glass window, except it consisted of part music, part color, and part something else infused with sensuality. She wanted to explore it, to glide into it like a mote of dust. But it would distract her too deeply and she might blow whatever chance she had of picking up more information about the Steeles. So she directed her attention to the photos in the album.

Labeled with names and dates, most depicted a younger Rae during the years she had worked at Manatee Correctional. In one photo, Rae sat in an office, laughing and hamming for the camera, surrounded by eight young men in prison blues. The photo was labeled: *me & education aides, 6/79.*

"Look at this," Rae said, handing him the picture.

Sheppard studied it a moment, then pocketed it. "Now look at this." The photo he passed her showed a small cabin shrouded in pines. "Is it what you saw?"

She looked at it more closely. The pines seemed taller than what she had seen, and the cabin looked smaller, more compact, older. "Damn close."

He glanced back at the album and read the label: 112 Pirate's Cove Lane. "No city, but it's a start. You feel like continuing?"

"Is this stuff useful to you?"

"You're doing fine. My job is figuring out how things connect, then putting them together into a whole."

Rather like a tarot reading, she thought. The cards spoke in an archetypical language that the reader had to interpret and then connect to the client's life.

The Hanged Man. The Lovers. The Tower. The eight of swords, the eight of cups, the ten of swords, the Wheel of Fortune. She kept the cards in mind as Sheppard picked up the box and got to his feet. She shut her eyes, grounded herself again. Heat throbbed like a heart at the base of her spine. She pulled the heat up, pushed it into her limbs.

Downstairs, the internal voice said.

She opened her eyes, scooped up her shoes, moved out into the hall. She felt an internal nudge that caused her to pause in the doorway of Carl's room. Except for the size, which was at least 20 x 20, the room might belong to any small child—the pet net jammed with stuffed animals; the posters of unicorns and

Disney figures; the Power Rangers; the kid's beanbag chair; the baseball bat and balls and toys. She didn't have to step inside the room to read it. Carl's energy breathed everywhere, curious and exuberant.

But fear suffused this room. Fear that something might happen to his mother or father or to both of them and that the only life he knew would collapse like a house of cards. This kind of fear in someone as young as Carl usually came from the parents, psychic debris the child absorbed like a sponge.

Mira turned away from the room and went downstairs. In the living room, she twisted her bare feet against the floor again. Nadine had taught her to do this. She claimed it helped create a kind of psychic circuit with the earth which rooted you, replenished you, kept you from burning out. Mira didn't know if it actually worked. But she did it because she felt a need for ritual.

She circled the silhouette on the floor, rubbing her hands together to work up a heat. She imagined a white light around herself, a buffer between her and whatever physical sensations she might pick up. Then she knelt at the silhouette's head and pressed her palms to the floor within the chalked lines.

Mira immediately felt a pressure in her chest, a tightness that she knew was the gunshot which had killed Steele. But this wasn't the agonizing pain she had felt Thursday morning; this was only its phantom. She rolled back onto her heels, stood, moved around the room until she found the residue of Rae's energy, a slipstream, tendrils that drifted through the air like an invisible fog. She stepped into it, moved with it.

And suddenly she is swept up into a maelstrom so fierce, so violent, she can't breathe, can't scream, can't move. She struggles against him as he pins her arms behind her. Kicks as he slaps a wet cloth over her face. Shrieks into the cloth as he lifts her off the floor, lifts her from the back with one arm squeezing her waist and the other hand holding the cloth over her nose and mouth.

She is still shrieking when he carries her outside, but the chloroform on the cloth is beginning to work and her shrieks weaken until they are choked, pathetic whimpers. Some deep pocket in her mind remains alert enough to order her body to stop struggling. To hold her breath. To fool him.

And just when she is sure her lungs will explode, the cloth slips away. She gasps, sucking at the fresh air, and twists her body savagely to one side and jerks her arm back hard and fast. It sinks into the man's gut, she hears him grunt, a pig's grunt. For seconds, precious seconds, he loses his hold on her and she lurches away from him, stumbling through the dark, a scream frozen in her throat.

If she can get to the end of the driveway. If she can reach the street. If she can flag down a car. If if, faster faster faster . . . He tackles her. She slams down into the bushes and he rides her like a horse, his fingers knotted in her hair, yanking her head back, back, back until she is certain her neck will snap.

Then she plunges through the looking glass, into a dark silence, and shrinks until she is a tiny white dot, floating in a black vastness.

14

Sheppard felt like a character in an existential play, the guy who knew he wouldn't find a way out but went looking for it anyway.

He helped Mira up and walked her into Steele's house. Her legs worked, her eyes were open, she was conscious, but she didn't seem to be here. After she settled in the recliner that faced the ocean, he went into the kitchen for a glass of water. Upon his return, pink splotches dotted Mira's cheeks and the inside of her left wrist looked as if it had been burned by rope or metal. Sheppard had seen this kind of injury on shackled cons during transfer from one jail or prison to another.

"Drink this," he said. "It's cold water."

Her fingers closed around the glass. She sipped, paused, sipped again. "That hasn't happened in a long time."

Even though he had a clear impression of what had happened—the physical events, her rapid movement from the house to the outdoors—he knew she referred to her total immersion in her impressions.

"Rae Steele was kidnapped by the man who killed her husband. I think she and Steele had had an argument and she took off and was nabbed before this guy killed Steele. It was dark when it happened. He had a cloth soaked in chloroform or something, but she fought it and got away at one point. He ran after her and caught her. Now she's surrounded by water."

He wanted to dismiss her impressions as colorful fiction. But the event she described might be a possible version of what had happened. He couldn't discount it because it bore too many similarities to what Carl Steele had told them.

He didn't comment when she finished; she apparently interpreted his silence as disbelief. "Shit, this is why I hate working with cops. We don't speak the same language."

"Then teach me your language, Mira."

"Right." She drew her fingers through her hair, pulled her knees up against her chest, looked away from him. "Spare me the Mr. Sincere routine, okay? That was what Guy Hotchkiss used to pull. 'Tell me what you see, Ms. Morales. Describe it to me, Ms. Morales.' "

"Hotchkiss is an asshole."

"At least we agree on something."

The angles of her face seemed less sharp now, her eyes looked less black, her expression had softened. Sheppard hoped she wouldn't choose this second to poke around inside his skull, because the green shoelaces would be the first thing she found. He touched her left wrist and turned it over, exposing the abrasions.

"What's this about?"

Mira drew her fingers over the skin. "He restrained her with handcuffs that have injured her wrists."

"But why do *your* wrists look like raw meat?"

She rubbed her eyes with the back of her hand; he sensed she'd explained this to people before. "I'm empathic. If the emotions are strong enough, I feel what other people feel and sometimes take on their physical symptoms. It's gotten better than it used to be, but I still can't disassociate myself completely."

"Like a stigmata." As a lapsed Catholic, he could at least relate to a stigmata, even if he didn't understand it.

"Sort of. Except there's nothing religious about it." She smoothed her hands over her jeans. "When my husband died, he had this rash under one of his eyes. I think it was from stress. Anyway, the rash appeared on my face about a day before he was killed." She paused again. "I don't even know why I'm telling you this."

Crouched in front of her like this, her presence swept him up. Her scent drifted toward him, a different cologne than what she'd worn yesterday, light but erotic. It stirred the slumbering beast of his libido, deprived too long. He had an overpowering urge to run his hands along the sides of her denim-clad legs and press his face into her lap. He quickly stood, jammed his hands into his pockets, and walked over to the huge picture window. Ocean. Beach. Sun. Zen, for Christ's sakes. His continued employment depended on it.

When he was sure he wouldn't do something stupid and offensive, he turned. "I'm curious about how this ability of yours works. If Steele or his wife had come to you for a reading, would you have picked up on his murder?"

"If anything, I might have seen violent death as one probability. But nothing's written in stone, okay? At any point, the soul has a choice."

You choose your parents, your siblings, *and* your death? Sure thing. And you also choose imminent unemployment, credit card debt, and the other depressing details that prevailed in his life now. Yeah. And if he believed that, he might as well hang it the fuck up.

Something of what he felt must have showed on his face, because she asked, "You think everything is external, Shep?"

"Some things are."

"Like what?"

He gestured toward Steele's chalked silhouette on the floor. "Like Steele's murder. It was an external event, something thrust on him from outside forces he had no control over."

"And what I'm saying is that Steele's deepest beliefs attracted this experience and at some level he chose to die this way. Our core beliefs *create* our reality. Everything begins inside."

He shook his head as he paced the length of the window. "I don't buy it. It means the guy living in a box under the bridge has chosen to be homeless."

"At some level, yes, he's chosen it."

He stopped, looked at her. His physical attraction to her had obviously impaired his judgment; she was a complete nut, a fruitcake. "C'mon. No one would *choose* that."

"*You* wouldn't choose it and neither would I. But we can't speak for other people. The homeless person, the battered wife, the homicide victim: their core beliefs attract particular experiences. But at every step of the way, we have the free will to make choices, to alter those beliefs, which alters reality."

He shrugged, hands at his sides, palms turned up. "A lot of people would disagree with your basic premise."

She laughed. "Most people."

"How does it fit in with horrors like the Holocaust?"

"I guess it was a collective decision to participate in that experience."

"Why?"

"To learn certain lessons, to teach other people something. It was a mass event, something that brought the issue of human rights into mainstream consciousness. The O.J. trial was the same thing. Regardless of whether he was innocent or guilty, the trial and the verdict brought attention to race relations, spouse abuse, corruption."

"How do you reconcile your beliefs with what happened to your husband?"

Her response didn't come as quickly this time. "I'm still working on that one. Let's keep it simple. What would you like most to be doing?"

"I'd like to own an import shop."

"Neat."

His ex had never used that adjective, he thought.

"What kind of shop do you imagine?"

He described it to her: the Guatemalan *huipiles* sharing space on the walls with hand-carved paddles from the Amazon; the varied pygmy figurines of gods and goddesses the ancients had worshipped; more modern items carved from jade and lapis.

"How big a store would it be?"

He had never thought of the physical store, only of what it would contain. "I don't know."

"I think the secret to manifesting anything is to visualize what you want, to see the outcome in detail. If you can do it with high expectations and a great deal of emotion, it'll come about."

Shades of the nine insights in *The Celestine Prophecy*, he thought. He had read the book only because it supposedly took place in Peru. But from the beginning, it had been obvious to Sheppard that the author hadn't ever stepped foot in Peru. He failed to describe or even name a plant or tree; he didn't possess so much as a tourist's sense of Hispanic passions; and he had his Indians all mixed up. The ruins in Peru had been built by the Incans, not the Mayans.

For Sheppard, these discrepancies had detracted from the insights, made them seem as fraudulent as the Peru the author described. Too bad. He stood at a point in his life where he could use a little magic, a few synchronicities.

"You think it's all bullshit," she said.

"Maybe not all of it."

He had a sudden, vivid image of himself and Mira making love. Her black hair fanned out against a pale sheet, her skin looked soft, drawn snugly over the exquisite geometry of her bones. At this very second, this image represented what he wanted most. The Zen of desire, a result of wild hormones and a pathetic sex life.

The visage, though, seemed so clear and real to him, it created an intense, powerful heat that started in his groin, sped up his spine, and seemed to leap away from him and into the space between them. She felt it, he could see it in her eyes, in the sudden tension in her body. Then he moved toward her, his feet gliding inches above the floor, his desire burning like a sun in the center of his chest. But before he reached her chair, the doorbell rang.

The intrusion shocked him and he stopped where he was, the echo ringing in these silent rooms, their eyes locked together. The second peal snapped him back completely into the moment. He nearly had made a fool of himself.

"Pizza Hut," he quipped. "Be right back."

He hurried up the hall to answer the door, grateful now that the bell had rung. Just what the hell had he thought he was going to do, anyway? Drop to his knees in front of her chair? Gather her into his arms? Right.

The woman on the front porch looked too well-heeled to be selling anything door-to-door. She wore black slacks and a red blazer that accentuated the paleness of her skin. Only true snowbirds had skin as pale as hers. Her light blonde hair, straight, thick, and chin-length, had been cut to move as she moved, with exquisite grace. Her sunglasses, designer chic, had cost probably three hundred bucks. He knew because his ex-wife had owned a pair. Her entire outfit, in fact, from the sunglasses to her shoes and black leather purse, had probably cost a cool grand.

A rich snowbird. Maybe a friend of the Steeles? Only a rich woman in her late forties would have the body of a thirty-year-old.

"Yes?" he said.

"Uh, hi." She smiled quickly and planted her sunglasses firmly on the top of her head. Her eyes, a mesmerizing mix of green and blue, regarded him as though he were an annoying insect. "Who're you?"

"Who're you?" he shot back.

"Lenora Fletcher, FBI."

The name slapped him in the face like a wet towel. Fletcher the Quantico legend? The only woman in the history of the Bureau to head up the training center at Quantico? Here? Why?

She slipped a badge from her blazer pocket, flashed it in front of him, then stepped past him and into the house. Her lovely eyes swept from wall to wall, down the hall, then fixed on him. "So, let's start over again. Who're you?"

"Wayne Sheppard, Broward County Sheriff's Department."

"And you're in charge of the Steele homicide, Mr. Sheppard?"

It wouldn't take much to dislike this woman. "That's right. What's the FBI's interest in this case?"

"I'm not at liberty to say." She started down the hall, her leather pumps tapping against the marble.

Sheppard blocked her in three strides. "You need a warrant to search this house, Ms. Fletcher."

She smiled all too sweetly, revealing a mouth filled with Pepsodent-bright teeth. "I have a warrant." And out of her blazer pocket it came, signed and stamped by a federal judge in Miami. "Now if you'll excuse me."

"I'll need to verify your badge number before I can accept the warrant."

She laughed out loud. "Really. Well, verify away." She proffered her badge again and he jotted down the number. "Where would you like me to wait while you waste my time?"

"In the living room."

Her shoes clicked down the hall. She nodded hello to Mira, who murmured, "Hi," then asked Sheppard where the bathroom was.

He pointed to his right. "Down that way."

Mira left, Fletcher perched her dainty little ass at the edge of a rattan couch, and Sheppard went out to the car to get Gabby's cellular phone. Although her search warrant had come out of Miami, he suspected D.C. was her territory and in D.C. he knew of one man to call for the answers.

Patrick O'Malley's number rang twice before his booming Irish voice answered. "O'Malley."

"Shep here."

"You're shittin' me." He laughed and Sheppard could see his freckled face and the flaming red hair now paling to gray at the temples. "We've been doing e-mail so long, it's weird to hear your voice, man. You in town?"

"No such luck. I need a favor. Could you run a Bureau badge number for me?"

"Shoot."

Sheppard glanced at Fletcher as he ticked off her badge number. She looked both amused and bored, like the kind of woman who would now pull out her nail file and go to work on her manicure.

O'Malley sucked in his breath. "Jesus, man. Fletcher? *The* Lenora Fletcher? What's going on?"

"Good question."

"You can't talk freely."

"Right."

"She's nearby?"

"Uh-huh."

"Christ. Listen real good, Shep. The last guy who fucked with her ended up in Alaska for a couple of years, you hear what I'm saying?"

"Loud and clear."

"She's Krackett's right arm and the grapevine is saying that Friday night Krackett made the unofficial announcement that she's sliding into his spot when he retires. So if she's down there, it's major."

But what the hell did it have to do with Steele? He couldn't ask right now, not with Fletcher in the room. "Thanks, buddy, that clarifies things."

"I can give you more if we talk later, Shep. Better yet, check your e-mail."

"Will do. Thanks again."

He hung up and Fletcher stood. "Satisfied, Mr. Sheppard?"

"For now."

"How long were you with the Bureau?" she asked.

"Long enough to find the answers I need."

She smiled affably and twirled her sunglasses with the deftness of a cheerleader manipulating a baton. "Then you were also there long enough to know that some answers can be detrimental to your well-being, Mr. Sheppard."

And he, the man who could be unemployed by the end of the week, just grinned. "Alaska would be fascinating."

Fletcher's eyes widened slightly, the only hint of a reaction. She started to say something, but Mira returned just then, her purse over her shoulder, everything about her shouting that she was ready to leave.

"I didn't get your name," Fletcher said, looking pointedly at Mira.

"Jane Doe." She looked at Sheppard. "I'll be outside." And with that, she headed for the door.

"You're welcome to stay while I conduct my search," Fletcher said.

"I don't think so," Sheppard replied and strolled up the hall with Fletcher's eyes burning holes in his back.

From where he stood, Hal could see Rae, stretched out on a towel in the sun, her body like some lovely dream he had begun to recall.

After *Body Heat* had finished, he had fixed them a late lunch and she had wandered out to the platform. She looked as if she had dozed off, but it might be a trick, he couldn't trust her yet.

So he shut his eyes and *reached,* hurling a part of his consciousness into her.

She lingered at the edge of sleep, images flicking through her with startling rapidity. Thanks to Steele, Hal knew these were hypnogogic images, mind pictures the psyche tossed out as a person sank toward the first stage of sleep. A beach. Rae tossing a ball to her son. The two of them splashing in the surf. Nostalgia.

He pulled back, opened his eyes. He hadn't solved the problem of the son yet. Rae's separation from her son, her gloom and doom, would separate her from Hal as well. But worse, he didn't know where the kid had been when he'd shot Steele. He couldn't understand how he had overlooked such a vital detail, especially since he had spent the last year watching her, following her, learning her routines and habits. Suppose the boy actually had seen something? Suppose he had seen enough to describe Hal to the cops? He needed to know what was going on *out there,* in the world beyond the chickee.

Hal glanced around, checking for anything she might use as a weapon, went into the den, and shut the door.

On those nights when loneliness suffused him like some ancient curse, he only needed to turn on the TV, aim the dish, and presto, he had his targets. He didn't know why, but he found it easier to *reach* when he had an image of the person or place in front of him—a photo, a videotape, a drawing, nearly anything would work.

He turned on the TV, adjusted the knob for the dish, popped a fresh tape into the VCR, and switched it on as well. He tuned into a local tri-county news station, the best bet for what he was looking for.

After ten minutes of weather news, a photograph of Steele filled the screen. Hal quickly raised the volume.

"The investigation into the murder of prominent criminologist Andrew Steele continues. His body was discovered Friday morning by the family housekeeper, in his home in Fort Lauderdale. His young son was rushed to the hospital in a coma and his wife, Rae Steele, a high school teacher, is still missing."

Hospital. That confirmed his impressions about the boy.

"Wayne Sheppard, a detective with the Broward County Sheriff's Department ..." Steele's photo vanished. In its place appeared a shot of a tall, lanky man in jeans and a cotton shirt, reading from a prepared statement.

No suspects at this time ... more details will be forthcoming ... Blah, blah, blah. Hal leaned close to the screen to study Sheppard's face. To memorize it. Once he had committed a face to memory, he could *reach* without a photo or a picture, and *reach* nearly as far and as deeply.

The newscaster's face appeared again. "It isn't known at this time how Steele's son was injured or what his condition is. Police are asking that anyone who has seen Rae Steele to please call the Broward Sheriff's Department." Her photo now came on the screen; it didn't do her justice. She looked uncertain, almost frail, a face in a prison mug shot.

Hal turned the TV to the VCR mode, rewound the tape, and played it to the point where Sheppard began speaking. Then he froze the image and peered into the cop's eyes. *Give me what you've got, fucker.* He *reached* hard, stretching himself to the very limit of his ability.

At first, he heard only loud, irritating static, the incessant chatter of the man's inner world. Hal pushed deeper, deeper, until he touched the place that mattered. In every human being such a spot existed, a soft, tender field that yielded treasures if you applied the right pressure in the right way. And now that he had found Sheppard's spot, he pushed harder.

The images coursed fast and furiously through Hal. He encountered useless shit about Sheppard's car, his home, his lack of money, about the absences in his life. But Hal found a couple of gems that stunned him: images of the tarot cards that he had sent Rae and the face of the attractive young woman to whom Sheppard had taken the cards.

The psychic.

He reached more deeply to find her name, but only came up with "one" and "mirror"—or a word that sounded like that. A starting point. He ejected the tape, put it in the drawer with other tapes, turned off the TV.

Hal opened the door to check on Rae. No change. She hadn't moved from the towel. He went over to her, stood at her feet.

His eyes followed the long, graceful contours of her bare legs, the sweet curve of her buttocks, the angles her arms made to her body. Christ, just looking at her made him hard. He wanted her so badly he could taste the need.

But the first time had to be perfect. Nothing forced. He wasn't a rapist, like Manacas.

Hal returned to the den, left the door open a crack so he would hear her when she woke, then sat in his rocker. The routine for a "real-time" *reach* was simple. Bare feet flat against the floor. Palms resting lightly against his thighs. Eyes shut. Conjure the face. Sheppard's face. Now he filled in the details—the sandy color of the man's hair, the thrust of his jaw, his mustache. Now *reach* beyond the video image, the chickee, the Everglades, *reach* beyond the river of grass. And the *reach* swept him away.

15

Sheppard's place surprised Mira. She'd expected the impersonal digs of a bachelor cop. Instead, his town house looked like a cluttered import shop. Most of the pieces he'd collected reflected his upbringing in South America, where his father had worked for an oil company. Woven Ecuadorian rugs. Shards of ancient pottery from Mexico. Religious icons from Peru that looked as old as the planet itself. Hand-carved paddles from the Amazon. Colorful Indian necklaces from Colombia. A blowgun from Brazil, complete with the bark pouch that held curare-dipped darts.

"This is one of my favorites," said Sheppard, tour guide. He plucked a chunk of rock off one of the shelves that lined the hall. "It's from the top of the tepui where Angel Falls begins."

"And this fellow?" She pointed at what looked like a shrunken human head. "Is it what I think it is?"

"Yeah. It came from a tribe of cannibals in the Venezuelan interior."

"Jesus, Sheppard."

"I know, I know. My ex wanted to burn it."

"That's not what I meant." She leaned against the wall, her thumb moving over a lapis penguin from Chile. "You're a cop with the heart of Indiana Jones. How the hell can you stand it?"

"I can't."

The plaintive nakedness in his admission made her want to slip her arms around him, pat him on the back, and assure him everything was going to be okay. "So get out of law enforcement."

"And do what? Become a lawyer? No, thanks. Open my

import shop? That takes capital." He set the chunk of rock from Angel Falls back on the shelf and leaned against the wall next to her. "Look, it's great to believe that everyone can follow a dream and make a living at it. But in reality, it's just not that easy to do."

"That's just a belief. Change it and the reality changes."

Old hurts echoed in his smile. "That's too simple. It's not how things work."

The skeptic's lament, she thought. But she'd had this same argument with herself over the years, particularly after her husband's death. In her heart she believed what she said, but in the mundane world of bills to pay and deadlines to meet, she played in Sheppard's court.

"If you try it first with something small, Shep, you'll see that it *does* work. The problem is us. How we've conditioned ourselves to think. We seem to believe that we have to suffer and struggle to get what we want."

"Okay, something small. I'll start small."

"What?"

He reached out, his fingers slipped into her hair, and he drew her face toward his. His mouth tasted exotic, of the places he'd been, of the dreams he had dreamed, and that taste literally transported her.

Mira suddenly caught a whiff of fog, cold, biting fog, felt the scrape of a beard against her cheek, and knew that he wore a cloak that billowed out around him like a sail filled with wind. His hair seemed darker, he wasn't as tall.

London? A life in London?

His hand found the bare skin at the nape of her neck, his fingers slid through her hair, and she began to ache all over inside. Their bodies pressed together, her hip bones cutting into him, his hands at her back, her hips, her ribs, her breasts. They stumbled through the hall and into his bedroom, groping at each other's clothes as they fell onto an unmade bed. His mouth crushed hers, they rolled across a comforter until she lay beneath him. He lifted up on his elbows, smoothing her hair away from the sides of her face. His eyes locked onto hers, eyes that she sank into, blue that she swam through with the ease of a fish.

Their clothes melted away. When the AC clicked on, he yanked the comforter up over them and she filled herself with the smell of his skin, an odor of untamed wildness, Sheppard the traveler, the seeker, the nomad. He sculpted her with his hands, played her like a piano, explored her as though she were an exotic country he had landed in and intended to savor.

His fingers slipped into her and out again, seeking the perfect rhythm, finding it, driving her to the edge. She gasped at the exquisite sensations, feelings she hadn't known since Tom had died. Her body moved against his, arched into his, begging, pleading to be taken over the edge, into some dark, pulsating sea of unimagined pleasure. But he held her there, trapped her within the almost unbearable pressure, and let his mouth glide down the center of her, pausing at her hip, a freckle, her navel.

Her senses had been hurled open by then and impressions rushed into her and through her like a warm, salty tide. Sheppard the serious kid, the rebellious teen, the young adult with big questions in his heart. She glimpsed his days on the Miami streets, his years with the FBI, his failed marriage, his travels, his threatened job, his debts.

Mira knew he felt her inside of him, zipping herself into his skin. She knew because she sensed him quickly nailing shut a place he didn't want her to visit. He pulled away from her physically and she locked her hands in his hair and pulled his head toward hers. "No," she whispered hoarsely. "No walls. I don't want walls."

He slipped away from her, his tongue in a slow freefall, circling a nipple, licking at the sweat on her belly, falling lower. His mouth fastened against her, his tongue slid over her, into her, claiming her. And just like that, she was gone, her body stripped and raw, a mass of nerve endings that twitched and jumped and leaped like an impaled frog. Her hands fell away from his back, her fingers sank into the mattress, a white heat filled her head. *No more no more no . . .*

She started to shudder, her bones collapsed, her hands flew away from the mattress, and clutched his head, holding it there. She cried out when she came, a long, broken cry that echoed eerily in the quiet room, but Sheppard wasn't finished. He hadn't even begun.

He slipped into her with the unconscious ease of a man who had been there before and moved with a maddening slowness, a salmon swimming upstream against impossible currents. Her awareness blinked off and on like a strobe, her body turned inside out, the world spun crazily inside her head. She soared.

She liked the fact that he didn't roll over afterward and fall asleep. He held her hand and they talked. "Have you ever been to London?" she asked.

"I spent two days there, then left the city." He glanced at her. "Why?"

"Just curious."

"You ever been?"

"No."

"Don't bother. It's just another city. The best part about England is Stonehenge."

Long before she had read Brian Weiss's *Other Lives, Other Masters,* her past life impressions of people had been vivid but infrequent. She rarely trusted them unless she also got names, dates, details that might be verified. In all these years, she'd found concrete confirmation only once, with a life her daughter apparently had lived in New York in the late 1880s. She'd been a minor player in the suffragette movement, a footnote in a history book.

She felt tempted to dismiss the earlier image as fantasy. But she couldn't shake the impression of Sheppard in that cloak. *Give it to me,* she thought, and the images leaped into her head, disconnected and erratic, like frames of a poorly made film.

"You lived there," she blurted. "In London. I think you were a merchant trapped in an unhappy marriage. You just wanted to be at sea."

He looked—what? Stunned? He lifted up on an elbow and, to her complete astonishment, asked, "Do you have any idea what year it was?"

Timing, Christ, what was the timing? "Early 1800s, maybe the 1820s, I'm not sure."

"Queen Caroline died in the 1820s. So did John Keats. Simón Bolivar defeated the Spanish army at Carabobo and ensured Venezuela's independence."

She laughed. "You sound like a history lesson."

"I've always had a fascination with that period of history. After I left the FBI, the first trip I took was to Great Britain. I wanted to see Stonehenge. I had to go through London and from the instant I stepped off the plane, I had trouble breathing. I couldn't sleep. I couldn't wait to get the hell out.

"I rented a car my second day there and left the city. I got lost and ended up at a bed and breakfast inn, a three-hundred-year-old house somewhere in the boonies. As soon as I walked into the building, I knew I'd been there before. That night I dreamed about this guy who wore a black cloak and traveled between London and South America selling spice or something. I'm pretty sure I was him. Or he was me." He shrugged, offered a sheepish smile. "You're the only person I've ever told that to."

And suddenly, the air between them surged with that weird electrical charge. "You make me nuts," he said hoarsely, and started to kiss her. Suddenly, he jerked back, hands mashed to his forehead, a low, terrible groan issuing from his mouth.

Mira bolted upright. "What is it?"

"My head." He stumbled to his feet, hands still gripping his head. "Jesus, it feels like—" His knees buckled and he sank to the floor, his body doubled over. A drop of blood bloomed like a rose at his right nostril. And then another drop. And then a stream of blood poured from his nostrils.

Mira, alarmed and terrified that he was having a stroke or something worse, helped him into the bathroom, slammed the lid on the toilet, and told him to sit on it. She jerked a towel off the rack, soaked it in cold water, and pressed it to his nose.

"Put your head back, Shep. It'll stop the bleeding."

His head dropped back, he held the towel in place, and raised his eyes. Something or someone else peered from his eyes, a malign presence that brought goose bumps to her arms, a chill to her spine.

She felt an overpowering urge to cover herself and yanked the other towel off the track and wrapped it around her body.

Just that fast, the *other* withdrew. It was as if some massive shadow had dissolved.

Sheppard leaned forward, turned on the faucet, and ran the towel under the water. "A nosebleed. Christ." Then he glanced at her and grinned. "See what you to do me?"

Mira's laugh sounded forced, even to her. "Is the pain in your head gone?"

"Except for a twitch right between my eyes."

"Has anything like that ever happened to you before?"

"Nope." He wrung out the towel and draped it over the top of the shower stall to dry. "I was feeling sort of queasy, so I got up to get something to drink. Then suddenly my head felt like it was going to explode."

"This is going to sound nuts, but when you raised your head, I had the distinct impression that someone else was looking out at me through your eyes."

"Great. Now I'm possessed."

"No, it wasn't like that. It was . . ." What? Now she couldn't say for sure what she'd seen or sensed.

He approached her, ran his hands over the towel she had wrapped around herself, then unfastened the top and the towel slipped to the floor. His hands slid over her hips, she locked her arms at his neck, and surrendered to the soft nuzzles at her throat.

"If I get another nosebleed," he said, "I'll know it's you. "

Sheppard's voice, Sheppard looking out of those eyes, and yes, the hands that raised heat in her blood definitely belonged to Sheppard, not to the *other*. But she felt a sudden urge to get out of here, run from the bathroom, the apartment, and flee back to the safety of her own world.

But now they stood in the shower, hot needles kneading her shoulders and back like fingers. Steam drifted up around them, a jungle heat. The night that Tom had died, the heat had been like this, so intense she'd tasted it in the air as she waited in the car for him. The parking lot had been awash in the glow from the sodium vapor lights, crickets had cried for rain, and suddenly the man had hurried outside . . .

Sheppard, perhaps sensing that her thoughts had left him,

cupped his soapy hands at the sides of her face and kissed her. And just like that, she knew why she'd tuned in on the murder of a man she hadn't known.

Mira jerked away from him, her hands fumbling for the spigot, shutting off the water. She backed up to the wet glass door, her head spinning but her thoughts utterly clear, singular, as though she peered through a telescope that brought the most minute details into complete focus.

"What's wrong?" Sheppard asked, frowning. "What is it?"

Her words slapped the air. "When were you going to tell me?" She groped behind her for the latch to the shower door. "Or were you going to tell me at all, Sheppard?" The door swung open and she backed out. "You could've said something. You could've told me about the goddamn shoelaces."

Fighting back tears, struggling with all the old pain, Mira hurried into the bedroom and scooped up her clothes.

"Hold on a second, will you?" Sheppard followed her. "Give me a chance to explain."

"Explain what?" Her voice hit a high note that made him wince. She yanked on her clothes and he danced around on one foot, trying to pull on his gym shorts. Tears coursed down her cheeks, he blurred. "It's not like you didn't have a chance to say something."

"I didn't even find out until I was going through the file on your husband's murder."

She slung her purse over her shoulder, wanting only to get away from him as fast as she could. "Then you should've told me before we even stepped foot inside Steele's house."

"How the hell could I do that, Mira? 'Oh, by the way. There's one little detail you should know. The guy with the green shoelaces also killed your husband.' When could I have said that to you?"

"I can think of several times since we got here when you could've brought it up."

He grabbed her arm as she started out of the room. "That's unfair."

She jerked her arm free. "What's unfair is that you knew and didn't tell me."

She shot out of the bedroom, her wet hair plastered to the

sides of her head. Sheppard didn't follow, didn't try to detain her or argue anymore. When she reached the parking lot, she remembered she hadn't driven here. But she refused to go back inside and ask Sheppard for a ride to the store.

So she started walking, walking fast through the afternoon light, out of the complex and into the neighborhood. She didn't pay any attention to where she was, she had no destination. Only physical movement mattered, the hard concrete under her feet, the sun's warmth beating against her head. Her anger rattled around inside of her like a loose metal ball. But it had less to do with Sheppard's omission than it did with her own bad judgment.

The bottom line hadn't changed: she shouldn't have gotten involved in the murder investigation and she shouldn't have slept with Sheppard. Never mind that she had enjoyed it; he had spelled trouble since the morning he'd walked into One World. Because of him, she now knew what she didn't want to know, that Tom's killer was alive and linked to her life once more through another murder. She had her answer about why she had picked up on Steele's murder, but what the hell good did it do her?

When she finally got tired of walking, she glanced around for a public phone she could use to call a cab and realized her feet had led her into the past. The convenience store where Tom had been shot stood right in front of her.

Even though she had driven past this place in the last five years, she hadn't been here since that night. It looked unchanged, stuck in a perpetual twilight zone where it catered to the same endless stream of humanity—blacks, Cubans, Haitians, Anglos, even a spattering of Asians. A wino shuffled out clutching a brown paper bag, climbed onto a rusted bike, and weaved off into the late afternoon. Tourists didn't wander into this neighborhood unless they took a wrong turn off the interstate.

Mira knew she should turn around and walk in the other direction, but she didn't. She couldn't. Her legs carried her forward. A pulse beat in her throat. The night Tom was shot, she had lowered the windows in the car because of the heat. The air had felt slick and sticky, she remembered. She had been beat from Annie's birthday party, her eyes had begged to close.

It had been noisy that night, too. Cars whizzed past on the road, music blasted from radios, distant laughter trilled through the air. And yet inside the store, Tom had been shot with a silenced 9mm. These two extremes, one containing the other, had always bothered her. There should have been noise, the shock of an explosion, the shattering of glass, something to warn her. Instead, she'd felt only a sense of utter wrongness, of time stretched to almost unbearable proportions.

Since Annie had been sleeping in the backseat, Mira had stayed in the car longer than she would have otherwise. Perhaps that had saved her life. But after a certain point, the *wrongness* had started to eat away at her and she decided to lock Annie in the car while she went into the store. Just as she rolled up the windows, the man in the mask hurried out. A Big Bird mask.

He had whipped it off, broken into a run, and sprinted around the corner of the building. She never got a good look at him. But she'd recognized the familiarity of everything and realized the dream that had haunted her during her pregnancy with Annie three years earlier had sprung up around her. She'd known what she would find when she burst into the store.

She almost expected to see the same thing when she entered the store this time, as though the violence had been suspended all these years, lost in some sort of dimensional warp. But no bodies littered the floor, no black man sprawled at the end of an aisle, there was no Tom lying in a pool of blood. The stink of burned coffee tainted the air, the floor looked scuffed and dirty, customers waited at the register. The store could have been anywhere.

Mira stepped into the aisle closest to where Tom had been lying that night. She remembered the angle his body had made against the floor, the blood that had turned his shirt from yellow to crimson. She'd known immediately that he was dead because his phantom self, his soul, his spirit, whatever you wanted to call it, had hovered just over the body, visible to her, as transparent as glass.

She'd screamed and Tom's phantom self had looked up, eyes stricken with astonishment, shock. And then he had started to rise like a balloon and she'd watched until he vanished through the ceiling.

Mira rubbed her eyes and struggled against the urge to flee. She needed to work through this, to understand whatever she was supposed to understand. She picked up a Peppermint Patty so large it would catapult a kid into sugar psychosis, and got in line.

She thought about the young clerk who, five years ago, had gone into the freezer to get ice cream and had come out to find two people dead and a woman weeping hysterically over one of the men on the floor. The clerk had been in the right place at the right time, so she had survived. Tom had been in the wrong place at the wrong time, so he had died. Hotchkiss had written it off as a random act of violence and chalked up the death to another miserable crime statistic on the Florida peninsula.

She paid for her merchandise and hastened outside, her head aching with indecision. She dug into her wallet for a quarter to call a cab and moved toward the phone. Then she saw a silver Porsche parked at the far side of the lot. Sheppard stood out, leaning against the door, hands in the pockets of the navy slacks he now wore.

They regarded each other across the concrete that separated them, neither of them moving nor speaking. She was suddenly certain that he hadn't simply followed her, that somehow he'd known where she would go, known it even before she had.

"Want a lift?" he asked.

A simple question, with simple choices. If she shook her head and continued to the phone, the door to her husband's killer would shut ever so softly. There would be no definitive closure to the past. If she accepted the ride, then she would be agreeing to see this through to the end. Her choice, either/or, a crossroad. She hesitated, but not for long.

"Yeah, I'd like a lift."

For the first few minutes in the car, she felt awkward, tongue-tied. Then Sheppard broke the ice. "Twenty minutes after you'd left, I figured out where you were going."

"That's more than I knew. I was just walking."

"I intended to tell you, Mira. I just didn't know how."

She gazed out the window, unable to forgive him. "It explains why I tuned in on Steele's murder."

"There has to be a personal connection for you to pick up something like that?"

"No. But my impressions were so vivid I figured there had to be a connection of some sort."

"It couldn't just be random."

The derisive note in his voice pissed her off. "No," she snapped. "It couldn't just be random."

"Look, I didn't mean it that way. I'm sorry."

She rubbed her hands over her face, regretting that she had snapped at him, but not quite able to forgive his omission, either. "Ever since Tom died, I've been grappling with the notion of random anything. If I accepted his death as random, as something over which he had absolutely no control, then I have to integrate the random factor into everything else, too. In the most personal sense, that would invalidate what I do."

"As a psychic, you mean."

She nodded. "A psychic connects with certain patterns and deciphers them. No patterns are fixed. They're constantly shifting, changing, in the process of becoming something else. But the strongest patterns represent the strongest probabilities, the events that are most likely to occur as a result of the person's root beliefs. Like we were talking about yesterday, I believe that birth and death and everything in between are choices the soul makes. Nothing is random or accidental."

"If you really believe that, then it means at some level Tom chose to die as he did and you, as his wife, agreed to those conditions."

She nodded.

"But why would he choose to die like that?"

This remained the toughest part of the equation and the most difficult for her to accept. But over the years since his death, she believed she had worked out a possible explanation, for whatever it was worth now.

"I think Tom was afraid of getting old. He was afraid of being handicapped in some way, afraid that I would die first and leave him alone. So he chose a death in which he went out fast at the age of forty-two."

"Why didn't you see it coming?"

"I did." She told him about the repeating dream she'd had during her pregnancy with Annie, nearly four years before Tom was shot. "By the time it was happening, though, I didn't recognize it as the dream until it was too late."

"Look, if you'd rather not do any more of this, I'll understand."

Another choice. If she walked away from this, her life would be easier, she could return to her usual routines, the hard knot of fear in the pit of her stomach would vanish. But she might feel she'd cheated Tom by not pursuing it to the end. She desperately needed closure, a resolution, before she could move on with the rest of her life.

"I'd like to keep doing this, Shep, giving you whatever impressions I get. But I can't if we're sleeping together."

He looked over at her. "Why not?"

Because it would betray Tom. Because it would dilute the passion of her memories, of her loss. "Because it might confuse whatever information I pick up about this man."

"So I either accept it or no deal?" His voice sounded injured. "Is that what you're saying?"

"It's not an ultimatum. I'm just telling you what my limits are."

"You're doing this because I didn't tell you about the green shoelaces."

"I'm doing what I can live with."

He didn't say anything. The streets of Fort Lauderdale blurred in her peripheral vision. She leaned into his silence, trying to read him, but ran into a wall he had erected when she'd walked out of his town house. She couldn't tune in on him. In some oddly perverted way, it balanced things between them. She rejected an intimate relationship and now she couldn't read him.

He pulled into One World's parking lot, but didn't turn off the engine. "I'll give you a call sometime tomorrow," he said.

His voice sounded cold, detached, completely indifferent. He had become someone else, that man from the London life, the seafaring merchant. Mira got out of the car and watched as the Porsche sped off, a streak of silver in the October light.

III: The Talents

"Psychic abilities are being developed
in government-sponsored research
programs in both the United States and
the Soviet Union. Yet, despite
decades of research that has produced
better and better results, most people
have been led to believe that psychic
abilities and experiences simply do
not exist, or at least are beyond their
understanding."
—Russel Targ and Keith Harary,
The Mind Race

16

Mira woke suddenly, her eyes seizing the dark, frantically searching for some small bit of light. But blackness suffused the air and pressed down against her chest like a giant hand, trapping her against the mattress.

An electrical blackout, she thought.

But she couldn't shake the creepy feeling that someone watched her. She sat up and patted the mattress around her, certain she would find one of the cats. She didn't. She patted her way across the mattress to the nightstand, slid the drawer open, groped for the flashlight. She turned it on and shone it around the room, through the doorway into the hall.

Nothing. She slid off the bed and moved quickly across the hall to Annie's room. She had kicked off the covers and thrown her arms out to her sides, as if to receive something. Seuss, her little guardian, had curled up alongside her legs and lifted his head when the beam of light hit him. He yawned, flopped over, went still again. Seuss would sense it if something were in the house.

Her animals were her eyes and ears.

Mira went into the kitchen. The battery-operated clock on the wall read almost five. Outside, the moon had set and the streetlights had gone out. The dusting of stars cast enough illumination for her to see the surrounding houses and the fence around the neighborhood pool at the corner.

The phone rang, startling her. She hurried away from the window to answer it before it pealed again and woke Annie. She guessed it was Nadine, struggling with a bout of insomnia, but hoped it was Sheppard.

"Hello?"

"I knew a Morales once," whispered a male voice. "Tom Morales. I had to hurt him because he interfered. If you don't back off, Mira, I'll hurt you, too."

A pain exploded in her right temple; it felt as if dozens of needles had been stabbed into her skull at once, all in the same spot. The agony literally knocked the air from her lungs. She wrenched back, her hands flew to her head, the flashlight clattered to the floor, and the receiver banged against the wall.

The pain raced across her forehead, then melted like hot wax over the top of her skull. A thick, debilitating nausea swept through her, her stomach heaved, she barely managed to make it to the sink before she threw up. She splashed cold water on her face, but the pain kept throbbing. Hot splinters of glass pierced her eyes.

Ice, she needed ice. She lurched blindly toward the refrigerator, yanked open the door to the freezer. She groped for a handful of ice, wrapped a dish towel around it, held it against her forehead. She stumbled back to the counter, leaning into it for support, and tried to breathe deeply. But with every breath she drew in, the pain burned and burned, a bright, cruel flame between her eyes.

She sank to the floor, rubbing the ice pack over her face, the back of her neck, holding it between her eyes, where the pain now burned like heat. An unbearable pressure filled her skull; it was as if her brain had suddenly expanded and now pushed against walls of bone, struggling to burst free. She felt a warm stickiness just under her nose. Blood, Christ, it was blood. Like Sheppard. She suddenly knew the source of this powerful energy emanated from the dangling receiver.

Her head spun, she couldn't get to her feet. So she crawled over to the wall, yanked on the cord, and the phone popped off the wall and crashed to the floor.

As the pressure in her skull eased, something dark and incredibly powerful swept through her. She felt invaded, penetrated, violated, as though invisible hands had thrust down deep inside her brain, probing it, scooping her skull raw and empty, until it was just a husk of bone and bloody tissue.

Mira started to sing. She sang any stupid ditty that sprang to mind: Row your boat, jingle bells . . . it didn't matter. Over and over again, she repeated the same tunes, the same words, faster and faster . . .

She heard a sharp popping sound inside her head as the presence flew away from her. If felt as if her skull had been punctured, releasing pressure, agony, the presence itself.

For seconds she didn't move, couldn't move. She sucked air in through clenched teeth, every muscle and fiber in her body pulled taut in anticipation of another assault. But nothing happened.

Mira reached for her flashlight, gripped the corner of the counter, and pulled herself to her feet. Blood streaked her hands and arms, spots the bright, deep red of menstrual blood trailed across the floor. Mira quickly sat down again, scooped up her ice pack, tilted her head back, and pressed the ice to her nose.

He is able to project his consciousness in a highly unusual way . . . dear God, was this what Nadine's channeled buddy had meant? It amounted to psychic attack, something she'd heard and read about but which, until now, she'd dismissed as a colorful myth.

When the bleeding stopped, she made her way into the bathroom. Her hands trembled as she washed the blood off her face and hands and arms. But she could still feel him on her skin, inside her head. She turned on the shower and scrambled under the spray without removing her T-shirt.

Her fingers twitched tightly around the bar of soap, she rubbed frantically at her body. Not enough. She felt dirty, spiritually raped. She stripped off her clothes, scrubbed herself with a long back brush, washed her hair. It helped, but she still didn't feel clean.

She slammed her fist against the faucet, turning off the water, and quickly got out. She jerked the towel off the rack, picked up the flashlight, and hurried into her den. Sage, she needed sage. It would purge the rooms, a spiritual enema.

Mira searched the shelves along the east wall that held most of her psychic tools and found a single cluster of sage. She broke it into four smaller clumps and lit one in the kitchen, her den, her bedroom, and outside of Annie's door. Smoke drifted through the rooms, the scent calmed her. After awhile, she put the phone back onto the wall. A bright, tiny point of pain burned at the crown of her head as she punched out Sheppard's home number.

7:55 A.M. She drove the Explorer toward school, an ordinary event. The sun shone now, cars crowded the road, the only menace was traffic. But she felt weird, disconnected. She kept glancing at Annie, reaching out to touch her hair, her arm, a reassurance that she was real.

Annie finally said, "You okay, Mommy?"

"Tired, that's all. Just tired."

Psychic attack. The very term smacked of superstition, New Age dogma. Years ago, Tom's mother had told her about an incident that had happened to her when she was a young girl in Cuba. Her black nanny, from whom she eventually learned the secrets and rituals of Santería, had been attacked psychically one night by a powerful *mayombero*, a practitioner of the black arts. She'd gone into convulsions and nearly died. Mira had never believed such a thing was possible. Until now.

How does he know about me?

She continued to puzzle over this after she'd dropped Annie at school and drove on toward the store. An hour later, she still felt deeply unsettled, as if she'd waded out to a sandbar at low tide and now the tide had risen and water slowly swallowed the sandbar.

Mira went through the messages on her desk, most of them concerning the street fair, but her mind fixed on the man's voice. *I'll hurt you . . .*

Cards, she thought. The cards would talk to her about what had happened. She needed to feel them in her hands right now, needed their language, their reality, their mystery, their unerring truth. She brought out one of her favorite decks, Tarot of the Cloisters, a stunning round deck with a stained glass motif on each card. She shuffled it a couple of times, asking silently about the incident, then pulled one card.

Hanged Man.

It was one of the seven cards Sheppard had found at Steele's. Did it refer to the man who had killed Steele and Tom and psychically attacked her and Sheppard? It made sense, but terrified her at a level too deep for words. She couldn't defend herself against someone like this, someone with the ability to affect *living matter*.

Telekinesis, psychokinesis—the label mattered less than the ability itself, the least common of all types of psi and the most difficult to test in a laboratory setting. In Mira's opinion, Uri Geller remained the most controversial telekinetic, what with his spoon-bending and watch-stopping stunts and the accusations that he was just a clever trickster. But there had been others.

In the sixties, a Brazilian healer, Arigo, had astounded American physicians with his apparent ability to transmute pain and cure diseases in his patients. Nina Kulagina, a Russian woman whom some Western researchers and parapsychologists considered the best telekinetic in the world, could reverse the spin of a compass under rigid laboratory conditions.

But this? Someone who could actually harm another at a distance? Who could rupture vessels in a sinus cavity? Create such excruciating pain in the skull? What the hell kind of power was that?

"Just one card?" asked a voice behind her.

Mira spun around in her chair. Lenora Fletcher strode over to the desk in brown khaki slacks, a red cotton print shirt, and brown flats. She carried a large shoulder bag with many zippered compartments. She moved through Mira's office with the easy confidence of someone who believed she had every right to do so. It didn't just irritate Mira, it pissed her off big time.

"Learn to knock, Agent Fletcher."

"I knocked. You didn't hear it." She plucked a card from the fan of cards on the desk and dropped it face up in front of Mira. "There's the real answer."

The Moon. Deception. Disillusionment, feelings of foreboding. But the card also symbolized feminine power, the psychic, the hidden.

"How long have you been reading tarot?" Fletcher asked, lighting a cigarette.

"I own a bookstore," Mira said, gathering up the cards.

Fletcher ignored that part of it. "A bookstore owner who reads tarot."

"I teach tarot. I've also taught yoga, natural healing, the I Ching, and astrology. So maybe you should burn me at the stake while you have the chance."

Fletcher laughed, a rich, robust laugh that surprised Mira. "Wrong century, too bad."

"So what is it you want?"

"I'm a little vague on why you were at Dr. Steele's yesterday."

"I'm sure Detective Sheppard can tell you whatever you need to know." She set the deck of cards in her briefcase and pushed to her feet.

"I'm asking you."

Mira faced her. They stood eye to eye, with the smoke from Fletcher's cigarette drifting toward her. Myra waved her hand through it and jerked her thumb toward the NO SMOKING sign on the wall. "I'd appreciate it if you'd smoke outside. Excuse me."

She started out of the room, but Fletcher said, "Just a minute." Said it in a tone of voice that could cut through two miles of ice in seconds. "Let's get straight on the basics. As of today, the FBI is in charge of the investigation into Dr. Steele's murder."

"So?"

"That means the sheriff's department has to turn over everything related to the case to us. That would include whatever you picked up psychically at Steele's home."

"Who says that's why I was there?"

Her smile flashed in a blur of white, perfect teeth. "You've helped local cops in the past. Your most recent—"

Mira interrupted. "I know my own history. And I didn't pick up anything at Dr. Steele's home." Then she carefully plucked the butt from between Fletcher's fingers, dropped it to the floor, ground it out with the heel of her shoe. When it was dead, Mira picked it up and handed it to her. "Next time smoke outside. I really need to get to class."

Fletcher slipped the crushed cigarette into her pocket, smiled like she had all the answers, and left without another word.

* * *

Pete Ames had a secret.

He sat on the other side of their cramped office, gloating like a cat with a dead bird buried under the carpet. He held a pastry in one hand and smacked his lips as he chewed with his mouth open. Sheppard finally gave up pretending that he didn't notice Ames's deplorable table manners.

"Christ, Pete. Shut your goddamn mouth when you chew."

He shut his mouth, but his gloating smile didn't vanish. "You heard the latest?"

"No, but I'm sure you'll tell me."

"A fed named Bruce Laskin marched into the captain's office at seven-thirty this morning and informed him the FBI is taking over the investigation into Steele's murder."

Sheppard saw his future sucked down the drain; his stomach did a steep roll. "On what grounds?"

"The abduction of Rae Steele."

"What abduction? There hasn't been any ransom demand."

Ames shrugged and bit into his pastry again, some sort of flaky croissant that oozed stuff the same color and consistency of pus. Sheppard felt nauseated just looking at it; he imagined the shit building up in layers inside of Ames's arteries. In twenty years or less, Ames would be a candidate for open heart surgery.

"Look, Shep, I'm just passing on the rumors. I had to give him the phone log, so by now he knows about the psychic's call."

"He knew about the psychic call because of the statement in the paper by an *unnamed* source, Pete."

Before Ames's lazy computer of a brain had a chance to process the remark, Sheppard got up from his desk and walked down the hall to Gerry Young's office. He paced back and forth across the room, the receiver mashed to his ear, and gestured for Sheppard to sit down. He felt too restless to sit. His future had backed up into shit's creek, Mira had been psychically attacked, Rae Steele's mother had been breathing down his neck, he needed a goddamn vacation.

Elizabeth Baylor had called him shortly after he'd spoken to Mira this morning and demanded to know what he and the rest of the department were actually doing about tracing her daughter. What leads did they have? How much longer did he expect this to take? Why hadn't she been apprised of where things stood and where they were going?

Sheppard, hung over from lack of sleep, anxiety, and every other thing that had gone wrong since Steele's death, had been tempted to hang up on the bitch. But he figured if he did, he might get his pink slip sooner. So he played the public relations routine, trying to mollify her. Yes, Dr. Baylor. No, Dr. Baylor. We expect something to break soon, Dr. Baylor.

Forget Baylor.

He focused on the view below. The river glinted off to the left, the bridge started to open, a line of cars snaked away from it on either side: life reduced to a game of tiddly winks.

"I was just about to buzz you when that call came through," Young said.

Sheppard turned. "Is it true? Some dork named Laskin from the Bureau?"

Young touched a finger to his mouth and motioned toward the door. They walked into the hall, over to the water fountain some distance from Young's office. "Yeah, it's true. What I know right now for sure is that Steele was involved in a high security government project. I'm not sure what it concerned. But Laskin wants your file on Steele."

"What file? I've barely had time to take a shit, much less write up my notes on Steele."

"Good. Create something to give him. Then we're going someplace where we can talk freely. And Shep, don't make any important calls from your phone, don't say anything in your office that amounts to a hill of cow turds. And whatever you do, don't include anything in your report about this cabin Rae Steele supposedly went to."

If a cabin existed, he hadn't found it yet. He still didn't know the city location for Pirate's Cove Lane.

"Look, things are going to improve," Young said, as if to break Sheppard's gloom.

"Optimist," Sheppard muttered.

"What the hell, Shep. After two divorces and innumerable

relationships that went nowhere, it was either get some optimism or stick a fucking gun in my mouth."

The resignation in Young's voice briefly distracted Sheppard from his own misery. Young rarely talked about his personal life, even in a general sense. "Weren't you seeing someone last spring?"

"That ended in the spring." He shrugged, seemed deeply uncomfortable, and leaned over the water fountain, signaling an end to the personal side of their conversation.

When Sheppard returned to his office, Ames glanced up from his bag of peanuts, a shit-eating grin on his face.

Fucker, Sheppard thought at him, and sat down again.

17

Fletcher had a special fondness for this particular Hispanic neighborhood, a crowded, bustling area south of Miami. It lay within several miles of where she'd lived for more than a decade of her childhood. Jammed into its half dozen blocks were Cuban cafés and restaurants, *botánicas*, clothing shops, shoe stores, and sidewalk windows where a cup of rich coffee cost less than a buck.

Her destination, a pretty yellow restaurant on a corner lot, resembled a Spanish hacienda. It sat back somewhat from the road and dense Arica palms surrounded it on three sides and shaded the outside patio. She parked across the street and spent a few minutes primping in front of the mirror.

Fresh lipstick. A comb through her hair. Remove the emerald post earrings and snap in a pair of braided gold hoops that were less flashy. She unbuttoned the jacket of her turquoise business suit and exchanged her flats for a pair of low heels. She felt like a young girl preparing for her senior prom, not a woman in her late forties about to perpetuate a lie.

The crowd inside El Gringo had spilled onto the back patio, where ceiling fans whirred quietly, keeping the air cool and fragrant. The fronds of the lush palms curved over the railing, potted plants separated the tables from each other, a Spanish singer crooned from a jukebox. A gringo named John Bennet owned this slice of Cuba. Hal's old man.

He knew her as Lia Fraser, a business executive with IBM. He believed she'd lived with his son when he'd been released from prison and that her life had fallen apart when Hal had disappeared. She checked in with him periodically, the bereaved ex-girlfriend who clung to a hope that Hal would come home.

She spotted him out on the patio, sitting alone, a man with a bald, very tan head, bushy white brows, and eyes as blue as the Caribbean. His bold, uneven features radiated a kind of Sean Connery charisma. In foreign ports, he would be the guy who drank the local beer, bedded the señoritas, and sailed off into a Jimmy Buffet sunset.

It had been six months since she'd seen him and he hugged her hello like a father, then stood back, his hands still on her arms. "My God, you look wonderful, Lia. It's been too damn long. C'mon, sit down. Would you like coffee? A guava turnover?"

"Both, thanks." She lit a cigarette as John signaled a waitress. "Business is still booming," she remarked when the waitress had left.

"I've got no complaints. How've you been?"

They chatted amiably for a while, fiction rolling off her tongue as smooth as honey. Her promotion, lots of traveling, new computers, new software, busy busy busy. John Bennet listened raptly, his blue eyes so much like Hal's she felt the old longing deep inside her chest.

It disgusted her, this longing. She considered it her greatest weakness, a failing that nearly had proven to be her nemesis. Hal Bennet might still prove to be her nemesis. Fletcher hadn't seen Hal in three years now, but her memories remained bright, vivid, rendered in excruciating detail: the long nights in the Coral Gables house, her obsession with his body, his talent, his essential *difference* from others.

The physical relationship had lasted a long time, longer than Fletcher had been married to either of her two husbands. But the chemistry had begun long before that. The first job he had done for Delphi had been a kind of test and proved to be a biggie.

At the end of 1979, Hal Bennet had *reached* into the mind of a suburban housewife in Virginia, prompted her to load the .357 her husband kept in a nightstand drawer, and to head into D.C. There, in a busy subway station during rush hour, she'd opened fire on the crowd. Five people had been killed and a dozen others had been injured before the cops cut her spree short with two shots to the heart. The fact that the woman had been one of the least likely individuals to do something like this had impressed Richard Evans. Not long afterward, funding for Delphi had been doubled.

In early 1980, she and Steele had created specific targets and goals for Hal that had helped train and hone his ability. He'd failed some and succeeded at others. But from these trial runs they'd learned the parameters of his ability. He worked best, for instance, when he could see the target or had a photo or video clip of it. Strong intent and desire or any deep emotion could propel the ability faster and more powerfully.

In one experiment, they'd given Hal photos of a primary transformer in a South Florida neighborhood and told him to blow it out. He couldn't do it. So Fletcher had driven him to the neighborhood and told him to do it with the transformer in sight. Nothing. But when she poked fun at him and threatened to toss him back in prison, he'd gotten angry and had blown the transformer in a few minutes.

In March of that year, Krackett said he wanted something major that would topple the Carter presidency. He and the director had despised Carter for the very humanity that had made him an outstanding ex-president.

A month later, on April 24, 1980, Hal Bennet, working with just a photo, had *reached* into a chopper pilot who was part of the battalion of eight that were supposed to pull off the rescue of hostages in Iran. That chopper had collided with one of the six C-130 transports. No one could trace the chopper's crash to its source because the pilot had been killed. If he'd lived, though, he might have described the chaos in his brain as he flew his mission—the abrupt, excruciating pain in his skull, the way his eyes had begun to leak blood, the state of his intestines.

She could still smell the sweat on Hal's skin as he had come out of it in that miserable trailer in the park behind Manatee prison. He'd been hooked up to machines that read his every vital sign, his every brain wave, machines that told them he was approaching adrenal exhaustion, that his *reach* had eaten up even his reserves. He'd spent a week in the compound clinic.

For months afterward, she and Steele had played it safe. No

big jobs for Hal. Instead, they'd concentrated on Manacas and Indrio. Then, in early 1982, Evans had urged her and Steele to test Hal again and had provided the target: a federal building in Minneapolis.

She'd sensed that Evans had his own agenda in mind and had argued with him about that one. But he threatened to cut the Delphi funding if she refused. So in March of that year, without advising Krackett about the new target, she and Steele had paired Hal and Manacas.

Manacas had been instructed to find an employee within the office building who fit certain parameters. Evans wanted someone whose random act of violence, like that of the woman in the D.C. subway station, would be totally out of character. The least likely person. Hal, working from a photo of the individual, would screw with the person's head and make him or her do something extraordinary.

Problems had developed right from the start because Evans had insisted on an event that would grab national attention. The upshot had been an explosion that had killed and injured dozens of people, including children who had been touring the building on a school field trip.

The repercussions for the FBI, which had investigated the incident, had been considerable. Despite all their sophisticated equipment and knowledge, they failed to determine the cause of the explosion or to make an arrest. It made the Bureau look very bad.

She'd accused Evans of engineering the incident for precisely that purpose—to tarnish the Bureau's image. He'd denied it, of course, but her suspicion remained.

And yet, despite all this, she benefited professionally from Delphi. In the fall of 1984, for instance, Indrio, now on parole, had been sent out to read an FBI agent who was believed to be spying for the Russians. Indrio used coordinates that Manacas had supplied and several minutes after the guy had passed documents to two Soviet emigrés, Hal had rendered the man incapable of movement.

Acting on information Hal and Manacas had supplied, she'd

been a major player in cracking the Cali drug cartel, a victory that had put her in the running for the deputy director slot.

Successes like this one had advanced her career and Krackett's. Because of the talents these three men possessed, separately and in unison, her beliefs about the way things worked had been shattered and rebuilt. Thanks to Hal Bennet, Delphi hadn't been just a project she oversaw. It had consumed her nearly as deeply as Hal himself.

He'd walked out on her three years ago—*three years, two months, and ten days ago, to be exact, but who the hell's counting?*— and simply vanished. Several years before that, Manacas and Indrio had also disappeared, but Hal's disappearance had struck much deeper. He, after all, formed the very core of Delphi.

And when he'd vanished, Evans had pulled the funding on the project, Krackett had immediately distanced himself from it, and she'd been left to clean up the mess alone. Specifically, this had meant getting rid of the other four members of the project.

Fletcher had never thought of herself as a killer. She still didn't, even though she'd been directly responsible for the deaths of the other four participants. The rational, ambitious part of her knew the deaths were necessary to ensure her future with the Bureau.

But another part of her suffered enormous guilt. It surfaced from time to time, particularly when she spun her lies with Hal's old man.

"I don't suppose you've heard from Hal," she said, working it casually into the conversation.

"Actually, I have. I called you at the Boca office after I got the first postcard several months back, but they didn't seem to know who you were."

"I've been working out of the New York office and I'm not there very much."

"Let me get the postcards."

She waited impatiently, her stomach in knots. In her mind, she saw Hal's beautiful, powerful hands against her body. She stabbed out one cigarette and lit another. John returned several minutes later with half a dozen postcards. He set them in front of her. "You're welcome to them, Lia. I don't need them."

She tried not to appear too eager as she glanced through them. They had all been mailed from Flamingo, a town at the very tip of the Everglades National Park. A chatty quality marked them— been here, done that. But several struck her as oddly pensive, written in a neat, tiny script. Hal hadn't mentioned her, but why should he? He had no idea that she knew his old man.

"Has he ever called?" she asked.

"Yeah, on my birthday a couple of weeks ago. He said he'd been moving around a lot, didn't have a mailing address or phone, but that he'd be in touch. Typical stuff."

Fletcher jotted her cellular number on a scrap of paper. "If you hear from him, John, give me a call. I'll be in town for a while. I'd really like to talk to Hal."

John nodded, folded the paper, slipped it in his shirt pocket. "Lia, honey, you'd be better off finding yourself some nice young man and settling down. Hal's no good. He's never going to change."

She shrugged. "I just want to ask him to his face why he left." That much was true.

"What good is that going to do?"

"At least I'll know."

John squeezed her hand and shook his head, as if to say he would never understand the vagaries of the human heart.

She left a while later with the postcards tucked inside her purse, weighted with the past.

The Elbo Room stood on the corner of Sunrise Boulevard and A-1-A, a Fort Lauderdale icon that had rocketed to fame more than thirty years ago in *Where the Boys Are*. It had been modernized since then, but the basics hadn't changed: cold beer, loud music, a hot spot for tourists and locals.

Fletcher walked through the place, memorizing the lay of the rooms. *If* Indrio kept his appointment with Sheppard Thursday night, she could take him into custody. Once Hood got finished with him, they would know everything that Indrio knew about Hal and Manacas and why Indrio had contacted Sheppard.

On the other hand, she had no legal ground for taking him into custody, except as a possible link to a murder suspect. He'd done his time and completed his parole. The only crime he'd committed would never hold up in court: he'd split from a covertly funded project that had put him to work for seventy grand a year when he'd been paroled.

She would come here Thursday night, disguised as Indrio certainly would be. If anyone approached Sheppard, she would have to determine on the spot if the person was Indrio. If so, then she would—what? Shoot him when he went to the men's room? Drop arsenic in his beer? Blow the place up?

Sure. And kill a hundred tourists in the process.

She would follow him when he left and worry about Sheppard later.

At the height of Indrio's involvement with Delphi, his telepathy had worked best the closer his proximity to a person. But perhaps it had developed to the point where now he only had to be in the same room with whoever he wanted to read. Or on the same block. Or the same city. She could jam his "signal" with the ELF, but maybe Indrio's ability had expanded to the point where he could work his way around such an obstacle. If so, he might sense a tail.

If this, if that. Her head ached with the numerous possibilities, none of them good. The Frankensteins she and Steele had created had grown well beyond her control now, maybe even beyond her knowledge of what was possible. And that terrified her.

"Lenora, it's Keith Krackett. Please give me a call."

Beep.

"Keith again. Is your voice mail working? I haven't heard from you, Lenora. Call me ASAP."

Beep.

"It's eleven Sunday night. I need to speak to you immediately. Call me."

Fletcher stood next to the phone in her hotel room, listening to the voice mail. Krackett had called a total of twelve times, each call progressively more demanding. The last call had come in about two hours ago. Relentless fucker, she thought, and deleted the messages. She would call him tonight, after she'd picked up Evans at the airport and had a chance to talk to him.

She stripped off her Lia clothes, left them where they fell, and went over to the closet for jeans and a shirt. Casual for Evans. Florida casual. She needed to do what she did best, figure the angles, play the possibilities. Evans would help her do that.

But she knew that if she didn't call Krackett, he would keep calling her, leaving messages that eventually would collapse into outright threats. If she didn't respond, he would send one of his lackeys down here or fly here himself. And that would be bad, very bad.

Call him, get it over with, stall for time.

She dressed, then picked up the phone, punched out his private number. He picked up on the second ring. "Keith, it's Lenora. What's up?"

A brief, terrible silence, then: "What's *up?*" He hissed the words. "Since Saturday I've left Christ knows how many messages on your machine and this is the first call I've gotten, Lenora. That's what's *up*. What in the hell is going on?"

His tone rankled her, but she managed to keep her voice calm when she spoke. "I haven't called because there's nothing to report, Keith. We're working on several possibilities."

Keep it vague and brief, she thought. The less Krackett knew, the better off she would be. She hit the high points and none of the explosive details, like Indrio's call to Sheppard or what she had learned from Hal's father.

"Tell me more about this feeling you had that you were being scanned," Krackett said.

"There's nothing to tell. It was Manacas, I'm sure of it. And if he's in the vicinity, then I'm sure Indrio and Hal aren't too far away."

"I want this matter wrapped up in a few days, Lenora. I don't care how you do it, just *do* it."

She needed more time, but she didn't say that to Krackett. "I'll do my best."

"And I'd like a progress report each day."

"I'll call when I have something to report, Keith. Talk to you soon." She hung up before he could say anything more and sat there, clenching and unclenching her fists, anger smoldering inside of her.

* * *

Fletcher spotted Evans as soon as she entered the airport. He waited at the baggage carousel and, except for the laptop slung over his shoulder, he might be just one more elderly tourist in a cotton shirt and chinos. She thought he looked better than he had when she'd seen him several days ago in D.C.

"I bet you thought I'd forgotten you," she said, coming up behind him.

Evans glanced around and smiled. "Not a chance you'll ever forget me, Lenora."

She laughed and hugged him hello. "I'm really glad you came down here. I could use some help." And, despite his retirement and illness, she still felt protected in Evans's presence.

"I'm anxious to hear what's been going on." He stepped away from her to pluck his bag off the carousel. She took it from him and slung it over her shoulder. "My car's just outside."

He paused in the late afternoon light, his head thrown back, his eyes drinking in the sky. "My God, it smells good here. The air in D.C. stinks in comparison."

"It's the politics that stink, Rich."

Evans looked at her. "Now more than ever. Your boss called me early this morning and wanted to know if I'd spoken to you. He said you weren't returning his calls."

"I'm not feeling very friendly toward Krackett right now," she replied, and unlocked the car and got in.

"He isn't happy that the Bureau has had to take over the investigation down here," Evans remarked once they were on the highway.

"And he would be even less happy if Hal and his buddies got away from us again. I didn't have any other choice. I hope you didn't tell him you were coming down here."

He seemed amused. "Of course not. My calls will be forwarded. Did you find anything useful on those disks I gave you?"

"Not really." She'd gone through them last night, hoping to find something that would give her an idea of where Hal might be hiding. "There wasn't anything on there that I didn't already know."

"That's going to change."

"How do you figure?"

"About a month ago, I got a call from Andrew Steele. He wanted to meet somewhere. He said he had some loose ends he needed to tie up concerning Delphi."

"Why the hell didn't you tell me this the other day, Rich?"

"Because it would open up a chapter you didn't know about and, quite frankly, given the state of my health, I wasn't sure I wanted to get involved. Anyway, I flew down here and we met for dinner on the beach. He said his wife had been receiving anonymous gifts in the mail and each one had a tarot card with it. He felt sure that she was being stalked by Bennet."

"Because of the tarot cards?"

"Yes. He was the only one of three who had any interest in tarot. And in his other life as Reverend Hal, he read tarot professionally. Andrew was afraid to go to the police because he thought they might uncover something about Delphi. Anyway, he was very paranoid about everything and asked me to keep his computer records on Hal."

"How do they differ from what's on the disks?"

"You'll see."

"And what's the chapter you didn't want to reopen?"

"For a period of about six months, Andrew and I worked privately with Hal."

"Privately." She repeated the word slowly, as if she'd never heard it before. "Privately when? Where the hell was I?"

He ignored her question. "Turn left on A-1-A."

She turned, then he directed her to an older neighborhood at the south end of the county. She wanted to repeat her question, but knew he wouldn't answer it until he wanted to. It disturbed her to think of Evans and Steele working privately with Hal; that hadn't been part of their arrangement. But the more she thought about it, the less surprised she was. Honesty never had figured into the equation.

They headed up a quiet road where the trees hadn't been cut down and bougainvillea vines grew wild, their thorny stems bursting with crimson buds. At the end of the street, Evans directed her into the driveway of an old, modest apartment building on the beach.

Tangled seagrape trees bordered it on one side and pines sprang up on the other side. It reminded her of the Florida of her childhood, old Florida before the million-dollar condos had been built. No security guard, no gates out front, an unlocked lobby door. In an odd way, it seemed fitting that Evans would use this simple place as a hideaway.

"There are six furnished condos, all vacant now."

"You own the building?"

"It's under my wife's maiden name. The Agency rents the condos from time to time."

Yeah, she got the picture.

They took the elevator to the penthouse apartment. Except for the magnificent view of the Atlantic, the penthouse seemed as simple as the rest of the building. The furnishings smacked of this same simplicity: rattan furniture with tropical-colored cushions, Mexican tile floors, pine bookcases. Evans turned on the master electrical switch, spun a faucet under the kitchen sink that turned on the water, then opened the sliding glass doors.

He remained in the doorway, breathing in the sea air. For moments, as he stood there against the afternoon light, he seemed almost like the Evans she remembered. Then he turned and went over to the bookcase. "You aren't going to like what you're about to discover, Lenora. But at this point, what you don't know may put you at risk."

He removed several books from the shelf, exposing a security pad. He punched in six numbers, ran a security card through the slot. He crossed the room and knelt in front of an electrical outlet that had popped out of the wall. He reached inside, withdrew an oblong cedar box, and snapped off the lid. He brought out a pair of three-and-a-half-inch computer disks.

"The original and a copy of the disk Andrew gave me." He loaded the disk onto his laptop, opened a file, and patted the cushion beside him on the couch. "Take a look."

"It'd be easier if you'd just tell me what's on the goddamn disk, Rich."

"Humor me, all right?"

So she sat beside him, put the laptop in her own lap, and began to read. And when she surfaced two hours later, the light in the room had waned, her head pounded, her stomach rolled with nausea. She didn't know whether she felt enraged or betrayed or both. She raised her eyes and looked at Evans, fiddling with the knobs of the TV on the other side of the room.

"I already suspected that the Agency's primary purpose in all this was to do things and create events that would make the Bureau look bad, Rich."

He came back across the room and sat in a nearby chair. "I don't deny that anymore. With the Cold War over, we figured there would be cutbacks. We had to do what we could to keep our jobs."

"Look, Rich, I've accepted that part of it a long time ago. But my God." She leaned forward, whispering. "You're responsible for the death of a former First Lady. Hal made her kill herself." Hal had pierced the mind of one of the most powerful and beloved women in the country and had cut her down like she was nothing. "For what? What did it prove?"

"That we could do it." A beat passed, his eyes held hers. "That we had a formidable weapon. Up to then, we knew that Hal could influence what people did, that he could even kill by causing a brain aneurysm. But this?"

Evans leaned forward, his eyes bright. "Think of it, Lenora. To seize control of another so deeply that he could make the person go against his or her own instinct for self-preservation. Christ almighty. Imagine what kinds of possibilities this opened up. A legitimate suicide. Nothing to track down. Nothing to prove, other than the suicide itself. The perfect murder."

He spoke like a god who had discovered the depth of his own powers and couldn't wait to use them. Something clicked into place at the back of Fletcher's mind and she suddenly knew why Evans had come here. "And now you've got an old score to settle with someone. That's why you want to find Hal. You'll entice him with a deal—his freedom in return for the suicide of whoever you're after."

"C'mon, Lenora. I'm too sick and old to be *after* anyone."

"Don't feed me horseshit," she snapped. "You could be on

your deathbed and it wouldn't make any difference if you had a score to settle."

The sharpness in her voice shocked her. She'd never spoken to Evans like this before. Then again, they'd never been equals until her promotion had been announced the other night. She knew that he expected to gain from her rise in the Bureau—information, favors, all the usual political machinations. In return, he would connect her to his vast network of contacts, which would make her privy to almost unimagined power.

But until now, she hadn't considered the possibility that Hal might be part of their unspoken deal. "And just so we're clear on where things stand with us, Rich, don't expect me to turn Hal over to you before I take him in."

"I don't *expect* anything."

With that, he moved over to the laptop, popped out the disk, and deleted the file with three clicks of the mouse. Poof, you're gone. Had the former First Lady died that quickly? *Will I?*

As she drove back to her hotel a while later, those two words bounced around in her skull like Ping-Pong balls. *Will I? Will I? Will I?*

18

The light in the lagoon this morning deepened the green of the mangroves, the blue of the water, and darkened the stain of Big Guy in the distant shadows. The stillness imbued Hal with an odd sense of peace. He felt as if he'd crossed some invisible boundary during the night and had emerged recreated on the other side.

He reached into the bucket of squirming minnows that separated him and Rae. She sat very still, eyes fixed on the water, her bare, shapely legs swinging slowly, like a pendulum. "You ever fished before?" he asked.

"No."

"But you live on the ocean."

Rae shrugged. "Andy isn't interested in fishing and it isn't something I ever feel like doing by myself."

"What did you two do when you weren't working?"

Her eyes narrowed against the light as she raised them. "Before Carl was born, we used to travel a lot. After . . ." Her voice trailed off and she shrugged again. "I don't know. Our personal lives got lost." She looked over at him. "Like prison, I guess."

The minnow Hal plucked from the bucket squirmed fiercely as he tried to fit it onto the hook. He felt a little sorry for the goddamn thing, but not sorry enough to quit. He slid the hook through it.

"That's the reason I never wanted to fish," she said, watching the minnow. "Maybe because that's how I've felt for most of the marriage."

The remark revealed more than she realized. He didn't have

to *reach* into her to sense that in the five days she'd been here, she'd been mulling over her marriage. She obviously had reached some conclusions.

Hal cast the line and scanned the periphery of the mangroves, searching for Big Guy. He'd come closer to the chickee, just his snout visible above the surface.

"Why doesn't the gator go for the bait?" she asked.

"I fed him earlier."

She nodded, watching the gator, the line, the mangroves, then dropped her head back and peered up through the holes in the braided branches, into the sky. "Are we going to eat the fish you catch?"

"Sure. The lagoon is loaded with bass."

"I thought there was mercury poisoning in the Glades."

"Not in my lagoon."

"How have you managed to live out here all these years?"

"I just did it."

She turned those magnificent eyes on him again. "Yeah, but how? It takes money to buy supplies, to maintain a boat, to have what you have here. Were you working? Did you have a job? What?"

"I saved a lot of what I earned as a psychic consultant. I also picked up a few stock tips right after I got out and a woman I knew played them for me. Now and then I go into Miami to the track and do well enough, but not so well that any red flags are raised."

"And all your money is here on the chickee?"

"It's the safest place I know of." He stared at her knees. Most women had ugly knees. But Rae's reminded him of sculptures, round and tan, shapes that promised something.

"So you don't need ransom money."

"I told you, Rae, this isn't about ransom." Something tugged at the line and Hal reeled in a clump of weeds. The minnow had vanished. "Shit. Something got it." He started to reach into the container for another minnow, but she thrust her hand inside first.

"Let me try," she said.

"They're slippery little devils."

"Sort of like you, Hal."

He laughed. He liked the analogy, liked that she tried to figure him out. "Go for one of the larger guys."

She went after the minnows in earnest then, seventy or eighty that he'd scooped out of the lagoon with a net. She rolled her lower lip between her teeth as she groped in the writhing mass. "I got one!" she squealed, and brought her hand out, fingers clenched around it.

"Okay. Good. Hold it for a second."

He removed the clump of weeds from the hook and showed her how to slip the minnow onto it, how to cast the line. "Now what?" she asked.

"As soon as you feel a tug on the line, give it a quick jerk and reel it in."

He enjoyed just sitting here with her and hoped the earlier difficulties lay behind them. She seemed to have adapted to the situation and he intended to make sure that continued.

He hadn't restrained or drugged her last night, the first time since he'd brought her here. And nothing had happened. He knew she'd slept deeply and soundly throughout the night because he'd checked, *reaching* into her, traveling the rich ocean of her dreams and the strange landscape of her sexuality. It had invigorated him, aroused him, and he had awakened this morning with a longing to touch her, to make love to her.

Part of his longing, he knew, resulted from what had happened a couple days ago, when he had *reached* into Sheppard as he and the psychic had gone at it. It had turned him on, he had pushed too hard and too deeply, and something had popped inside Sheppard's skull. But in the seconds before he'd pulled away from the cop, he'd found the name of the psychic's dead husband, Tom Morales, a man he had killed.

The coincidence shocked him. But it also left him with an overpowering curiosity about the psychic. So before dawn yesterday morning he'd gotten her number from information and had called her.

He rarely *reached* over the phone, but found it surprisingly easy with her, hooking into her voice as though it were a current. He had frightened her, especially when he had pushed hard, just as he had done with Sheppard. But he didn't know if he had frightened her deeply enough so that she would back off. If she didn't, he would be forced to push at her until a vessel in her brain popped.

Hal knew that Steele had been aware that he could *reach* in this way, that if he pushed too hard he could create tremendous pressure inside the cranium, that he could pop blood vessels, squeeze organs to mush, that he could do major damage. Steele and that spook Evans had encouraged him to do this on several occasions. But the ability remained as erratic as it had been in the past. He could rarely control it. Until the incident with Sheppard, it hadn't happened in months.

Unfortunately, Mira had broken the connection between them before Hal had gotten the information he wanted. He suspected it would be easier with physical proximity.

But he didn't want to leave Rae alone here and he didn't want to drug or restrain her just when things between them had begun to improve. Yet, he couldn't risk her escaping, either. No matter what precautions he took, escape remained a possibility as long as she had the freedom to move around the chickee.

"Did Andy have other spies?" Rae asked suddenly.

"Yeah, there were others, in different prisons."

"How many others?"

"Six others."

Something tugged on her line, she jerked it up, and reeled in weeds. Hal removed the stuff, baited the hook again, and she cast in another direction. She remained standing and his eyes slipped up her tan, shapely legs.

"You knew them, these other six?" she asked.

"Two of them. I was aware of the others. We were connected in a weird way." He couldn't take his eyes off her legs. He especially liked the backs of her knees, the soft, white skin in the crease. It made her seem vulnerable somehow, as though that crease were her Achilles' heel. He wondered if Steele had ever kissed it.

The thought made him feel like puking. He had never understood how any woman, much less Rae, could possibly find Steele attractive enough to fuck him. Yeah, he'd been good-looking, smart, he had dressed right, he had dough. But so what? He had no sense of humor, he didn't know a damn thing about movies, and the only music he liked was Bach. He'd possessed all the sensuality of a rock.

"Is Andy still doing it?" she asked.

Not now. "I don't know. I haven't had any contact with him since I got out."

"I guess what puzzles me is that Andy's the type of man who always has a specific purpose for anything he does. He wouldn't do it just out of curiosity, to satisfy some deep intellectual yearning."

Hal watched beads of sweat forming on the backs of her knees, glistening like raindrops. He imagined licking them away, making love to this part of her body with just his tongue.

He knew from *reaching* that sex had been absent in their marriage these last months, that she was, in fact, hungry for intimacy. He also felt there had been someone else for a while, a man she had seen on the sly. But Hal hadn't been able to find out anything about him; she kept that memory locked up too deeply for him to plunder it.

"Hal?"

He realized she had asked him a question. "Yeah?"

"Was Andy doing this work for someone else?"

She posed the question easily, casually, following the pattern they'd fallen into out here on the platform. But Hal recognized it as a ploy to get information out of him.

"Why do you think that?"

"Things have happened that don't make sense."

"What kinds of things?"

She shrugged and glanced back at the lagoon. "Calls in the middle of the night. Charges on the fax line to a D.C. number that Andy claimed had to do with some inmate transfer. Sudden weekend trips out of town. Stuff like that. For a while I thought he was having an affair." Another shrug. "Maybe he was."

"Would that bother you?"

"It's sort of beside the point now."

Not to me. But he didn't say it. He didn't want her to think he was going to rip off her clothes and rape her. He didn't want her getting any ideas that he might pull a Manacas. "You were having an affair, so it would even things up if he was, too." Hal *reached* gently in the hopes that the memory would be more accessible to him now.

But she slammed a door on the memory and buried it under so much debris he didn't have a prayer of finding it. Her glance was quick, sharp. "How did you—"

"It doesn't matter." He withdrew and changed the subject. "Want to watch *Pulp Fiction* after we catch lunch?"

"Sure." Her smile was sly, secretive.

He wanted to smile along with her, but sensed he might be the brunt of her joke. "What's so funny?"

"I just realized I never knew you were so into movies."

"They never had any movies worth a damn when I was in the joint." Showing *Pulp Fiction* or *The Shawshank Redemption* at Manatee would be the same as showing *The Langoliers* on a 747, he thought.

"That's because Andy used to select them."

Hal laughed. "That figures."

She started to say something, but a hard tug on her line cut her short. Rae jerked the rod up, her legs braced wide apart, and struggled to reel in whatever it was.

Hal leaped up to give her a hand, but the rod wrenched and she lurched forward, reeling frantically, and fell right off the end of the platform. She splashed wildly, her screams echoing across the lagoon. For moments, Hal froze in abject terror, reliving the incident with the college coed.

Then he saw Big Guy whipping through the water, aimed straight for her. His feet tore loose from the platform, he flew to the edge of it, leaped into the water, and lunged for her. But Rae, a nonswimmer terrified of water, had moved beyond panic. Her arms flailed, she shrieked, he kept losing his hold on her, and she went under.

Hal dived for her, his powerful arms propelling him deeper and deeper. When he grabbed her by the hair, she already had lost consciousness. He wrapped an arm around her neck and swam hard and fast toward the ladder at the front of the chickee.

But the gator swam faster, a silent missile headed straight for them, now less than ten yards away.

Floodgates inside of Hal slammed open, adrenaline pumped through him. He swam as if water were his element, reached the ladder with seconds to spare. He grabbed onto the lowest rung with one hand, gripped Rae at the waist with other arm, and slung her over his shoulder. He clambered up the ladder, heaved her onto the platform, then dropped to his knees beside her.

Jesus God, she wasn't breathing. Training kicked in, a CPR course he had taken in prison. He opened her mouth and breathed into her, paused, pressed down on her chest, breathed into her again. And again. *C'mon, please, breathe.*

When she started coughing, relief flooded through him. Even though he got her into a sitting position, she kept coughing and gasping for air. Then she toppled forward like a wet rag doll, shuddered, and vomited.

Hal stumbled into the chickee for a blanket and a bottle of water and made it back onto the platform before she had even raised her head. He draped the blanket around her shoulders, smoothed her wet hair away from her face, and coaxed her to sip from a bottle. She straightened up, coughed again, wiped her mouth and face with a corner of the blanket, and whispered hoarsely, "I'm okay. I'm okay now."

He hesitated, not wanting to leave her. Then he shot to his feet and ran over to the platform. Big Guy lurked four or five feet away, eyes and snout poking up out of the water. Gloating fucker. A tidal wave of rage swept through Hal's mind, emptying it of everything except a pure, reptilian fury. He reached under the platform, pulled out the wooden paddle he'd hidden, and hurled it, shouting, *"Get the fuck out of here!"*

The paddle struck the water and Big Guy's massive jaws clamped over it. He sank from sight and only the noisy silence of the lagoon remained.

At eleven-thirty Tuesday morning, Pete Ames strolled into the office with his hand inside a bag of Doritos. He mumbled something around a mouthful of chips that Sheppard didn't understand.

"What?" Sheppard asked.

Munch, munch. Ames finally swallowed his mouthful of chips and said, "I ran into Pikolo downstairs. He wants you to stop by the lab as soon as you can."

Good, Sheppard thought. The perfect excuse to leave while Ames finished his bag of chips. He took the stairs so he wouldn't get stuck in the elevator with someone who had heard his job would be history on November 1.

It had happened several times already—the sympathetic looks, the inevitable questions about what he would do, where he would go. He felt sure that Charlie Pikolo wouldn't mention it, that he probably didn't even know. The boys in the crime lab, Pikolo in particular, tended to live in their own little world, their jobs as secure as the pope's.

"Hey, Pick," he called, walking into the empty lab.

Pikolo's youthful face popped up from behind a counter. Although he'd just turned twenty-five, he looked about eighteen, a computer nerd with dark, disheveled hair and wrinkled, mismatched clothes. His eyes blinked constantly because he had just gotten contacts.

"Hey, Shep." He stood, brushing at his clothes. "Question. Didn't you tell me that the little black box you dropped by here on Friday was on that Steele fellow?"

Sheppard had forgotten all about it. "Yeah, in the pocket of his pajamas. Why? What is it?"

Pikolo blinked. "The real question is what the hell Steele was using it for." He opened a drawer and brought out the device. Today it more closely resembled a pager than a TV clicker. "This thing emits extremely low frequency radio waves. ELF, for short."

"So?"

"Well, I had to ask myself why someone would carry one of these gizmos around, okay? I know that some years back, the government was experimenting with ELF on submarines and as a possible means for riot control. Given Steele's line of work, I figured he might wear one whenever he was in a maximum security prison. But to bed?" Pikolo wrinkled his nose. "Not reasonable. So I started looking for unreasonable explanations."

He turned the contraption on. "Right now, it's emitting signals that oscillate between one and three cycles per second, the lowest frequency there is. It's the same frequency as the theta waves the brain produces during deep sleep and in early infancy. It can also be indicative of a brain tumor."

Another twist of the knob. "Now it's emitting signals that oscillate between four and seven cycles per second, the equivalent of the brain's delta waves. Deltas are dominant in kids between the ages of two and five and in psychopaths. They can be evoked by frustration."

"Steele worked with psychopaths," Sheppard said. "And his wife had been getting weird shit in the mail."

"Exactly." Pikolo's thumb stroked the device as though it were the hand of a woman he loved. "I got to wondering if the ELF's signals could jam the emissions from a psychopath's brain. This led me straight into Steele's early research in psychic phenomena."

The books from Steele's den, Sheppard thought. He had paged through them, read the material with great interest, but he still didn't see the connection. "Explain."

"Well, I'm no expert on this stuff, okay? But from what I understand, Steele learned that during certain types of psychic episodes, the brain emits theta or delta waves. Suppose those were the signals he was trying to jam?"

Interesting, Sheppard thought. Nadine had told Mira that the man with the green shoelaces had some sort of unusual psychic talent. If Steele had known that, then perhaps Pikolo's musings weren't so outrageous.

"Tell me more."

"This device creates a shield of white noise," Pikolo said. "Of static. In a sense, it jams signals of the same frequency that are emitted from another source."

"You mind if I borrow this for a while, Pick?"

"No problem."

Sheppard didn't have any idea what the hell any of this meant. But before this was over and done with, he would.

* * *

The peal of a phone woke her. Rae sat up, confused, groggy, sweating beneath the blanket, her son's face bright in her mind. She had been dreaming of Carl, Carl when he was an infant, Carl as a toddler—dear God, Carl, what was happening to Carl?

She wanted to fall back into the dream, seek refuge within it, romp with her dream son on a dream beach. Maybe when she woke again she would be in a hospital, recovering from a car accident she didn't recall. Yeah, fat chance.

Rae threw off the blanket, heard the phone again, and got up to see where the ringing was coming from. She stopped just outside Hal's den, where the door was cracked open enough for her to catch snippets of the conversation. Ed. Fletcher. Mira. The pub.

Rae stepped quickly and silently away from the door, her heart pounding, and weaved back through the light to the futon cushion in the main room. Kathleen Turner, she thought. *Body Heat.*

She knew it would be her only way out.

19

Around twilight that evening, a cold front swept into South Florida. It brought a sudden, hard rain that Mira knew would kill business until One World closed at nine. She figured she might as well close early and join Nadine and Annie upstairs.

Just as she began to tally the day's receipts, the bells on the door jingled and a man came in, stomping his feet and shaking the water from his rain slicker. He filled the doorway of the front office, a bald man with a muscular body and a rather handsome face. He asked for Mira.

"I'm Mira," she said.

"I'm on the Navy ship that pulled into Port Everglades. And a buddy of mine gave me your name. I was wondering if I could get a reading tonight."

"I was just about to close. I'd be glad to schedule you for tomorrow."

He looked disappointed. "My ship pulls out tomorrow and it's really important. I'll pay you double whatever you charge. My daughter is sick and I—"

"Okay." She had a soft spot for troubled strangers in need of answers about their kids. "Sure, I guess I can squeeze in a reading. Pull up a chair, Mr. . . . ?"

"Ed, just call me Ed."

Mr. Ed, like the talking horse. "Have a seat, Ed."

"I sure do appreciate this, Mira."

She brought out a deck she loved, The Universal Tarot, an idiosyncratic deck that seemed appropriate for Mr. Ed. "Cut them into three piles, then shuffle and think of your question. The more specific, the better."

"Do I tell you the question?"

"No, you don't have to."

As he cut and shuffled, she grounded herself with slow, deep breathing, then took the deck and dealt six cards off the top. Mira laid them out side by side, two for the past, two for the present, two for the future. Her left brain instructed her to look for something about his sick daughter, but she didn't see a single card in the six that indicated children.

Right brain, she thought. *Let the cards speak to you.* But the longer she stared at them, the more silent the cards became. She drew a complete blank about the simplest definitions, couldn't even remember the key words for these particular cards. A slow panic built inside of her.

"Are they bad?" he asked.

"No, it's just been a long day. Draw one more card."

He drew the Devil, which in this deck depicted a bestial figure standing in the center of a pentagram, surrounded by a pair of flies and a bound man and woman. Lust, bondage to the past, focus on materialism, yes, okay, it got her started. "The root of your question, Ed, has to do with some unpleasant event or experience in the past that you haven't been able to put behind you."

Now she moved to the original six he'd drawn and read them as a continuation of the story. "The event involved or resulted in legal problems for you. In the present, there's an older woman, an authority figure connected to the judicial system. Considerable animosity exists between you and it goes back a long way. Does this make sense to you?"

"Yes." He looked—what? Surprised? Shocked? "Go on."

"In the near future, the ten of swords marks the end of a cycle you've been in. It may happen through a stab in the back by someone you thought you could trust." She tapped the king of cups. "This man is in his forties and may be psychic himself. He's the one who betrays you somehow."

His eyes bored into her, small strange eyes that made her squirm inside. An image flashed through her head of a woman sprawled in mud near a fence. A pair of panty hose was tied around her throat and from the waist down, she was nude. Mira didn't have any idea what it meant, where it fit in a time sequence. But it definitely concerned Ed.

"What's the final outcome?" he asked.

"Draw one more card."

The Death card.

"The outcome will be an unexpected and sudden reversal in affairs for yourself or whoever your question was about."

He studied the cards. Her unease swelled. She heard Nadine or Annie walking around upstairs, a roll of thunder outside. A biting chill licked the back of her neck.

What did that image mean? she asked silently. But her inner voice remained mute. She scooped up the cards, shuffled them, fanned them out again. "Let's do one more spread for clarification. Choose five cards."

Ed's hand glided through the air, an inch or two above the fan, a way to sense energy or heat from a particular card. It indicated he wasn't the neophyte he pretended to be. His hands looked like those of a laborer, the nails blunt, cut straight across, dirt beneath several of them. But he didn't speak like a laborer, didn't dress or act like one. He didn't impress her as the military type, either.

He handed her the cards and she put them face down, four in a row, one beneath them. The Path Spread packed a lot of information into five cards and was versatile enough for either a general reading or one that answered a specific question. Ed's cards, five majors, indicated violent change, upheaval, deception and disillusionment, anguish, ruin, devastation.

Mira always tried to put a positive spin on a reading, but no matter how she interpreted these, Ed's life charged toward disaster. "My best advice to you is to take careful stock of your life. Decide what your priorities are."

"That's not what those cards say."

She didn't like the sharpness in his voice. "That's what they say to me."

"What's this position?" He tapped the first card.

"The path you're on."

"The Tower. That's about violent reversals in fortune. And this second position?"

"The lesson you need to learn."

"The Moon." He laughed. "I need to learn how to see deception."

"That isn't the only meaning."

"And this third position?"

"What you're moving toward if you take no action."

"The Death card again."

"It doesn't mean physical death."

"Bullshit."

The sharp nastiness of his tone set off major alarms inside her; Mira just wanted him out of here. She started to gather up the cards, but Ed slapped his massive hand over them. "Leave them." A pulse throbbed at his temple; his weird eyes pierced hers again.

"The reading is over," she said.

"It's not over until I say it's over." His eyes fastened on hers, a slow smile crept across his face.

Mira stood, heart drumming in her chest, fear pounding in her throat, and stepped away from him. She reached for the phone and punched out 911. Ed swept his arm across the desk, knocking most of the cards to the floor, and shot to his feet. Rage burned in his eyes, blood rushed into his face. "You haven't seen the last of me," he spat, then spun and charged for the door.

"What's the nature of the emergency?" asked a male voice on the other end of the phone.

Her voice sounded choked. "Uh, no emergency. I dialed the wrong number. Sorry." She hung up, ran into the hall, flipped the dead bolt on the front door, and sank against it, her knees like Jell-O.

Outside, she heard his car speeding away.

A lunatic, the first lunatic in the history of the store. Yet, she sensed that Ed hadn't just wandered in off the street—or off a Navy ship. The attack on Sheppard Sunday, the attack on her early this morning, and now this: she felt sure the events were connected.

What did that image mean?

Her inner voice didn't reply, but the image she had glimpsed earlier filled her head, as if in response. The woman sprawled in the mud, nude from the waist down. She suddenly knew the woman had been strangled and raped.

Is the woman me? Is this what might happen to me?

The voice came through loud and clear this time, as if to reassure her. *Another woman. It's already happened.*

And Ed had done it. The impression had been a warning not to continue the reading. She felt there was more to it than that, more about who Ed was and why he had come here, but the answers hovered just out of her reach.

Nadine's cane tapped through the hall. "Mira?"

She stepped unsteadily away from the door, as if she had spent the day on a ship at rough seas and hadn't found her land legs yet. "Right here."

Her voice sounded okay, but Nadine apparently read something in Mira's face because she looked at her hard, frowning. "What's wrong?"

"I just had a difficult client."

Nadine regarded her silently for a moment, her dark eyes piercing the half-truth, riddling it with holes. "One of the three," she said softly.

"What?"

Her grandmother's eyes had glazed over, her breathing had changed. In the hallway light, she looked almost mythical, as though she had risen full-blown from some invisible sea. Mira realized she'd gone into trance, that Ben now spoke through her. "He's one of the three I mentioned the other night. It would be best if you left town for a while, Mira. You, Annie, Nadine. Certain events have been set in motion and will now follow their own line of probability."

Riddles, Ben always spoke in riddles. "Christ, don't talk to me in riddles, okay? Give me information I can use."

Thunder rolled through the subsequent silence. They stared at each other. Then the phone rang. The noise pinged against the silence like a chunk of hail as it bounced off a tin roof. It didn't snap Nadine out of trance, Ben simply withdrew, gently.

Her grandmother blinked and said she would get the phone, said it as though there had been no lapse since she had asked

Mira what was wrong. "Nadine, wait." Mira touched her shoulder. "Ben just came through."

Nadine looked surprised. "He did? What'd he say?"

Mira repeated Ben's message. "You didn't realize it, did you, Nadine. Ben was just suddenly there."

"Then you'd best heed what he said," Nadine replied, and shuffled into the office to answer the phone.

You haven't seen the last of me. Ed.

Mira rubbed her hands over her face.

Utmost caution. Ben.

I'll hurt you, too. The caller.

"Shit," she said into her hands.

Sheppard had spent several hours this afternoon in the county offices, searching for property records on 112 Pirate's Cove Lane anywhere in Broward County. He found nothing under the address and nothing under Hartmann, the name Mira had come up with.

But he'd gotten luckier at Steele's home. He'd found a record on the computer for a property purchase for 112 Pirate's Cove Lane NE, bought by Rae Hartmant—not Hartmann—three years ago. It was located in a town forty miles west of the Lauderdale airport.

By the time he called Mira and convinced her to read the cabin for him, the rain had started. Now it swept across Alligator Alley with the fury of a living thing. He couldn't see a foot in front of him. The Porsche's headlights bounced off the rain as though it were a giant sheet of aluminum. The wipers whipped across the glass, a monotonous melody.

They didn't talk much; the events of Sunday still stood between them. Besides, Sheppard knew she didn't really want to read the cabin, that she didn't want any further involvement in the investigation. He believed she'd agreed to do this because of what had happened earlier this evening with "Mr. Ed."

"How much farther?" Mira finally asked.

"It should be just ahead."

Sure enough, half a mile later, he spotted the street sign and swung onto a dirt road. Branches braided overhead, creating a canopy dense enough to shield the car from most of the rain and wind. An eerie quiet closed around the Porsche and seeped into the car with them. When Mira shifted in her seat, the sound seemed abnormally loud, almost abrasive.

The Porsche hit potholes, bounced through deep puddles. He shifted into first gear. Now the banyans gave way to the scrubby Florida pines Mira had described. He saw A-frames, cottages, snug little cabins nestled in the evergreens. Number 112 stood alone in a cul-de-sac, set back from the road in the dim glow of a single streetlight.

Sheppard pulled into the driveway, stopped, but kept the headlights on. "Is this the place you saw?"

She rubbed her hand in small, tight circles against the fogging windshield. "Yeah, I think so. There's the mailbox." She sat back, shook her head. "I had absolutely no sense that there were other houses around. My impression was of complete isolation."

"Let's take a look."

She didn't exactly break any records getting out of the car. But hell, after what had happened when she'd read Steele's place, he didn't blame her. The cabin, locked up tight, had been sealed against whatever Rae Steele had imagined might harm her. In the end, though, locks hadn't protected her from anything.

While Mira waited on the front porch, Sheppard went around to the rear of the cabin to find a way in. His flashlight located the pond she'd described, an erratic circle of water in the trees at the foot of the slope. It spooked him, she spooked him, he admitted it. The world she lived in bore no resemblance to his own. He felt like an ill-prepared tourist every time he visited her world.

None of this stopped him from trying to break in to a place that had been discovered through a psychic channel, not through maps, microfiches, interviews, or any other tangible source. Confronted with the verification of a psychic vision, Sheppard felt a part of himself coming unhinged, swinging in the dark wind like an old, creaking gate.

He broke in, finally, through a kitchen window, and crawled over the sink. The air, wet and intrusively cold, the way cold could be only in a temperate zone, smelled stale, shuttered, of some secret hidden in an attic in a Gothic novel. The electricity worked and he turned on lights as he made his way up the hall to the front door.

Compared to Steele's beach mansion, the decor here was bare bones: a worn couch with an afghan thrown over the back of it, a faded recliner in front of the TV, a cheap, nicked coffee table. The stone fireplace, with its broad hearth and pine mantel, held ashes and a partially burned log. He noted the photos on the mantel, but didn't pause long enough to look closely at them. He wanted to get Mira inside before she bolted.

She unzipped her raincoat as she stepped inside. Raindrops glistened and winked like sequins against her dark hair. Her eyes darted around the front room, then she took a long, deep breath, exhaled slowly and said, "She used to meet a man here . . . I don't get a name."

Off came her shoes. She swiveled her bare feet against the old wooden floor and moved toward the fireplace. "They made love there." She pointed at a throw rug in front of the fireplace. "When it was cold outside." She rubbed her hands over her arms and stood for a few minutes, staring into the empty fireplace.

It had begun so quickly, it took Sheppard a few minutes to get the recorder on. He moved closer to her and asked her to describe the man.

"I can only see the back of his head." She looked at the rug, as though she could actually see Rae and this man making love there. "His hair is going gray."

"Is it Steele?"

"No, definitely not Steele. The energy pattern isn't the same." She rubbed her hands over her arms. "It's really cold in here."

"I'll make a fire." Sheppard set the recorder on an end table, knelt in front of the fireplace, and began sweeping the ashes to one side. He found the butt of a cigar and the blackened remains of a photograph. The only visible image on the photo showed Rae. He put the cigar butt and the piece of photo into an evidence bag; he figured the butt belonged to whoever Rae had been seeing. He pocketed the bag, then pulled logs and twigs from the basket next to the fireplace. "What else do you pick up?"

"This is her refuge." Mira turned right, toward the hallway, but she didn't move toward it. "Her private space. She wanted to divorce Steele."

He made a Boy Scout's fire, a nest of twigs, burning hot and bright, then several logs. "How long ago was this?"

"I don't know."

You've got to know, he thought. "Years? Months? Two weeks ago? What?"

"Months, yeah, I'm pretty sure it was months."

Now she stepped forward, her feet seeming to glide over the floors, into the kitchen. Sheppard, recorder in hand, trotted after her, noting the sweet curve of her denim hips. Sunday seemed like lifetimes ago, but it had been only two days. His memory remained so vivid he could still feel her skin under his hands, could still taste her.

Can't sleep with you . . . Why not? Why the fuck not? He was in love with this woman, he—

In love?

Not likely, not damn likely. Hormones had loud, noisy voices that insisted on being heard and yes, the chemistry between them bristled and yes, she was . . .

paradise

Ridiculous. She was difficult. She was weird.

and . . .

". . . stood here in front of the window," she was saying, standing at the very spot she referred to. "He was weeping, she didn't know it."

I'm weeping, I'm weeping, Sheppard thought, and moved closer to her. The warmth of the fire didn't reach into the kitchen. He knew she was cold, chilled, he could see it in the press of her lips, in the way she tucked her hands inside the sleeves of her raincoat.

"They were standing here when she told him she couldn't see him anymore." She walked over to the rear door, unfastened the chain, opened it, stepped onto the small porch. "She stood out here after he left that night."

Sheppard came up behind her, listening to the rain falling through the trees, to the wild beat of his own heart. He reached out to touch her hair, but she turned abruptly and moved back into the cabin. He followed, shut the door, fastened the chain again, and hurried after her, into the front room.

The fire had caught, a delicious warmth suffused the damp air. Mira stopped in front of the fireplace, lifting the framed photos, searching for something. "There should be a key here somewhere. He returned the key she'd left him."

She couldn't find it. Mira held her hands up to the fire, rubbed them.

"Anything else?" Sheppard prodded.

She shook her head.

"Would you mind helping me out with something?" he asked.

She turned, hand on one hip. "Isn't that what I've been doing?"

"I don't mean with this. I need to test a, uh, theory."

"A theory. Okay, what's the theory?"

He reached into his pocket and felt the ELF device. He flicked the switch on. "Try to read me."

"I don't have my cards with me."

"Clairvoyantly."

She hesitated, then said, "Let me have your hand."

Mira took his hand and began to breathe deeply. He sensed the moment when her consciousness shifted. She started to frown. "Weird. I can sense the feeling tones that are yours, but I'm not picking up anything."

Sheppard turned off the device. "Now try it."

Mira altered her breathing, deepened it, and ran her thumb slowly over his knuckles, the back of his hand. She suddenly smiled. "I'm picking up something, but I don't know how to interpret it. It sort of looks like a TV clicker. A remote control thing."

"Like this?" Sheppard removed the device from his pocket.

"Yes."

"Now watch. I'm hitting the ON switch. Now try to read me again."

She took his hand once more, altered her breathing, and after a few moments shook her head. "Static, a wall of static. That's all I get. What the hell is that thing?"

"This was found on Steele." He explained the rest.

"You're talking way over my head, Shep. But there was a definite difference. I went from a complete blockage to a bright, vivid image."

"You prove the theory. Now if I can just figure out what he was using it for, I'll be in good shape. Let's try it once more." He turned it off, Mira took his hand again, and this time he visualized the two of them making love here in front of the fire.

Mira suddenly laughed and dropped his hand. "So embarrass me some more, Sheppard."

He slipped the device in his pocket again, slipped his arms around her waist, and pressed his face into her hair. She didn't do anything, didn't move or speak or return his embrace. Then her arms came up around his neck. Firelight flickered across the planes and angles of her face, rendering her features in a surreal, breathtaking beauty.

"That London life ended badly," she said softly. "I don't want to repeat those patterns."

Of all the things she might have said, he hadn't anticipated this remark. "I don't understand."

"I think I was the wife you were always running from."

"I'm not running now."

Her features softened, she laughed. "Yeah, I guess not."

"Give it a chance, Mira. That's all I'm asking. I'm sorry that I didn't tell you about the goddamn shoelaces, but I honestly didn't know how to say it."

She touched her finger to his mouth, whispered, "It's okay," and kissed him.

And then they, like Rae and her mysterious lover, sank to the rug in front of the fireplace. Sheppard's heart soared.

Fletcher huddled beneath the pines in the dark on the other side of the road, watching their shadows against the blinds. When the shadows sank from sight, she tightened the hood of her rain slicker and resigned herself to the wait.

The cop and the psychic, she thought. Goddamn fools. Had they really believed she wouldn't put two and two together? No one pulled anything over on Lenora Fletcher, at least not for any length of time.

She lit a cigarette and crouched down behind a clump of palmetto bushes, her patience like some sort of penance that she had to endure to get what she wanted. But it would pay off, it had to. In the end, one way or another, even Hal would get his due.

20

As soon as Hal walked into the bar at Pier 66, he spotted Manacas and Indrio seated at a back table. They blended with the rest of the crowd, an ability they'd learned in prison, where you never wanted to be singled out.

Indrio, smoking furiously, looked as nervous and uptight as a bird that expected to be stalked. Manacas, who had always been the calmer of the two, sucked on a slice of orange from whatever he was drinking.

Male bonding, Hal thought. They expected him to sit down and go through the macho shit that would renew their collective commitment to The Plan. But Manacas and Indrio had bonded years ago, in the joint, and even after all these years, Hal knew that he remained the third wheel. They already had decided on whatever scheme they would present to him. His acceptance or rejection of that scheme would make little difference unless they needed him to pull it off.

He also knew that bonding had little to do with tonight's meeting. This centered on commitment to The Plan. He didn't have to *reach* into them to know that.

Five years ago, he had backed out of a scheme the three of them had concocted to pull off a bank heist using their combined talents. Their intention had been to practice on several convenience stores first, to see if they could make the clerk walk away from the register without locking it.

In the first store they'd targeted, a 7-Eleven in a suburban Miami neighborhood, they'd succeeded in getting the clerk to leave the room without locking the register. Indrio had monitored the operation, Manacas had taken the money, and Hal had succeeded in keeping the clerk away from the front room for eleven-and-a half minutes.

They had pulled two similar jobs after that, failed at one, and succeeded at the other. After that, Indrio and Manacas were ready to move on the bank. But Hal had put them off for a while so that he could test himself, alone.

He knew they couldn't pull the heist without him. Neither of them had the ability to force the clerk to do anything. And yet, he wasn't sure that he could pull a heist alone, either. It required enormous concentration to *reach* deeply and to hold the reach for any length of time. It meant that while he *reached,* he didn't have much energy left over to be consciously alert to danger; he needed someone to watch his ass. So the solo job had been intended to define his own limits.

He targeted a L'il General here in Lauderdale and it bombed big time. Yes, he got the clerk to leave the register unlocked and walk out of the room. And yes, he had held her away. But he'd been so focused on the clerk, he'd failed to realized that two customers had come in.

He'd killed them both. One had been Mira's husband.

The incident freaked Hal and he backed out of the heist. He hadn't seen Manacas and Indrio for a long time after that, several years. Then he and Manacas had run into each other one day at the beach and that meeting eventually led to a reconciliation with Indrio. Hal wasn't sure when they had started talking about killing Steele and Fletcher. Maybe the obvious had simply become more so, that they wouldn't be completely free to pull any sort of job, much less get on with their lives, unless Steele and Fletcher were dead.

So here they met, a trio of misfits bound by their personal history and little else. As soon as he joined them at the table, he felt their suspicion, a rippling undercurrent that he could practically taste and feel, a fourth presence here at the table.

"I checked her out," Manacas said without preface.

"Checked who out?"

"The psychic, man. Mira. Nice-looking woman. And she's no phony."

Then he proceeded to relate his experience with the psychic.

Hal felt like choking the asshole, shaking some sense into him. When Manacas had mentioned Mira earlier today on the phone, Hal hadn't suspected he would do something like this. Stupid, stupid, stupid. It seemed so obvious to Hal; how could it not be obvious to Manacas?

"Let's worry about Fletcher right now," Indrio said.

He puffed furiously on his cigarette; a cloud of smoke hovered around his head. Hal coughed and waved at the smoke with his hand; Indrio didn't get the fucking hint. He glared at Hal and said, "We didn't think you were going to show, Hal." Hostility radiated like an odor from him.

"Chill out, Vic. I'm not that late."

Indrio tapped the face of his watch. "Forty minutes."

Manacas rolled his eyes. "Cut the shit, man. He's here. It's a waste of time to argue about it. Fletcher's in a penthouse suite, Hal. When I scanned the place, I got the sense that hers is one of the two that faces the canal."

"You don't know which one?"

"I will once we're up there. The door I saw has some sort of gold-plated object on the knocker."

"She's not up there now," Indrio said. "Or if she is, she isn't answering the phone."

Hal wanted to be done with this, to get back to the chickee, to Rae. She'd been sleeping when he'd left and rather than drugging her, he had padlocked the door to the chickee's main room. "So what's the plan?"

Indrio snickered. "We break in and leave her a calling card. This would all be much easier if you'd just give her head a good squeeze, Hal."

Jesus, Indrio just didn't get it. "I guess you didn't hear me the first six hundred times I said this, Vic. I've never able to reach into Fletcher or Steele. You couldn't read them, either." *Never* wasn't quite true. He'd managed a few times.

Indrio pointed his cigarette at Hal. "We're talking about *you*, man, not me. Your ability has always been stronger than what Ed and I do."

Manacas, peacemaker, held up his large, powerful hands.

"That's it, *amigos*. You want to argue, fine, do it on your own time. I'm outta here."

He pushed back his chair, but before he could rise, Indrio grabbed his arm. "Okay, no arguing. Go ahead with what you were saying."

"The only point I'm trying to make," Manacas said, "is that whenever I looked for Steele or Fletcher, I located them by the static. So I couldn't—can't—read them either. Except for the other night. When I scanned the penthouses, I found her easily enough. Weird."

"Maybe because she was sleeping," Hal said. "Her guard wasn't up."

Manacas shrugged, unconvinced. "I don't know. Let's talk about now. About how our calling card is going to do major damage."

Indrio snickered. "For sure."

Manacas plucked a large canvas shoulder bag off the floor. "Out where I live, Hal, buildings go up overnight and the wildlife is scrambling to find new places to live." He set the bag on the table, unzipped it. Hal peered inside.

The snake, coiled in a small wire mesh container, reared its head and hissed. Hal wrenched back. "Jesus," he whispered. "A coral snake?"

Manacas looked pleased with himself and quickly zipped the bag shut. "Its bite is fatal within minutes. The closer the bite is to the heart, the quicker you die. I figure we'll just leave it in her bed."

"What the hell do you need me for?"

Indrio's face tightened. "We agreed we'd do this together. That's what."

"I did my part," Hal snapped. "And I did it alone. You two do Fletcher."

"Bullshit." Indrio stabbed out his cigarette and leaned so close to Hal he could smell the smoke on his breath. "The only reason you did Steele alone is because of his wife. But she doesn't have squat to do with Ed and me. So you're either in this or out of it completely, Hal. What's it going to be?"

Indrio, hothead asshole. Hal glanced at Manacas. "You agree with what he's saying?"

"Look, man, I don't give a shit one way or another about you and Steele's wife, okay? If it was me, I'd probably have done the same thing."

Yeah, Hal thought. Manacas, rapist.

"But Vic's right about our original agreement. We're in it together or forget it. You pulled out of the heist; you owe us, Hal."

"I've already risked my ass."

"So you're out? Is that what you're saying?"

If he said yes, then he would be out for good. He wouldn't be able to change his mind and go back. Indrio and Manacas, he knew, would vanish as completely from his life as they had before. Although he didn't need them to carry out his own plans, he knew that his new life with Rae, whatever shape it took, would be easier without the specter of Fletcher hanging over him. So why not go along with it? Why the fuck not?

"Okay, I'm in. How do we get into the suite?"

Indrio patted his jacket pocket. "That's my department. Once I get the door open, I'll watch the elevator and stairs. You and Manacas deal with the snake."

Hal pushed to his feet. "Then let's get going."

None of them spoke once they got in the elevator. But Hal felt a brief, insistent nudge inside his skull as Indrio tried to worm his way in. It pissed him off.

Ever heard of knocking, Vic?

Indrio grinned. *Just checking to make sure you're all here. No hard feelings, huh? About what I said earlier?*

You said what you had to say.

Manacas couldn't eavesdrop on the exchange, not unless he'd learned some tricks over the years that Hal didn't know about. He sensed it, however, and knew them well enough to figure out what it concerned. "Hug and make up, *amigos*, we're almost there."

As the elevator slowed, Indrio tucked an unlit cigarette behind his ear and removed a leather pouch from his jacket pocket. "I should have this door open in about sixty seconds. But in case it takes longer, watch the stairs, the elevator, and the doors to the other suites."

Teamwork, Hal thought. If he'd resorted to teamwork that night five years ago, Mira's husband would still be alive and maybe his life would have veered in another direction. A saner direction.

The elevator stopped. Hal pressed the HOLD button to keep the doors open and stepped out into the corridor after the others. Fletcher's energy drifted through the air like a faint residue of stale perfume.

He pulled it deeply into his lungs. An image took shape in the upper corner of his right eye: Fletcher dancing the merengue one night in a Latino bar in Miami, her hair long and loose, whipping around her head as she snapped her hips this way and that. She'd had too much to drink and there had been a primal wildness about her that he'd liked. It was the night they'd become lovers. Lifetimes ago. The image disturbed him, but he didn't know why.

Manacas had identified the right door, and Indrio went to work on it. Hal positioned himself where he could keep an eye on the elevators, the stairs, and the doors to the other penthouses. It took Indrio about forty seconds to get the door open, then he motioned them inside, his small, dark eyes darting nervously about.

"If I whistle, that means get out fast," Indrio said, and stepped out into the hall without shutting the door all the way.

Hal and Manacas snapped on latex gloves as they crossed the main room of the suite. Fletcher's energy felt much stronger in these rooms, intense, irritated, unpleasant. It reminded Hal of all the reasons why he'd split from Fletcher's world and obliterated whatever nostalgia he'd been feeling out in the hall. The bitch deserved a coral snake, a fer-de-lance, a goddamn python.

Manacas set the canvas bag on the floor next to Fletcher's bed. A king-size bed. Too much room for a snake to move around in. They had to narrow the parameters. "Let's put it in a pillowcase," Hal suggested. "A bite to the face will kill her faster."

Manacas grinned, a malicious glint in his eyes. "Good idea. He'll stay where it's dark and warm." He pulled on a pair of heavy-duty gardening gloves and tossed Hal a pair. "The fingers are lined in lead. Get that pillow ready, man. I don't want to hold this sucker any longer than I have to."

Hal put on the gloves. They made his hands feel large and clumsy. He picked up the middle pillow, pinched the pillowcase between his index fingers and thumbs and held it out to Manacas.

Manacas unzipped the bag, unlatched the wire mesh cage, and reached in for the snake. When he brought it out, he had it clasped behind the head, making it nearly impossible for the snake to bite him. Good thing, too. The snake hissed and thrashed like a live fucking wire, its tiny bright eyes possessed of a malign intelligence. Manacas kept his arms extended well in front of his body as he positioned it over the open pillowcase, then dropped it inside.

The snake fell to the bottom of the pillowcase and whipped wildly about. Hal's heart sprang into his throat. He cast the pillow between the other two and wrenched away from the bed. He yanked off the heavy gloves, stuffed them into Manacas's bag. "I'm gone."

"I can just see it," Manacas said, excited. "Fletcher gets back, she's bushed, she flops into bed, and feels this burning sting at her neck. By the time she gets the light on, she'll be on her way out."

"And if it doesn't happen that way?"

"Then it'll happen some other way. The snake's going to get her."

Hal hoped so, but he, better than anyone, knew just how lucky Lenora Fletcher could be.

They slipped back into the hall, where Indrio had worn a path in the carpeting with his incessant pacing. The hall stank of cigarettes. He didn't stop moving or puffing on his cigarette even when he saw them. He simply moved faster, toward the EXIT sign.

"We take the stairs, get off on different floors, then take the elevator the rest of the way down."

"Fuck the elevator," Hal said. "The stairs are safer."

Indrio grabbed his arm. "It's not just you involved in this, Bennet."

Hal wrenched his arm free and flung himself into Indrio, *reaching* so hard and suddenly that Indrio looked as if he'd been kicked in the balls. His eyes bulged, he gasped, his hands flew to his head, and he stumbled into Manacas.

Squeeze till it bleeds. Steele's voice, then Fletcher's, then the voice of that Agency spook Evans, all three voices merging into one.

Manacas slammed into him, knocking Hal against the stairwell door. It flew open and Hal fell through it and struck the concrete landing on his back. His breath *whooshed* out of him. He just lay there wheezing like an asthmatic, Manacas looming over him, his bald head reflecting the dim light like a mirror.

"Don't you ever pull that shit on us, Bennet."

Indrio limped up behind him, holding a handkerchief to his bloody nose. His weird, insectile eyes met Hal's, then flicked to Manacas. "Told you he was a motherfucker," he muttered, and headed down the stairs.

Manacas held out a hand, Hal grasped it, and pulled himself up. He rubbed at the center of his chest, coughed. Manacas suddenly looked remorseful. "Look, man, Vic's uptight."

"He's had a hair up his ass since I told him about Rae."

"Shit, he's probably jealous. Let's get outta here."

They didn't say a word during the first two flights. Hal heard Indrio somewhere ahead of them, smelled the smoke from a fresh cigarette. Manacas stopped on the seventh floor. "I jump off here," he said and flung an arm around Hal's shoulders. "Call me in the next day or two. There should be news on Fletcher by then. Don't worry about Indrio. He won't do anything stupid."

"He's a wild card, Eddie. More than either of us."

Manacas's smile smacked of prison camaraderie, resigned, maybe even a little sad. "He says the same thing about you, *amigo*. Talk to you soon."

With that, Manacas the pragmatist, the peacemaker, vanished through the doorway to the eighth floor. Hal couldn't shake the certainty that he wouldn't see him again, that he had chosen sides the instant Hal had *reached* into Indrio.

* * *

Smoke. Fletcher smelled smoke as soon as she stepped off the elevator. It wasn't real strong, but it didn't have to be. To an addict, the barest whiff smacked of paradise.

But as of this evening when she'd left, the only other smoking suite on this floor, the one next to hers, had been vacant. That bothered her. It bothered her even more when she unlocked her door and realized the odor of smoke in the hall smelled stronger than the smoke in her suite. More recent.

Fletcher shut the door and stood for a moment with her back to it, listening for noises. Nothing, not even a hiss of air from the vents. She opened the door again, sniffed at the hall, shut the door and sniffed at the air in the front room. Definitely stronger out there.

A hotel employee was up here sneaking a smoke. So what?

She threw the dead bolt, the security lock, tossed her purse in the nearest chair. After Sheppard and the psychic had left, Fletcher had gotten into Rae Steele's cabin for a look around. The only item of interest she'd found was an unsigned love letter to Rae that had been hastily scribbled and filled with flowery prose. Not Andrew's style at all. She wondered who Rae had been seeing, if Andrew had known. One more loose end to worry about.

She turned on a lamp in the living room, shrugged off her jacket, and flung it onto the couch. Scotch, she thought. She needed one of those little bottles of Scotch from the bar and a long, hot bath.

She noticed the blinking light on the bedroom phone. Krackett, she thought. Or Hood and Laskin. Or perhaps Evans. She didn't want to talk to anyone.

She started the water for her bath, then went into the bedroom and stripped off the rest of her clothes. She unclipped the ELF from her belt, but didn't turn it off. Didn't dare. She set it on the bed, then switched on the lamp and turned to rummage in her suitcase, which rested on the floor against the wall. Something moved in her peripheral vision, her head snapped toward it.

Shadows, just shadows. Christ, she was jumpy.

She gathered up her toiletries, clean clothes, and the ELF

device, and went into the bathroom. She dropped everything on the bath mat, turned off the faucet, opened a fresh bar of soap. She spent several minutes at the sink, brushing her teeth and applying a face mask that she used religiously once a week.

Hal used to poke fun at her about it, called it one of her "little vanities," like her penchant for nice clothes, for quality makeup, for certain creature comforts. He'd given her a facial one time as she'd soaked in a hot bath and because she hadn't been wearing the ELF, he'd been able to *reach* into her while he was doing it. He had *reached* so deeply that she had come without him ever touching her in a sexual way. She missed that. She hated to admit it, but there you had it.

She stepped into the bath with the mask drying on her face, tightening her skin, and sank down into the water. She shut her eyes, drifting in the luxurious heat, and dozed off. She came to suddenly, listening for whatever had awakened her.

There. A rustling sound, the noise palm fronds make in the wind. She sat straight up, her heart thumping, and reached down to the bath mat for her towel. She whipped it up and stood, wrapping it around her. She brought one foot over the side of the tub and, as it brushed the top of the mat, a snake's head poked out from under the folds.

Fletcher shrieked and jerked her leg back into the tub just as the snake struck the side. It whipped away from the tub, across the floor. The red, yellow, and black bands around its body seemed to blaze, visible long enough for her to identify it as a coral snake. Then it vanished through the door, into the bedroom.

She scrambled from the tub to the lid of the toilet and looked frantically around for a weapon. But her gun lay in the bottom of her purse in the bedroom. Just the thought of stepping down to the floor terrified her.

If she could get to the doorway, if she had a clear view of the bed, if she could run fast enough . . . *Do it, just do it.* Fletcher reached across to the counter, to the pack of hotel matches in the ashtray, then plucked the nail polish remover from her makeup kit. She set them on the back of the toilet, grabbed a towel from the stack on a shelf behind her, and paused, trying to steady her hands.

Get it right the first time, Lenora. You may not get a second chance.

She saturated most of the towel with the polish remover, lit a match, held the flame to the end. It caught fire and burned like money, hot and furiously, emitting a putrid smoke. She climbed down, darted to the bathroom door, paused.

Her eyes swept through the room. Too many places to hide, not enough light, too damn far to the bed, sweet Christ . . . She slammed her fist against the door, it banged against the wall. *Now.*

Fletcher lurched for the bed, her bare feet slapping the carpet, the flames hissing and climbing up the towel, closer and closer to her hand. Her eyes watered from the smoke, the room blurred. The bed seemed to move farther and farther away from her, like an object in a dream. Then she saw it, the coral snake whipping toward her from the left. She flung the burning towel at it and leaped onto the bed.

She dropped to her knees and grabbed wildly at the spread, gathering it to the center of the mattress so it wouldn't touch the floor. The rug where the towel had fallen had begun to smolder. She didn't see the snake. She couldn't reach her purse. She scrambled back, scooped up the phone, punched 0 for the operator.

Three rings, three long and endless rings, then a soft female voice said, "How—

"Snake!" she screamed. "A snake's in my room! Ten-oh-two! Penthouse! Hurry, please!"

Seconds passed, seconds in which she stood with her back plastered to the headboard, smoke thickening in the room. Her eyes fastened on the door, the locked, dead-bolted door and the continent of space between it and the bed, between the bed and her purse, the gun inside it.

I can't I can't . . .

Banging at the door. Someone shouting.

Leap to the chair. Yes, she could make it.

She leaped, the chair tilted, and she tumbled over the back of it. She landed on her knees and sprang forward, her panic like some terrible curse, hurling her forward, forward. She stumbled toward the banging, the shouting. She coughed and wheezed from the smoke that rolled thickly through the room. She didn't see the door until it practically reared up and smacked her in the face.

She fumbled with the locks, her head whipping around again and again, trying to see the floor around her. She threw the door open and charged into the hall, a hysterical woman wearing nothing but a white facial mask.

21

At nine Wednesday morning, Sheppard went to the property room and signed out the baggie that contained what he'd found at Rae's secret cabin. The nub of a smoked cigar, a charred photo, a few other odds and ends. To this he added a copy of his report concerning the cabin, which noted that the forensic results would be available in a day or two. Then he searched out Gerry Young.

Sheppard found him in the fax room, his eyes ringed with circles, his fatigue as obvious as chicken pox. "Gerry? You got a minute?"

"About that."

It suddenly occurred to Sheppard that Young's personal stake in this investigation exceeded his own. He had five dependents—two ex-wives and three children between the ages of seven and sixteen—who each got a cut of his paycheck. In contrast, Sheppard didn't pay alimony, had never paid alimony, and there had never been any kids to support. For some reason, though, he had the distinct impression that Young's fatigue could be blamed on more than just the specter of unemployment.

"Sure, what's up?" Young asked, poking his finger toward the ceiling, then gesturing to the hallway.

As they stepped outside the room, Young whispered, "We're sweeping the building for bugs. I think Fletcher's people may still be listening in."

No surprise, Sheppard thought, and followed Young to the door of the men's room. "I found the cabin," Sheppard said.

An odd, indecipherable expression flickered across Young's face. "And?"

"It didn't yield much." He pulled the evidence bag from a

windbreaker pocket. "Both items were in the fireplace, in the ashes."

He held the bag up to the florescent light so that Young could see the butt of the cigar and the remains of the blackened photograph. Young took the bag, turned it around in the light.

"Any idea who he is?"

"Not yet."

"Forensics find anything?"

"We won't know until tomorrow sometime."

Young pocketed the evidence bag. "You need backup for tomorrow night at the Elbo Room?"

The act of pocketing the bag punctuated the end of the discussion for Young about what Sheppard had found at Rae's secret cabin. But Sheppard wasn't ready to end it. "No, I don't want backup. And I wasn't finished. Mira described a guy with graying hair—not Steele."

"That's it? That's all she got?"

"She feels the affair ended some months ago."

"That isn't much to go on, Shep."

"She gets what she gets."

"There's one possibility we haven't really considered about this mystery man you're meeting with, Shep."

"Just one?" Sheppard replied dryly.

"He could be the guy who killed Steele."

Sheppard had considered the possibility—and dismissed it for the same reason he dismissed it now: it *felt* wrong. He couldn't explain it beyond that. "I don't think so."

"I'm going to back you up tomorrow night, Shep."

Sheppard shook his head and leaned back against the wall in the hallway. "I do this alone or I don't do it at all."

Young looked at him as if he'd lost his mind. Then he laughed, a loud, robust, incredulous laugh that echoed through the hallway. He rocked forward, into Sheppard's face, his eyes drawn closely together, as dark and impenetrable as a dense forest.

"Let's get something straight here, Shep. If I want to back you up, I'll back you up. If I see fit, I can yank you off this case so fast it'll make your dick spin. We understand each other?"

Sheppard's anger shot out of him, as abrupt and extreme as Young's. He sank his index finger into Young's chest. "Then go to it. I don't need this goddamn shit. Take the case, Gerry, and good fucking riddance."

Young stepped back, Sheppard's arm fell to his side. For a long, tense moment, neither of them spoke. People passed them in the hall, rookies in some training class. Then Young hissed, "What the fuck's with you, anyway?"

"Hey, I could ask you the same question."

Young's eyes dropped to the floor. He drew his fingers back through his thinning gray hair and shook his head. "It's too complicated to go into."

Sheppard had the distinct impression that Young wasn't talking about the investigation, that there was, in fact, something else involved here. Something very personal. But he wasn't about to prod.

"This isn't the guy who killed Steele, Gerry. I can't tell you how I know that, but I do. I also know that if you're there, he's going to sense it and things will get fucked up. He'll bolt. We'll lose him."

Young folded his arms across his chest, the corners of his mouth plunged. "So now you're psychic, huh?"

"Let me do it my way." He showed Young the ELF and reiterated what Pikolo had told him the other day.

"Then wear it tomorrow night," Young said. "And call me as soon as you get in."

Just that fast, the issue of backup had been settled. "I'll call you," Sheppard said and started to turn away. But Young wasn't finished.

"We answered a call last night at Pier 66. There was a coral snake in Lenora Fletcher's penthouse suite."

"Looks like Fletcher has some enemies we don't know about."

"Unfortunately, it didn't bite her."

"You're a sick fuck, Gerry."

"Don't I know it."

Sheppard left with the ELF device in his pocket and a thousand questions in his heart.

Lenora Fletcher stood at the crest of the sand dune and glanced up and down the beach, a hand shading her eyes. She spotted Evans down near the water's edge, a frail man walking with the aid of a cane. Other than several fishermen standing on shore, the beach looked deserted.

She removed her flats and padded across the warm sand, grimacing as grains stuck between her toes. She disliked the beach, except from a distance, as something to look at. The idea of sunbathing or swimming in salt water held no appeal whatsoever. Hal used to kid her about being squeamish of critters— sharks, insects, snakes.

She wondered where he and the other two had gotten the coral snake. Just the thought of it brought a chill to her arms. The hotel management, probably anticipating a lawsuit, had moved her immediately to another suite, their most secure suite, they assured her, with three nights free of charge.

Evans saw her before she reached him and lifted his cane in greeting. He'd gotten some sun since she'd seen him last and looked almost healthy. "You're up and around early," she remarked.

"Down here, the sun wakes me. Didn't you get my phone message?"

"I didn't pick up any of my messages last night."

As they walked up the beach, she told him what had happened. He didn't speak immediately. "So they've definitely targeted you, Lenora."

"Sure looks that way. But tomorrow night Indrio is meeting with a local cop at a bar on the beach. I intend to be there. He'll know where Hal and Manacas are."

"You want company?"

"Thanks, but I can handle myself just fine, Rich."

He chuckled. "There's never been any doubt about that. Indrio might recognize you, but he's never seen my face, so I might provide a necessary cover."

Fletcher hesitated, then detoured. "I'd like an honest answer about something, Rich."

He raised his eyes from the sand and smiled. "I know, I know. You've spent the last few days mulling over our conversation and you want to know what I'm up to, right?"

"Something like that."

He glanced out at the ocean, nodding to himself. "I used to

believe I'd die fast, from a bullet or an accident. Given my druthers, it would be preferable. No pain, no time to think about what I would have done differently in my life. But that isn't how it worked out. So now, there are certain favors I'd like to repay before I die. Through Hal, I can repay two of them."

"By using Hal's ability to get rid of someone."

"Yes, that's one of the favors. The other favor involves you. If you allow me access to Hal once you find him, I'll make sure that you become the director of the Bureau, then attorney general. I don't doubt you'll eventually get there on your own merits, Lenora. But I'll hurry the process along."

She knew he could do exactly that. But could she believe him? More to the point, could she afford *not* to believe him? "How long would you need him for?"

"Twenty-four hours at the most. I could work right from my condo."

"And what guarantee do I have that you wouldn't turn me over to Hal?"

She expected him to protest, to act shocked. But he merely shrugged. "None. I'd be a fool to try to convince you of anything that went contrary to your own beliefs. But I'd have nothing to gain by your demise, Lenora, and everything to gain by your position in the Bureau."

Of all the things he might have said, this smacked of the sort of logic that had ruled Evans's professional life. It convinced her he was being honest, at least as honest as he could be *at this moment*. And in her business, it didn't get much better than that.

"Okay," she said. "Then we have a deal. But I want to do tomorrow night alone, Rich. You're safer staying in the background."

"I understand. Call if you need anything. We have a number of people down here who can help, Lenora. You don't have to bring any of them in alone, especially Hal."

Fletcher hooked her arm through his and bussed him quickly on his cheek; it felt like dry paper.

22

Lightning burned blue across the sky, thunder rumbled like some discontented god, it had begun to sprinkle. But impending rain hadn't deterred business in the Elbo Room this Thursday night.

When Sheppard walked in at nine-forty-five, music blared from the jukebox, the air smelled of smoke, people jammed the bar. He waded into the thick of the crowd, hoping to find a vacant table. No such luck. He returned to the bar and eased his way to the front, where he ordered a cranberry juice with a slice of lime.

The mini cassette recorder in the pocket of his raincoat felt weighted and obvious. Ninety minutes worth of tape, ready and waiting. In his other pocket, he carried the ELF device.

Someone tapped him on the shoulder, a tall, scrawny guy, an Ichabod Crane with thinning hair and an ugly scar along one side of his face. "It's not safe here, Sheppard. Let's move down the street."

"I'm not going anywhere until I get your name."

The man fidgeted, twitched. "The only thing that's important is what I have to tell you about Steele. I'd rather not do it here because I think we're being watched."

Outside the windows, lightning stripped away the blackness of the sky. Seconds later, thunder rolled. The lights in the bar blinked, the skies opened up, rain smeared against the glass. "We can go out the back way," the man said hoarsely, his eyes still darting about.

Sheppard didn't budge. "Just who do you think is watching us?"

"Probably one of Lenora Fletcher's boys."

"Hey, man, for all I know, you're working for her."

The man laughed, exposing a row of stained, crooked teeth. "Not fucking likely. You coming or not?"

"Not without a name."

"Vic, okay? Call me Vic."

"And how did you know Steele?"

"First I was his guinea pig, then I was his gofer. You need to know what I know, Sheppard." His head seemed to swivel on his shoulders. "I really have to get outta here."

He turned quickly away and Sheppard followed, his hand inside his jacket pocket, resting lightly against his 9mm, a compact P239.

They threaded their way through the crowd and stepped out into an alley behind the building. Sheppard raised the hood of his windbreaker, but it didn't offer much protection from the rain.

The wind whipped through the alley, driving the cold rain at an angle into his face. Vic, who wore no windbreaker or raincoat, seemed to barely notice the weather. He loped several paces ahead of Sheppard, hands thrust in his pockets, shoulders hunched slightly. He looked like some wino who hoped to find five bucks on the ground that would buy him a gallon of rotgut for the night.

They rounded the side of the building and emerged on A-1-A. Rain swept through the glow of the crime lights, traffic had slowed to a crawl. Vic darted between the cars with the quickness of a snake, then hit the sidewalk on the other side at a swift trot. He didn't slow down until he reached a brown Pontiac parked at the curb.

Sheppard moved the tape recorder from his right pocket to his left, turned it on, zipped the pocket shut. Then he got into the passenger seat and Vic pulled sharply away from the curb, the wipers whipping across the windshield. A horn blared behind them.

"Fuck off, asshole," he muttered, glancing in the mirror. Then, to Sheppard: "We should be pretty safe as long as this line keeps moving."

"Safe from Fletcher, you mean."

"For starters, yeah." He pushed in the lighter on the dashboard, slipped a cigarette from his shirt pocket, and cracked his window as he lit it. "You mind?"

Yeah, I mind. But hell, it was his car. "No."

Vic inhaled the smoke as though it were oxygen, drawing it deeply into his lungs, then blowing it out softly, so that it sounded almost like a sigh. "Christ, now that we're in here, I'm not sure where to start."

"Tell me about being one of Steele's guinea pigs. That'll do for starters."

The headlights of oncoming cars flashed like strobes in the windshield. The wipers continued their maddening, rhythmic swishing across the glass. Sheppard cracked his window to let out the smoke that drifted toward him.

"In the late sixties, Andrew Steele did his psychiatric residency at Duke University. His specialty was parapsychology. He tested hundreds of volunteers for their psi-Q—psychic potential. They ranged from students and stockbrokers to housewives and convicts. He found that as a group, cons seem to do better than average. He figured it had to do with living by your wits, living at the edge. Street smarts, in other words. He also found a high psi-Q among cops."

He braked for a light, tossed out his cigarette, checked the rearview mirror. The traffic ahead began to thin, the beach lay behind them now. "So go on," Sheppard said. He shifted his body so the recorder was in a better position to pick up Vic's voice.

"Anyway, Steele eventually narrowed his research exclusively to cons. He published some of it, but the reaction in the academic community was real negative. Now a Harvard prof writes a bestselling book on alien abductions and who gives a shit?"

"Harvard gave a shit."

Vic laughed, a short, harsh sound that sent him into a coughing fit. "Good point. The academics weren't crazy about Steele's research, but the government took notice. By 1977, Steele wasn't publishing; he was head shrink at a federal prison in

Virginia. That's probably where he made his connections with people like Fletcher."

"Like Fletcher or *with* her?"

"Both, that's my guess. In 1978, he went to work at Manatee Correctional and implemented Delphi. Fletcher was the federal watchdog. Manatee was their base, but Steele recruited from prisons around the state."

"And you were part of Delphi?"

"Hell, I was their first recruit." He lit another cigarette, eyed the mirror again, worried his lower lip. "A session with Steele was part of the intake routine when I arrived at Lake Butler."

"What were you in for?"

"Drugs, theft, a shitload of charges." He shrugged his bony shoulders. "Whatever. I got seven years, did four and two years of parole. When I was sprung, Sheppard, I was pulling in seventy grand a year working for Delphi. I had a conch house in the Keys, drove a Mercedes, did just fine. Except that I felt more like a prisoner than I had in the joint. When Fletcher wanted answers, she wanted them yesterday. Basically, I sold my fucking soul."

"I'm not real clear on what it was that you did, Vic." Or why the government would pay him seventy grand a year to do whatever it was he did.

"I spied for the feds."

Like it was obvious what he was talking about. "I definitely missed something here."

When he glanced at Sheppard, the pupils of his deeply shadowed eyes suddenly glimmered like wet streets. "Delphi was about using psychics to obtain information. We did the dirty work. What the hell do you think I've been telling you?"

"So you're psychic?"

"I'm a telepath. It started when I was a kid. Steele taught me what it was, Delphi taught me how to use it."

"Give me an example of how you used it for the feds."

Vic stabbed a thumb to his right and Sheppard realized they were passing Steele's slice of paradise, the mansion dark and empty now. "We're going to talk about her, too, Sheppard. About Rae."

"You were going to give me an example."

Vic shifted his body, crushed out his cigarette, and fastened both hands to the wheel. "Okay. Let's say there's a political fund-raiser in D.C. Big party, lots of important people. Fletcher wants to know how some senator is going to vote on a particular issue. So she and I go to the party. During the evening, I stand a couple feet away from the senator and skim whatever's at the surface of his mind. Then I give Fletcher the info, she or Hal or one of the others verifies it. That's a simple example."

"Who's Hal?"

"One of the seven. I'll get to him in a second."

"The seven what?"

"There were seven of us in Delphi."

The seven tarot cards?

"All of us were cons handpicked and trained by Steele, used by Fletcher, and funded by a shadow budget that probably originated with one of the spy organizations. Once we got out, Fletcher set us up in a life. We were like fucking indentured servants, okay?"

Jesus, I've walked through the looking glass.

Vic snapped his fingers. "Alice."

"What?"

"Alice Through the Looking Glass. One of my favorite kid books."

Sheppard realized Vic had just read his mind. It spooked him so deeply he couldn't think of a damn thing to say. He reached into his pocket and switched on the ELF device.

Vic lit another cigarette. "That's more or less how it works for me. I catch bits of the white noise that floats through people's heads." Another glance in the mirror. "We each had a specialty, I guess that's what you'd call it. Telepath. Clairvoyant. Remote viewer. Lucid dreamer. Telekinetic. Whatever. They were innovative in how they used us."

"I was in the FBI for five years, Vic. I never heard squat about anything called Delphi."

"I'd be worried if you had. Even at its height, there were probably less than a dozen people who knew about Delphi. But it was one of the most generously funded covert projects of any kind.

"But I'm telling you, it got old fast. I did it for five years and I was on complete burnout. By then Fletcher trusted me, so she sent me to the Caribbean for a break. I met a woman, got myself a new life, and here we are."

Not quite, Sheppard thought. "Did Steele use tarot cards in his therapy?"

Vic looked surprised. "Yeah, how'd you know?"

Sheppard told him about the seven tarot cards he'd found in Steele's desk drawer. "Each of them was sent with a gift to Rae Steele."

"What were the cards?"

Sheppard ticked them off. He knew them by heart now.

"What a sick fuck he is," Vic muttered.

"Who?"

"Hal. He must've sent the cards. See, Steele had each of us pick a tarot card that we felt represented who we were. It was part of our routine for self-examination or some shit like that. Mine was The Tower. Hal's was the Hanged Man. Hal must've sent her the cards knowing that Steele would recognize them as the ones that represented the seven of us in Delphi. Christ, I bet it made him incredibly uptight. He couldn't go to the cops; he'd have to explain about Delphi. So what happens? Hal kills Steele and nabs his wife."

Onto the tape, Sheppard thought, right where it belonged. "How do you know that?"

"I know, okay? I just know."

They reached Delray Beach and Vic turned west over the bridge. He followed the road through the refurbished downtown, an area of several blocks that had always reminded Sheppard of the small towns in Stephen King's books, places where nothing was what it seemed.

"Don't you want to know more about Hal?" Vic asked.

"I figured you were getting around to that."

Vic laughed. "Yeah, eventually." The car bounced over the railroad tracks and into a rundown section of town. "Almost from the beginning, Fletcher and Steele recognized that me, Ed, and Hal were the best of the seven. They put us together on projects, shit like that. Anyway, I was the first one to vanish.

Fletcher tried to get the others to look for me, but they gave her bad information or no information at all. Ed and Hal finally split, too.

"Not too long after we'd split, one of the women in Delphi was killed in a car accident outside of Durham, North Carolina. It wasn't any accident, she was murdered. Then another guy in the program bit the dust—an apartment fire supposedly caused by a space heater. By then, we'd realized they were eliminating the players. Now we three are the only ones left out of the seven."

He drove up and down side streets and kept leaning forward to rub at the fog on the glass. "Let's stop until the rain lets up," Sheppard suggested.

"Uh-uh. I think we've got a tail."

As Sheppard turned to look out the rear window, he unzipped his pocket and stuck his hand in, fiddling with recorder to turn the tape over. Vic was so uptight about being followed he didn't notice. "If someone's tailing us, he's invisible," Sheppard remarked.

"A car was back there when we were going through downtown Delray."

"You think Fletcher knocked off the other four in the program? Is that what you're saying?"

"I don't know if she actually did it, but she was responsible for it. When the three of us split, the funding started drying up and the people who knew about Delphi were getting real nervous about how they were going to continue to control ex-cons. So it was decided the whole thing, participants included, would be scrapped."

"You think, but you don't know for sure."

"I know for sure, man. If you don't want to buy it, fine, suit yourself. But I know what I know. I also know that some spook from another agency had a lot to say about what happened and didn't happen in Delphi. For awhile, Hal worked exclusively with him and Steele; I don't think Fletcher even knew about it."

"What was the spook's name?"

"Richard. That's all I could ever pick up. He was a honcho in one of the security organizations, I don't know which one."

"That's damn vague," Sheppard remarked.

"Yeah, well, a lot of it was vague from where I stood."

"Why did Hal kill Steele?"

Vic wasn't quite as quick to answer this time. "It's complicated, Sheppard. Originally, we talked about killing both him and Fletcher, to be free of them." He lit another cigarette. "You don't know what it's like to have to live with eyes in the back of your goddamn head. That's how Fletcher made us feel.

"Anyway, I never really thought it would happen and frankly, I wasn't all that keen on the idea. I have a fine life now, why fuck with it? I can live with the paranoia. But then Hal did it and when we met, he told Ed and me about Rae. That's when I realized all along that he's had this private agenda. Kill Steele, nab his wife. He claims he still wants Fletcher dead and that's supposedly what he's gearing up for. Maybe it's true, maybe it isn't, I don't give a shit. I just want out of the whole fucking thing."

"Where did you meet with Hal?"

"Bay Pub, a hangout in Florida Bay. I don't know for sure, but I think he lives somewhere in the Glades. I got no idea where Ed lives and he and Hal don't know where I live. We figured it was best that way." He had turned east again, slipping into the stream of traffic.

"What's Ed's last name?"

"I can't tell you that. Ed and I have had our differences, but I got no problem with him. I know Hal's got a cellular phone, because that's how he and Ed stay in touch. Then Ed passes stuff on to me."

"I thought you said you kept in touch telepathically or something."

"Hal's the only one of us who can reach far enough to do that. His talent is like a wild mood swing, okay? It isn't always there, it isn't always something he can control. But when he's hot, watch the fuck out. If he really extends himself, he can make the inside of your head feel like it's going to explode. If he keeps it up, capillaries in your cheeks burst, your nose starts to bleed, you're literally crippled with pain."

He's describing what happened to me. And to Mira.

"The attack lasts about thirty seconds to a minute. If it continues for another three to five minutes, you begin to bleed internally. In six to eight minutes, your spleen bursts or your intestines rupture. In fifteen to twenty minutes, you're dead. That's how Delphi used him best. It's called telekinesis, Sheppard."

"A bullet killed Steele," Sheppard said flatly.

"Only because Hal can't do this with everybody. He could never reach into Fletcher or Steele, we don't know why."

Sheppard knew why; he felt the weight of the ELF device in his pocket. "So whose brain did Hal turn to mush?"

"The list isn't that long, but it's impressive," Vic said dryly, and proceeded to tick off the incidents.

A chopper pilot in Iran. A suburban housewife who opened fire in a D.C. subway station. A federal building in Minneapolis. The suicide of a key figure in the Senate.

The whole thing smacked of conspiracy theories, too far *out there*. It sounded, in fact, like Forest Gump. Pick an event and the deadly trio had been involved.

"There were other things, too. Things Hal has never admitted that happened when he was working with Steele and this Richard spook. Now and then I got a glimmer of something from that time."

"Like what? Can you be specific?"

"The death of a former First Lady that was actually suicide. Hal messed with her head."

Sheppard started to say something, but Vic suddenly hissed, "There it is. The pale sedan three car lengths back. I'm sure it's the same car I saw before."

Sheppard glanced back, Vic pressed his foot to the gas pedal. The car shot forward and Sheppard's head snapped around. Vic swerved into the other lane and charged toward the intersection, tires shrieking against the wet pavement.

He raced through the red light, dodging oncoming cars. Horns blared, Sheppard shouted at him to slow down. But Vic drove like a madman, lost in his own world, his body hunched over the steering wheel, his face seized up with a kind of wildness. The engine roared, the speedometer needle leaped past eighty.

Just ahead, red lights flashed, their glow washing across the windshield like blood. It took Sheppard a moment to realize they had circled and reached the bridge again, that the red lights meant the bridge was about to rise.

"Don't do it!" Sheppard shouted, and lunged for the steering wheel, trying to seize control of the car.

One of Vic's bony arms crashed across the bridge of Sheppard's nose. Pain lit up the inside of his sinus cavities and the car weaved like a drunk across the road. Sheppard grabbed Vic by the back of the neck and slammed his head into the steering wheel, knocking him out. Sheppard pushed him aside and grabbed onto the wheel, but it was too late. The tires struck the incline of the bridge as it began to rise.

The engine sputtered and died, the wipers quit, the car was airborne. He didn't feel any sense of motion and yet, wind whistled past the windows. He felt like he was suspended inside some lightweight bubble, drifting in a hot air balloon. And then everything inside of him screamed, *Get out get out* and he kicked open the passenger door.

Wind and rain rushed in, the blackness of the intracoastal waters swirled below him. The car's nose suddenly plunged forward, everything inside rattling, sliding around, tumbling. Sheppard leaped.

He struck the water feet first. The impact jarred him down to his very cells, knocked the air from his lungs, and he sank through the wet blackness. He hit bottom and his feet sank into muck, trapping him. His brain shrieked for air, adrenaline raced through him. He somehow got his shoes off and swam frantically for the surface, swam against the weight of his gun, his clothes, the current.

As his head broke through the surface, an explosion rocked the air. Flames and plumes of black, greasy smoke sprang toward the sky.

Sheppard treaded water, staring at the fireball, filling his lungs with air, then he dived and swam away from the bridge, swam as fast as his arms and legs would carry him, swam until he could swim no more.

23

Fletcher stood at the edge of a seawall with several dozen other people, watching the frenzied activity on the bridge and in the water below. Fire trucks and ambulances had arrived within minutes of the explosion. Cops, paramedics, and firemen now swarmed like ants over the bridge. Coast Guard cutters cruised through the debris.

She couldn't very well identify herself; she didn't want to be associated in any way with what had happened here. But she needed answers. She needed to know if Indrio and Sheppard had both been in the car when it had exploded.

She moved along the seawall, rain drumming the hood of her raincoat. The flashing lights from the emergency vehicles on the bridge washed through the air, illuminating the faces of bystanders huddled beneath umbrellas. The rain had put out the fire, but the air smelled scorched, ruined.

Fletcher pulled out her badge as she neared the bridge and hoped that whoever she showed it to wouldn't remember her name. She just wanted to cross the bridge and get a look at the remains of the car.

She walked over to one of the cops and held up her badge. "Anything I can do to help, sergeant?"

"Thanks, ma'am, but we're doing okay."

"What happened, anyway?"

"The bridge operator says the driver tried to beat the bridge as it was going up. Damn fool."

"Just one person inside?"

"I really don't know, ma'am. The paramedics are going through the debris. You might talk to them or to the bridge operator. He's over in the ambulance now. We're damn lucky it was raining and traffic was nil."

"Mind if I take a look?"

"Go ahead. Watch where you step. Pieces are strewn all over the place."

The car had struck on the east side of the bridge, just beyond the point where the asphalt began. She had seen the explosion and pieces of flaming debris shooting out in all directions. But up close, the grim sight chilled her, particularly because she knew she was partially responsible: the smoldering ruin of scorched and twisted metal, the carpet of glass shards, the stink of smoke. The rain had helped contain and squelch the fire and now firefighters poked through the largest heap of debris. She walked past them, anxious to speak to the bridge operator first.

The ambulance was parked down near the roadblock, the rear doors open. An overweight Latino in a rain slicker, jeans, and a Marlins baseball cap was inside. He held an oxygen mask over his mouth as a paramedic took his blood pressure.

Fletcher stuck her head inside the door. "Excuse me." She showed her badge. "You mind if I ask him a few questions?"

"No problem," the paramedic replied, and spoke to the man in Spanish.

The bridge operator nodded and kept sucking greedily at the air.

"How many people were inside the car, sir? Could you tell?"

He held up two fingers, a peace sign, then slipped the mask off his face. He sounded short of breath, as if he'd been running. "Maybe two, I not sure. It happen too fast, *me entiende?* I be in bridgehouse, the bridge it be coming up, then . . . the car it flies off the bridge . . ." His hand cruised through the air in front of him, then his fingertips plunged downward. "I see something, I not know what, falling out of the car. Then . . ." He clapped his hands together, a sharp, startling noise. "Boom. *Un explosion.*"

"Do you think this falling object was a person?"

"*Nosé.*"

A traumatized man who could barely speak English was about as reliable a witness as a drunk. "Are you sure something fell? It was raining awfully hard, it was dark . . ."

He tapped the corner of his eye. "Juan know what he see, eh? Something fall. If it a man, I hope he has wings."

She wasn't going to get any farther with this guy. Fletcher thanked him and went over to one of the firefighters. Badge, greeting, the same routine. The badge didn't impress him and the interruption obviously irritated him. Tough shit, she thought. "Have you found any bodies?"

"Nothing whole," he replied.

"Is there enough to tell whether the body is male or female? Black or white?"

A veil of water poured over the end of the visor on his helmet. "Have a look." He motioned toward a body bag at the side of the road.

"May I borrow your flashlight?"

He handed it to her and turned away, making it clear she was on her own. Fletcher went over to the body bag, untied it, and shone the flashlight inside. Her stomach heaved. The mass of scorched flesh and bone was probably a limb, but she couldn't determine the gender or the race. She quickly tied the bag, returned the firefighter's flashlight, then hurried away from the ruin, off the bridge and across the shopping center parking lot to her car.

Chilled and beat, she stripped off her raincoat, her running shoes and socks, cranked up the car and put on the heater. She sat there for a long time, eyes burning, stomach cramped with hunger, shivering as the warm air poured through the car.

The windows fogged up and her view of the outside world shrank to smears of red and blue from the lights of the emergency vehicles. It was as if she had suddenly developed cataracts that, second by second, swallowed her sight.

You fucked up big time, Lenora. The voice was her own, but she heard it as Krackett's.

For the first time in years, she felt deeply and desperately afraid that she wouldn't be able to fix what had gone wrong.

Thunder woke her, tremendous booms that echoed in the lagoon with frightening clarity. Lightning lit the inside of the chickee in a strange, watery blue that possessed weight and texture; it felt as cool as a mother's hand against her face. Rain tapped against the chickee's thatch and tin roof, an oddly soothing sound.

Rae, no longer restrained and not drugged, pushed up on her elbows. She glanced in Hal's direction. In the flash of blue light, she could see only his head, poking out from under the sheet that covered him.

He saved my life.

Fact.

He kidnapped me.

Also a fact.

She'd spent a lot of time the last few days examining these facts from every conceivable angle, then applying them to her plan. Of the two facts, the first seemed the most important now. Would her husband have saved her life in the same situation? She didn't think so. Andy's primary concern in life was Andy, bottom line, end of story.

The realization filled her with relief. It made her feel better in an abstract, dreamy kind of way, as though she had carried the question around inside of her for years, an embryo so small she'd been barely aware of it.

She pulled her legs to her chest and clasped her arms around them, thinking of the Rae she had been. That woman, Andy's wife, had been a fictional person, a personality patched together from what she'd believed Andy wanted in a wife. She was no longer that woman. She didn't know who she was now or what she was becoming, but she knew she wasn't fictional.

Wind blew through the open windows, a wet wind that smelled of the Glades, a rich, almost menstrual odor. All that wilderness, she thought. All that water. She didn't know her specific location within this wilderness or if it even showed on a map. *If* she could find the paddles to the boat and escape, where would she escape to? The mangroves? And then what? How far could she get before he *reached* and found her? A mile? Two? Five?

You don't have a choice. Not if she wanted to see her son again.

Rae rolled onto her knees and peered across the chickee. She could detect his shape on the mat where he usually slept. For a split second, she considered killing him as he lay there. But with what? Her bare hands? The only object within easy reach was the rocking chair. If it creaked, if the floor creaked, he would be instantly awake, he was a light sleeper, a part of him remained forever alert, vigilant.

And if he didn't kill her, it would mean the handcuffs again, the drugs, everything like before.

Forget it. Rae got to her feet, unzipped her shorts, rolled them off over her hips. She drew her T-shirt over her head. A part of her mind worked frantically, sealing up the truth and burying it so deeply even God wouldn't find it. What would happen next would be buried in the same place, forever beyond the light of day.

Rae stepped forward, away from her futon cushion, the wet wind licking her back. Lightning flashed against the walls, illuminating Hal's drawings of her, dozens upon dozens of drawings. Rae in her car. Rae at the mall. Rae with her son. That other Rae, living a lie. It disgusted her.

She knelt beside him, staring at his head. Her heart slammed around like a tennis ball in her chest. Then she folded back the sheet, exposing the curve of his spine, a country of skin, and stretched out alongside him.

Hal dreamed of the spook that he and Steele had worked with for a while, an aging fart with hard eyes and difficult targets. Then he felt her hands, Rae's hands, on his back, and they drove the dream out of him and brought him fully awake.

He didn't move, barely breathed. She fitted her body to his, molding her legs to fit the shape of his, spoons in a drawer. She drew her nails lightly through the hair at the nape of his neck. He was simultaneously aware of the lightness of her touch, of the persistence of the rain drumming against the roof.

Hal rolled onto his back and she loomed above him, her silken hair falling at the sides of his face. Transformed, she became Kathleen Turner in *Body Heat*, Uma Thurman in her best moments in *Pulp Fiction*, Grecian in her beauty, everything about her larger and more magnificent than anything he had ever imagined.

"I didn't thank you for saving my life," she said.

It smacked of Heathcliff, the moors, Scarlett to Rhett, a music that made his throat go dry, a narcotic that infused him with passion and hope. Hal slipped his fingers back through her hair, something he had always wanted to do. It felt surprisingly cool and thick and a little wild. He drew her head toward his own and when his mouth found hers, he *reached.*

A thick fuzziness, a delicious warmth. He felt as though he drifted in some sweet, magical sea, that he was about to become the man he had imagined he might one day be. Her inner voice was soft, surprised. *I like this . . .*

Her arms slid around his bare back, his hands explored the mystery of her flesh, her bones. Curves. Angles. The sharp points of her ribs, lined up like a series of exclamation marks. They rolled, legs scissoring together, Rae now on her back. He could just make out the mole next to her breast, staring up at him like a small, perfect eye.

He lowered his mouth to that breast and *reached* harder, deeper. But instead of her voice, he found the voice of Manacas on the phone this afternoon, informing him of a short piece in the local paper about a coral snake found in a penthouse suite at Pier 66. No injuries.

Lucky Fletcher.

Keep doing that . . . Rae's voice now, soft and seductive, curling through him like tendrils of smoke. *Yes, like that. Andy won't lick them. He thinks it's dirty or something.*

He drew his tongue in sharp, tight circles around the nipple, then nibbled at it like a tiny fish. Her skin tasted warm and damp and sweet, like sweating fruit. She gasped, he liked the sound of it, liked that he made her feel this way.

. . . top, I want to be on top, Andy won't do it like that, do everything to me he doesn't like . . .

Hal rolled, taking her with him, and she lifted up, straddling him, hands stroking him, her mouth touching his face here, there, her hair caressing his skin. His hands slipped over her buttocks

. . . make me come like this . . .

and he drew his fingers between her thighs, teasing, promising,

. . . inside me . . .

and her tongue twisted against his, she moaned into him,

breathed into him. His fingers were inside of her, her hips thrust against the pressure

... *ohgodohgodoh* ...

Suddenly she lifted her hips slightly and guided him inside of her. He died, he went to goddamn heaven, he was gone. She reared up, her chest slick with sweat and rain, her skin glistening in the explosion of lightning.

... *harder, faster, there, wait, hold it, oh oh*

And he came, just like that he came and she didn't, she tottered at the hot, electric edge ...

... *No, Christ, no* ...

Hal rolled again, they were on their sides, her chest heaving, and he coaxed her onto her back and pulled out of her and kissed his way down her body.

... *Don't stop don't stop* ...

He licked at her skin, circling a hip, inscribing a secret language against the top of her thighs. He parted her with his fingers and fastened his mouth to her. The sweet, secret taste of her was forbidden knowledge, what had gotten Adam and Eve expelled from the garden. It seemed he had yearned for it his entire adult life.

But he had *reached* so deeply inside of her the border between them got swallowed up, he felt devoured, subsumed. It had never happened to him before and it terrified him.

He thrust himself inside of her and rolled again so she was on top. Their bodies slapped together, sharp, wet sounds that echoed against the darkness, against the flashes of lightning. She raised up, he gripped her hips and ...

... *please* ...

when he came it was a small death. He was flung away from her, hurled out into the blackness of the lagoon, hurled upward through the hole in the branches. He shot toward the sky, the hidden moon.

The storm shook the chickee like a dog with a bone. Wind knocked the shutters closed and whistled under the eaves. Water slapped the wooden pilings. Rae wanted desperately to shut her eyes and drift in the sounds, but she couldn't. Not now, not yet.

"Are you doing it now?" she asked.

"Doing what?"

They lay on their sides, facing each other. His fingers, lost in her hair, smoothed strands away from her face, smoothed until she thought she would scream with the repetition. The border between pleasure and pain had blurred for her; her skin felt so sensitized her nerve endings seemed exposed, raw.

"Doing whatever it is that Andy was so interested in."

"He called it *reaching*. And no, I wasn't doing it."

"But you were doing it earlier."

"Yes."

I should feel violated. But she didn't. How could she? If Andy could do this, perhaps their marriage would not be what it was now. What she felt most of all was a strange and thrilling curiosity about his talent. "It works just like that?" She snapped her fingers.

"Sometimes it doesn't work at all, sometimes it works better than it does at other times. In the beginning, when Dr. Steele started with the photos, it was unpredictable. There was all kinds of interference. Like static. He taught me how to turn down the static, how to focus."

"Have you ever *reached* into him?"

"I never got past the static. There're others like that, people I just can't get into. They're locked up tight."

"Did you reach into me when we were on the compound?"

"What do you think?"

That he had. "There were times when I'd be sitting alone in my office and I'd have the sudden feeling that I wasn't alone." She thought of that day the two of them were in her office and her head had started to pound and the pain had peaked into a migraine. She'd been too turned on earlier to notice what the *reaching* felt like. Now she needed to know if there was any sensation when he did it, if she felt any differently. "Do it now, Hal. *Reach* into me."

"Think of something," he said.

She conjured memories of the two weeks she, Andy, and Carl had spent in Barbados last winter. The hot sun. The turquoise waters. The sea urchins in rainbow colors. The dock where they had dived for sand dollars.

Then she felt it, a small, dull ache at the back of her skull, as though she had eaten something that hadn't agreed with her and any second now her stomach would revolt. A wave of heat washed through her, the pressure at the back of her head deepened for fifteen or twenty seconds.

"An island," he said.

"What else?"

"Dollars." He laughed softly. "And urchins. I kept seeing street urchins. The street urchins asking for dollars?"

Not quite, but close enough.

"Did you feel anything?" he asked.

"Not really," she lied. "Tell me more about these photos that Andy gave you. What did you do with them, exactly?"

"The photos were just part of the whole thing, Rae, and we used them only in the very beginning."

"What'd you do after that? Give me an example."

"An example," he repeated, mulling it over. And then he started talking, as if unburdening himself.

Her mind went numb. She couldn't think of anything to say even after he'd finished.

"No comments at all?" he said.

Yes. That she suddenly detested the man she'd been married to for fourteen years. "What did you get in return for doing this work?"

"When I was still in, I got privileges. The guards never hassled me, there were never any surprise searches of my room, I became a trustee. Once a week, Superintendent Russo signed me out for work on an outside ground crew and we went over to one of the trailers in the employee park and I had several hours alone with a woman."

Fascinating. She'd spent four years at Manatee and had known none of this. "Who was the woman?"

"This lady from Miami who wrote me out of the blue and we started exchanging letters."

Lightning flashed, followed some time later by a distant roll of thunder; the storm was on the move again. The wind had cooled and Rae drew the sheet up over them."Where is she now?"

"Dead."

"Dead? How?"

"They killed her."

"Who killed her?"

"The people in charge of Delphi."

"Andy? Is that what you're saying? That he killed her?"

"No, not him. He knew about it, he knew about all of it. But he didn't kill her. That wasn't his role. My guess is that Lenora Fletcher had the woman killed because she was afraid I might have told her what was going on. She was the fed in charge of Delphi."

"And Andy knows about this."

"You're not getting it, Rae. He and Fletcher worked this project together. And later, your husband and a CIA spook named Richard Evans worked with me, without Fletcher knowing about it. Some team they were," he added, and talked again.

I'm his confessor, Rae thought. A week ago she wouldn't have believed this story. "What happened when you got out?"

"Fletcher was waiting for me. She drove to this upscale neighborhood in Coral Gables and stopped in front of this Spanish-style house. There was a sports car in the driveway, a black lab pup in the yard, clothes my size in the closet.

"She told me I had the place rent free and that the feds would be paying me about seventy grand a year to gather information for them. That was just how she put it: *'gather information.'* " He laughed. "Like it was that harmless. But hell, I didn't have any better offers. By then, your husband was pretty much out of the picture."

"How long did you work for them?"

"Too damn long." His voice sounded resigned, as if he'd made his peace with his failings long ago. "If you count the time at Manatee, it was close to thirteen years. I should've split before I did, but Fletcher and I were sleeping together, I had a lot of freedom, and I didn't mind the work. Toward the end, I was fixing this place up, getting ready."

Lightning flashed again, throwing neon blue against the walls.

"With Fletcher, I always felt like a butterfly under glass, one of those poor suckers pinned to a piece of velvet, marginally alive, an exotic curiosity."

"What happened when you vanished?"

"Nothing. I just left."

"But were the feds looking for you?"

"Sure. They still are, but not in any official capacity. This was a covert project and there are three of us missing and still free."

"So you're in touch with the other two."

"Yes." He was stroking her hair, combing it with his fingers, and it felt good, it aroused her. She suddenly wanted him again, wanted him to *reach* into her again, unearthing more of that dark sensuality, the dangerous pleasures, that had never existed in her marriage.

Hal began to touch her once more and Rae shut her eyes, surrendering to her body's treachery.

IV: Impossible Things

"I've often believed six impossible
things before breakfast."
                                    —Lewis Carroll

"Consciousness is the creative element
in the universe. Without it, nothing
would appear."
                          —Fred Alan Wolf,
                          Taking the Quantum Leap

24

The sharp, incessant ringing pierced her eardrums like barbed arrows. Mira groped blindly for the receiver.

I'll hurt you . . .

She bolted out of the dream, her heart racing. The doorbell. Real world. The digital clock read three a.m. Nadine? Not at this hour. It seemed unlikely that someone who intended to harm her would ring the bell, but Steele's killer had done it. She ran into the closet for Tom's gun.

He'd bought the Cobra .357 after he'd received a threatening note from a former disgruntled client. It had seemed extreme to her at the time, a gun so powerful that even a psychopath wouldn't argue with it. Now she felt grateful that it wasn't a puny .22 and that she'd learned how to shoot it.

Safety off. She slipped silently to the door, where the cats sniffed around, and peered through the peephole. Despite the dimness of the outside light, she recognized him by his height and unlocked the door. Sheppard looked like he was coming off a four-week drunk. Damp, stained clothes. No shoes. Scrapes and cuts on his body.

"You look like hell, Shep."

"Nice touch." He motioned at the gun. "I hope to hell you know how to shoot it."

"I do."

"I thought you didn't lock your doors."

"I didn't until I met you. C'mon in."

He slouched against the wall and only then did she realize he was hurt. She took hold of his arm, helped him inside. He pressed his left arm tightly against his body even when he sank to the couch.

"Frankly, Shep, I'm afraid to ask."

"Cab's out there. I lost my wallet. May I borrow the fare from you? I'll pay you back tomorrow."

"How much?"

"Sixty-eight and change."

"Jesus, where'd you come from?"

"Boynton Beach."

Up the coast a good piece. "Go sit down. I'll pay him."

"I'll take the gun," he said.

The gun. She'd forgotten about the gun. She handed it to him and he leaned back into the shadows. Mira hurried into the bedroom, pulled on a pair of gym shorts under her T-shirt, counted the money in her wallet. $52.76. She stuffed the bills in her pocket, then went into Annie's room to scrounge up the difference.

The tin box on her toy shelf held her allowance money, which she'd been saving for the Crystal Skull CD-ROM. Mira felt guilty scooping out a wad of bills and a handful of quarters. Outside, the rain had stopped, the air felt chilled, water dripped from the trees and plants. The cab stood silently at the curb, engine and lights off, the young Cuban driver leaning against the door, smoking. He waited patiently while she counted money into his hand.

It pissed her off that Sheppard had put her in this position. That she'd allowed him to do so. She'd known the man less than a week and he was already borrowing money from her and doing it in the middle of the night.

In Spanish, she told the cabbie to keep the change, the equivalent of a ten buck tip. "And make up an address, okay?" Just in case Fletcher checked with the cab companies.

"No problema. Gracias, señorita."

She returned to the house, threw the dead bolt, turned on a lamp. Sheppard's head rested against the back of the couch. His eyes had shut, he still hugged his arm to his side. Mira didn't see any blood, but her own ribs began to throb in sympathy.

"Shep, do you need a doctor?"

"No." His eyes opened. "Gauze. I think I screwed up a couple of ribs."

Mira shut down so she wouldn't feel his pain.

"I've never borrowed money from a woman, Mira. I'm sorry you had to be the first."

She needed to hear the words, but it didn't change the resentment she felt right this second. "So am I."

"I'll repay you tomorrow."

"That's not the point, Shep."

"Yeah," he said softly. "I know it's not."

"I'll be back in a minute."

When she returned with an Ace bandage and scissors, he held a mini cassette recorder and a tape. He fiddled with one, then the other. "The recorder's shot. But maybe the tape's not."

"A hair dryer might work."

She returned to the bathroom, jerked the hair dryer off the bathroom counter, marched back into the living room, and dropped it in his lap. "I told you from the start that I didn't want to be involved in this, Sheppard. But at every step of the way you've pulled me in deeper and—"

"You're absolutely right. I'm a selfish fuck."

The rest of her little speech evaporated. She dropped to her knees, pressed her face to his chest. He stroked her hair, rested his chin on the top of her head, and started talking. The man named Vic, his plunge from the bridge, Delphi, Fletcher, and the name of her husband's killer.

Hal Bennet. She said the name to herself, broke it down into syllables, shuffled the letters around to form other words, put it together again. A name personalized it.

Hal, whose buddy Vic had snitched on him, and another buddy named Ed. Maybe the same Ed who had come to the store the other night for a reading? *Is that too crazy?* She pulled back; Sheppard turned on the hair dryer and aimed it at the tape.

"Remember I told you about the guy named Ed who came into the shop for a reading the other night?"

He turned off the hair dryer, set the tape aside. "Ed who looks like Kojak." He nodded. "Sure. You think he—?"

"Yeah, I do." She gestured at the tape. "Is it dry?"

"It will be by tomorrow. I just hope there's something still on it." He reached into his shirt pocket, pulled out a soggy notepad, dropped it onto the couch, and proceeded to empty his pockets. "Did Ed have any scars or tattoos?"

"I don't think so."

"Would you recognize him from a photograph?"

"Sure."

"Good. I'll try to track down a mug shot through the Department of Corrections. In the meantime, it'd be a good idea if you and Annie go somewhere for a few days."

"Go? You mean, like leave town?"

He nodded.

Echoes of Ben's warning, she thought, and rocked back onto her heels. "C'mon, Shep. I've got a business to run and a street fair that starts tomorrow. No, today. I can't just walk out of my life."

"This guy Ed already knows where you work, Mira, and Bennet has called you at home. I can't tell you how to run your life, but I know if Annie were mine, I'd take her someplace safe until this thing is played out."

"You're frightening me," she said softly.

Mira walked away from the couch and stopped in front of the sliding glass doors. She peered out through the Levalors, into the wet darkness, a black hole, a riddle as incomprehensible and terrifying as Hal Bennet. She finally said: "Annie could stay with Tom's folks or one of his brothers."

"Can you do it today?"

"In the morning."

"It *is* morning."

"When the sun comes up, I'll call Tom's mother."

"Use your cellular phone. Your home phone may be bugged. I'm pretty sure my office is. That's the only way that whoever was following Vic's car could've known where and when we were meeting."

The reality of it all seeped into her like some toxic gas. She suddenly felt so tired she could no longer think straight. "I need to get some sleep. You'll have to sleep on the couch, Shep. With Annie here, I don't think it's . . ."

"I understand."

"I'll get sheets for the couch and some of Tom's clothes. You're taller than he was, but there might be something that will fit you."

She knew she was babbling, but couldn't help it. He had succeeded in frightening her and she only wanted to grab enough sleep so she could think straight. She picked up the Cobra and carried it into the bedroom with her. She put it into her purse with a box of ammunition, set her purse by the bed, and gathered up bedding and a towel.

She kept some of Tom's things in a bottom drawer of her dresser, clothes and personal items that she still couldn't bear to part with. She went through them, looking for a shirt and jeans that would fit Sheppard. Everything she touched was connected to a memory that the passage of time hadn't dimmed, memories that reminded her of the dream a few nights ago. Tom on the hillside, Tom saying that he liked Sheppard. She buried her face in one of Tom's shirts and a hole a mile deep tore open inside of her.

She didn't know how long she stayed like that, on her knees in front of the drawer, her face pressed into the shirt. She didn't hear Sheppard come into the room, didn't know he was there until he slipped his arms around her and pulled her against him. She clung to him as though she were drowning, and he just held her tightly, rocking, rocking gently until her sobs subsided.

Omens and dark visions consumed Sheppard's dreams, the primal stuff of nightmares. He woke exhausted, light streaming over him, his ribs aching, his neck and back stiff. As he sat up, Suess stepped carefully over the blanket and flopped down in Sheppard's lap.

"Just you and me here, huh, big guy?"

He stroked the cat. The silence in the rooms crowded around him, urging him to get up, to move. His ribs shrieked when he finally stood and kept right on shrieking as he went into the kitchen to make a pot of coffee.

Afterward, he unwound the gauze from his ribs. The skin had turned an ugly purple and looked even worse once he had showered. He nearly passed out when he wrapped fresh gauze around his ribs.

He didn't like wearing clothes that had belonged to Mira's dead husband. It made him feel like an impostor, some asshole who had blown into town and turned the widow's life inside out like a dirty sock. The shirt fit too snugly and the jeans, four inches too short, looked like pedal pushers and squeezed his balls. He put his jeans and the rest of his clothes in the washer and returned to the kitchen wearing just his briefs and Tom Morales's shirt.

Three cups of strong coffee and a note from Mira tacked to the fridge ushered him back into the human race. *If you need a ride to your car, call Nadine, she's willing. I'll be back sometime this afternoon. Annie wanted to wake you and talk about those pink dolphins. I left the cellular phone for you to use. M*

He smiled at the part about the pink dolphins, started to fold the note to keep it, then tore it into shreds and flushed it down the toilet. He called Gerry Young first and reached him at home.

"Young here."

"It's Shep."

"Christ almighty. I've left fourteen million messages on your goddamn answering machine. Where the hell are you?"

Sheppard told him briefly what had happened last night. Young reacted with silence, not a good sign.

"Fuck," he said finally.

"I can think of more appropriate adjectives, Gerry."

"Fuck," he said again. "I'll check with the sheriff's department up in Palm Beach County. In the meantime, let's fly out to Florida Bay to poke around at this pub. Get the directions, Shep."

"Right. And I need to access the DOC computers."

Young reeled off several numbers and codes. When they hung up, Sheppard went into Mira's den to use her computer. A Pentium, equipped to the hilt—CD-ROM drive, scanner, an oversized monitor screen. He figured she wasn't in debt, that she hadn't gone into debt to buy this computer, her car, or anything else. He was damn sure, in fact, that Mira's books balanced and that she would be appalled to know the truth about his financial condition.

But since she was psychic, maybe she already knew the truth about his finances.

He connected his cellular phone to the computer, then called one of the numbers Young had given him. It gave him access to the DOC computer in Tallahassee and the code took him into the heart of the system.

Of the fifty states, only New York, California, and Texas presently had more people in jail than Florida did. But that had not been true in the eighties, when Florida had bounced back and forth between the second and third slots, thanks in large part to the drug trade and the influx of Cubans from the Mariel boatlift. He had a shipload of names to check.

He didn't know whether Bennet's name had double Ns and double Ts or singles of one or both, so he conducted a global search for the various spellings. He narrowed the time frame to ten years—1979 to 1989—and found nearly a hundred Bennets under the different spellings, but no one with a first name of Hal. He requested a list of Bennets who had done time during those years at Manatee Correctional and that narrowed the list to six.

Sheppard had no idea what Bennet had done time for or how long a sentence he'd gotten. Short of going into each file, there didn't seem to be any way to narrow the list even further. So he started with the first of the six names, opened the file, began to read.

It was immediately obvious that he wouldn't have to wade through mountains of notes to eliminate a name. This Bennet, for instance, had been only fourteen when he entered the system, which would make him less than thirty now. Sheppard had gotten the impression from Vic that Hal was closer to Vic's own age, older than forty.

Twenty minutes later, he had one possibility simply because the guy fell in the right age group. As soon as he opened the file, he knew he'd found his man. Richard Halbert Bennet had gotten seven years for psychic fraud.

Sheppard downloaded the entire file and requested a mug shot. The face that came up astonished him. At some level he had formulated an idea of how he thought Hal Bennet would look and this didn't fit. This guy could pass for a stockbroker, an attorney, a physician. He looked blessed with the proverbial silver spoon. His face seemed vaguely familiar, but Sheppard couldn't say why.

As he downloaded the mug shot into Mira's computer to print it, he suddenly remembered where he'd seen Bennet's face. He'd been in that group shot taken years ago at Manatee, one of a handful of inmates standing around Rae Steele. A photo from her album.

He printed out the mug shot and studied it as if it might tell him where Bennet had taken Rae. But the photo mocked him, reminded him that Rae Steele had a private life every bit as secretive as her husband's. While Andrew Steele had been consorting with the psi boys, his wife had been holed up periodically in her cabin, screwing her brains out with some other guy.

Did it have any bearing on the investigation? Would it provide any leads to where Bennet had taken her? Sheppard didn't know and because he was sick to death of questions he couldn't answer, he turned his attention to Vic and Ed.

Without their last names, Sheppard knew he would have a tough time tracking them down. Even with the ten-year parameter, he ended up with nearly three hundred names, permutations of Edward and Victor. It would take him days to go through that many files. He left them alone for now and disconnected from the modem. He made three backups of the files, put two of them in separate envelopes and addressed one to his home address and one to Young's house.

He called information in Flamingo, a town in Florida Bay, a punctuation point at the end of the only road that angled through the Everglades National Park. Through a series of electronic menus, he got directions to the pub via channels and waterways that placed it about twelve miles east of Flamingo.

He called Nadine last, to tell her he didn't need a ride, to thank her for offering. He intended for the conversation to be short and sweet, but Nadine had a few things to say.

"I want you to know I blame you for Annie's absence."

"I'm trying to *prevent* a problem, Nadine."

"If that were true, you wouldn't be involving Mira any further in your investigation."

She hung up before he could say another word. Sheppard felt an overpowering need to defend himself and started to call her back. But the bottom line, he thought, was that she was right. He had *not* tried to keep Mira out of this. If anything, he had drawn her into it more deeply every step of the way. He practically had bullied her into reading Steele's home, had asked her to read Rae's secret cabin, and had come to her last night when he should have gone to Young's place or home.

He used the hair dryer on the tape again, popped it into the mini recorder on Mira's desk, and hit PLAY. The voices sounded like they had laryngitis, but they were clear enough. He listened to the tape as he waited for the captain to arrive, his eyes fixed on the printout of Hal Bennet's mug shot.

Fletcher spotted Hood's white van, parked just outside of Sheppard's complex, in the shade of a tremendous banyan tree. Fletcher pulled alongside and Hood stuck his head out the window. Bits of the gooey pastry he held in one hand clung to the corners of his mouth. Fletcher hoped that Sheppard had a comparable fatso in his life.

"No sign of him yet," Hood said. "And I've been here since four this morning. His car's not there, either."

"I'm going in. If you see his car, use the radio. I'll have mine on."

He nodded, popped the rest of the pastry in his mouth, and raised his window again.

An eight-foot wall surrounded the complex like a little Jericho. The security guard in the guardhouse looked so far past his prime he probably couldn't remember his prime.

She stopped at the gate and lowered her window as the old guy stepped up to the car. "Morning," she said.

"Morning, ma'am. Who you visiting?"

"Actually, I'm not visiting anyone." She flashed her badge, echoes of last night on the bridge. "I'll be talking to some people here in the complex. I'd appreciate it if you would keep this to yourself."

His eyes lit up as if this was the most exciting thing that had happened to him in fifty years. "Sure thing, ma'am. You go on through."

He raised the guardrail and she drove into the complex. She parked on the far side of the pool and clubhouse, where her car wouldn't be visible to the guard. She slipped her radio out of her purse, tuned it to the channel she and Hood used, and said, "Testing, Jim. You read? Over."

"Loud and clear. Over and out."

She reached into the glove compartment for a small tool pouch and a pair of latex gloves, put them in her purse. If Sheppard wanted to play with the big boys, she thought, he would have to pay the price.

The empty parking spaces in front of his building told her that her timing couldn't be better. Just about everyone had left for work. The courtyard in the center of the four-story building exploded with tropical plants. The foliage shielded her from the windows on the opposite side of the courtyard, but not from the apartments in the connecting corridor. That could be a problem.

She walked around to the side of the building, where each of the apartments had a small balcony. Thick ficus hedges separated the apartments from each other and provided ample privacy on either side. Several porches, including Sheppard's, boasted tall hedges at the front. She would be virtually invisible behind that wall of green.

Fletcher darted to Sheppard's gate, unlatched it, slipped inside. Sliding glass door, a window on either side. The door would be her best bet. The locks on these suckers usually turned out to be substandard, one of the ways developers cut costs. She worked the gloves over her fingers, got out the tool pouch, selected a nifty little pick that a locksmith in Virginia had made for her.

If you're caught, Lenora, you'll be in very deep shit.

And if Sheppard got to Hal first, she would be in even deeper shit.

How much did Indrio tell you, Sheppard?

Christ oh Christ.

It took her fifteen seconds to spring the lock and another

thirty seconds to knock loose the steel peg at the top of the door. Then she slipped inside.

The light on the answering machine blinked steadily, the digital counter read 13. If nothing else, she would get some idea of when Sheppard had last been home. She punched the PLAY button. An electronic voice announced the date and the time of each call. The first four, hang-ups, had come through between seven and midnight last night. But after that it got more interesting.

At 12:37 A.M., Captain Young had left a brief, cryptic message: *"Waiting to hear from you, Shep. Call me as soon as you get in."* He'd called again at two, three, five, and at six-thirty this morning. If Sheppard hadn't been here when the first hang-up had come through, it meant he'd been gone since at least seven last night.

Fletcher turned up the volume on the machine so she would be able to hear it as she searched the place. Shelves lined the hallway, all of them crammed with miniature figurines made of clay and ceramics. They looked old, fragile, authentic, pre-Columbian artifacts from a lost time. Sheppard's treasures, she thought, and slammed her fist against the underside of the top shelf, tilting it. The figurines tumbled to the floor, shattering on impact.

Oops, too bad.

She upended another shelf. Then another. Pretty soon, all the lovely icons lay in a shattered heap on the floor. Tough shit, Sheppard.

She grabbed a broom from the pantry and continued into the bedroom. Computer first. She didn't find a file on Steele, but that didn't surprise her. Sheppard had impressed her as the kind of man who either kept the facts in his head or scribbled them in notebooks.

She checked his e-mail: zip. Had he downloaded any files? She went into the directory and perused the space each of the files had taken up. ASCII files generally consumed a lot of space, but nothing stood out. It pissed her off. She hated stupid, local cops.

Clutching the broom near the bottom of the handle, she stepped away from the desk, and swung it at the monitor with the zeal of a kid going after a piñata. The glass exploded and tinkled like wind chimes when it hit the floor, a sweet, satisfying sound. It made her feel so good she whipped through the room, smashing whatever the broom handle struck.

She fell into a mesmerizing rhythm—swing, hit, smash, over and over again. Each swing took her back to the day Hal had left, when he'd walked out of the house and out of her life, gone wherever. She had taken a knife to his things that day, the knife her father had given her on her twelfth birthday. She'd shredded his clothes, his drawings, his paintings, her arm rising and falling, her spirit locked into the rhythm of annihilation.

Cut, slice, kill. Her fever swept her up, lifting her higher and higher until she soared. The room began to bleed. The blood leaked from the corners up near the ceiling, seeped from the baseboards, beaded like sweat on the walls. She could smell it and the odor fueled her fever. Cut. Slice. Kill. More, again, yes—

The phone rang and she whipped the knife upward, severing the line. Then her arm froze where it was, raised straight up like the arm of a clock stuck at midnight. She couldn't remember what she'd been doing, why her arm was raised. Confused, she looked slowly around. This was the house where she lived with Hal. And Hal was gone. He'd walked out on her. That was it, wasn't it?

She had the note right here in her hand. *Can't handle it, babe. Adios.* But when she looked at her hand, her fingers clutched the handle of a knife. Her knife. She dropped her arm to her side, not wanting to look at it. A tidal wave of panic slammed into her and she spun and charged down the hall, through the ruin, to find her purse.

In the bedroom, she dug through the ruin like a dog through garbage and finally pulled her purse out of the mess. She shoved the knife down inside the bag, leaped off the bed, ran for the door.

She had run halfway across the cobbled road when she realized she still wore the latex gloves. She stripped them off, shoved them in her purse, and didn't stop running until she reached her car.

As soon as she got inside, she locked the doors and began to shake. A terrible cold licked at her spine. She needed heat. She had to get the fuck out of here.

Key, ignition, stop shaking, hand, stop shaking. Car moving now, don't go too fast, wave at the old fart . . .

She sped away from the guardhouse and swerved out into the road. When she saw the white van, she heard something shift in her brain, and suddenly she felt better. Not great, not okay, but better.

She waved at Hood as she flew past.

25

At noon, the chopper lifted off the pad at a small county airport. Despite his extensive travels, Sheppard didn't like to fly. But his stomach only lurched once, a compliment to Gerry Young's skill as a pilot. Young held instructor and instrument ratings for four types of planes. But Sheppard trusted his ability because flying was as necessary to Young's survival as traveling was to Sheppard's.

When the Everglades came into view, it looked like a panorama of incredible blues and greens, a vast and mysterious wilderness. Sheppard felt as if they had discovered a new continent, a new world.

The chopper hit rough air, his stomach plunged to his toes, he grabbed onto the edges of the seat. "It's just clear air turbulence," Young said.

Yeah, a silent killer, like cholesterol, Sheppard thought. "Are we almost there?"

"Not much farther. You got that ELF turned on?"

Sheppard patted his shirt pocket. "It's on." And it emitted signals at four to seven cycles per second. He just hoped it was the right frequency.

Young pointed at the dark stains in the distance that floated like oil spills against the breathtaking blue of Florida Bay. "Ames will be there with a boat."

Ames. Yeah, he would believe it when he saw it. He pressed his hand to the nagging ache in his ribs and wished he'd stayed home. No job was worth this shit.

Young had gotten the scoop on last night's explosion and it coincided with what Sheppard had suspected. The driver of the sedan had been killed. But the cops didn't have any idea who he was because they hadn't found the license plate or any I.D. and there wasn't enough left of the body to take prints. No one on the ground had been killed and the driver was believed to have been alone in the car.

Eventually, Sheppard knew, the incident would be written off as one more tragic highway statistic. The only question now was whether Fletcher knew he'd been in the car when it had flown off the bridge.

They landed on a helipad in the tiny town of Flamingo, an outpost comparable to something out of the old West, except that water surrounded it completely. It hardly qualified as an island; it was more like a Pacific atoll, the result of some geological accident.

In the late 1800s, it had been the only settlement in the area, occupied by a few hardy pioneers. Now it was the southernmost headquarters for the Everglades National Park and was still occupied by hardy pioneers. So much for history, Sheppard thought.

Ames waited for them, grinning like a loon as he consumed a bag of sunflower seeds. He cracked the shells incompletely with his teeth, then slobbered as he spat them out. "I was beginning to wonder if you'd make it," he remarked as they climbed down from the chopper.

"Why the hell would you wonder that?" Young shot back, putting him in his place.

"I thought you'd be here earlier," he replied lamely, and didn't have much to say after that.

He'd failed to procure an airboat, Young's first choice, but seemed mighty proud of the puny skiff with the puny outboard that he'd rented. "For Chrissake's, Pete," snapped Young. "The water around here is too shallow for an outboard."

"Not with all the rain we've gotten. The water's close to a foot higher than it should be for this time of year."

They got into the boat, Ames propped his fat ass near the engine, and they chugged off into a wilderness of blue.

As soon as Sheppard glimpsed the Bay Pub, he knew it fit Bennet as a hangout. Surrounded entirely by mangroves and water, the shack looked like it had been slapped together with driftwood and spit. Spidery wooden pilings elevated it from the water. The place seemed as forlorn and frail as some of the centenarians that Willard Scott featured with his weather forecasts.

Ames agreed to wait in the boat while Sheppard and Young went inside. Despite the pub's isolation and the hour of the day, people jammed the place. No stools, no tables—even the open areas along the railing had been claimed. A single, sweeping look told Sheppard everything he wanted to know about the Bay Pub. He had seen hundreds of bars like it in the Caribbean, a harbor for sailors, misfits, and drunks.

He and Young made their way to the end of the bar and ordered two iced teas and a bowl of you-peel-it-shrimp. When the bartender brought their order, Young showed him the computer printout of Bennet's mug shot. "Has this guy been here recently?"

The bartender, a crusty old conch with a white ponytail and starbursts of wrinkles at the corners of his eyes, scowled at the printout as though it were some hideous insect that had dared to crawl across his bar. Then he looked up at Young and Sheppard. "Who's asking?"

"Long lost friends." Young flashed his badge.

The bartender's attitude didn't change, but his scowl vanished. "Yeah, he's been here in the last week."

"Alone?" Sheppard asked.

"Nope. There were two guys with him, one tall and thin, the other bald and big."

Vic and Ed? Sheppard wondered. "How often do they come here?"

"They're not regulars. Sometimes just one shows up, other times there's two, sometimes all three."

"Any idea where they live?" Young asked.

"Nope. Excuse me, I've got thirsty customers. If you're fixing to stick around, there's a table out yonder." He gestured toward the other side of the room, then moved away before either of them could ask him anything else.

The table faced the west dock, where the smaller boats tied up. Ames stood down there, yukking it up with another boater and popping sunflower seeds into his mouth. Beyond him, spits of land trailed through the shimmering waters like a string of dark pearls. The color of the water changed where the bay met the Gulf, a clear line of demarcation, like a border between countries.

"Now what?" Sheppard asked, tracking an airboat that raced into his vision from the north.

"We enjoy our shrimp," Young replied, and plucked out one of the plump little suckers and started peeling.

By the time Hal shoved off, Rae slept peacefully, a drugged sleep brought on by the Darvon he'd sprinkled like an herb in the soup she'd had with lunch.

He hadn't given her as much this time. A mistake, maybe, but he didn't think she would try to escape now, not after last night. For the first time since he'd seen her on the compound lifetimes ago, he believed it was possible that Rae might grow to love him.

But he still had to do something about her son and about Fletcher. Also, the dream he'd had about that spook Evans nagged at him, demanding that he pay attention. He wondered if Steele's murder might have brought Evans here, too.

If Evans had come to Florida in the wake of Steele's murder, then it meant he somehow intended to extract one more impossible task from him, one more goddamn miracle, one more quick death to even some score in the murky world he inhabited. Well, no thanks, Evans.

Three miles from the chickee, he exchanged the canoe for the airboat. Then he sped across the open waters of Florida Bay, headed for the pub. Manacas and Indrio probably had a new half-assed plan about how to finish off Fletcher, but its success would depend on Hal's willingness to go along with it. The Steele plan had depended on that as well, which was how Indrio and Manacas had always worked their best games: get someone else to do the shit work.

He tied up at the pub dock and spotted Manacas standing alone at the railing in a fishing cap and sunglasses, bleached-out jeans and a purple and black batik T-shirt. Style had never been his strong point.

Hal tied up the airboat, trotted up the stairs. "We may have a problem," Manacas said without preface. "Indrio hasn't been home since yesterday afternoon. His girlfriend said he was going up to Lauderdale to meet someone. She figured it was me."

"Where in Lauderdale?"

"I don't know. That's what worries me. Like I told you on the phone, I tailed Fletcher to the Elbo Room the other day. And then Indrio heads off to Lauderdale and doesn't come home. It's the kind of coincidence I don't like, Hal."

Hal laughed and shook his head. "Christ, you're making something out of nothing. There's more to Lauderdale than the Elbo Room. Besides, she was there on Monday. Indrio went up there yesterday."

"Suppose Fletcher knew Indrio was going to be there and was scoping out the place?"

"How the hell would she know that?"

"Christ, who knows. With Fletcher, anything's possible."

"You're worrying about nothing."

Manacas whipped off his shades. The fierceness in his eyes matched what Hal imagined had been there when he'd raped and murdered the woman whose death had put him in prison. "Let's get something straight, man. Anything that involves Fletcher is important. We were ready to help you with Steele. You knew that. The only reason you took care of him yourself was because you wouldn't have been able to nab Steele's wife with us around."

"So what? The bottom line is that you guys got what you wanted without the hazards. I told you I'd help you waste Fletcher, but you can forget the snake bullshit, Ed. You want to kill her, we do it right."

Hal's bluntness seemed to mollify Manacas. He laughed and shook his head. "Same ol' Hal, always going his own way and fuck the rest of us. Let's get something to eat."

As they made their way through the crowd to the west side of the pub, Hal sensed a *wrongness* in the air, something clearly out of whack. But what? He stopped, looked around slowly.

At least a hundred people crowded the pub today, too many for him to get a fix on whatever it was that felt so *wrong*. He flung part of his awareness out over the crowd like a net, but a loud, irritating babble filled his skull, a buzzing human static that made his head pound. He dismissed the *wrongness* as paranoia.

But as he hurried after Manacas, the skin at the back of his neck prickled and itched. He couldn't shake the bad feeling in the pit of his stomach.

Sheppard crossed the pub, headed for the rest room, when a waitress with a pitcher of beer bumped into him. Beer spilled down the front of his shirt; he leaped back and she rushed forward, thrusting napkins at him, apologizing.

The crowd parted like the Red Sea to accommodate them, a corridor lined by legs and shoes. At the end of it sat two men who looked like a couple of tourists whiling away the afternoon until they sailed off into a tequila sunset.

But at precisely the moment that Sheppard saw them, the larger of the two men removed his fishing cap, exposing the pale curve of his bald head and a face that belonged to Kojak. Sheppard's heart literally leaped into his throat; he hastened back to Young.

"Kojak's here with Bennet," he said softly, tilting his head toward them. "Table at the railing, in the corner. Bennet's mine."

Young stood. "I'll circle and come up behind Kojak."

They moved into the crowd. Floodgates had slammed open inside of Sheppard, adrenaline coursed through him, a metallic taste coated his tongue. His muscles had tightened like cords, his body literally hummed. He could see the back of the other man's head now, the pale hairs that curled against his neck.

The attack lasts about thirty seconds to a minute. If it continues for another three to five minutes, you begin to bleed internally. Or maybe your intestines rupture. Vic's words swarmed inside of him like angry bees; he slipped the ELF out of his shirt pocket, clipped it to his belt.

Sheppard saw the man's hand, kneading the muscles in the back of his neck. He stood close enough to see the freckles on the back of Bennet's hand.

This one's for Mira, fucker.

The man's head snapped around, almost as if he heard Sheppard's thought, and suddenly everything assumed a weird, hallucinogenic quality. The noise in the pub dimmed to a dull, pounding ache in his ears, his peripheral vision melted away, his arm rose too slowly, as if trapped in molasses. Then the inside of his skull went ballistic. Bright, blinding explosions of light seared through the depths of his brain, short-circuited synapses, and scorched a pathway to the very center of pain.

Wrong frequency, wrong wrong wrong.

This thought slammed through his head with a pain so extreme that language alone could never describe it. Beyond migraine, beyond agony, beyond torture, beyond anything he had ever experienced or imagined. It drove him, shrieking, to his knees, his arms wrapped around his head, his reasoning mind wiped out.

Instinct seized him. He rolled to put distance between himself and Bennet. But panic had broken out in the pub and people scrambled over him. He couldn't reach the ELF to adjust the frequency, the pain was too extreme. Blood poured out of his nose. The horror in his skull had stolen most of his vision. He raised up on his hands and knees and shook his head like some wild, wounded animal, trying to clear his vision, vanquish the agony, trying to breathe.

Someone yanked him to his feet and he swayed, the pub tilting to one side, people slamming into him from behind. Then, just like that, the pain snapped away from him, he could see again, and thought poured back into his head. He spun, searching the frantic, undulating sea of faces for Bennet, the bald man, Young.

He must have looked like some wild primitive, blood staining his face and the front of the shirt, because people leaped out of his way. He made it to the railing and glimpsed Bennet charging down the east dock, where the airboats and larger vessels were tied. Sheppard vaulted over the railing and moved, hand over hand, along the outer edge so he wouldn't have to fight the panicked crowd.

He jumped the final yard, his ribs squealing, and landed on

his feet like a cat. He tore straight down the middle of the dock, shoving people out of his way. Bennet had leaped onto an airboat when Sheppard tackled him from behind. He fell face forward into the water, taking Sheppard with him.

They sank, locked together like mismatched lovers. Sheppard was taller and weighed more than Bennet, but Bennet was faster and imbued with the shocking strength of a man desperate to remain free. His knee sank into Sheppard's groin, air rushed from Sheppard's lungs, his hands slipped, and Bennet shot away from him.

When Sheppard's head broke through the surface, the roar of the airboat's engine deafened him. It sped away from the dock, spewing a curtain of water behind it, racing ahead of the other boats that were fleeing the chaos.

Sheppard made it to the dock, heaved himself over the side, and couldn't get up. Whatever reserves of energy he'd been drawing on were now exhausted. His head felt like it might lift off his shoulders in the next breath of wind. He just lay there, watching the airboat as it shrank to a pinprick of glinting metal in the distance.

Hal didn't slow down until he reached the mangroves where he'd hidden his canoe. He pulled into the dense shadows beneath the sagging branches and killed the engine. Fast, he thought, got to move fast. He expected to hear the chatter of a helicopter within minutes and he wanted to be hidden deep in the maze of channels by then.

He paused long enough to cover the airboat with a dull green tarp and tossed fallen branches over it. Then he threw his pack into the canoe, shoved off, and leaped inside. He paddled hard and fast, a man possessed by the demons of his past. Manacas, Indrio, Fletcher, Steele, the names charged through him, screeching like a pack of hyenas.

Several times he heard a chopper sweeping in low over the mangroves. Its shadow seemed to fall across the water and trees like some mythical cloud of doom. He couldn't be sure it belonged to the cops, but he wasn't about to risk being seen. It chilled him to think how close he'd come to being caught.

The only thing they knew was that he'd headed north. Even if they'd caught Manacas, he couldn't tell them where Hal lived because he didn't know. He had the number for Hal's cellular phone, but that wouldn't be of much use to them once he ditched it. For now, he was safe.

And tomorrow? Would he still be safe tomorrow?

When he'd *reached* into Sheppard, in the moment or two before he had begun to squeeze, he'd found Indrio's face floating in a sea of other confusing, disconnected images. Now he pulled those images closer and scrutinized them, chewed at them, and started to piece them together.

He likened it to sketching, a slow act of creation, except that it wasn't done in any particular sequence. It was nothing as simple as the shape of the face, the beauty of an eye, the perfection of a mouth. It hurt to scoop the information out of himself, hurt when he understood that the image of the exploding car was how Indrio had ended up, hurt most of all because he knew that Indrio had betrayed him.

But it didn't surprise him.

How much had he told Sheppard? Enough, at any rate, so that Sheppard knew about the Bay Pub.

What else did you tell him, you fucking creep? About Rae? Did you tell him about her?

Sure, why not? Why would he withhold something like that? Indrio's point had been to give Sheppard enough to track him down. All this because he'd taken Rae when the only thing he was supposed to be doing was killing Steele. Indrio hadn't trusted him since he'd turned down his girlfriend's offer for a new identity all those years ago and went his own way.

If he was caught this time, they would throw away the fucking key. He would get the chair. But first they would have to catch him. Indrio the creep got what he deserved.

And so, Hal thought, would he.

26

Her eyes opened into a hazy, ephemeral light. Death, she thought, and wondered when someone would appear. Her father, perhaps. Or her grandmother. She'd read those books, seen those people on *Oprah*.

But she heard the soft intake of her breath and when she blinked, she felt the movement of the muscles. Then the air snapped into astonishing clarity and she saw the bands of afternoon light falling through the slats in the wooden shutters.

The chickee, not death, not yet, no matter how much her traitorous body wished it.

"Hal?" Her voice shot off into the stifling room, a probe seeking the presence of another body. It found only emptiness.

He had drugged her again, but hadn't given her as much this time. Or maybe it had been a different drug, milder. She had vague memories of waking, of wandering out to the Jiffy John, of sipping water, of corn flakes floating in powdered milk and water. The drug had brought on the thick, crippling lethargy that she hadn't been able to shake off earlier. But the sex had made her lazy, sated. Good sex did that to her.

She knew he had left and since he hadn't shackled or restrained her in any way, she got to her feet. She didn't have any idea where he'd gone or how long he would be away, but she intended to make good use of his absence. She'd gotten what she wanted: time.

Rae threw open one of the shutters to admit fresh air, but didn't open all of them. He would be alert for something like that, for some change from the way he'd left things when he'd split.

She realized, suddenly, that she didn't hear the generator. As far as she knew it hadn't been turned off since he'd brought her here. Maybe he'd done it to preserve fuel. Why keep it running with him gone and her dead to the world and all the perishable foods used up? Logical, certainly. But she doubted it was the only reason.

If nothing else, Rae had learned that Hal always had multiple motives for doing something. So when she found his note in the kitchen, explaining that he'd gone into town for supplies, she knew it wasn't the only purpose for the trip.

The real question, the only one that mattered, concerned time—how much of it she had and how much of it she needed to escape.

Rae took a quick shower, changed clothes, brushed her teeth. These acts humanized her, cleared her mind, and washed away the remnants of Hal's touch. That most of all.

Afterward, she walked out to the edge of the platform. Fish jumped in the lagoon, she didn't see the gator. The skiff was gone. She couldn't swim to the mangroves, so she would have to find some other way off the chickee.

Rae found a backpack in the kitchen and stuffed it with things she would need. Then she headed into Hal's locked room, the backpack slung over her shoulder. He'd apparently had other things on his mind when he'd left; he'd neglected to snap the padlock. She turned the knob, but didn't push the door open.

The right to privacy had been so ingrained in her that even under these conditions she hesitated violating it. Although she had searched Andy's things several times in ten years—his desk, his bureau, his files—she had always felt guilty afterward. And if she entered this room, would Hal sense it?

She nudged the door open with her toes. It swung inward, creaking. She stepped inside, her eyes skipping across the hand-made furniture, the TV, the braided throw rug, the shelves crammed with videotapes. He'd taken the cellular phone, but who would she have called? The cops? Hell, she didn't even know where she was. Andy? *Hi, hon. I got laid last night and came so many times I lost count.*

She moved farther into the room and began pulling the tapes

out at random, one here, another there. She checked the labels, not entirely certain what she sought, but equally certain she would recognize it when she saw it.

He'd arranged the movies alphabetically by titles, except on the bottom shelf, where several dozen movies had been grouped together. Rae recognized some of the titles—*Resurrection, Poltergeist, The Dead Zone, The Fury, Siesta, Carrie.* Psychic phenomena movies, she thought.

Maybe Hal had an unwritten script inside him that he was acting out, maybe that was what this was all about. Or maybe these events she had been living were scenes from a movie that already existed.

Psychic mutant abducts wife of prominent psychiatrist, imprisons her in Everglades, breaks down her resistance, makes love to her.

National Enquirer stuff. What seemed more likely was that, consciously or unconsciously, Hal had adapted scenes from any number of movies and put his own twist on them. Rae might be Patty Hearst, Hal could be the telekinetic freak in *The Fury.* The most vital point to her own well-being centered around what he envisioned for the two of them.

The only inkling she'd gotten about his future plans was a remark he'd made last night, while they lay in the dark, whispering back and forth. *If you could live anywhere in the world, where would it be, Rae?*

The mountains. Colorado, the Andes, the Himalayas, it wouldn't matter as long as it's high. What about you?

The same.

She shook the memory away; her fingers moved more quickly through the videos.

Next to the psychic films, she found several labeled only with numbers. She slipped them out of their boxes, saw that the tapes hadn't been labeled, either, and knew she'd found what she was looking for. Rae hurried back into the kitchen to start the generator.

A few minutes later, she returned to the den, shut the door. She selected tape #1, popped it into the VCR, turned on the TV. A home movie. The camera zoomed in on a woman in a bikini, sunbathing by a swimming pool. Hal's voice, off camera, said,

"And here's Lenora Fletcher, grabbing some sun. Smile for the camera, Lenora."

She shot him the bird and Hal laughed, zooming in on her belly button and the finger of his own hand inscribing circles around it. Then his finger slipped inside the waistband of her bikini. "Cut it out, Bennet," she snapped, but didn't slap his hand away.

"C'mon now, babe, just one little smile." The camera moved to her face; she stuck her tongue out at him. "Got to do better than that." And the camera moved back to the bottom of her suit, his hand now moving inside of it, burrowing between her thighs like a small rodent.

Fletcher's thighs opened wider and her hand came down over his, covering it, guiding it, her hips moving against the pressure until Rae could hear her rapid breathing. Then the camera tilted, static filled the screen.

Rae fast-forwarded the tape, hit PLAY again. The sight of herself and her son on the screen stunned her. They held hands and walked into a playground near the house. Her flesh literally crawled as she kept watching.

There: herself and Carl strolling past shops in downtown Lauderdale, romping in the surf, feeding seagulls, leaving the day care center. And there, she and Carl were having a picnic one afternoon several months ago at a park in Palm Beach County.

Dear God. To know that he had followed her and watched her was one thing. But this made her feel as though her life had been invaded, violated in the most intimate way.

She watched the tape to the end, certain she would see a shot of the cabin, of the secrets she'd lived there six or seven months ago. Her heart twisted at the thought. *I ended it because I was afraid Andy would find out, that he would divorce me and sue for custody of Carl.* Now look at her.

By now, her ex-lover certainly knew she was gone. What did he believe had happened? Had he gone to the cabin, perhaps thinking she had fled there?

Rae rewound the tape, popped in another, a news broadcast from a Fort Lauderdale station, something the satellite dish made possible. A minute or so into the broadcast, Andy's photo flashed on the screen and Rae hiked up the volume. ". . . body of Andrew Steele, a prominent Fort Lauderdale psychiatrist, was found Friday morning by the family housekeeper. His four-year-old son is in a coma . . ."

Blood rushed into her head, pounded in her ears. She watched in stupefied horror until the tape ended and snow filled the screen. A thick, terrible sound suffused the room, a moan of exquisite pain. It was coming from her.

She felt filthy, defiled, violated. She stumbled to her feet and tore at her clothes as she ran for the shower. *Water, soap, oh God what have I done . . .* Rae stood under the tepid spray for a long time, sobbing, scrubbing herself furiously, until she no longer felt the phantom touch of his hands, his mouth, until she'd been emptied.

Then something cold and bright clamped down over her, an unnatural calm. It was as if she had been injected with a massive dose of a painkiller; she was aware that her emotions clamored deep inside of her, but they no longer seemed to be a part of her.

She put on clean clothes, returned to the den to put the tapes back in order, and left the padlock exactly as she'd found it.

She needed a weapon. Kitchen, she thought. Surely there would be something in the kitchen that would serve as a weapon. But from the beginning, Hal had used only plastic utensils, paper plates and cups. No metal knives. The pots and pans were iron, but too cumbersome. She needed something smaller, something she could hide in her clothes.

She searched the pantry, his belongings, the cabinets. She pulled a chair into the main room of the chickee and checked the spaces in the corners up near the ceiling. Too obvious. Hal would be innovative, particularly if he were hiding something potentially lethal. He would choose a spot that she would be afraid of searching.

Water.

She ran out to the platform, to the ladder. She scanned the lagoon first and spotted Big Guy out near the mangroves. Far enough away, she decided, and dropped her legs over the side of the platform. She climbed down to the third rung, stretched her arm between the rungs and shone the beam around. Her heart leaped ecstatically. There, tied to a beam and resting against one of the horizontal planks, was a dark drawstring bag. But she couldn't reach it from here. Rae ducked her head under the platform and swung around to the other side of the ladder. She hooked her left arm between the rungs and reached with her right. Her fingers brushed the bag, but she still couldn't grab it. She had to get closer.

She positioned both feet on the bottom rung, the water lapping at her heels, grasped a higher rung with her left hand, and stretched. She stretched until the muscles in her arm felt as though they were tearing away from the bone. Her fingers closed around the bag, she yanked hard, the string snapped, she grasped it.

Suddenly, she heard wild splashing behind her and her head snapped around. The gator sped toward her with all the precision of a missile, its tail thrashing, jaws opening. Rae swung around to the front of the ladder, scrambled to the top, and hurled herself onto the platform. She lay there gasping for air, blood thundering in her ears.

She still hadn't moved when the gator's massive tail slammed against one of the vertical wooden posts that elevated the chickee from the water. The entire structure shuddered, trembled, swayed. Rae leaped up and ran into the kitchen. Feed the fucker, she thought, and opened two cans of beans. She ran back out to the edge of the platform and tossed the cans into the water.

Rae backed away from the edge and loped back into the kitchen. She emptied the contents of the drawstring bag on the table and pawed through her treasure. Screwdrivers, pliers, fishing line, hooks, nails, a small hammer.

Which will hurt him?

Hurt him? Who the hell was she kidding? If she could hurt Hal, then she had to be prepared to kill him. Because if she didn't, he would kill her. He would *reach* so far inside of her nothing would be left when he finished.

She picked the longest nail, which measured about half the length of her index finger. It wouldn't do much damage unless she hit him in the eye. Forget the nail. The hooks were too small to be of any use. She might be able to strangle him with the fishing line, but she wouldn't bet the farm on it.

Screwdriver, then. Flat-edge or Philips?

Philips. It was longer, it had a better grip, and the end, though rounded, seemed more likely to penetrate skin than a flat-edge. But where on the body? The base of the neck? The crotch? Maybe just a hard, driving blow to his spine would do it. Would he sense what she had done as he approached the chickee? Would he be ready for her when he docked? Would he squeeze and squeeze . . .

She would use the mental room again. It had kept her true feelings away from him last night, otherwise he wouldn't have left her unrestrained.

Rae found a comfortable spot on the platform, sat down Indian-style, shut her eyes. Piece by mental piece, she constructed her magical room, her refuge. She fine-tuned the image, embellished it. Then she put her secrets inside of it and encased it in steel and cement, sealing the room completely.

"I want to call my attorney," Manacas shouted, beating his fists on the glass of the one-way window.

Sheppard glanced at Young, seated next to him. The captain puffed on his cigar and blew a smoke ring at the glass. "The fucker really does resemble Kojak. How long has he been in there?"

Sheppard glanced at the clock on the wall. "Eighteen minutes."

"Long enough. Let's see what we can find out before Fletcher gets here."

"Fletcher? Why the hell did you call her?"

Young finally looked away from Manacas. "I haven't called her yet. But officially, the feds are still in charge of the investigation, Shep. I've got to call her or pay the fucking price."

"Give me fifteen minutes."

Sheppard pushed to his feet, his body aching from his confrontation with Bennet, and went into the holding tank next door. Manacas paced like a caged beast. "So what's your lawyer's name?" Sheppard asked.

Manacas glanced at him. "I can't remember. I need a phone book."

"He probably knows you as Nick Laker. That *is* the name you're going by now, isn't it, Mr. Manacas?"

"I did my time, I got paroled," Manacas said hotly. "And there I was, having a beer with some guy I'd met and suddenly that other cop's got me in a necklock." He stabbed a finger at Sheppard. "You guys fucked up, not me."

"You were with a suspected murderer, Manacas."

"I just met the guy, for Christ's sakes. We were having a beer."

"Richard Halbert Bennet did time for fraud. You two were participants in a project called Delphi. He was their star teleki-netic, you were their remote viewer, and Vic was their telepath. Does that ring any bells, Manacas?"

Manacas looked as if he had swallowed his tongue. His expression made it clear he suddenly realized his future and his freedom might vanish faster than the Brazilian rain forest. "I, uh, we . . ." he stammered.

"Let's cut the bullshit. Either you talk to me or you talk to Lenora Fletcher. Take your pick."

He paled visibly. "Who?"

Sheppard lost his temper. "Get Fletcher on the phone, Gerry," he called. "And give us audio in here so our friend Manacas can hear the conversation."

Young's face came through the mike. "Got it."

The noise of electronic dialing filled the room, a tape recording. But Manacas didn't know that. He ran over to the glass and banged his fists against it again. "Hey, hold on a minute!"

The noise stopped. "Found your memory?" Sheppard asked.

Manacas whirled around, his face bright red, a vein throbbing at his temple. "Bernet killed Steele and nabbed his wife. He's got her in the Glades, he lives out there somewhere, that's all I know."

"Oh, c'mon," Sheppard said. "You were Delphi's star remote viewer. If anyone knows where Bennet is hiding, it's you, Manacas."

Manacas squirmed inside his shirt, as if it were too small for him. When he spoke, it was obvious he didn't know how much to say because he didn't have any idea how much or how little Sheppard knew. "I never . . . I mean, I, uh . . . Christ. I never tried to find him. I didn't want to know."

"How often have you seen Bennet in the last few years?" Young's voice boomed over the mike.

"A beer, dinner, nothing regular. That's not against the law. He didn't tell me about Steele and Rae until today. He's nuts, man, totally fucked."

Sheppard detested liars. "I hear from Vic that you guys planned all along to knock Steele off."

Something tragic happened to Manacas's face. His jowls sagged, the corners of his mouth plunged, disbelief swept through his eyes. "Indrio?" He whispered it.

"Who?" Sheppard mocked him.

"But *why?*"

"Because his heart wasn't in it, Eddie. The past was dead for him. And he didn't trust Bennet."

"Then it's true. He's dead. I knew it. I knew the bastard was dead." He whispered these words, too, his voice crackling with emotion.

"Why did you go to the bookstore for a reading?" Sheppard asked.

Manacas rubbed his hands over his face, then sat back, his hands dropping to the table. He looked resigned now, defeated, exactly where Sheppard wanted him.

"We thought we should check out the psychic, see whether we needed to worry about her. I shoulda told Hal to do it."

For the space of several seconds, his eyes glazed over. Sheppard felt a distinct and sudden emptiness in the room, as if Manacas had stepped out for a smoke, leaving his body behind. He snapped back just as abruptly, dropped his body into the chair, and said, "I can help you. But in return, I want your word that you won't turn me over to Fletcher."

Sheppard started to reply, but Young beat him to it, his disembodied voice filling the room. "Let's see what you've got first, Manacas. Then we'll talk about deals."

Manacas obviously wanted more. But Sheppard suspected his fear of the alternative— of being turned over to Fletcher— would convince him to cooperate. "I need paper and a pencil."

Sheppard tore out sheets from his notebook and handed Manacas a pen. He jotted down a cell phone number and stared at it, his lips moving as he repeated it silently to himself. "In the old days, Steele used random numbers for a particular target. I don't know why, but it acts like an e-mail address for whoever's given the numbers."

"That's a cell phone number," Sheppard said, sitting across from him.

Manacas nodded. "Hal's. It's probably useless as a phone number now, but it might work for my purposes."

Then he fell silent, his eyes glazed over again, and he began to sketch, slowly at first, then picking up speed. When he finished, he'd filled three sheets, front and back. He had numbered each one and handed them to Sheppard in order. "He's living in some sort of structure that's elevated out of the water. I'm picking up a lot of water and not just because it's in the Glades. It's like it's . . . I don't know . . ." He shook his head. "Surrounded by water? Yeah, surrounded. That feels right."

"The Glades is pretty goddamn big, Manacas. You've got to do better than that," Sheppard said.

Manacas slapped down the next sheet of paper. "A trail. A canoe trail through the mangroves. That's what this is." He stabbed his finger at the sketch. "Bay, I kept picking up the word bay, I don't know what it means. But the trail leads to it."

"And what you've drawn here is a map?"

"Yes, but the way I see things and the way they exist when you're there differ somewhat."

Sheppard studied the sheet and pointed at a series of squares and rectangles. "What're these things?"

"They have numbers on them, going from low to high. I think they're mile markers. The trails out there have mile markers."

"You know that from drinking at the pub."

"Look, I'm not the wilderness freak that Hal is. I don't go canoeing around in there. I get to the pub by airboat, a straight shot from Flamingo."

The door to the interrogation room slammed open and Young hurried in. He dropped a map of the Everglades in front of Manacas and leaned into his face. "You want protection from Fletcher? Then make it worth my while to put my ass on the line for you." Young's fist slammed down over the map; his voice reached a fever pitch. "There's Florida Bay and there's Hell's Bay, Eddie. Which bay is it, asshole? You're supposed to be one of the best."

"Jesus, man, take it easy." Sheppard grabbed Young's arm and pulled him back.

Young wrenched his arm free of Sheppard's grasp, his face still livid. He blinked hard several times and stepped back from Manacas, aware that he'd lost it.

"I'm doing the best I can," Manacas said quietly.

"It's not good enough," Young snapped.

Manacas's eyes glazed over once more. He picked up the pencil, made another sketch. "I'm not getting a name, but there's a large hammock of trees near the entrance to this place, where you put the canoe in. That's all I'm getting."

"Is Hal there now?" Young asked.

"I didn't pick up anything psychically. But after what happened today at the pub, I doubt it."

Young stared at him a moment longer, then asked Sheppard to step outside with him. When they were in the hall, he said, "What do you think? Is this all bullshit?"

"He was definitely tuning in on something," Sheppard replied. "But he's also a liar. It's your call."

Young thought about it, but not for long. "We keep him a day or two, while we check out his maps or whatever the hell they are. We'll go in tomorrow at first light."

"What about Fletcher?"

"I'll tell her we caught him, then lost him and Bennet. He'll be in protective custody for forty-eight hours."

"You're putting our collective ass on the line, Gerry."

"Only until we know for sure. If nothing comes of it, we turn him over to Fletcher and good fucking riddance."

27

The turnout for the fair that evening surpassed Mira's expectations. The unofficial count so far stood at about fifty thousand, many of them in costume. She felt the turnout boded well for the success of the fair over the course of the Halloween weekend.

The only problem seemed to be at One World's booth. Since five that afternoon, when she'd returned from dropping Annie in Miami, she and Nadine had been reading almost nonstop for customers. She didn't think they would be able to sustain this same pace tomorrow, when the crowd would be double or triple what it was tonight.

"Annie would enjoy this," Nadine remarked during a temporary lull in customers.

Mira agreed, but she didn't want to talk about Annie. She knew it would lead back to an earlier disagreement, when Nadine bluntly expressed her contempt for Mira's decision to take Annie to Miami for the weekend.

"I hope she'll at least get to go trick-or-treating down there," Nadine went on.

"Tom's family is taking about twenty kids trick-or-treating, Nadine. Don't worry about it."

"You're missing the point."

Mira rolled her eyes.

"You gave in to your fear, Mira, which means you'll attract reasons to be afraid." With that, she pushed to her feet and announced she needed to eat. "What can I get you?"

"A slice of veggie quiche."

Nadine nodded and walked off. Mira reached under the table

for her cell phone. She hadn't heard yet from Sheppard and felt uneasy about it, uneasy in a vague, nonpsychic way. She started to punch out his number when two people in costumes and masks stopped at the table. The man, dressed like Zorro and wearing a mask, seemed much older than the woman. He said, "We'd like readings."

"I'm working the booth alone right now. One of you will have to wait."

"That's fine. How much?"

"Twenty for fifteen minutes."

He handed her a twenty, gestured to the woman, and they ducked under the canvas awning. They sat down at the small, circular table where Mira had been doing her readings. She picked up a deck of tarot cards, set them in front of the man, and he cut them without her asking him to. She fanned them out. "Pick six."

He selected his cards quickly; she noticed that his hand trembled and wondered if he was ill or just nervous. Almost immediately, she felt a vague pain in her groin and suddenly knew the man had prostrate cancer. She also realized the woman's silence irritated her. Dressed like a witch, she wore a full mask and a black cloak that covered her from the thighs up.

Mira placed his cards in a straight line, two for the past, two more for the present, and the last two for the future. But when she turned them over, she didn't know what to say. Nothing good appeared in these cards.

"Christ," the man laughed. "That doesn't look too promising."

"You need to take better care of yourself," Mira began, then something inside her clicked into place and she slid The Hanged Man out of the spread. "This man may present a danger to you. He . . ."

"In what way?" the woman asked.

Mira raised her eyes, looked at the woman, then reached out and pulled her mask down. Lenora Fletcher just smiled and lifted the mask off her head. "So they caught Manacas and lost him. Detective Sheppard tangled with Bennet and lost him, too. But I suppose you haven't heard any of that."

"Why should I? I'm not a cop."

Fletcher leaned across the table. "When you speak to Mr. Sheppard, do tell him that if he's interfering in a federal investigation, I'll make sure he gets nailed for it." With that, she got up. "Let's go, Rich."

The man had tilted his mask up, revealing small, pale eyes and a sharp nose. "Tell me what danger this man presents to me," he said, pointing at The Hanged Man.

"He fulfills your expectations." Mira didn't know what the hell that meant. But he apparently knew, because he simply smiled, thanked her, and followed Fletcher out into the noisy crowd.

"Maybe it's time to hang it up," Evans said.

"I can't do that." Fletcher hooked her arm through his as they made their way through the street fair crowd. "I'd be admitting that Hal won."

Evans gave her arm a squeeze and she realized she'd just passed one of his little tests of fortitude or resilience or some goddamn thing. "Exactly," he replied. "What's good about the situation is that the local cops have done the hard work. They've flushed Hal out of the Everglades."

"Or driven him deeper inside of it."

"I don't think so. Even in the old days, Hal could be pushed only so far. He'll be spooked now, ready to run. And he'll do it with or without Rae."

"So what're you suggesting?"

"That he's going to finish what he started. You and Steele were his primary targets. Steele's dead. I think he's going to come after you now and that you need to be ready."

Fletcher hated to admit it, but she felt he might be right. "What do you have in mind, Rich?"

"A plan," he replied.

Sheppard felt like the old man in the nursery rhyme, the guy who just wanted to fall into bed and pull a blanket over his head and not wake up till morning. But he still needed to pack the gear they would need in the morning. He also wanted to study the sketches Manacas had made and compare them to a map of the Glades. Then, if he still had the ability to move, he intended to drop by Mira's and repay the money he'd borrowed.

He entered the dimly lit courtyard of his building, where most of the windows had been opened to the cool night air. He heard televisions, kids, the sounds of family life. A part of him envied his neighbors. A week ago, his biggest worry had been losing his job; now he worried that he if he had another run-in with Bennet, he wouldn't survive it.

He unlocked the door, turned on the hallway light, stepped inside, and stopped dead. His living room looked as if it had been torn apart by dinosaurs on a rampage. The couch cushions had been shredded, foam leaked from them, feathers littered the floor. Books were strewn everywhere, covers ripped off, pages ripped out. The answering machine had been destroyed, the phone wire cut. The Guatemalan *huipiles* that had hung on the wall had been reduced to ragged strips of colorful cloth. And that was only the living room.

It got worse in the hall, where his artifact collection lay in a crumbled ruin on the floor, the sun god from Peru, the masks from Colombia, the icons from Ecuador. His bedroom was uninhabitable, the mattress sliced open, lamps broken, his computer monitor reduced to a gaping hole with glass strewn around it.

Sheppard sank to the corner of the mattress, trying to compute the damage in dollars and cents. He had insurance, but not enough to compensate for all this. Rage smoldered inside of him and he shot to his feet and returned to the living room. He found the spot where the sliding glass door had been jimmied. But so what? What the hell did it tell him? Not a name, not a face, nothing immediate.

Sheppard slammed the door shut, took one sweeping look around the room, and dug out his cell phone. Young answered on the second ring.

"It's me," Sheppard said. "I'll be ready to leave in two hours."

"I was just about to call you to suggest the same thing."

"Should we take a chopper?"

"I don't know. There's a storm moving this way. The seaplane might be better. We'll play it by ear."

"I think we should try Hell's Bay first."

"Then with luck, we'll launch the canoe by midnight at the latest. We may not get far in the dark, but at least we'll be there."

"See you then."

"Hey, Shep?"

"Yeah?"

"Why the sudden rush?"

Sheppard looked slowly around the room again. "I'll explain when I see you."

Rae never saw the airboat, but she heard it, the roar of its engine like bursts of gunfire that filled the silence between rolls of thunder. She could almost see it in her mind, skimming the surface of the water like some primitive beast with wire mesh wings. The airplane engine at its rear propelled it forward at speeds up to a hundred miles an hour. Park ranger? A fisherman? Tourists? Or Hal?

No, it couldn't be Hal. He didn't have an airboat, did he? The only boat she'd seen was the canoe, tethered to the ladder, bobbing in the water without its paddles because he had hidden them.

Hidden them so I couldn't escape.

Well, guess what, Hal. She didn't need the goddamn paddles to get out of here. She had the screwdriver.

Just in case the airboat belonged to Hal, she moved quickly around the main room in the chickee, closing the shutters. The smell of impending rain filled the air and the stink of her fear trailed closely behind it.

Fear he would sense.

As she closed the last shutter, she glimpsed the sagging dark clouds that hung over the mangrove like some Biblical sign of doom.

She stopped next in the kitchen, where she turned off the generator and switched on her flashlight. Her eyes swept through the room, making sure nothing was out of place. The table, set for two, held an unlit candle and cheap plastic placemats marking his place and hers. He would see it as soon as he entered the kitchen and believe that she had planned a homecoming for him.

Should she lock the padlock on the den door? Or had he left it that way as a test?

Leave it. You're ready.

As ready as she would ever be for this.

Rae rushed back into the main room of the chickee, shut the door, and realized she no longer heard the airboat. Had it passed? Had the driver turned off the engine? *What?*

She strained to hear something beyond the shutters, some small sound that would tell her for sure he was headed this way. Thunder sounded, drumrolls that got louder and closer with every second.

He would be using a flashlight when he came in here and would see the futon. She'd covered it with a blanket and stuffed clothes and a pillow under it. She just hoped it would look like a body to him.

Will any of this fool him?

A sour lump of fear slithered up her throat, a wave of cold washed across her back. Her resolve nearly deserted her. *I can't fight someone like Hal, I can't I can't . . .*

You will, whispered the voice of reason. *You don't have a choice.*

Rae moved the futon closer to the window, so the beam of his flashlight wouldn't strike it directly when Hal opened the door. Then she scurried into the shadows to the left of it, where she would be hidden by the door when he walked in. And there, heart beating wildly, the screwdriver clutched in her hand, she stood with her back to the wall and waited.

Almost immediately, the fearful part of her hurled *what if's* at her. What if he sensed something wrong, what if he had already *reached* into her and found the truth . . . No, he hadn't *reached* yet. She knew what it felt like and she hadn't experienced it since he'd left.

Rae squeezed her eyes shut and conjured her sealed room, the seamless walls, the perfect corners, not a nick or a crack in its structure. She shoved her fear down deep inside and filled her mind with pleasant, dreamlike images.

She heard splashing in the lagoon—Big Guy? No, no, not the gator. The paddles. The canoe now rounded the chickee, gliding along the right side. When it bumped up against the ladder, the vibrations raced like electricity through the floor of the chickee and coursed up through the soles of her feet to her knees.

Moments ticked by, each more excruciating than the one before it. Then: "Rae?" The echo of his voice hung in the air, as thick and oppressive as August heat.

She shut her eyes and focused on the dreamlike images. A heartbeat later, a liquid warmth moved through her, just beneath her skin, as if she had stepped into a steaming bath scented with sweet, erotic oils. This, she knew, was how Eve had felt that first time with Adam, this quickening of the blood, this sense of wonder, this strange and terrifying ecstasy.

He was *reaching*.

Her consciousness split down the middle like an atom. Part of her clung to the dreamlike images, the other part hunkered down in the shadows, silent, waiting. When he withdrew, her heart raced, dampness spread between her thighs, her shirt stuck to her skin like adhesive.

He said something aloud, she couldn't hear what it was. She didn't have to hear it. Just the sound of his voice triggered images of their lovemaking, of the things he had done to her, the way he had made her feel. The hidden part of her recoiled in disgust; the other part of her savored the memories, felt drugged by them, and wanted more.

The floor creaked, his footsteps receded. The muscles in her right hand, the hand that clutched the screwdriver, began to ache and twitch. Her tongue slipped along her lower lip, moistening it. She heard other noises now, clumps, thumps, bumps, sound effects in a silly Batman movie. Hal was unloading the canoe.

"Rae?" he called again.

Sweat rolled into her eyes, she raised her arm. It seemed that her joints creaked so loudly that even God could hear them. The door squeaked as it yawned inward. Light pierced the room like sharp, metallic arrows.

"Hey, babe, we've got to talk."

He pushed the door open wider; a carpet of light widened at his feet. His shadow fell across it like a coffee stain, fell just in front of him where she could see it. It eddied, moving like some huge, grotesque protozoa, farther into the room where she could see it.

The shadow loomed larger and taller than she remembered, an optical illusion of some kind. A joke. A trick. Then she could see him, the physical Hal, the real Hal, the motherfucker who had uprooted her life, invaded it, and nearly succeeded in rewriting the script with himself in the lead. Not goddamn likely, she thought. And her rage broke free of the sealed room and exploded out of her.

Rae lunged at him, the screwdriver suspended above her head like a bright new moon, the tip of it aimed at the soft, tan flesh at the back of his neck. Then her arm began to fall.

At the last possible second, Hal spun around, threw up his arms to protect himself, and deflected the blow. The screwdriver sank into the fleshy juncture where his arm connected to his shoulder and the impact jarred Rae to the tips of her toes. Her hands flew away from the screwdriver's handle and she stumbled back, his shriek ringing in her ears.

Hal fell to the floor. She stumbled once more, unable to wrench her eyes from the sight of him, writhing on the floor, one hand clasped around the screwdriver. She couldn't tell whether he was attempting to pull it out or just trying to decide what the hell it was. His beautiful face had turned monstrous.

She whirled around and ran for the ladder, the canoe, the lagoon, the mangroves, ran to reclaim the life he had stolen from her. She scrambled down the ladder, and leaped into the canoe. It tipped, it rocked, a scream raced up her throat and exploded into the air, raw shards of noise. She grabbed onto the paddles, but went nowhere.

The rope, oh Christ, the rope was still tied to the ladder. Her fingers fumbled at the knot. She got it loose, tore it off the rung, and it dropped into the water.

Then she paddled furiously, madly, without looking back.

Hal, Hal, Hal.

The mangroves moved closer.

It started to rain, slow, hard drops at first. Faster, faster, oh God . . .

The canoe began to fill with water. It lapped at her feet, rose over her heels. Rain rolled into her eyes and she kept blinking and paddling, blinking and paddling, her body approaching adrenal exhaustion.

Then the green closed around her, branches snapped back in her face and clawed at her clothes.

Faster.

Faster.

When she looked back, she could no longer see the chickee. She could no longer see anything.

Gone, the bitch is gone.

He knew it as soon as he came to, lying on his back on the open platform, rain pouring into his face, the screwdriver sticking up out of his right shoulder. He saw it in a corner of his vision, standing upright like a flagpole, a big chunk of the metal embedded in him. Blood stained the fabric around it, most of it from when he had tried to jerk the screwdriver out earlier and had passed out from the pain. The rain had turned his blood pink and it ran off of him, diluted, anemic.

Hal rolled onto his left side, then pushed up very slowly to a sitting position. Bad, but not so bad that he would pass out again. Rain lashed his face as he pushed to his feet. He stumbled into the kitchen, under cover, and swayed. He felt so dizzy he thought he would puke. He gripped the edge of the counter to steady himself and stared out through the curtain of rain that swept across the lagoon.

Darkness.

Rain whipped sideways across the water in a shimmering curtain that reduced his visibility to practically zilch. He tried to *reach* for Rae, to find her beyond that curtain of water, somewhere out there in the mangroves. But he was too weak. And he would remain weak until he took care of his injury.

His shoulder had become a hot, oozing throb. He lit a lantern, then unlocked the drawer where he kept his first aid supplies. Weaving like a drunk, he carried them over to the table. He eased himself into one of the chairs.

He picked out everything he needed, bottles of this, jars of that, a needle and thread, scissors, and a dozen penicillin tablets.

The first thing he did was cut away his shirt, exposing his shoulder. His head spun when he saw just how deeply the screwdriver was buried in him. At least three inches. Blood seeped around it.

Had it hit an artery? If he pulled the screwdriver out would it be like pulling a plug? But he couldn't travel with the goddamn screwdriver sticking out of him. *Do it.*

He swabbed the area with alcohol, then betadine, wrapped a sterile cloth around the base of it, then began to ease it out very, very slowly. Hot agonizing shoots of pain raced down into his arm. His vision blurred from the pain. Twice he nearly passed out.

He stopped frequently to check the bleeding. Worse, but he saw no sudden spurts, nothing to indicate the metal had punctured an artery. *A little more, just another inch.* Jaws clenched, he eased the metal out the rest of the way. Stars exploded in his eyes, he dropped the screwdriver and collapsed against the table, panting from the waves of pain that crashed over him.

After a time, with his hand still pressing the cloth tightly over the wound, he lifted his head from the table.

Fresh cloth, he thought.

Rae did this to me.

Peroxide, more betadine, sterilize the needle in alcohol.

But Fletcher is responsible.

He worked now like a man possessed, doing what needed to be done. He handled it okay until the instant when he poked the needle through the inflamed flesh around the puncture wound and then he lost it big time. He shot out of the chair, howling, the needle still stuck in his skin, swinging like a miniature pendulum. The sudden movement caused fresh bleeding and when he fell back into the chair, blood rolled down his arm.

In all, he took eighteen tiny stitches with heavy duty black thread. It stopped the bleeding but not the pain. The shoulder pulsed and throbbed like an abscessed tooth, a steady, maddening beat without relief. He bandaged it, swallowed two more penicillin tablets and three Tylenols with codeine.

The rain still came down, a tempest. Rae wouldn't get very far in it and neither would he. But he didn't have time to wait now. Fletcher would pay for this, for all of it. And then he would vanish like Houdini again.

As for Rae, let her rot. He didn't want her anymore. She'd tried to kill him. And she wouldn't get out of here alive, anyway. Not only was she terrified of water, she would be terrified by everything else out there, too. Her panic would do her in and the Everglades, cruel and eternal, would do the rest.

By then, he would be gone like the wind.

28

Hal left the chickee on a puny Zodiac raft that Big Boy could have punctured in seconds if he'd been in the lagoon. It had been strapped to the roof, where Rae couldn't get to it. He hoped the blinding rain had driven the gator farther into the mangroves and that it made a meal of Rae.

The Zodiac putted through the canopied tunnels to where he'd left the airboat. He loaded his belongings on board, then headed out across Hell's Bay.

The rain swept in great, shuddering sheets across the bay, biting his face, soaking him through his poncho. Bolts of lightning spilled electric blue light across the water, allowing him to see where he was going. The noise of the storm nearly swallowed the roar of the airboat's engine.

By the time he neared shore, exhaustion suffused him. He wanted desperately to climb into someplace warm and dry and fall asleep. Instead, he forced himself to keep moving. As long as he moved, he could hold back his fatigue.

He tethered the airboat in the mangroves, unloaded his belongings, and hiked along the edge of the road to the hammock where he kept his truck. He unlocked it, tossed his things into the passenger seat, and scrambled inside.

He pulled dry clothes from his bag, changed, chewed three more Tylenols. Then he cranked up the truck and pulled onto the road that led out of the park. Traffic didn't exist at this hour in the park and the storm only reinforced that. He got out of the park in forty minutes, but on the open road his visibility shrank to just about zero.

Hal pulled off into a cluster of trees and brush, killed the engine, and sat back. Rain drummed the roof of the truck and streamed over the windshield. He felt used up, depleted, directionless. Even though he'd considered the chickee only a temporary home, it had been home in the deepest sense of the word, a place that grounded him, a refuge to which he could return. Now that had been ripped away from him.

He pressed the heels of his hands into his eyes and an image of Fletcher took shape inside of them. Fletcher with her coy smile, her hard eyes, her relentless agenda. And suddenly his consciousness sprang away from him, *reaching* for her, yearning to squash her like a goddamn bug.

But he couldn't find her. His fatigue was too great to reach vast distances right now. She might have moved out of Pier 66 after the coral snake incident, but even if she had, he would be able to locate her once he got within the city limits. He would find her the way he always had, through that irritating static, that envelope of white noise that seemed to surround her.

The same noise, he realized, had surrounded Sheppard out at the pub, but not in the same way. With him, the static had pulsed erratically, allowing Hal to squeeze inside it and turn on the pressure in his skull. He sensed the difference was significant, but had no idea why.

He pulled back into the road, puzzling over this apparent contradiction. In the past, the only times he'd been able to *reach* unimpeded into Fletcher had been when they had sex or, less frequently, when she slept. It used to bug him, but he eventually wrote it off to some quirk that she and Steele had shared. But now the whole question took on new meaning and urgency.

The rain abated somewhat as he neared Lauderdale. Streetlights swung eerily in the wet wind and water from standing pools splashed against the sides of the truck. He crossed the bridge that led to Pier 66, swung into the lot, and nosed into a parking space. He turned off the engine, shifted his body into a more comfortable position, and *reached* for Fletcher.

Nothing. Not even the white noise.

He *reached* again, tossing out a wider net. He caught the flotsam of dreams, orgasmic rushes, drunken gropings, laughter, cruelty, love, a vast emotional spectrum. But he didn't find Fletcher.

He didn't think she'd left town, but knew of one sure way of finding out.

Hal reached into his bag and brought out a notepad where he'd scribbled phone numbers, addresses, impressions, ideas for photos. He flipped through the pages until he found the address he was looking for. Then, smiling to himself, he backed out of the parking space and turned north on U.S. 1.

Thanks to the weather, they didn't get off the ground until nearly one A.M. As soon as they reached a thousand feet, turbulence gripped the seaplane and Sheppard's stomach rolled over. He suddenly wished he'd driven.

Fighting a headwind and rain, it took them twice as long as it should have just to reach the outer fringes of the Glades. Once the park lay beneath them, Young brought the plane down to 800 feet, but the visibility here wasn't any better than it had been higher up. Surrounded by a wet darkness, Sheppard suddenly knew how Jonah felt in the belly of the whale.

Young had to resort to instruments to find Hell's Bay. When they were supposedly right over it, Sheppard peered down and saw only blackness. "Maybe your instruments are wrong," he shouted over the noise of the engine.

"It's down there," Young shouted back.

He dropped down to 150 feet and flew over the frothing bay. Manacas had said the trail markers nearest Hal's hideout were in the higher digits; according to the park map, the higher digits lay on the west side of the lake. Sheppard pointed westward. "Land over there. I don't want to cross this shit in a rubber raft."

Young nodded, pulled back on the wheel, and the seaplane lifted suddenly, leaving Sheppard's stomach behind. He gripped the edges of his seat as Young swung around again and came in for his final approach. Rain hammered the windshield. The wind kept catching the right wing and tossing it upward, as if to flip the plane over on its back.

Then the pontoons struck the surface of the water. Struck

hard. Sheppard's body snapped forward, his stomach revolted, and he doubled over and threw up on the floor at his feet.

"Shep, take this. Drink it." Young shoved a bottle of Gatorade at him.

Sheppard lifted his head, wiped his arm across his mouth, took the bottle and sipped at it. The plane bobbed on the surface of the water. Young had turned on a pair of spotlights that illuminated a shimmering curtain of rain. Beyond it, mangroves embraced a small cove.

He throttled back on the power, nosed carefully into the cove, and killed the engine. In the noisy silence, water splashed against the pontoons. Neither of them moved. They just stared out the windshield as the vast, impenetrable blackness of the mangroves. Then Young threw open his door.

"I've got to secure the plane."

Sheppard released his seat belt and opened the passenger door. He stepped out onto the pontoon, his eyes fixed on the twin beams of the spotlights. Brilliant lights. But they barely dented the blackness.

No way, he thought. He slipped back inside the plane and crawled into the rear. They'd removed the backseat, but even so the inflatable dinghy and their supplies took up most of the space. Sheppard pushed everything around, found his rolled-up sleeping bag, and propped it against the side of the dinghy, and laid down.

He heard the door open, heard the rush of wind, then Young said: "Hey, Shep."

"What."

"C'mon, let's launch the dinghy."

"I'm not launching a fucking rubber dinghy in this weather, to go into a black swamp where we'd be as good as blind, Gerry. And I don't think Bennet is going anywhere, either. It'll be light in a few hours. We can go then."

Young scrambled into the back, grabbed the front of Sheppard's jacket, jerked him forward, and hissed, "Rae Steele has been missing for nine days, Sheppard. We're going in."

In the glow of the spotlights that spilled through the front window, his face looked wild, almost manic. Sheppard threw off Young's hands and shoved him away. "What the fuck's wrong with you? Flashlights won't do shit in those mangroves. And if we're lost in there, what the hell good are we going to do her?"

Young's face suddenly sagged in the jowls, as if weighted by excessive gravity. The glow of the spotlights deepened the lines at his eyes, his hair looked grayer. He seemed to be aging as they stared at each other. Then he held up his hands, patting the air and nodding. "You're right. You're absolutely right. We'll wait for the storm to let up. We'll grab some sleep. Yeah." He kept nodding to himself as he crawled into the front and turned off the spotlights. "Good idea. Sleep an hour, then do it." His hands burrowed through the supplies and yanked out the roll of his sleeping bag. He put it at the far end of the plane and sank down against it.

In seconds, his snoring punctuated the splash of water against the pontoons. Sheppard puzzled over what he'd glimpsed in Young's face, something that didn't fit. But he couldn't seize it and finally surrendered himself to the slow rocking of the plane.

She woke suddenly, inexplicably, her eyes snapping open to the darkness of her bedroom. Before she even blinked, a dry, calloused hand clamped down over her mouth and a muscular arm locked around her neck, immobilizing her, nearly choking her. Mira's senses blew wide open; a thick, crippling miasma rushed into her.

It's him. Bennet. Hal Bennet.

An alarm shrieked inside of her and she immediately threw up a wall around her fear, sealing it away where he couldn't find it.

"You scream, you're dead." He whispered it, his voice as slippery as moss.

She nodded slowly and he removed his hand from her mouth, but the pressure around her throat remained. "I can hardly breathe," she rasped.

He eased up on the pressure, then his head loomed above her, a dark, featureless shape. Smells assaulted her, his smells, of wind and water, sweat and smoke and sex, a thick, suffocating stink. She felt like vomiting.

Behind the scents, she felt *him*, the feeling tone unique to Bennet, the sum total of who he was. And it, this presence, this psychic gestalt, seemed to dissolve as soon as she perceived it, seeping through the pores of her skin like some noxious gas. She felt the moment that it came together again inside of her and molded itself to her, to the shape of her soul.

"Now, first question." His breath warmed the side of her face. "Is Lenora Fletcher still in town?"

"Yes." She felt him inside of her now, weighing her answer, reading it, scooping her out with his psychic hands. "She was with a man I read for at the fair tonight."

"You mean last night. It's nearly five A.M."

"Yes, last night."

"What fair?"

"The Lauderdale street fair. We ... I ... my store ... has a booth."

"Where you do readings and shit."

"Yes."

"And she was dressed like ..." He paused and Mira felt him swimming through her, looking for Fletcher. "A witch?" He exploded with laughter. "Who was she with?"

She blurted, "If you can see her as a witch, then you can see who the hell she was with."

His essence exploded inside her, infecting every cell of her being, every crack in her soul. A terrible throb mounted in her skull, right between her eyes. She winced with pain, then gasped, every muscle in her body twitching hard, as if she'd been splayed like a frog and pinned to a strip of velvet.

It ended just as abruptly as it had begun; it was like having a rug literally pulled out from under her. She fell through a sudden void, a weird and terrible emptiness, fell the way she sometimes did in dreams, slowly, with the world spinning crazily around her. Then she slammed into the walls that hid her fear and lay there, wounded and breathless.

Bennet grinned and said, "You're kidding. Evans?" As if

nothing unusual had happened. "An old guy with gray wisps of hair and small eyes? Him?"

The pressure around her neck had vanished. He no longer restrained her in any way. "His first name was Rich." She coughed and rubbed her neck. "That's what she called him. He wore a Zorro costume." She coughed again and he turned on the floor lamp.

"You can sit up," he said. "But do it slowly."

Mira pushed to a sitting position, but didn't turn to look at him. She couldn't look at him just yet, couldn't stare into the eyes of the man who had murdered her husband.

"What were the old guy's cards?" Bennet sat at the corner of her bed now.

"The only card I remember is The Hanged Man."

"That's my card."

She didn't comment.

"Do you remember what you told him?"

"That The Hanged Man represented danger for him."

"Look at me," he said.

Fuck you.

"Look. At. Me."

And he *reached* into her, seized her, and forced her to turn her head. *Forced her* like an abusive parent grabbing a child's chin, except that he didn't touch her physically. Her head turned until she stared into the face of Tom's killer. His fathomless blue eyes held hers, then she wrenched her gaze away and looked down at his shoes.

Green shoelaces.

Sweet Christ.

Tears brimmed in her eyes. She blinked them back and met his gaze. "You've already taken everything you can take from me, Mr. Bennet. It's Lenora Fletcher you want, not me."

He leaned back, his eyes unnaturally bright despite the dark circles under them. "You're right. Absolutely right. And you're going to bring her to me. Her and Evans."

Within the sealed room inside herself, Mira's thoughts raced. She knew if she made a break for it, he would run her down physically or psychically, either way would be fine with him.

Her best stab at survival lay in going along with whatever he said and seizing the first opportunity that came her way. As long as he believed he needed her, he wouldn't kill her.

He got up and paced restlessly alongside the bed. The distance, small as it was, allowed her to see him clearly for the first time. His clothes looked slept in, his hair desperately needed shampoo and a comb, mud had caked around the edges of his shoes. He favored his right arm and kept rubbing at his right shoulder.

When she opened just a little, she felt a hot, throbbing pain around her own right shoulder. She sensed the injury involved a knife and knew that with very little effort, she could pick up other information about what had happened. But she hesitated opening herself more fully. She felt that if she did, he would swallow her completely.

"Fletcher wants to find me as badly as I want to find her. Did she give you her cell phone number?"

Her impulse screamed for her to say no. But she knew that if she did, he would either find the truth himself or kill her now. "Yes."

"So you're going to call her and tell her you've picked up some information about my location. You'll . . ."

"She's not going to listen to me, Mr. Bennet."

He stopped pacing. A sly, terrible smile touched the corners of his mouth and he leaned toward her, palms pressed against his thighs. He brought his eyes level with hers, then locked onto them. In a very soft voice, he said: "You'd better make sure that she listens to you, babe. Because your life depends on it."

She couldn't tear her eyes away from his, couldn't even blink to break the connection between them. He'd seized her again, gripped her brain with nonphysical hands, and now he held her immobilized, suspended between one moment and the next like a fly caught in honey.

The air turned tight, hot, electric. Suddenly, the blue leaped out of his eyes and sprang into her pupils and plunged through them, down into the darkness five years in the past. Images poured through her, but each unrolled separately, in a horrifying slow motion.

Bennet in a mask. Bennet walking into a convenience store. *That* convenience store. His green shoelaces. The pretty little clerk behind the counter. The expression on her face as Bennet seized her mind. Now Mira saw the clerk walking away from the register, leaving the cash drawer open. She went into the freezer, sat down on a bench, and clutched her arms to her waist, her teeth chattering from the cold. She saw Bennet scoop money out of the register drawer and then, behind him, the glass door swung inward and Tom walked in.

Her Tom.

Five years dead but here he stood in front of her, real enough to touch. She could even smell his cologne.

A scream clawed at the back of her throat, a scream Bennet tried to kill but couldn't. The horror of that night propelled her scream and it exploded out of her.

His hand slapped down over her mouth with such force it snapped her back against the bed and impaled her. Her eyes flew open and his head swung in close to hers. He straddled her, a rider on a horse. Her right arm got trapped under her own body and he pinned her left arm with his other hand. Then he leaned in so close to her face she could smell the madness in his breath.

"Don't make me pull an Eddie Manacas," he hissed, and shoved an image at her of a woman with a stocking tied around her neck. A woman naked from the waist down. The woman Mr. Ed had raped and strangled. "Just do what I tell you and you'll live to see your kid grow up."

She wanted to nod, but couldn't. *Anything, I'll do anything,* she thought at him.

He took his hand away from her mouth, then went into her closet, swept hangers off the bar, dropped everything on the bed. "Find something to wear. Something casual. Jeans, a T-shirt. And wipe your nose."

He tossed her a wadded-up handkerchief. She touched it it her nose and it came away bloody.

"C'mon, get up, get the fuck up. It'll be light soon."

Mira pushed up on her elbows, swung her legs over the side

of the bed, and ran the back of her hand under her nose. Less blood now.

"You're going to tell her that I called you, attacked you psychically. And when I did, you picked up information about my location."

"She'll wonder why I didn't go to Sheppard."

"You can't get in touch with him. You're also going to tell her the information concerns someone whose name is Evans. You don't know whether it's a first or a last name."

The gun. If she could get into the closet where she'd hidden the gun . . . "She'll want me to give her the information over the phone."

"You tell her you have to show her on a map."

Mira held her jeans and a T-shirt up against her. "Do you mind if I step into the closet to change?"

"Don't bother." He turned so his back was to her.

Mira quickly pulled on the clothes, then he turned around, his eyes sweeping from her head to toes and back to her face again. "Good, that's good." He glanced at the clock on the nightstand. "Lenora is an early riser. You'll call her at six-thirty. And while we wait, you'll fix me breakfast."

Then he stepped to the side of the door and gestured grandly for her to precede him to the kitchen.

By six-thirty, fatigue had settled like lead in Hal's bones, weighting him, pulling him down. He didn't trust his psychic reflexes enough to rely solely on *reaching* to control her. So he brought out the gun and gestured toward the phone.

"Time to do your thing, babe. And make it good." He set the kitchen phone in front of him and punched out the cell phone number on the business card Fletcher had given Mira. He handed her the receiver and quickly turned on the remote phone so he could listen in without leaving the room. Then he aimed the gun at her chest.

She picked up on the second ring. "Lenora Fletcher."

At the sound of her voice, his blood began to boil. He *reached* ever so slightly, just enough to find the white noise, then quickly withdrew.

"Ms. Fletcher, this is Mira Morales."

"Oh. Ms. Morales. Well, this is a surprise. What can I do for you?"

"I've got some information on Hal Bennet's whereabouts. I can't seem to get ahold of Detective Sheppard, so I thought I'd better pass it on to you. It also involves someone named Evans. I don't know whether that's a first or last name or a nickname. Maybe you know."

"So this is psychic information."

"Yes."

"What is it?"

"I need to show you on a map."

"I'll be right over. Are you at the bookstore?"

"No. I'm at home. And frankly, I don't want you here. My store hasn't been the same since the day you walked in there and offered your opinion on the cards I'd drawn. So no, I'll come to you."

Fletcher chuckled. "Suit yourself. Take down this address."

As she gave Mira the address, Hal scrawled it on a nearby wall calendar.

"I'll meet you in an hour," Fletcher said.

Mira glanced at Hal, who nodded. "That's fine," she replied. "See you then."

Mira hung up. "Now what?"

"When did she come to your store?"

"The day she decided the feds were going to take over the investigation. She left bad vibes all over the place."

"Yeah, that sounds like Fletcher. You know where this address is?"

"South of here, over on the beach somewhere."

"You have a map of Lauderdale?"

"In my glove compartment."

"Let's get it." As he gestured toward the garage, a cat poked its head out from behind the couch. Hal bared his teeth and hissed at it; the cat ducked behind the couch again.

Mira opened the utility room door and they stepped out into the dark garage. He hit the wall switch and a dim overhead light came on. "Hold it right there," he said, and she stopped. "I'll get the door."

Hal opened the passenger door and gestured for her to get in. He considered shooting her now. But the address Fletcher had given included an apartment number and he didn't intend to knock on the door himself. "Sit in the seat," he told her.

She sat and he reached across her knees to open the glove compartment. No gun, no weapon of any kind that he could see. Just a stack of maps. "Okay, find the right map."

Mira brought out the maps, went through them, handed him one. He reached out and stroked her cheek with the muzzle of the gun. She didn't flinch, didn't react at all. She just stared at him, venom in her eyes. "You think I wanted to kill your husband?"

"Whether you meant to or not, he's dead."

"And you'd kill me in a heartbeat for it."

"Kill you?" Her mask cracked. "I'm not the killer, Mr. Bennet. You are."

"They made me into a killer." He gestured for her to get out of the Explorer. "That's what everyone overlooks. Steele and Fletcher trained me to kill and when I didn't want to do it anymore, my name went on the shitlist." He motioned her into the house and followed closely behind her. "Steele deserved to die. And so does Fletcher."

"What a waste," she said softly. "Your talent could be used to make a difference and instead, you sold out."

Bennet slammed the utility room door, grabbed her arm and spun her around. She winced and drew back, arms clutched against her. "Let's get something straight. I never had the advantages you were born into. When I was Reverend Hal, I changed lives, I diverted some personal tragedies. Yeah, I overcharged for what I did. But people could've gone elsewhere. And they didn't because I gave them answers. I gave them something to believe in. I wasn't born a killer."

Her gaze disturbed him. Then, in his head, he heard her words as clearly as if she'd spoken them aloud. *But you're a killer now.*

His anger leaped away from him. "What the fuck do you know," he shouted, and shoved her away from him.

She stumbled back into the table, her eyes bright and liquid with emotion. Finally, in a strangely calm voice, she said, "If we're going to make it to that address in time, we'd better leave."

"What makes you think you're going anywhere?"

"You need me to ring the doorbell, Mr. Bennet."

"Very good," he mocked her. "And then what?"

"Then I guess we'll find out if I'm right."

The phone rang before Hal could say anything. "Who would be calling you this early?"

"My grandmother."

"Let it ring. She'll think you're still asleep." Hal reached into the basket on the counter, and grabbed her keys. He tossed them to her. "We're going to take your Explorer and put my truck in your garage. You can wear those boots in the garage. Let's get going."

29

Four hours after they putted away from the plane in the rubber dinghy, after they took innumerable wrong turns and battled mosquitos and insects that looked like remnants of the Jurassic era, they followed a pair of dolphins from the dripping mangroves into a deeply shaded lagoon. The sounds of wildlife broke up the eerie stillness—clicks and hums, buzzes and splashes. Otherwise the place seemed untouched by time, outside of time.

Sheppard ducked as they passed under a drooping copse of trees, Spanish moss hanging from the branches. The dolphins circled the Zodiac once more, then shot away, headed in the direction from which they had just come. Sheppard, at the rear of the boat, stared after them.

"Something spooked them, Gerry."

"Yeah. That."

Sheppard turned to face the front of the raft again and saw what Young meant. The chickee rose out of the lagoon on eight-foot stilts, a solitary structure with walls, windows, shutters, and a small satellite dish perched on its tin and thatch roof. Through the space under it, Sheppard could see part of an extended platform and a ladder. No boat was in sight, there didn't appear to be anyone within a hundred miles, but they both drew their weapons.

Young motioned to the right, indicating they should approach from that direction, the farthest distance between the chickee and the mangroves. Sheppard set his gun beside him and started paddling. Young dropped to his knees, sighted down the barrel of his gun, and swung it slowly from the far left to the far right, scanning the lagoon.

Frenzied splashing erupted to their left, but it happened too quickly for either of them to see what had caused it. They came up behind the chickee and tracked alongside it. Branches braided together overhead and cast such deep shadows he couldn't distinguish the shapes of the trees to his right. They just melted together, a looming emerald mass that seemed to lean in toward the water as if to embrace it.

Suddenly, something crashed into the raft on the left, rocking it so violently that Young got thrown off balance. He struck the side, his gun slipped out of his hand, and a wild thrashing erupted beneath the raft. It heaved in the middle like a mound of earth surrendering to extreme internal pressure; Sheppard was hurled back.

"*Gator!*" Young shouted and grabbed his paddle off the floor of the raft and swung it over his head.

Sheppard scrambled for his gun, scooped it out of three inches of water, rolled onto his knees. He clutched it in both hands, sighted on the froth, prayed the gun would fire.

He squeezed the trigger.

Nothing, Christ, nothing.

Young yelled at him to shoot the fucker, shoot, *shoot*, and Sheppard squeezed the trigger again. The blast sounded like the end of the world, echoing across the sheltered cove and springing into the surrounding mangroves like a living thing. The gator's wild thrashing caused the raft to pitch furiously in the frothing water and Sheppard fell back, bounced against the slowly deflating side of the raft, and rocked onto his knees again.

He had somehow managed to hold onto his gun this time. The skin on his palms had grown into it, into the handle, into the heart of the gun itself. It would fire again. It had to. The gator, still alive and enraged, closed in on them. Young beat the paddle against the water; Sheppard sighted on the gator again, pulled back on the trigger.

Click.

Again.

Click.

Again.

The explosion resounded inside his skull, slamming around

between his ears like some giant tennis ball. A vague awareness crept into him that the thrashing had stopped and the raft no longer pitched. Air hissed out of it so fast that he could feel the side he leaned against getting lower, softer. Water seeped over the side.

"Where's the gator?" Sheppard shouted.

"It sank."

"Is it dead? Did I hit it?"

"Jesus, I don't know."

Sheppard tossed his gun to Young. "Cover me." He shucked his windbreaker, tore off his shoes, and eased over the side. He grabbed onto the rope and swam toward the chickee's ladder.

"I didn't need saving," Young muttered, scanning the water for some sign of the gator.

"I'm saving the raft, Gerry, not you. Unless we can patch the hole, we won't be getting back to the plane before dark. And I really don't want to spent a night out here."

"Good point. Swim faster."

Before Sheppard reached the ladder, the gator's corpse floated to the surface. Sheppard went around it and swam faster to the ladder. The side of the raft that continued to lose air now resembled a huge cellulite dimple in a very large and fleshy thigh. Sheppard grabbed onto the ladder first, climbed halfway up, then Young got out, clinging to the ladder like a giant spider, and together they hauled it out of the water to an open platform.

They sank to their knees, stupefied, taking in everything. The kitchen, the table, a door with an open padlock dangling from it, and a door farther back in the shadows that stood all the way open. "Rae?" Young called, stumbling to his feet. "Rae, you here?"

The tight, uneasy silence caught his voice and tossed it back as an empty echo. "Jesus, we're too late," Young said softly, his face the color of old bread. "She's dead."

Something about the way Young said it bothered Sheppard, but he didn't have time to think about it. He reached the open doorway and stopped, balking at the dozens of sketches that papered the far wall. They featured Rae Steele in multiple poses, multiple moods.

Some of the sketches had gaping tears in the center, as if Bennet had slammed his fist through them; one had a penknife impaled in the center of it.

"Jesus God," Young breathed, stopping next to him.

They went into the room, neither of them speaking. Young made a beeline for the closest shutter, threw it open, and leaned out into the fresh air. Sheppard heard him suck the air in through clenched teeth, struggling not to puke.

It puzzled Sheppard because there wasn't any corpse, any blood, nothing so blatant that would make a man feel like puking. Unless he had a personal stake in whatever had happened here. Unless his imagination churned, filling in the blanks.

A man with graying hair who isn't Steele: that was what Mira had said. A man who smoked an occasional cigar. A man who rarely talked about his personal life. A man, Sheppard thought, whose significant relationship had ended last spring.

"Fuck," Sheppard said. "You and Rae Steele, Gerry?"

Young turned slowly, like a man in trance, his eyes wide with shock, with pain, with emotions that burned as brightly as sunlight against snow. And then he covered his face with his hands, his shoulders slumped, and for long, terrible seconds he said nothing, did nothing. When his hands fell away from his face, tears glistened in his eyes.

"It ended seven months ago," he said, his voice little more than a whisper. "It isn't in her nature to sneak around. She wanted to leave him, but she was afraid he would win custody of Carl. It was a mess, Shep, the whole fucking thing was a mess from beginning to end, but I was so goddamn in love with her it didn't matter."

"Christ, Gerry. You knew about the cabin. You could have at least given me some hint about the goddamn cabin."

"How the hell could I do that without telling you the rest of it? It would look like I killed him, for Christ's sakes. I didn't kill him, Bennet did. But you wouldn't have believed me if you'd known about me and Rae."

"Bullshit. I know you're no killer. Give me credit for that much. Your problem is that you can't trust anyone enough to open the fuck up to them, Gerry."

Blood rushed into Young's face, he glared at Sheppard. "What horseshit."

"Go fuck yourself," Sheppard snapped, and turned away to search the rest of the chickee.

Everything here smacked of an odd precision: the way the shutters fit, for instance, the hinges exactly right, the edges sealing seamlessly. Each piece of handmade furniture was a work of art, a thing of exquisite beauty and ultimate practicality. It was as if Bennet had discovered the better part of himself out here and it had found expression through his hands.

They loaded Rae's clothes and what remained of the videotape collection into large garbage bags to take back into town. They removed the sketches from the walls and packed them in Sheppard's waterproof bag. Bit by bit, they dismantled the chickee and packed up the evidence. And through it all, they spoke only briefly. Help me with this, do that.

Young heard the noise first, a kind of hapless squeaking too loud to be a rat. He hurried out onto the platform to investigate and Sheppard followed quickly. She climbed up the ladder, a woman with the gaunt, fallen features of a Holocaust victim. Her hair was slicked back against her head, but Sheppard couldn't tell if it was water or sweat. Her bare arms looked as if swarms of insects had feasted on them. One eye darted about wildly, desperately, the other was swollen shut.

The blood leaked from Young's face and he tore toward her. "Gerry," she whispered hoarsely, and collapsed against the platform floor.

"Christ," Young whispered, and slipped an arm under her head and with his other hand smoothed the hair away from her face. "Rae, come on, wake up, talk to me." His head snapped up. "Help me get her inside the chickee, Shep."

"My store hasn't been the same since the day you walked in there and offered your opinion on the cards I'd drawn . . ."

Fletcher kept turning that sentence around and around in her mind, examining it from every conceivable angle. But no matter how she looked at it, she came up with the same answer. Mira had been warning her.

The day she'd gone to the bookstore, Mira had been studying one card only—The Hanged Man. And in the old days, that had been Bennet's card. Maybe Mira didn't know that. Just the same, Fletcher felt sure she'd been telling her that Bennet was there, forcing her to make the call.

She walked out to the edge of the roof of Evans's building. From here, the dark, sagging sky looked close enough to touch. The drizzle had started again, a slow suppuration. Even if it started to pour, though, Mira's car would be visible as soon as it turned onto the street.

And then what, Lenora?

She signaled to Hood, who stood behind the far right corner of the roof with a high-powered rifle slung over his shoulder. Laskin waited on the beach, a barefoot fisherman in a raincoat. She switched on her handheld radio. "You guys copy? Over."

"Loud and clear," Hood replied. "Bruce?"

Laskin replied, "Okay down here."

"Rich? You with us?" Fletcher asked. "Over."

"I'm here, watching the road from the side balcony," Evans replied. "I suggest we all take our positions. Over."

Fletcher eyed the road again. "Let's go over it once more, people. Jim, you'll be the first to see the car. You alert the rest of us and keep your rifle aimed at Bennet. If anything goes wrong, you shoot him before he reaches the steps. But that's a last resort. I want him inside the building, preferably outside the apartment, before you open fire. Got that? Over."

"What's there to get?" Hood replied dryly.

"Bruce, as soon as the car stops out front, you start heading back toward the building. Jim will tell us when Bennet enters the building. Give him to the count of ten, then follow. He'll have to take the stairs because the elevator will be stopped up here. By then, Jim will be inside the elevator and we'll all be on an open radio channel.

"If the woman's with him, she'll probably be the one to ring the bell or knock. Either way, you'll hear me say, 'Just a second.' That'll be your cue, Jim and Bruce. You count to three by thousands and come out firing. Aim for his neck, chest, or upper back. The tranquilizer darts will work fastest there. Any questions? Over."

"Yeah," said Laskin. "What the fuck do we do if none of this works? Over."

Fletcher rubbed the bridge of her nose and squeezed her eyes shut. "It'll work."

"But what if it doesn't?" Laskin repeated.

"Then you pray, guys, and you keep firing until he's on the floor. Keep your ELFs on the pulsating mode. Over and out."

Fletcher took one last look at the road, flashed a thumbs-up at Hood, and hurried over to the trapdoor that opened to the roof. She slipped down inside it, lowered the hatch, and climbed down the ladder into Evans's pantry. He stood there, waiting for her, a gun tucked into his belt, another gun in his hand. He handed that one to her.

"No darts in these," Evans said. "If he makes it into the apartment, the fucker's dead." He started to walk back into the living room, but Fletcher caught his arm. "This better be worth it, Rich. I'm putting my ass on the line for you and the goddamn favor you owe someone."

Evans smiled, his eyes unnaturally bright, and patted her cheek with his hot, dry palm. "You're not doing it for me, Lenora. You're doing it because you want to head the Bureau or be appointed attorney general and you know that I can get you there faster than you can get there on your own merits. Now c'mon, let's get settled."

He turned away from her and strode into the living room.

The rain fell harder as they crossed the intracoastal bridge to the beach. The wipers whipped back and forth across the windshield in a maddening, metronomic rhythm. And to Mira, even the light seemed to grow dimmer, as if the devil's hand had grabbed the sun and slowly squeezed out the heat and radiance.

She somehow managed to keep her fear locked up, shoved down deep inside her. Now and then she heard the echoes of its shrieks, but mostly she heard the rain tapping the Explorer's roof. Bennet didn't say a word. He sat with his back to the door, the gun aimed at her and his psychic sentry standing at attention inside of her, watching, listening.

As soon as they turned onto A-1-A, he consulted the map folded open in his lap. Turn right, turn left, turn right again. She did what he said because she didn't know what else to do. And yet, she remained vigilant, alert for a chance, however small, to escape.

As they approached the street where they were supposed to turn, Hal said, "Keep going. You're going to turn after that cluster of pines just ahead. There should be a dirt road there that parallels the pines."

She passed the pines and turned onto a dirt road that angled between the pines and a small, deserted playground. The Explorer splashed through puddles, hit potholes.

"Pull into the pines and stop," Bennet said.

Mira stopped, turned off the engine, removed the keys from the ignition and started to pocket them.

"Uh-uh. Give me the keys." He extended his hand and she dropped the keys into them. He put them in his pocket, then unsnapped a pouch at his waist and brought out a roll of heavy electrical tape. "Give me your hand."

"For what?"

He grabbed her wrist and wound a length of tape tightly around it. He wrapped the other end around his own wrist. "I can't worry about you bolting. Now pull your hood up and get out nice and easy."

She pulled the hood of her rain slicker over her head; Bennet did the same with his raincoat. They slid out of the car together, the tape binding them more closely than handcuffs. He kicked the door shut and they headed into the trees.

"I want a look at the building first," he said.

"You think it's a trap?"

"I think that Fletcher's a very bright woman who's always prepared."

He *reached* into her then, grabbing, and she heard his voice in her skull, as if they'd fused, merged, melted together. *Act normal. Do what I say. If you try anything at all, I'll squeeze.* And he squeezed just to show her what he could do in spite of his fatigue, a squeeze of agony so intense she gasped. Then it vanished, leaving only a trickle of blood trailing an erratic line to her chin.

"Any sign of the car, Jim?' Fletcher asked. "Over."

"Not yet," Hood replied. "Bruce? Is the beach still clear? Over."

"Clear and wet," Laskin replied. "Over."

Fletcher frowned and glanced at Evans, who paced across the living room. "If anyone appears on the beach, Bruce, and gets too close to the building, you'll have to turn them away. Over and out."

30

Hal's shoulder ached; the painkillers had begun to wear off. But adrenaline pumped through him now, abrading the fatigue that had dogged him since he'd left the Glades. It sharpened his senses, heightened his awareness, and would make *reaching* easier.

He stopped at the edge of the pines and, still holding the gun on Mira, *reached* into the building. Static seemed to fill the place. Instead of withdrawing as he'd done in the past, he embraced it, sank into it more deeply, tried to work with it.

Gradually, he realized he could sense several different pockets of static. Two pockets emanated from an apartment on the top floor. Another seemed to be located above the apartment, on the far side of the roof. A fourth felt more distant, out on the beach somewhere. He sensed no other people in the building.

He withdrew and hurried through the trees, to where they grew the thickest. Only five or six feet of exposed area stood between them and the side of the building. Hal figured the person on the roof wouldn't spot them from here and if they moved along under the building's awning, they could make the front door without being seen.

"Fast," he hissed, and ran out from under the cover of the trees, Mira stumbling alongside him. When he reached the wall, he jerked her toward him and pushed her up against the wall. "Stay under the awning."

"Look, let me go," she said. "You don't need me for this."

Hal grinned. "You're my insurance." With that, he crept along the side of the building, moving toward the front door.

* * *

As Young helped Rae Steele climb into the back of the plane, Sheppard's cell phone rang. He dug it out of his backpack. "Sheppard."

"This is Nadine, Mr. Sheppard. I've been calling Mira's house since early this morning and she didn't answer, so I . . . I came over here. I think something has happened."

Sheppard's chest tightened. "She's not at the street fair?"

"She was supposed to pick me up. One of the screens has been removed from a window, the locks on the window are broken, and the blood . . . I also found an address scrawled on her wall calendar. It's not her handwriting."

Sweet Christ. Bennet. Bennet got to Mira. "Give me the address."

She ticked it off, he told her he would be in touch, and hung up. Then he shouted at Young.

Mira saw the man first, darting up from the beach, through the rain. He clutched a fishing pole in one hand and held a radio to his mouth with the other hand. Before she could react, Bennet's head snapped around, the man stopped, stared, then suddenly the air turned tight, electric, as if its molecules had sprung to life.

The man went for his gun but never retrieved it. His hands flew to his head, the fishing pole struck the ground, and he stumbled back, his raincoat hood slipping off his head. In a single blinding moment that would be burned into Mira's memory as long as she lived, she saw blood pouring from the man's nostrils and oozing from his ears and the corners of his eyes. Then he just fell over backward and lay there, twitching.

A scream raced up her throat but Bennet slapped his hand over her mouth before it reached the air. "You want to end up like him? Huh? Do you?"

She shook her head and he took his hand away from her mouth. Even as they moved toward the man, Mira sensed he was dead. Bennet leaned over to scoop up the guy's radio and gun. Every time he moved in a direction that she didn't, she felt the electrical tape loosening slightly, and it buoyed her hope.

Bennet examined the gun. "Tranquilizer darts. Like I'm some kind of fucking animal." He went through the man's pockets, found three more loaded darts, and a black device that she recognized. An ELF device. Bennet fiddled with the ELF's knobs, turned it off. "The white noise," he muttered, and dropped it to the ground, slamming the heel of his shoe over it.

Static crackled from the radio. "Bruce, do you copy? Over."

Fletcher's voice. Bennet smiled, turned the radio to RECEIVE, and lowered the volume. He put it in his raincoat pocket, then pulled Mira back to the side of the building, around the corner, and up the steps. She stumbled intentionally and went down on one knee, hoping the tape would tear. Bennet didn't seem to notice; he jerked her to her feet again, shoved open the front door, and they stepped into the lobby.

"Bruce, do you copy? Over."

Silence.

"Jim, you copy? Over."

"Hood here," said a male voice. "No car in sight yet. I walked the perimeter of the roof and didn't see anything unusual. Bruce's radio probably went on the fritz. It wasn't working so good. Over."

"I'm going down to check on him. He should be inside the building now. Over and out."

Bennet hesitated a moment, glanced at the elevator, then at the door that opened to the stairs. He quickly pressed the elevator button, but nothing happened. He grinned. "She's got it stopped up there. She'll be coming down on the elevator. I'll stop her on the next floor."

"You can't—"

He jammed the gun to her neck. "Move."

Fletcher, Evans, and Hood stepped out into the hallway. She gestured for Hood and Evans to take the front stairs, she would take the back stairs. But first, she flicked the STOP button inside the elevator and punched the button for the first floor. She stepped back, the doors whispered shut, and the elevator started down.

Fletcher ran silently across the hall to the service stairs. Her heart *knew* that Bennet was down there, that he planned to ambush her when she stepped off the elevator. Fat chance.

As she started down to the second floor landing, she heard the distant creak of the elevators cable's and pulleys, unoiled for probably fifty years. It wouldn't be long now, she thought, and relished the taste of her victory.

As Mira pushed open the door to the second floor, she felt Bennet extending himself, *reaching* to stop the elevator, *reaching* so hard he momentarily forgot about her. So she spun and brought her right knee up, slamming it into Bennet's groin.

He gasped and fell back, jerking her toward him. Mira wrenched her arms upward with such force she felt tendons tearing in her shoulder. But the tape ripped, freeing her, and Mira tumbled back into the door. It swung all the way open and slammed against the wall in the hallway.

Bennet, eyes bulging in his sockets from the pain, charged her. Mira leaped up, threw her weight into the door, and caught his arm as the door slammed shut. His gun fell to the floor. He shrieked like a panicked pig and Mira screamed, *"Second floor, help, someone, help!"* She tried to reach the gun, but couldn't stretch far enough without moving away from the door.

Then he hurled himself at her, *reaching* with such raw power that pain exploded inside her head. For seconds, it literally blinded her. She struggled to keep her weight against the door, so he wouldn't get his arm loose, and tried to deflect his attack by singing "Jingle Bells" at the top of her lungs.

She felt a sudden lessening of pressure in her head, heard a man on the other side of the door scream, then he came after her again, seizing her. His full weight slammed the door; she couldn't hold him off any longer. She leaped back, scooped up the gun, and he fell into the hallway, an enraged giant. He weaved toward her, one hand struggling to pull a tranquilizer dart from his shoulder, his eyes fixed on her, the pain pulsing erratically inside of her now.

Mira raised the gun, clutching it with both hands, and fired once. She missed, Bennet still lumbered toward her. Just as her finger twitched against the trigger again, someone shoved her from behind and sent her sprawling to the floor. The gun flew out of her hand.

As she dived into the elevator, Fletcher shouted, *"That's far enough, Hal!"*

Bennet *reached* for Fletcher, struck the wall of white noise, and dived through it. *Not so fast, Lenora. You're not going to shoot me.*

He felt her panic, saw her hand dart to the black device hooked to her belt, and tasted her fear when she realized it couldn't protect her anymore. *Drop the gun, babe.*

"Don't shoot him," shouted someone behind Hal.

Hal knew that voice. It broke his concentration and his head snapped around. Evans, Richard Evans. He tried to reach for Evans, but couldn't. The tranquilizer now coursed through his blood and he didn't have the energy to hold Fletcher and Evans at the same time.

Fletcher shook herself from a stupor and stammered, "Hood, where . . . where's Hood?"

"Dead. Where's the psychic?"

"In the elevator."

Hal released Fletcher and dived through the surface of Evans's thoughts and intentions and suddenly realized what was about to happen. "Richard Evans," Hal said, vaguely aware that his words had begun to slur. "Out of retirement for the likes of me."

"Don't flatter yourself, Bennet," snapped the old man.

Hal didn't hear the rest of what he said; he shouted silently at Mira.

In the mirror mounted near the top of the elevator door, she saw Evans, Fletcher, Bennet. She pressed her back to the wall and stood slowly. Get the doors shut, get outta here, she thought.

Then Bennet's voice boomed in her skull. *He's going to kill you. Get outta here, now, fast!*

All the terror she had kept locked up inside of her since early this morning sprang to the surface. Adrenaline poured into her. She lunged for the control panel, slammed the heel of her hand over the CLOSE button. Nothing happened.

In the mirror, she saw Evans moving toward the elevator and heard Fletcher say, "What the hell are you doing, Rich?"

"Taking care of business."

"What business?" Fletcher sidestepped toward him. "What the hell are you talking about?"

Mira kept punching the CLOSE button, begging the doors to shut, anxiously scanning the control panel for a master switch.

"Krackett, I'm talking about Krackett." Evans stopped and turned, facing Fletcher. "Krackett sent me down here, Lenora. To bring Hal back. And to kill you." Then he fired.

Fletcher fell back in a spray of blood, her head struck the wall, and her gun hit the floor and spun across it. Evans kicked it out of the way and continued on toward the elevator, toward Mira.

Their eyes met in the small round mirror at the top of the door and she leaped upward, knocking loose one of the lighting panels in the ceiling. She grabbed onto the metal bar and jerked her legs up toward her body; the first blast tore through the back wall.

Evans laughed and kept moving toward the elevator. Mira swung her body back to push off against the wall behind her, but a wave of energy slammed into the elevator, energy so powerful it exploded the mirror and every light fixture in the hallway. *Ping, ping, ping.* Glass and plastic rained down, the elevator doors slammed shut, the hulking heap started to move, and in her head she heard Bennet again.

I proved you wrong. Run like hell.

"Christ, Hal," Evans said, shaking his head as he turned to face him. "That was stupid. I'm prepared to offer you the world and you're helping the only person left alive who can threaten what we do."

"What *you* do." Everything had started to blur. "I'm outta the loop, Evans."

"Don't be a fool." He stepped over Fletcher's body as though it were roadkill. "We're prepared to offer a much more lucrative deal this time."

"Really. And what kind of deal would that be?" He remained on his knees because Evans found him less threatening that way. "I'm willing to listen."

"I think you're bullshitting me, Hal," Evans said, and shot him in the knee.

Hal already had *reached* for him and barely felt the pain. He *reached* with everything that remained inside him and seized the fucker's willpower and began to mold it, direct it, doing exactly what Evans and Steele had taught him so many years ago.

Even as Mira raced out of the building, into the rain, the connection between her and Hal Bennet remained. She saw what he saw, felt what he felt. When Evans shot Bennet in the right knee, her own knee exploded with pain and she rolled through the sand, clutching her knee, her mouth frozen in a silent scream.

She tried to sever the connection between them, but she didn't have the strength. She felt him *reach* into Evans, grab control of him, and saw Evans struggling against the awesome power that he had helped create. Then Evans sank to the floor, sobbing even as he jammed the barrel of the rifle into his own mouth.

She shrieked then, shrieked to break away, to separate, to sever, and suddenly she popped free and rolled through sand, sobbing and shrieking and still clutching her knee.

The final shot echoed out across the beach, vibrating against the wet air like some long, erratic musical chord. It faded and she heard only the hum of an approaching plane and the soft drumming of the rain against the sand.

A light drizzle still fell as the medics carried Fletcher and Bennet out of the building. Sheppard stood near the ambulance, watching.

Both of them were still alive, which was more than he could say for Richard Evans, who had left the building in a body bag. Fletcher was unconscious and Bennet was nearly there, his eyes rolling around in their sockets like loose marbles.

As they started to put his stretcher into the ambulance, he raised his hand and gestured at Sheppard. He stepped forward, but Mira came up behind him and caught his arm. "No," she whispered. "Don't."

He looked at her, hair wet from the rain, clothes soaked through, eyes filled with emotions he couldn't identify. "He's too drugged up to do anything," Sheppard said. "I'll be right back."

She grabbed onto his arm and went with him. They stopped alongside the stretcher and Bennet pushed his oxygen mask to one side. "Computer. In the chickee. An encrypted file. Everything . . . about Delphi." His eyes slipped to Mira and something passed between them, something Sheppard felt but couldn't decipher. Then the medics put Bennet in the ambulance and moments later, it sped down the driveway.

"What happened just then?" Sheppard asked her.

She pressed her folded arms against her waist and blinked back tears or raindrops, he couldn't tell which. "He said he was sorry."

"I didn't hear him say a damn thing."

"I know."

He glanced back toward the street, as if he expected the answer to be there, but the ambulance was gone. Mira reached for his hand and laced her fingers through his. Softly, she said, "Let's go home."